The Perpetual Journeys Series

The Maze | The Scarlet Phoenix

By John McClellan

For Jesus Christ
The greatest friend.
The greatest teacher.
The greatest hero.

&

For Trisha McClellan

Acknowledgements

I would like to thank a number of people as I continue on my way in the authorship of <u>The Perpetual Journeys</u>. First, and foremost, I'd like to thank my cousin, Caty, for providing a stunning cover for my compounded novel. Her tireless work while still raising two small toddlers single-handedly not only owes my respect, but that of everyone who will pick up this book. And while you two may not remember this, Garret and Connor, I thank you both for lending your mom to me! May the three of you and Jeremy enjoy these two works and may all of earth's blessings be abundant in your lives!

As promised, I would also like to recognize the small fan group entitled "Carter Members of the Perpetual Journeys." Thank you all for sticking with me for the past year and for your support in my process. While it would be imprudent for me to name all 42 of you, know that I could not have done it without each of you individually!

For my sister, Trisha, because of her full support. Trisha, to you and all of your friends, I owe this success. Your prayers and love is unmatched.

For my brother, Paul, who still, after nearly ten years, enjoys reading my works.

To my parents, thank you for your financial, spiritual, and emotional support.

To Jesus Christ, the one man to whom I truly owe everything, including my talents and success.

And for you, whoever is reading this book. I probably don't know you, but without fans like you who take the time to read a book, every author is worthless. You make dreams come true.

Now, what are you waiting for? Begin your own perpetual journey through your imagination! Get reading!

Table of Contents
The Maze:

The Scarlet Phoenix

Prologue

A man worked tirelessly on his experiment. He pulled wires, hooked up batteries and poured in chemicals, but only the greatest scientist in the world would know what he was making – that's the case because he is the greatest.

"Come on," he said impatiently. "I worked for years on you; don't break down."

He took the pliers and twisted two of the wires together. This made the machine roar alive. The man, called Zyno, leaned back in his chair and breathed in relief.

"Finally," he said. "I have used practically all my experiments on this thing. I wonder what I should call it…"

He picked up the small, spherical object and turned it around in his hand, examining it.

"I should call it, Roboblast," Zyno said. "With this, I can get revenge on everyone. The time has come."

Zyno left the lab. Outside, he took out a match and a bottle filled with liquid. He lit the match, put the match inside the bottle and threw it up into the air. It exploded, showing a bright green color that lasted for a few seconds. He paused for a moment and looked out in the distance. He heard a motorcycle start up far away. Zyno watched as a man tore down the road on a specially-designed motorcycle. This motorcycle had rockets built into the engine. The rider stopped very close to Zyno, got off and greeted him.

"Ben, nice of you to come," Zyno welcomed. "Now I have finished it. We must get the last piece out."

"You mean about the ad?" Ben said. "We have worked for seven years, Zyno; I am glad this has come to an end."

"Not yet," Zyno said. "Daniel will be our last part and I am betting he might put up a fight. Be sure and get our third one to come."

"You mean the magician?" Ben said. "I never really believed in that stuff, but whatever you say."

"And the station," Zyno said. "We need you to stay there until Daniel shows."

"And the ad? Would you like me to post that, too?" Ben asked.

"Yes," Zyno replied.

"Well, let me at least see it," Ben said.

"Of course," Zyno said. He strapped the machine to a floating hovercraft he had created. He pressed a button on the craft and the object floated around above him. Suddenly, Roboblast shot a small bubble into the air. It sank slowly, but when it hit the ground, the earth shook a bit, making them lose their balance.

"So once Daniel joins us, he can finish my 'Shrinky,'" Zyno said, "Then, we can take care of the rest of the world."

"Alright," Ben sighed in relief. "This greatest invention, what's its name?"

"Roboblast," Zyno said. "But it's not the greatest invention."

He was right. For behind them, the door swung open to reveal the greatest invention the world would ever see: The Maze.

1) Benjamin

"Wow, look at this!" Five-year-old Paul Quaill exclaimed to his 11-year-old brother, John. Paul was looking at a magazine.
"Wow is right," John exclaimed after he read the article. "This is amazing! Hey Jerry! Take a look at this article:

> *'Roboblast' is the newest creation of Zyno Wayne's lab. A bubble appears at the touch of a button. (Warning to all visitors: Do not touch the bubble). When the bubble hits the ground, the earth shakes and a crater is formed. This invention is a great stride in the field of geological science. If you want to see more inventions, visit Zyno's lab at 25 miles west of Cestorn.*

Kind of reminds you of our inventing uncle, huh?"
But their brother Jerry wasn't listening. The 14-year-old was playing his favorite video game. All he heard was "west of Cestorn," but that was enough to get him off of his game.
"Did you say 25 miles from Cestorn?" Jerry asked excitedly. Jerry's favorite video game store was in that direction.
"Yes, but where's Cestorn?" Paul and John said together.
"Ten miles from here, let's get going!"
John complained.
"That's 35 miles!" He said, "We can't go that far and we are too young to drive. But maybe if we had a four-wheeler, we could probably do it."
"How much does a four-wheeler cost?" Jerry asked, getting out his wallet.
"More then you think," John replied. "About $800 for a used one around here."
"I have two hundred and five dollars," Paul said, "But I am saving it for college. I'll let you borrow some though."

"I have three hundred and ten dollars," John said putting away his wallet.

"I have two hundred and five dollars also," Jerry said. "What does that equal Paul?"

"Seven hundred and twenty dollars," Paul answered quickly.

"Darn! We are eighty bucks short!" Jerry cried out. He sadly walked away. Just then, John remembered that his friend Jimmy had a four-wheeler.

"Maybe I could borrow Jimmy's," John said. "He owes me for the time I lent him my bike. Let's see if he would be able to loan it to us."

John called Jimmy and Jimmy said they could borrow it. John hopped on his bicycle. John didn't realize he had a flat tire until he had gotten halfway to Jimmy's.

"Dang it, this means I'll have to walk the rest of the way," John said angrily. "And it's still another mile away."

After John finally got there, Jimmy was outside waiting. He was standing next to the four-wheeler, which was blue with green stripes.

"Hey man," Jimmy said. "Here she is. Try and take good care of her, she's not very old."

"I will," John said, breathing hard. "Thanks. In case you were wondering, the reason why I need this is so I can go to Zyno's lab."

"Zyno? That name rings a bell," Jimmy said. "Where does he work?"

"Twenty-five miles west of Cestorn," John replied. "Pretty far from here; I doubt that you know him. By the way, nice four-wheeler."

"Thanks. It was really blue when I bought it. It looked so dull, plain and pathetic. So I said, 'I want to make this thing look alive.' I got some green paint and painted streaks. My dad's a painter; free paint comes in handy."

"Hey Jimmy, not to be rude, but Zyno's lab is about to close. Can I come back later?" John asked.

"If it's about to close, you must go!"

John waved goodbye to his friend and sped off. He was so happy that he was carelessly driving the four-wheeler. Jerry was pleased that John was able to get it from Jimmy. Paul and Jerry got on. They started off to Zyno's lab. Since Jerry was the oldest -- at 14 – he got to drive it (though John and Jerry argued for 15 minutes until Paul said that Jerry, being the oldest, should drive. John agreed, not because he was generous, but because Paul was a 5-year-old boy-genius). They were very happy.

"Jerry, do you exactly know where Cestorn is?" Paul asked

Jerry stopped so suddenly that John and Paul were nearly thrown off the four-wheeler. " … Er … um...west two miles … no … um … well, not really … "

"WHAT?!" John yelled, as Jerry sped up again. "Then how did you know that it's 10 miles from were we live?!"

"I heard mom say it when she was going to drive to the video game sto-" he stopped quickly, but John caught every word.

"So you were just going to drop us off at the lab and go to the video game store?! Well let me tell you something: GO SINK YOUR SKULL INTO A CEMENT BLOCK! You're coming with us!"

Paul and Jerry were shocked at what John had said. He normally would never say something like this. But Jerry turned around and said, "And how are you going to make me go? You can't even-"

Before he could finish, John had Jerry in a headlock.

"What was that, dear brother? You asked me how I'm going to make you?! Well you just better do it or there might be consequences!"

"John! Let him go!" Paul screamed.

"Why?"

"He needs to drive! We're going to crash!" But it was too late. The four-wheeler was going full speed straight at a pole.

SMASH!

Paul and John went flying off the vehicle and Jerry went face first into the pole. John got up, rubbing his elbow while Paul got up and limped back to the four-wheeler.

"Oh, won't Jimmy be ecstatic when we bring back his beautiful vehicle with a huge dent," John said.

"You distracted Jerry, this was your fault!" Paul said. "Hey! Can you believe our luck? Look what we ran into!"

They had crashed into a gas station.

"I will go inside and buy supplies," John said.

"Good idea. Zyno's article in the magazine said to bring some," Paul said.

John reached into his pocket to get his wallet and—

"My wallet!" John exclaimed. "I must have left it at home!"

He looked at Paul and opened his mouth to speak, but Paul cut him off.

"Uh-uh, you aren't getting any money from me! Sorry, saving up for college. Try Jerry."

John looked around for Jerry and found him passed out behind the four-wheeler. All of a sudden, a man ran out of the building towards them. John's eyes widened as he recognized the man.

"Excuse me, I just heard a crash, is everyone okay? My name is Benjamin. I run this gas station."

"We're okay. I'll be in there in a second," John replied.

The man smiled. He turned around and went back into the building.

"Why didn't you tell him about Jerry?" Paul asked.

"I met him before, when I was five. Don't you remember the story of Uncle Dan and Ben? He is evil. If I told him that one of us was hurt, he might tell us that he would help us and then kill Jerry."

"Then why are we going to buy stuff in his store? Wouldn't he poison some of the stuff or something?"

"I don't think he recognized me. But he would recognize Jerry, so we better not tell him. We better play along like it's just us," John said.

While John went inside, Jerry came around. Paul told Jerry everything. Jerry checked the fuel gauge. It was almost empty. Jerry got a gas hose and started filling it up. John came back out with a screwdriver, magnifying glass, three bags of chips and a liter of soda.

"Is that all you got?" Jerry asked, halfway done filling up the four-wheeler.

"It was the only things I could afford. I had to use my emergency money; I always put it in my shoe. I only had seven dollars. I thought the chips might be enough to feed us. A magnifying glass will help us take a close look at Zyno's stuff.

After I told Benjamin about Zyno's lab, he said I might want to have this," John said, holding up the screwdriver. Jerry knocked the screwdriver away.

"What did you do that for?" John asked. He picked it up.

"It might be a bomb! How dumb can you get, John? This man wanted me dead ever since I was little! Do you think he's changed? No, of course not," Jerry said angrily.

"He doesn't remember me, Jerry!" John said. "I was barely in the picture in the conflict between Uncle Dan, Benjamin and you. It was you and Uncle Dan and no one else. I remember it like it was yesterday. Uncle Dan was one of the best scientists of his day. Benjamin asked Uncle Dan if he would like to join his team of scientists. When he refused, Benjamin got angry and threatened to kill Uncle Dan's nephew (because Uncle Dan has no children). That nephew was you! But seven years passed and he still didn't kill you. We had forgotten about the threat, until one night he came to our house with a knife. Uncle Dan picked up his gun and fired a few bullets at him, but he wasn't a very good shot. But it did cause Ben to drop the knife and run off."

John finished the story and added, "Did I mention myself in the story? No, I didn't. So I bet he won't remember me."

"But why would anyone suggest buying a screwdriver? I mean come on-"

"What do you think, Paul?" John interrupted.

"I think you both got a point," Paul said. He took the screwdriver from John's hand and examined it. "We also haven't seen our uncle in quite some time. But one thing's for sure: there is no bomb in this."

Jerry took the hose out of the four-wheeler and reached into his pocket for his wallet. He left it at home as well.

"No. I tell you no!" Paul said, "I'm not giving you any of my money."

Jerry hopped on the four-wheeler and grinned.

"Hop on," He said to them

"I don't know, Jerry, we could get in big trouble if they catch us," John cautioned, but he get on.

"Okay ... but I'm not sure about this, Jerry," Paul said, though he got on too. Jerry started the engine.

"And where do you think you're going?" said a voice behind them. John groaned.

"STEP ON IT, JERRY!" Paul screamed. Jerry pulled on the handle. They zoomed out of the gas station. There were no cars on the road, so they had a nice get-away.

"Jerry, look!" Paul exclaimed. There was a building just ahead.

"That's it all right. We'll be safe there," Jerry added.

"Safe? Look behind us!" John exclaimed. They turned. In the distance, they could see a motorcycle.

"He can't do much. There's no way he'll catch us," Jerry said. But at that moment, fire came out of the motorcycle. Rockets! And within 30 seconds, he was ten feet away.

2) Starting the Maze

"We have to get to the building now!" Paul exclaimed. "Can't this thing go any faster?"

"No," Jerry replied. "This is as fast as it goes. I'm even having trouble controlling it. But I have an idea."

"Oh no," John moaned.

Jerry turned sharply left, off the road and into the soft dirt. Benjamin went speeding right past them. Jerry sped back onto the road and headed towards Zyno's lab. Benjamin looked behind him, confused. As he saw them going towards the building, he turned his motorcycle around and headed back in their direction. They hopped off their vehicle and ran right to the lab's front door. Locked! Benjamin smiled. He got off his bike and ran towards them. They gave the door one last push and the door finally gave way. They ran in and found another pair of doors. Luckily, these weren't locked. They ran in just as Benjamin headed for the first pair of doors. They quickly locked the inner doors by pressing a button. After many attempts at opening the door, Benjamin gave up and stormed out of the building. They all gave a sigh of relief.

"This is it. Zyno's lab," John said.

But it didn't look much like a lab at all. There was nothing in the room except a small door. They noticed there was a note on the small door. They had to get on their hands and knees to see the message:

Welcome to Zyno's Lab
Enter through these doors and be amazed at the great wonders of Zyno! But stranger, heed my warning. If all goes well, you will see great inventions. But fail and you may never see the outside world again! For I put before you a great maze. If you come to a dead end, just push the wall with all your might. Good luck!

"Maze? What does he mean, 'maze'? I'm not good at mazes! What maze is he talking about anyway?" John exclaimed.

"I think we're supposed to go through the door," Paul replied. He looked for a doorknob and found one the size of a toothpick. Slowly he turned it. It opened and they crawled in. They stood up and saw dark green walls all around them. The walls went up ten feet and connected to the ceiling. They had walked right into the maze!

Their first observation after this was that the building was very hot. They began to sweat within seconds.

"So, Jerry," John said, turning to his oldest brother. "Are you going to turn back to go to the game store or are you going to stay with us?"

"I'm going to go with you guys. Benjamin might still be out there," Jerry replied cautiously.

After walking for at least an hour, they came to a dead end. They did as Zyno ordered and pushed the wall with all their might. Suddenly the maze behind them left as they were sucked into the wall like a black hole. They all lost their stomachs as they felt a falling sensation. A twisted green color like the top of a cyclone appeared in front of them. They were about to pass out from shock when they hit the ground. Paul's glasses snapped in half. Slowly, they got to their feet. They looked like they were outside, but they had never been here before.

"Where are we?" Paul asked, holding up his glasses to his eyes.

"That is easy to answer," growled a voice from behind them. "The question is, what are *you* doing here?"

They turned around quickly. There, crouched down and bearing his teeth, was a leopard – only its fur was pink!

"Er … we are going through a maze, you see, and we kind of … er … got here," Paul said. "Please don't hurt us Mr. Leopard … "

The leopard growled.

"I—AM—NOT—A—LEOPARD!"

He pounced. Jerry stepped in front of John and Paul. The leopard landed on Jerry, and he and the leopard fought. Jerry, with his lightning-fast reflexes built from video games, avoided the leopard's slashing paws. Using his feet, Jerry pushed the leopard off with all his might. The leopard looked surprised. Then he smiled and bowed his head.

"I have met my match. So what do you need to know?"

They were all about to ask something, but Jerry spoke first.

"If you are not a leopard, what are you?"

For a second the leopard looked offended. But he quickly overlooked the insult and said, "A tiger. My name is Lino."

"Let me get this straight," John said, "You are pink, you have spots like a leopard, your name sounds like a lion name, but you call yourself a *tiger*?"

Before Lino could answer, Paul asked, "Where are we?"

"In a time portal," Lino answered. "You are in the future. Your time was eons ago. I'm not sure what time it is now. To answer your question," nodding to John, "any animal can mate with any other animal nowadays. Tigers in your world will mix with leopards. My dad was such a mix. My mom was a flamingo. And here I am."

"Your mom was a flamingo," Paul repeated in disbelief.

"How can you talk?" John asked, continuing.

"How can you?" Lino said.

"Well, I learned," John replied.

"Same with me," Lino said, laughing. "Nowadays, most animals speak."

"Do you know how to get back into the maze?" Jerry asked.

"Oh yes, indeed," Lino exclaimed. "But I must warn you, that it is very dangerous in the maze."

Jerry's stomach rumbled.

"Ah … can we have something to eat first?" He asked.

So they all ate their chips – Lino ate an innocent bunny hopping by – and then started off for the maze. After what seemed like an hour, Jerry got tired and collapsed to the ground.

"I'm tired guys, I need a break," he said.

"We can't stop now, Jerry, we have to get back to the maze!" John said impatiently.

"Well you guys go ahead, I'll catch up," Jerry said. John was about to argue with him, but then thought better of it. He turned around and left leading Lino and Paul.

They walked for a quarter of an hour before anything happened. They heard a high cruel laugh behind them. They turned around to see a big hyena with huge macaw, rainbow-like wings. Lino growled.

"It's you," he said. The hyena stopped laughing.

"It's nice to see you again, Pink Panther," said the hyena dancing. "It's been a long time since we've seen each other. Why don't you ever visit me?"

"Shut up!" Lino roared. "And you know I hate being called *that*!"

The hyena looked at Paul and John.

"And you didn't invite me to dinner," the hyena said. "I love raw human. But it's been over a year since they have been extinct. Leave it to the Pink Panther to find the last ones. Mind if I enjoy the feast with you?"

"I'm not going to eat them," Lino growled. "They happen to be my friends. Their older brother, Jerry, is quite a fighter too, he's the best … "

"THREE! THREE HUMANS FOR DINNER? FEAST!"

The hyena jumped into the air, flew over and snatched Paul and John by their necks.

"Come back here!" Lino yelled from the ground as the hyena started to fly away. The hyena looked down and laughed.

"Ah, we can't forget Pink Panther," he said.

He took from behind his wing what looked like a chain with thorns. He threw it at Lino, which bound him fast. Lino screamed. The hyena kept laughing.

"I'll bind you guys up, too," He said. "And then you and your brother will be my evening feast! HA!"

It was a long time before Jerry got up and stretched and began to walk. Thirty seconds later, the hyena jumped out of the bushes.

"Are you Mr. Jerry?" He asked.

"My name is Jerry Quaill. Who are-"

Jerry was cut off suddenly because the hyena jumped at him, grabbed him by the neck and flew off.

"Lino said you were a great fighter?! You were easier then taking carrots from a rabbit. But then again, Lino is a pathetic fighter." He laughed his hard cruel laugh.

When they landed, the hyena led Jerry inside an enormous building. As they walked in, however, it looked very small. He was so surprised that the building was huge on the outside and tiny in the inside that at first he didn't notice how cold it was. After a few seconds it became apparent. He looked at his watch.

The thing most unusual about his watch was not only did it contain the day of the week, time and date, but it had the temperature of the room (made by Paul of course): -41. Jerry didn't have to be a genius to know that just about 20 minutes in here and you could freeze to death. The hyena tied up Jerry's arms and hands. He started to lead him to another room, but Jerry slipped on a puddle and fell to the ground. The puddle contained an oily substance.

"Are you humans so uncoordinated?" The hyena said angrily. He brushed the substance off the ropes. "Your family members did the same thing!"

The hyena led him into a room where Paul and John were out cold.

"What did you to them?" Jerry asked miserably.

"Oh they are just cold, just like you will soon be." The hyena said happily as he quickly tied Jerry up. "Goodbye!"

And he flew out of the room. Jerry started thinking fast. He started wiggling and finally, his book bag fell off. He unzipped it with his hands behind his back. He went through it and finally found what he was looking for; the liter of soda had been there from over an hour ago and was very warm. Slowly he unscrewed the top and splashed it on Paul and John. John shook his head and opened his eyes a little. He still looked pale and cold. Paul hadn't moved at all.

"You okay, John?" Jerry asked. "We're going to get out of here in no time."

He splashed a little more on Paul. But already, the soda was getting colder. He splashed the rest on Paul and finally, he awoke.

" ... Jerry? ... Is ... that ... you? It's ... so ... cold." Paul shook as he spoke. Jerry rattled his mind for something. It would be a matter of minutes before they all died. He was already getting colder and weaker by the second. But John wasn't. Quite the contrary, he looked like he was getting stronger by the second. Yet he still looked very pale.

"Jerry, we've got to get out of these ropes," John said weakly. "There is a window right there, so that might give us a little bit of heat, but other than that, we have nothing. If only I had my pocket knife ... "

"Where is it?" Jerry asked at once.

"The hyena took it and threw it out the window," John replied sadly.

Paul was fading away fast. The sun just reached the window, giving off some of its energy, but had little or no effect on Paul.

"Can you go through your supplies again?" Jerry asked.

"I have a screwdriver, a magnifying glass and half of a bag of chips," John replied.

"Can you give me some of your chips? I bet they're warm." Jerry asked.

"Good idea, they're in my pocket." John said. So very slowly, with his hands tied behind him, Jerry took out John's chips from inside his pocket and gave them to Paul who bent down and ate them.

"Pretty warm, thanks guys," Paul said. "But not enough, we still need to get out of here."

"Do you think we could light a fire in here?" John asked.

"Probably not," Jerry said. "But what I don't understand is how the hyena didn't shiver when he came in here."

"Maybe it's because of his fur coat like the animals in our world," John replied.

"No, it wasn't that thick. I remember feeling his skin when he picked me up," Paul said. "Maybe he has pulled humans in here for so long, he's just used to it."

"But he said that humans were extinct over a year ago," Jerry said. "And pardon me if I am wrong, but not doing something for a year won't get you used to it."

"And another thing, why did he put us in here in the first place?" Paul asked. "Why doesn't he just eat us whole?"

"Well, I think to him this is a freezer and he already has something to eat," Jerry replied breathing hard.

"Jerry, you have been in here only a few minutes but look paler than me; I've been in here a lot longer," John said.

"How long have you been in here?" Jerry asked.

"Not sure of the exact amount," John said, "But I think I was in here about fifteen minutes when I passed out. Maybe half an hour."

"Do you know any way to keep yourself warm?" Jerry asked.

"I would probably know, but it feels like I have been brainwashed and I can't remember anything," Paul answered.

"Look, what we should concentrate on is getting ourselves out of here," John said

"I don't agree John," Jerry argued. "I think we should worry about keeping warm first.".

But Paul was thinking of something else. *Fail and you will never see the outside world again.* Jerry must have read his mind, for he said, "don't worry Paul, we will definitely get out of here. It's just taking some time."

Paul nodded. He was still worried. Even though Jerry kept saying things like, "It's okay, Paul," and, "We will find a way out." Jerry looked paler then ever. *It's over*, Paul thought, and just when he was thinking of what it would feel like to be dead, Jerry's face lit with excitement.

"John, I just thought of something," Jerry said quickly. "Could you get your items out with your hands behind your back?"

"I think so, why?" John replied.

"I think I've got the perfect plan. It's the only one I can come up with," Jerry said. "I can't see; is the sun still visible out the window?"

"Yeah, is that what your plan is … climb out the window?" John asked.

"No. John, can you get out the screwdriver and magnifying glass?" Jerry asked.

Again, slowly he unzipped the frozen zipper and it broke. He reached inside and felt around until he pulled out the two things. He threw it over his shoulder and Jerry caught them behind his back.

"Okay, Jerry what's up? Why do you need the magnifying glass and screwdriver?" John asked.

"To get out of here of course," Jerry replied.

"Well wasn't that specific," John said sarcastically. "Jerry we have a right to know what you're up to!"

"Yeah Jerry, tell us before we freeze," Paul pleaded. Jerry realized that both of them looked paler than death.

"Okay, here's the plan," Jerry began, and they both looked very still.

"Wait a second, Jerry ... " John said. They all heard footsteps coming. The door burst open and the hyena came in. He looked stunned that they were still conscious.

"Wow, still alive?" He said, but then seeing them pale he just grinned evilly and said, "Oh, well, it's just that no one has survived this long. I wanted to check on you. You will soon be reunited with your friend Lino..." – John's heart filled with anger when thought of him being wrapped up with chains – " ... and he will be dead when you do."

He grinned again and left.

"That was close," Paul said, giving a sigh of relief. "What where you saying, Jerry?" And then, "J ... Jerry?"

Jerry had fallen over and passed out. He had become completely frozen.

3) The Great Escape

"What happened to him?" John asked.

"He-he is f-frozen!" Paul shuddered. "We couldn't think of something fast enough. We're going to freeze soon too."

John thought of something.

"Paul, this is like a riddle! Why would he want to know if the sun is there? And the magnifying glass?"

"Well, there is only one thing I can think of," Paul replied. "If you hold a magnifying glass up to the sun, you can create a fire. But if he thinks he could burn our way through the ropes, he's wrong. It would burn us too."

" ... And fire can't burn through metal! Paul, we will hold the screwdriver in between the rope and us, the heat will burn the rope and nothing else! Not only that, the rope will be a lot more flammable since we both fell in the oily stuff outside, which I am guessing is gasoline. The hyena brushed off most of it, but it'll be just it enough for the fire to catch. It's a bit risky though ... "

"I'll say!" Paul interrupted. "If this fails, we will die! Excuse me, I would rather die frozen than burning up."

"But we have no other choice," John argued. "I think there is little chance of surviving this and no chance if we just sit here."

"Right," Paul gave in. "Hand me the screwdriver and the magnifying glass."

"No, sorry, I'll be doing it!" John argued.

"I'm going to—"

But it was too late. John had already gotten the magnifying glass and held it out. He put the metal part of the screwdriver in between his skin and the rope. He held the magnifying glass between the sun and the screwdriver. The sun's rays could now pass through the magnifying glass and could make a fire on the rope. Two minutes passed before the rope caught on fire. The screwdriver stopped the fire from reaching John's skin because the metal wouldn't burn. It burned enough that the ropes came off. It worked! John quickly untied Paul. Paul got up and congratulated John. John picked up Jerry and put him on his back, leaving his backpack up to Paul.

"How are we going to get out?" John said, seeing that the door was locked.

"I have an idea. Give me the burning ropes." Paul said. Then he shouted, "Boy is it good to be out of those ropes!"

His plan worked! They could hear the footsteps of the running hyena. The door burst open and the hyena stood in its place. Paul quickly threw the ropes at him and it coiled around the hyena's body, burning his skin. The hyena screamed like a banshee. They quickly ran out and found a huge metal door. They turned around. The hyena was recovering.

BAM!

They looked at the door. There was a huge dent in it.

BAM!

Someone was trying to break through. With one more smash the door came down upon them. They quickly jumped back as it came thundering down. Two kids about the age of twelve and thirteen were holding large sledgehammers.

"Jimmy! Tyler!" John exclaimed.

"No time for hellos. We need to get you out of here," Tyler said. He threw John his pocketknife. "Found this outside."

"You are right, we've got to get out of here," John said. "We need to save Lino!"

"Who's-"

"Never mind," Paul said, signaling they didn't have time to explain. They ran off. Suddenly, the hyena's screaming stopped.

"He's probably recovering, we have to hurry," John said. "We need to find Lino. I don't think we can find our way out ourselves."

John's back was aching because he was carrying Jerry the whole time. He was sweating harder than he ever had in the maze. He wished Jerry would just wake up. Tyler read his mind.

"John, give him to me," He said. "You have just come out of a huge freezer; you must be very tired and weak. I am stronger. Working with my dad carrying wood has its advantages."

John was very thankful for Tyler. He was a friend that he could always count on. He gave Jerry to him. Paul gave him his backpack.

After a long search, they found the pink tiger still struggling with the chain. There were huge cuts on him from wrestling with the chain because of the thorns.

"Lino, are you okay?" Paul said. Jimmy's eyes widened. Tyler let go of Jerry and Jerry fell to the ground.

"What a dumb question," Lino growled weakly, "Of course not."

"What are we going to do now?" John asked impatiently.

"Please," Lino moaned, "find the key to open this."

"What is going to happen if we can't find it?" John asked desperately.

"A scientist will come and finish me off soon," Lino moaned again. "He always does; animals that are still strong hide from him."

"Don't worry," Paul said grinning. "I'm a little scientist myself."

Everyone stared at him, even John. Paul took off his backpack and pulled out a laptop computer. He grinned again but nobody else did. John took the opportunity to give Paul one of his many lectures

"Paul!" John said sharply. "How did you get a laptop? They are over $2,000! And didn't mom say you couldn't have one?"

Paul's grinned faded. "For your information, John, I didn't buy it. Mom said I could have one if I could *make* one. And no other laptop in the whole world could match this one."

He turned it on. A hologram of a person suddenly appeared. He was saying things very fast in a different language that nobody seemed to understand except Paul. Paul typed for a long time, sometimes looking up and talking to the hologram in its language. Finally, Paul said something in English.

"*Activate key*!" He said. Another hologram came out. It was a piece of paper with words on it. He read it and started typing again. Five times he did this, until a key came out. He handed it to John and turned off the computer; the hologram of the person disappeared.

"Paul, what the—" John began, but Paul held up a hand meaning to stop talking. He looked at Lino and said "There isn't a lock on this thing."

"Put it in my mouth," Lino said and Paul did. "It's tiger magic. You'll see."

The chain disappeared. Lino got up and thanked Paul. Seeing Jerry, he asked "What's wrong with him?"

"He is basically frozen. We need to somehow unfreeze him. What do we have to do that?"

"I have a lighter, a pocket knife and scissors," Jimmy said.

"I only have walkie-talkies and a compass," Tyler replied.

"Well, we could make a fire and hopefully Jerry would warm up enough to wake him," John said doubtfully.

"I don't think we should stop," Jimmy said. "That hyena might still be out there."

"We might not get another chance to unfreeze him," Paul said, "John is right. We can fight. We have weapons." He grinned patting his backpack that held his laptop. John scowled.

"You win," Jimmy answered. He handed them his lighter. John shook his head.

"Jimmy, your parents didn't let you have you a lighter, did they?" he said. "How did you get it?"

Jimmy grinned. "Isn't it obvious, John? I smuggled it out of my dad's room. John, I don't see why you don't have your own family. You would make a great parent."

"No, I'm just very cautious, thank you," John said fuming.

"Then shut up and be a kid for another seven years." Jimmy said smiling at John's anger. John looked furious.

"Come on, Jerry, please wake up." Paul said. They had set up the fire and put Jerry very close to it. Paul was shaking him.

"What should we do?" He asked John.

"I don't think I heard anything in class about how to get unfrozen. ("That makes sense," Tyler said to Jimmy. "He always plays table-top football in Science class.") You're the boy-genus," John replied.

"I know I'm smart and all that," Paul said, "But I don't know everything."

All of a sudden, there was a cough. Then, a moan.

"Jerry! You're okay!" Paul said joyfully.

" ... Yeah ... where am I?" Jerry muttered smiling as Paul hugged him. And then he said, "Hey, how did you guys get out of that freezer?"

"Long story Jerry, I'll tell you later when we have time," John said. "Right now, we've got to get back to the maze. Lino, lead the way."

Lino turned and ran off. They could barely keep up.

An hour later, they got to a big metal door.
John said, "Hang on, there's a message:

Congratulations
You have gotten through the first world of the maze.
Once you go through this door you will be back in the maze.
If you do this maze correctly, there are only five more worlds
left. Enter through this door by entering the chip into the
slot.
Insert here→
"

"*Only* five," John moaned. "And what chip is he talking about?"

Nobody could answer him. There was a loud screech from behind them. They all spun around. The great hyena was flying towards them in the distance.

"The only chips I have are the ones in my bag," Jerry said.

"I have a chip that might be the one we need," Jimmy said. He took out of his pocket what seemed to be a small computer chip.

"Well, it's worth a try," Paul said. He took the chip from his hand. He was about to put it in when something hit him hard from behind and the chip flew out of his hand. The hyena had just pushed him. He flew fast over to where the chip had landed, but Jerry was faster. He quickly jumped on it. The hyena went full speed at him. Tyler got between Jerry and the hyena. Tyler got out his sledgehammer and gripped it tight. He swung it like a baseball bat with all his might. His aim was true. He hit the hyena in the head and the hyena fell to the ground unconscious.

"Nice shot," Lino said, admiring the damage.

"Okay, now that that's out of the way," John said, taking a breath, "let's get back to the maze."

He slid the chip into the slot. The door opened. They only saw the green swirl. They were sucked in again. After thirty seconds of free fall, they finally landed on the hard floor of the maze. Paul put away his snapped glasses and pulled out a new pair. The temperature felt very good to Paul, John, and Jerry after being in the freezer so long. Jimmy and Tyler however, were not in a freezer for an hour, so they didn't feel very good. Jimmy took off his glasses and wiped them off. Because he was sweating so much, the perspiration had fogged up his glasses.

"Jerry, how hot is in here?" Jimmy panted. Jerry looked at his watch.

"Ninety-one degrees," Jerry replied. "Wow! I didn't realize that it was this hot. We better get to a different world fast. We could dehydrate."

They kept walking until they came to a fork. They all looked at each other.

"I think we should split up," Jimmy said. "We will take different routes."

"Good idea," Tyler said. "We can each take one of my walkie-talkies."

"I don't think that would be smart, Tyler," Paul corrected. "Who knows what kind of worlds this maze possesses. We might be in a whole different dimension. Or we could be in a whole different century. I bet they would go haywire for either."

"Well, it's worth a try," Jerry said. He took one.

"Well, see you then," Jimmy said. They both took their different routes. John, Paul, Lino and Jerry went for a long time without seeing a dead end.

"When ... will ... this ... thing ... ever ...end?" John panted.

"There!" Paul pointed. "I see one to our right."

They ran towards it. They stopped right in front of it.

"I think we should call Tyler and Jimmy before we enter," Jerry said. He called and told them. He put the walkie-talkie away and put his hands up to the wall.

"Ready?" he asked.

"Hang on," Paul said. He took off his glasses and he too put his hands up on the wall. John followed suit. They all pushed.

For the third time, they all lost their stomachs. They felt like they were falling again, only this time it was a blue cyclone. They were gasping for breath. Just when they thought they couldn't last any longer—

CRASH!

They landed face-first on the ground. They got up, and Jerry said "Let's see who can actually land on their feet next time."

The four of them slowly got up and (after Paul put on his glasses) looked around. It was dark, damp and cold.

"Where are we?" Paul asked. All of a sudden something moved in the shadows. It came out into the light. They gasped. It was a pterodactyl. It was bigger than they had ever imagined.

"Um ... Paul? I know where we are," Lino replied. "We-we are in the past."

It swooped down towards them. They jumped to the ground. That is, all except Lino. Lino stood his ground. He waited until the last second before he pounced. The Quaills just laid there petrified. The pterodactyl bit Lino with its huge jaws. It ripped the skin. Just as Lino screamed, John jumped to his feet. He charged the dinosaur and pulled out his pocketknife; but Lino's paw slashed off its head.

"That was close," Jerry said, getting to his feet.

"Yeah," Paul agreed. "Let's look around for that chip."

"What chip?" John asked.

"Well, we had to get one in the first world, right?" Paul replied. "I bet you it's going to happen in this one. Why would Zyno change it around?"

"To throw us off course, as usual," John replied.

"What do you mean 'as usual'?" Paul asked testily. "He hasn't done anything to us."

"Let's count then," John said sarcastically, "Let's see now ... he made this complicated maze, he made a time portal that contains a hyena with macaw's wings and a tiger that's pink and has black spots like a leopard (Lino cleared his throat at this), makes metal doors that you need chips to open, another time portal that goes to the past, a ..."

"Oh, shut up, I get the point!" Paul said.

"He's right though," Jerry said. "Let's look for a chip."

They went around looking for it. They found no dinosaurs on the way, but they did see huge dinosaur eggs, which made them more nervous. Paul wanted to keep one *only* for research, but John stomped on that idea by pointing out that even a pterodactyl would be bigger than their house.

"But we could give him to the museum – or a zoo even – and we could get lots of money!" Paul pleaded.

"No, Paul, we are not bringing home a dinosaur egg and that is final!" John answered sternly.

"Hey! Look, there's a chip," Jerry said.

He bent down to get it, but John threw out an arm to stop him. His eyes were transfixed on something a few feet away, way up. Jerry followed John's gaze upwards. He looked into the eyes of the biggest and the most vicious monstrosity of a creature to roam the land. The Tyrannosaurus Rex! It was twice the size of an average T-Rex that Paul had read about in a book. The book said 50 feet. This one was at least 90. For a second, Lino, Paul, John and Jerry stared at the dinosaur and it stared back. Then they screamed and ran faster than they thought they could ever run. The dinosaur came rampaging right behind them.

"Quick! Get in the pit!" Jerry yelled. They all dove into a big hole in the ground. The dinosaur soon found them. It shot out its deadly jaws at them. They dove out of the way, but John wasn't so lucky. The jaws caught his backpack and the T-Rex dragged him upward. He was screaming very wildly, like a maniac. Thinking quickly, Jerry got out his walkie-talkie and pressed the "talk" button.

"Tyler, can you hear me?" he said.

"Loud and clear," came the response from the walkie-talkie.

"Ty, do you know the weakness of a T-Rex?" Jerry asked in desperation.

"Course' I do," Tyler replied, casually. "I actually pay attention in science class. Hit it in the only soft spot on its body: its eyes. There was that one story about the spikes of a stegosaurus hitting—"

Jerry turned off the walkie-talkie. He picked up a large stone. Then he found another problem.

"How am I going to throw it ninety feet?" He said. Paul shrugged. Jerry gave it one hopeless throw. It hit the dinosaur's chest and bounced off. The dinosaur looked down. He dropped John and bent down to get Jerry. They could hear John's leg crack and break. Jerry quickly dropped his back-bag and picked up the largest stone he could see. When he looked up, he saw that the dinosaur's head was 10 feet from him. He swiftly threw it at the dinosaur's eye. They heard a 'plop' and they saw milky-white liquid squirt out of the dinosaur's socket. The dinosaur roared. It turned its head so he could see Jerry. Jerry picked up another rock and threw it at its eye. They all heard another 'plop' and the dinosaur's eye exploded. The blinded dinosaur lifted its head to normal height again. Jerry ran and picked up John, leaving his back bag behind. The dinosaur tripped and came crashing down. Jerry dove out of the way, John still on his back. The T-Rex fell onto an unusually shaped boulder that punctured through the chest of the beast. The dinosaur gave one more deafening roar and then it died. Paul and Lino ran up to John.

"John, are you ok?" Lino asked.

"Yeah, Lino, I'm fine," said John, rubbing his ankle.

"No, really, I think you hurt your ankle," Paul said, looking concerned.

"Ya' think?" John said in an annoyed tone.

"Sounds like he's fine to me," said Jerry, grinning.

"No, I think he broke his ankle, or at least the dinosaur did," Paul said, getting something from his back pack. As John saw what it was, he moaned. It was his computer.

"Paul, really, I'm fine," John said, trying to get up. But he fell down again.

Paul opened up his laptop and turned it on. The hologram of a person came out again. He began talking in a different language. Paul spoke back. Then he nodded in John's direction. The hologram turned to John.

"Estey ler tiof, noha?" it said to John.

"What?" John muttered, confused.

"Tinke fourm laew englishe," Paul said. It nodded.

"What seems to be the problem?" It said.

"Ankle," John replied. "Who are you?"

"Hologram Saente Flaminetorela," it replied. "But you may call me Flaminetore. I'm here to help you."

"Okay ... uh Flamanatorrer. I guess I can trust you." John said.

"It's pronounced Flay-men-et-tor. It is very difficult to say in your language. That is one of the reasons why my master and I speak in a different language. Difficult words are very easy to say in our language."

John looked at Paul.

"Master?" he said. Paul grinned.

"What are you going to do to him?" Lino asked Flaminetore.

"Heal him as best as I can. I cannot fully repair a fracture," Flaminetore said. He turned to John. "Can you be careful on that leg once I heal it? You may still walk on it and, if you leave it alone for a while, run on it."

"Okay," John said. Flaminetore grabbed John's leg and lifted it. Paul typed something on the computer. John's leg vanished. John screamed. Lino pounced at the hologram. He went right through it. Instantly, John's leg was back and the pain was gone.

"Thanks," John said, feeling his visible limb.

"We shall meet again. Well, now how shall I put it? Oh yes, English. *Goodbye*," Flaminetore said, the last word sounding very familiar in computer speech. He disappeared into the computer.

John got up and pushed his extremely long, dark hair out of his eyes.

"Well, let's roll," Jerry said, picking up the chip from the ground. "Let's find that metal door."

They traveled for about five minutes, talking about Flaminetore.

"What languages were you and Flaminetore speaking in, Paul?" Jerry asked.

"Neptune's main language," Paul replied.

"And what's up with him calling you master?" John asked, close to laughing.

"Hey, I had nothing to do with that," Paul lied, trying to hide his guilty face.

They came to a small lake. The water looked clean ("Wow, at this time in the world?" Paul said) but they looked to see if they could walk around it. It was very long. The easiest way to the other side was to swim across.

"Should we swim across or walk around it?" Lino asked.

"The sooner we get out of this maze the better," Jerry replied.

Before anyone could stop him, he dove into the pond. He came up and he was shivering.

"Come on, it won't kill you," he said.

So they all jumped in and swam across. Small minnows swam away as they approached the middle of the lake.

"Do you smell something?" Paul said, making a face.

"No," they all answered. They reached the other end of the lake and they got out soaking wet. Jerry shook his head, brown hair no longer spiked. Then John informed them of another problem.

"I'm hungry," he said. Jerry and Lino agreed. Paul was about to argue when his stomach rumbled. He nodded weakly.

"Where are we going to find food?" Jerry asked.

"We could eat the dinosaur, that's … well, if you don't like my idea, you come up with one," John said. Everyone had made a face at the thought of eating a dinosaur. They all looked at each other and had to agree. So they turned around and swam back.

"I swear, I smell something gross," Paul said. Jerry treaded water and reversed his direction.

"There's nothing here, Paul," Jerry said. They all turned around and swam to the other side of the lake a little faster then usual. They got out and ran back to the war scene. They saw that the huge T-Rex was lying face down with other dinosaurs walking around it and eating it. Lino ran at them, growling. They all scattered. John took out his pocketknife headed towards it. Paul stopped him.

"John, wait," Paul said. "Raw meat is bad for you. You may get sick."

"No problem," John said, cutting off some skin. "We'll just ask Flaminetore to heal us or something."

"I know that he is amazing, but he cannot do everything," Paul said. John tried a piece. He made a face.

"It tastes like octopus," he said almost gagging.

"MMMM," Jerry said running over. Growing up on an island, Jerry loved the taste of seafood.

"I'll put some in my bag so we can still eat while we look for the metal door," Paul said, after eating some himself.

"Now that we've got something to eat," Lino said, eating a particularly large piece of skin, "let's plan where we should camp tonight."

"What?" John asked.

"Well, it is getting late," Lino said. "We should camp somewhere safe because I don't think this place is safe to sleep without shelter."

"Where should we camp though?" Jerry asked.

"Well, I saw a huge tree across the lake," Paul said. "Maybe it is hollow. If it is, let's sleep inside of it."

"Do you think there is enough room?" John said.

"It has to fit three kids and a tiger," Jerry added.

"I can't really remember how big it was exactly," Paul said.

"Well, let's try to retrace our steps because I didn't see any thick trees," John said.

"Right," Jerry said, taking another wad of skin and stuffing it into his mouth.

They came once again to the lake. They dove in and started to swim across. Then they all smelled it.

"It stinks," John said.

"What is it?" Jerry questioned. He turned around and gasped. He quickly turned back around and started to swim as fast as he could. He said, "Swim as fast as you can and whatever you do, don't look back; it will slow you down."

They did as they were told. Lino and Jerry got to the other side and leapt out. John was almost there. Paul swam very fast. When he got close to the end, he couldn't resist it. He looked over his shoulder. Some feet away from him, he saw something right under the surface of the water.

"Paul, don't look back, just swim!" Jerry yelled. John had just got out. Paul turned his head back and started swimming faster than he ever thought he could. He was only three feet from the edge now. He heard a huge snapping noise from behind him as though someone had just turned up the volume of someone who clapped. He jumped out. Not a moment too soon, too. The snapping noise happened again, and Paul finally got to see what it really was. It was a crocodile, at least 10 feet long. It turned around and fell back into the water.

"That was close," said John shivering.

"Amen," Paul said, wiping off his fogged-up glasses. "Let's find that tree now."

Suddenly, there was a long, low growl. They spun around. Nothing was there.

"Lino, stop scaring us like that," Paul said calmly.

"I swear I didn't do that," Lino replied, with a shaky voice. "Does this place ever sleep?"

They were all petrified. Slowly, they turned back around and started to walk at a slightly faster pace.

"There's the tree!" Paul said joyfully.

It was at least 50 feet tall and 15 thick. They ran up to it. Paul pounded on it. Inside they heard an echo.

"Yes, it's hollow!" Paul exclaimed. "Cut it open with your knife, John!"

John was about one quarter of the way done when they heard the growl again. They spun around.

"Uh ... Lino?" Paul said, panic-stricken. "I hope that is your ancestor."

For right in front of them was not a wild tiger known in their year. This was a saber-tooth tiger.

4) The Hyena, the Tiger, and the Door

For a moment all of them stood very still, but the saber-tooth tiger sank his sharp claws into the ground and crouched down. Lino pounced at the tiger first. The tiger jumped aside and Lino fell onto the ground. The tiger jumped on top of Lino. *The saber-tooth tiger has the upper hand*, they all thought. They were right. The tiger began scratching and biting Lino. Lino started to scream. Jerry tried to distract it by throwing a stone at it. For all the effect it had on it, it was like trying to push a giant T-Rex's heel off a cliff with a twig.

They all racked their brains to think of something. John looked at Paul.

"Can't Flaminetore do anything?" John asked almost pleadingly.

"Even if he could, it would probably be too late." Paul replied. John turned back to the war-scene. *There was only one thing left to do.* He took out his pocketknife and examined all of the knives quickly. He opened the sharpest one and took a step forward. Immediately, a pair of hands grabbed him by the shoulders and pulled him back. He turned to see that the hands belonged to Jerry.

"Are you insane?" Jerry whispered. "We will just have to leave it to Lino. You're going to get killed if you go out there."

But John wasn't listening. With huge strength he didn't know he had, he pulled off Jerry's hands and said, "I-DON'T-CARE!"

He ran towards the tiger with the blade in hand. The tiger looked over his shoulder. It was enough of a distraction. Lino rolled out from under the tiger. The tiger fell to the ground. Seeing his chance, John lunged. Before he could get any further, however, something hit him very hard in the back and he fell to the ground. Paul had tried to protect him by tackling him.

Lino jumped on the tiger and began to claw it. It looked like Lino had the battle won, but the saber-tooth tiger smacked a mighty paw at Lino. Lino staggered a little and the saber-tooth tiger wrenched free.

It was the most vicious battle that they had ever seen. When one had the upper hand, two seconds later, it was reversed.

There were some blood spots on the ground. Most of them, they noticed, belonged to Lino.

Now the saber-tooth was winning again. It was pouncing, scratching and biting Lino, who could barely defend himself, let alone attack. Both Jerry and Paul were holding back John, who was desperately trying to get back to the fight. The tiger showed no mercy towards Lino. Lino kept on screaming with pain. Each scream got John stronger. Finally, he broke away and started to run towards the fight. He jumped on the tiger. He wrapped an arm around its neck and stabbed him in the side.

"Get Lino and run!" he yelled to Jerry and Paul. "I'll hold him off!"

They both picked up Lino and ran towards the cut tree. Jerry released a moaning Lino and began pulling on the remaining strip.

John tightened his grip on the neck of the tiger and started stabbing it wildly and repeatedly. He thought he had gone crazy, wrestling with a full-grown saber-tooth tiger. But then he thought of himself trying to save Jerry, Paul and Lino. He couldn't give in. However hard the tiger was struggling, he had to hang on, or it will ignore him and attack Jerry and Paul.

Just then, the tiger struggled and the knife got knocked out of John's hands. Jerry saw this and snatched the knife.

"Get out of here," John said exhaustedly. "You've ... got ... to ... go! Can't ... hold ... him ... off ... much ... longer!"

Jerry turned and finished cutting a hole in the trunk. With enormous effort, he was able to drag in Lino. Jerry jumped in after. Paul yelled, "John, come on! Jump in!"

John jumped off the saber-tooth tiger and ran flat out towards the tree. He could hear the tiger behind him. He dove in and Jerry put the missing piece into the hole. They heard snarl after snarl as the tiger tried to slice open the tree trunk. It would not give up its meal so easily.

"It's nuts if it thinks it could claw its way through this," Jerry said pointing to the thickness in the trunk. John wasn't thinking about anything except the fact that he – an 11-year-old – just escaped from a fully grown saber-tooth tiger with barely a scratch on him. He came to his senses and asked, "How's Lino?"

"Hurt," Jerry said. "Paul, you need to get out your computer."

Paul reached for his back bag and saw it was unzipped. He searched for his computer, but found that it was missing.

"It's gone! I don't believe it! It must have fallen out!" Paul said stunned.

"You're kidding!" Jerry said, also amazed.

"How come you didn't notice?" John asked accusingly.

"I don't know, but look at this!" Paul said. They walked over toward the bag and found lots of little stones that looked soaked.

"That looks like some rocks floated right into your bag at the lake," John said.

"Don't be stupid, rocks don't float," Jerry said. "What if the computer fell into the lake and as you were getting out, your bag scraped the—"

"That's awful!" John said suddenly. "Your computer wouldn't work even if we still did have it. It would be so soaked-"

"Nope," said Paul as if John didn't know anything. "It's water-proof, fire-proof and bullet-proof. It's nearly invincible. The only thing it can't resist is a strike of lightning."

"Or you could have just dropped it right outside," Lino said hopefully.

"I'm not going out there," John said, as they heard scraping noises. "One fight with a saber-tooth is enough for one lifetime."

"Oh, don't mind me," Lino said sarcastically. "Don't mind me, I'll just die here and you can just watch."

"Lino, we tried everything, we—"

"I'll do it," said Jerry. "I'll go get the computer. I'll fight the tiger and find the ... "

"I'll find my computer," Paul said, interrupting him. "I'll look for the computer and Jerry should fight it. It should be simple for me to find my computer. It is gold on the outside with shiny-silver edges."

So though reluctantly, John gave Jerry his pocketknife and Paul left with Jerry. He was alone with Lino. John looked at him. When he first met him, he thought he would see nothing mightier, and when he starting to become their friend, he felt very much protected. Now here Lino was, defenseless and weak, not even able to squash a bug with his paw.

"What are you staring at?" Lino asked a little annoyed. John shook his head. He didn't want to look at Lino for a while. He concentrated on some termites scuttling by.

"Stupid things," Lino said, following John's gaze and saw the bugs. "How can they survive from here to my time? They should go, just like the dinosaurs."

He sighed. He rolled over on his side.

"Hey, Lino," John said. "Are you sure there's nothing I can do to help you?"

Suddenly Lino jumped up, startling John.

"Lino ... Wha-" John began, but Lino apparently couldn't hear him. His eyes went out of focus. He was saying over and over, "*Need ... blood ... can't carry on ... without it*!"

He started to head towards John who backed up.

"*Need ... blood ... can't carry on ... without it*!"

John felt his back hit the end of the tree.

"*Need blood! Need blood! Save myself*!" Lino was yelling, approaching John with hunger in his eyes. He was a couple of inches away when he stopped and his head drooped. He shook his head and then very suddenly fell to the ground. John crawled over to him.

"Uh ... Lino," John said cautiously. "Are you ok?"

"What?" Lino replied, groaning. "Of course not. I was the one that fought the saber-tooth tiger remember?"

"No, I mean right now you were acting kind of strange," John said.

"What do you mean?" Lino asked curiously. "Oh! I just tried to take a nap and I must have—"

"You weren't sleep-walking," John said nervously. "You ... you were chanting something about needing blood."

Lino's eyes widened. His expression looked as though he had forgotten something very important. He shook his head.

"Sorry about that," Lino said. "Nothing important. Sorry I scared you."

"What was that?" John asked.

"I said already, nothing important!" Lino snapped. But John didn't stop asking him. Finally Lino gave in.

"Yes, there is something that you can do to help me," Lino said. "If I mix a different animal's blood – a good amount – with my blood, all of my scars and wounds will disappear from the past 200 years. Two hundred years is a short while for us tigers." He added seeing John's stunned face. He shook his head again. "But you wouldn't ... you couldn't ... "

"I'll do it," John said at once.

"You're not going to give me some of your blood just for my health!" Lino said in a final tone, but at the end of his sentence, he grimaced in pain.

"Of course I'm not," John said, going over to Paul's almost empty backpack. "Some of the dinosaur's skin had a little bit of blood on it. How much do you need?"

"A lot, as much as you can scrape off of the skin," Lino moaned. "Good thinking."

So John gave Lino some dinosaur blood. Immediately, all of Lino's cuts healed and disappeared. All the drops of blood on the ground went back into him. Lino stood up and smiled at John.

"Thank you," Lino said. "And now I'm in your debt."

"Don't mention it," John said grinning. "You don't have to do anything for me."

"Ah ... but I do have to," Lino said, bowing his head. "You have just saved my life."

"Yeah, well, you kind of saved my life too," John said.

"How? That's twice you saved my life," Lino asked, taken aback.

"It was you who saved my life by jumping at the saber-tooth tiger and fighting him," John said. Lino grinned.

"I did that so I could actually have some dinner," Lino said. "I hated that dinosaur skin."

John grinned as well. He muttered, "Whatever."

Lino looked at the piece of trunk they had cut out.

"I don't hear any fighting going on," He said. "If I go out and, well, check on them for a second ... "

"No," John said, standing up quickly. "I'll check."

John popped out the "doorway" and looked out. Two figures were running towards them. They both jumped into the tree, Paul with his laptop.

"Triceratops! We only just got away. Jerry wasn't as lucky as me, though," Paul said. Paul was rubbing his arm, which was bleeding a little. Jerry was bending over, hands on his side.

"You ok, Jerry?" Lino said, looking concerned.

"Never mind me, Paul will fix me up," Jerry said, closing his eyes tightly. "But what about you?"

"Don't need to, Jerry, he's fine." John said. Jerry opened his eyes and looked at Lino. His mouth dropped. "How ... did you ... get ... healed?!"

John told Paul and Jerry about everything. Jerry was amazed.

"Wow! I wish we had healing powers like that!" he said.

"Well, let's get to it. Paul, Flaminetore if you don't mind," John said, rubbing his hands together. Paul nodded and turned on his computer. Five minutes later they were all healed. Before turning off his computer, Paul checked the time and Flaminetore got them all blankets and they went to sleep.

Jerry was up first in the morning. He stretched and pushed his hair out of his eyes. He crawled over and turned on Paul's computer. Flaminetore came out and was about to say something, but Jerry interrupted by saying, "English, please."

Flaminetore looked down and saw Jerry. He smiled.

"Of course, uh ... master's brother," Flaminetore said bowing.

"Just call me Jerry, ok?" Jerry said, embarrassed. Flaminetore bowed again.

"Okay, what would you like me to do for you, sir?"

"Do you have anything to eat? If I may, I would like scrambled eggs... "

"I am sorry, sir," Flaminetore said, shaking his head. "But I can't make anything that you call food."

"Nothing?" Jerry asked, surprised. Then Flaminetore looked thoughtful.

"Well," he said. "There were my experiments. Master didn't really teach me a lot. But I did manage to make a lemon last week. I can try it again."

"Ok, if that's all you can make," Jerry said, making a face. "But remind me to kill Paul for being able to make a machine that can make any key in the world but not even an omelet."

Flaminetore's face turned from friendly to angry.

"You shall not hurt my master," he said. "He thought it wasn't necessary for me to be able to make food because he thought he could always get food himself. But he thought it was necessary to get a key to unlock anything."

"What's all the noise for?"

Lino and John were getting up.

"What time is it?" John said, yawning. Jerry looked at the computer.

"Seven-thirty," Jerry replied. "I think we should wake up Paul. We should be on our way soon. I hope you guys like lemons. Unless you're going to eat that dinosaur skin for breakfast."

So they woke up Paul and ate their lemons quietly. Paul turned off his computer and they got out of the tree.

"Hey Jerry," John said suddenly. "Where was the saber-tooth tiger last night?"

"I got out of the tree and there was nothing there, so I decided to help Paul look for his computer," Jerry replied.

"What's that?" Paul said, pointing to something in the distance. It was running very fast and had huge macaw-colored wings.

"I don't know," Jerry replied. It was getting closer and they noticed it had a gray body. John threw out a hand to stop them.

"I don't believe it," he said, eyes widened. "But ... how?"

"What is it?" everyone asked.

"I ... I think it's the hyena from the first world."

He was right. As it came closer, they saw it more clearly. It had a black burn around its middle. Its face was beat up. It landed in front of them. It looked both tired and angry.

"If I weren't so tired, I would get revenge and kill you all on the spot," it said. "But I was up all night and the burn that you inflicted upon me hurts and I was attacked by a tiger just so I could find you."

"Like you could take us on anyway," John said, angrily reaching into his pocket.

"Oh yeah?" The hyena said. "I'd like to see you humans—"

John pulled out his pocketknife and opened one of the knives. Lino crouched down to pounce. Paul grabbed and opened his computer. Jerry put up his fists.

"What were you saying, dung breath?" Jerry said, grinning at the look of horror on the hyena's face.

"What do you want with us then, if 'you are too tired?'" John said, putting his pocketknife down.

The hyena grimaced. "Well, I was sent to warn you that if you injure another member of the pack, you will be killed."

"What are you talking about?" John said with frustration.

"The pack," the hyena said as though it was the most obvious thing on earth. "The pack! Don't hurt any more of the pack! You know, the saber-tooth tigers?!"

"Oh, we won't be messing with them anymore," Paul chuckled. "We are getting out of here."

"I know that you're heading out of here," said the hyena. "But there are not only saber-tooth tigers in the pack. Well, heed my warning."

He stretched out his wings and said, "Next time we meet, we'll finish this, Lino."

"You'd better count on it!" Lino said, as the hyena flew off.

"What was he talking about?" John repeated.

"I'm not sure myself," Lino said. "But I think he knew about the battle between me and the tiger."

"So he wants us not to attack another thing again, eh?" Jerry said with an edge to his voice. "We actually didn't attack anyone. We were defending ourselves."

"Well, I'm not going to listen to that little piece of scum," Paul said. "Let's just get out of here. I'm sick of living in the past."

"And once I catch up with that thing, I'm going to teach him a lesson for trapping us in that freezer," John replied.

"While we are on the subject, how did you get out of that freezer anyway?" Jerry asked. As they walked on, John and

Paul explained how they got out. When they had finished, Jerry smiled and said, "Good job! That was my idea too. I didn't think it would work either, but it was worth a shot!"

"When do you think we will get out of here?" Lino said.

"I don't know, but sometime soon, I bet," Paul said checking his watch. "We have been traveling for over an hour. We also traveled for over four hours yesterday, unless we are heading in the wrong direction, then we would ... "

Jerry rolled his eyes. "Paul, will you stop babbling? We are going to be there soon."

The words were hardly out of his mouth when John said, "Look! I think it's the metal door!"

They ran towards it. They stopped and found it in the bark of a tree. Jerry searched his pockets for the chip.

"Well, I'm glad we can get out of this place," Paul said shivering "It gives me the creeps. I hate looking over my shoulder everywhere I go."

"Do you think it's going to get any better in a different world?" Lino asked.

"Good point," John said. "Jerry, what's taking so long?"

"I know I put it in one of my pockets," Jerry responded. All of a sudden, they heard a big stomping noise nearby. They spun around. It was another triceratops. It was charging toward them.

"Jerry, hurry with that chip!" Lino yelled.

"Got it," Jerry exclaimed, pulling out a small chip from his pocket. He stuck it into the hole. The door slowly opened.

"Get inside!" John yelled, pushing Paul and Jerry in. He turned to Lino. "Lino, hurry!"

Lino jumped in. John was about to leap in when the dinosaur hit him from behind. He went flying into the air. He landed a few feet away from the dinosaur and the door. He got up, but had a terrible pain in his back. He looked at the dinosaur that came running at him. He looked behind the dinosaur and found the door closing. He jumped out of the way of the dinosaur, got up and ran flat out towards the door. It was almost closed, and he was almost there ...

He dove to get into the door but it had shut. He was stuck here ... stuck here with the triceratops.

5) The Third World

Jerry hit the ground. Paul smashed into him. Lino landed a few seconds later, three feet from them. They got up and looked upward.

"Where's John?" Paul asked.

"He was right behind me," Lino responded. "Let's give him a second."

They had just traveled through the metal door. They had the sensation that they had fallen through a blue tornado. Paul had forgotten to take off his glasses once again, and they had broken. He turned on his computer and got another pair from Flaminetore. They continued to wait for John for five minutes.

"He's not coming," Lino said. "Do you think he's stuck?"

"I hope not," Paul said nervously. "He won't last 10 seconds against that triceratops."

Jerry turned around and thoughtfully contemplated the wall.

"Come on, guys," Jerry said. "Let's push this wall and see if we can go back to the past."

They pushed the wall, but accomplished nothing. Paul kicked the wall.

"Do you think the chip will still be there for John?" He asked.

"I don't know," Jerry replied in a worried tone. "But if he doesn't get out of there fast, we could get Flaminetore to give us a key to go back in, right?"

"I don't think there *is* a key to go back," Paul said.

"Let's just hope John can get the chip out of the hole before it disappears or something," Lino said anxiously.

John threw himself to the ground once again. The triceratops continued its assault repeatedly. John couldn't take much more of this. His nearly-healed leg started to throb again. The pain in his back was worse than ever. His nose was bleeding from throwing himself to the ground to avoid the charge of the dinosaur. He couldn't fight this creature. Nothing he had could help him. Except ...

He pulled the walkie-talkie that Jerry gave him out of his pocket. He pressed the talk button.

"Jimmy, are you there?" he asked, diving out of the way of the dinosaur again.

"Yes, where are you?" Jimmy said.

"Dodging triceratops," John said, running to the metal door.

"Glad to hear it," Jimmy replied. "I'm still in the maze. What do you need?"

"The chip disappeared," John said in horror as he checked the slot in which Jerry had put the chip. "I need to get into the maze, but I can't. The chip is gone!"

The triceratops turned and charged John.

"I've got an idea," Jimmy said suddenly. "Is the triceratops charging at you?"

"Yes, he's almost at me," John said, preparing to jump.

"Here's what you do," Jimmy said. "You wait-CCCCCCHHHHHH"

The walkie-talkie's batteries must have died. *Think ...* John told himself. *What did Jimmy want me to wait for? The last possible moment? How would that help?* He turned around and saw the door. It clicked in his mind. Like a matador facing a charging bull, he would wait until the last possible moment, jump out of the way and the dinosaur would smash open the door. He would then jump through the door. He waited. The rampaging dinosaur was almost to him. It lowered its head to hit John. John dove out of the way. The triceratops crashed into the door with full force. The door flew open and the triceratops collapsed at the foot of the door. John just thought of something. What if the dinosaur was sucked into the maze? The others could get hurt. The vortex started to pull the triceratops inwards. Without even thinking, John moved between the dinosaur and the door and pushed the dinosaur with all his might. John started getting sucked in as well. He fell into the door. As he fell, he was able to stretch up and shut the door. He was alright. His brothers and Lino were alright. He landed with a thud on the ground. He got up and looked around for his brothers. They weren't anywhere in view.

"Jerry! Paul! Lino!" John yelled. "Where are you?"

"John? Is that you?" said a voice that John recognized as Jerry's. John looked around. Jerry, Paul, and Lino came running out from around a corner.

"What happened?" Paul asked. "We came out of the door and you weren't there. We waited for five minutes before we tried to reach you from another world."

As they walked, John explained to them what had happened. They were amazed, especially Paul.

"You opened the door without the chip?" he gasped. "I thought you could only-"

"So did I," John interrupted. "But Jimmy gave me the idea. Let's try to catch up with them. I think we owe them multiple 'thank-you's'."

They started running. They came to a dead end.

"Hold on," Lino said. "Should we go try to find our friends or try to get out of this place?"

"Let's get out of here," Jerry said. "I'm sick of being in this maze. It has to be a thousand degrees in here."

"I think we should worry about our friends as well," John said, trying to ignore Jerry.

"I think our friends can manage," Paul said, breaking the vote. "We can try to meet up with them later."

That settled it. Jerry, Paul, Lino, and – though reluctantly – John pushed the wall. As usual by now, they were sucked in. They fell into a red tornado. They were used to it by now. They landed. John, Paul and Lino slammed to the ground, but Jerry landed on his feet.

"I accomplished it," he said triumphantly. "I landed on my feet."

"Zyno has *got* to come up with a better way to travel from the maze to the next world," John said, getting up and brushing himself off.

"Yous 'ah knows our mastor?" a voice said from behind them that made them all jump. They spun around. There was someone right in front of them. Only ... beneath them. It was only three and a half feet tall. As they got a good look at it, they noticed it wasn't even close to being human. It had dark, tan skin. It had longer ears whose tips drooped down. It had completely big, black eyes with a little yellow dot for a pupil in each that was darting around at them all. It had very long, brown bangs that went down to his eyes. They saw that it had four long fingers on each hand. They also noticed that, though it was small, it looked as though it was full grown.

"We don't exactly know him," Paul said to the creature. "Who are you?"

"I'ne Victa, Victa. Yes, Victa!" it said in a high-pitched voice.

"Victa?" Lino said puzzled

"No, no, not Victa," it said shaking its head. "It's Victa!"

"Oh, I think it means Victor," John said. "Is that it, Victor?"

"Yes, yes," It said rapidly nodding. "It's Victa!"

Victor surveyed John, Paul and Jerry oddly.

"My, yous the most strangest Thogs I ever seen," Victor said, shaking his head.

"What?" Jerry said confused.

"I 'ah said yous are the strangest Thogs I is ever seen." Victor repeated.

"We are not Thogs," John said. "We are humans."

Victor's eyes widened.

"Oh! In thats 'ah case, come wis me."

He turned and ran. They glanced at each other incredulously: who was this excited creature? Without having a better plan, they followed it. Lino caught up with Victor and said, "What did you think I was?"

Victor turned and laughed. "Oh, I thoughts yous 'ah were a Liger!"

"He got me right then," Lino said to Jerry. Victor led them to a huge, oval-shaped building. He ran up and knocked five times. The door opened and they saw another Thog. It was a little taller than Victor. It looked very similar to Victor. Same color hair, same eyes and same ears. It looked at Victor with hatred in his eyes.

"These are humans, and they knows ours master!" Victor said, bowing. The Thog looked them over and nodded. They were very taken aback. The way Victor reacted when they told him they were humans was as if he had never met a human before. This Thog reacted as if he dealt with humans every day.

"Comes 'ah this ways," the second Thog said in a deep voice. "You, Victa, get backs to yours work!"

They followed the second Thog into a dark room. He shut the door and looked at them.

"Mista Victa just said you knows our master, Zyno. Is 'ah these true?" He growled.

"I told him, we don't know Zyno, we just heard of him," Paul said with irritation creeping into his voice.

"I see," the Thog said in a disbelieving tone. "An' I correct to say that 'ah yous peoples and liger are going through this 'ah maze?"

"Yes," Jerry said, amazed. "How did you—"

"Nevermind," the Thog said, waving a hand. "Yous will need a chip to get into the maze agaen. We have the chip," He pulled the familiar chip out from his pocket. "But wes 'ah will only geeve it to you if complete this task 'ah we;s give yous 'ah."

John and Paul looked at each other nervously.

"What task?" Lino said curiously. The Thog looked at him.

"You will not participate, you won't. This test is only fors the 'umans. Yous may watch if yous like,"

He then turned to Paul and said, "An' I correct to says that yous are the youngest?"

"Yes," Paul replied, staring at the ground in embarrassment.

"Then yous will be second to participate 'ah," said the Thog, turning to the wall. He slammed his fist against the wall. Three buttons suddenly came out of the wall, a red one, green one and a blue one. He pressed the blue one and a glass case came out of the wall. Inside stood a big ax. The case fell to the ground and shattered. The Thog picked the ax up and handed it to Paul. Paul looked in awe at it.

"Yous will gos outside and in sa' hall, there is another Thog. Takes 'ah what he has in his hands and drink it, gots it?" the Thog directed.

"Okay," Paul said, still staring at the ax. Paul left and the Thog looked at John.

"Yous will be the second youngest?"

"Yes, I am. Will I get an ax too?" John looked excitedly at the Thog who chuckled.

"No, no, yous 'ah will gets something else," he said as he pressed the green button. Another glass case came out of the wall, this time bigger, and again, the Thog made no attempts to catch it. As it broke, they saw a small sword with a gleaming gold handle. The Thog picked it up. "You will bes 'ah third 'ah to compete 'ah."

"Thanks!" John said, taking a few swings with his new sword. "This is cool so far!"

"Now goes out 'ah and yous 'ah listen to the Thog 'ah."

"Ok," John said.

The Thog turned to Jerry.

"And yous 'ah must be the oldest 'ah?" He asked.

"Yes," Jerry replied slowly.

"Then you will compete first 'ah," he said. He pressed the last button and another sword came out. It was bigger than John's. It had a shiny, purple handle and a long orange blade. It was very heavy.

"Should I go out with the others?" Jerry said, taking a few swings with his sword as well.

"Yes, and goods luck 'ah. Yours friend will be watching, I dink," he said, pointing at Lino. Jerry walked out of the room. He didn't see his brothers, but another Thog.

"Hello Victor," Jerry said, looking at the familiar face.

"I gots to get you!" Victor said jumping up and down. "I 'sa hoped I would one day get to get someone and I'm here! Well, I gots to give you directions don't I?"

"Er, I guess," Jerry said, confused.

"Whats you gots to do is face a creature and only use yours powers (Jerry looked at his sword and grinned). Only yours powers can defeat the creatures 'ah. We won't come to help you so yous got to figure it out how defeat it." Victor said. "Now drink this."

He handed Jerry a bottle with a green liquid inside of it. Jerry drank it and became and very sleepy. Without another word, he fell to the ground into a deep sleep.

Jerry woke with a start. He had a dream that he fought a creature and lost. He stood up and looked around. He was in a giant stadium. He thought he was dreaming again, but he looked up and saw many Thogs in the crowd and he saw the Thog that gave him the sword was in the top row. Jerry looked around.

Where was the creature? He turned behind him. A huge door was opening at the opposite side of the field. When it completely opened, Jerry saw a muscular Thog wrestling a leash made of chain. The Thog could barely control the creature that was at the end of it. The seven or eight-foot tall creature had long, strong arms, a hunched back, sharp teeth, two big, beefy legs, and orange skin with red spots. It seemed to want to get at Jerry. Jerry grabbed his sword off the ground, gripped it tight and prepared himself. The Thog let go of the chain and the creature lurched towards Jerry. Jerry jumped and slammed the blade of the sword at the creature's shoulder. The blade bounced off the creature's shoulder and Jerry fell to the ground. The creature jumped on top of Jerry and started punching him with his fists. Jerry spun from underneath it and swung his sword with full force at it. The creature ducked and kicked at Jerry. Jerry wasn't fast enough. The kick hit Jerry in the ribs and the sword flew out of his hands. The creature ran for the sword, but Jerry got up and jumped on top of the creature. He wrapped his arms around its neck just as John did to the saber-tooth tiger. The creature grabbed Jerry's hands and threw him off. Jerry hit the ground, bounced up and jumped over to his sword. The creature kicked the sword from his grasp and jumped at the sword. Jerry tripped the creature and got up and ran towards his sword. The creature grabbed Jerry's foot and pulled. Jerry pulled the other way. His shoe came off and he fell, landing a few inches from his sword. He got up, grabbed his sword and turned to face the creature that was also getting to its feet. Jerry thought for a moment. The sword couldn't be his power because Victor said his power would destroy the creature. The creature ran at Jerry and threw a punch at him. Jerry ducked, spun and tripped it. It fell and Jerry once again smashed his sword on his head. It bounced out of his hands and went about six feet away from them. The creature got up, pushed Jerry to the ground, and headed to the fallen weapon. Jerry jumped to his feet and ran flat out to his weapon. The creature noticed and threw a karate chop at his neck. Jerry couldn't stop so the creature's fist caught him in neck. He got clothes-lined. Jerry flipped to the ground and rolled to his knees. He knelt on the ground gasping for breath. It was the worst he had ever gotten the wind knocked out

of him in his life. He heard a *whoosh* of a sword above him, but
didn't look up. He felt that if he looked up, he might pass out
from fright seeing the creature with his sword. Another swing of
a sword, but Jerry felt no pain. What was going on? Why didn't
the creature hit him? At a snail's pace, he looked up. The
creature was heading towards him. It swung the sword over his
head and charged at Jerry. He swung it down toward Jerry's
neck.

6) Thogeens

With a sixth sense, Jerry spun out of the way. He still was gasping for breath and could hardly think. He looked at the creature as it tried to pull the sword out of the ground. *Why did it have to grab the sword before me?* He was very frustrated. He jumped up, the pain in his side to have gone. He ran towards the creature just as it pulled the sword out from the ground. Right as the creature took a swing at Jerry, Jerry leapt into the air, still frustrated with the creature. He kicked the creature in the face. The creature dropped the sword to cradle its head. Jerry grabbed the sword triumphantly and swung with all his might. The blow landed on the creature's chest and it staggered a bit. It regained balance and punched Jerry. Jerry fell to the ground. *That creature is too powerful*, Jerry thought. *I have the weapon, but he's killing me.* With the rest of his strength, Jerry swung his sword at the creature a final time. The sword hit the creature's waist and flames erupted from the blade. The creature fell to the ground, covered with flames. Jerry heard the crowd cheer from all around him. He had a bad cut on his cheek. He had a black eye and his ribs were very sore. He saw two Thogs running towards him. When they reached him, Jerry noticed that one of them was Victor, the other was the muscular Thog.

"Yous did it! Yous 'ah did it!" Victor said happily. "Yous 'ah found your powers 'ah"

"Yeah, it *was* my sword, wasn't it?" Jerry said.

"Its 'ah was not yous physical weapon," the other muscular Thog said gruffly.

"What do you mean?" Jerry asked, surprised.

"The captains 'ah will explain it to yous 'ah," Victor said. Jerry walked to the end of the field and went up some steps to the top row, where he found the Thog that gave him his weapons for the task. Paul was seated nearby.

"Great job, Jerry," Paul said with a dazed grin.

"Yous 'ah did very well," the Captain Thog said, shaking Jerry's hand. "Yous will now watch yours brother face that creature. He is very dazed. We gaves the littles one a sleeping draught and he just woke up to see you defeat the Thogeen."

"Thogeen?" Jerry asked curiously. "Is that the name of the creature I just faced?"

"Yes," the Thog said as Paul walked down towards the field. "Thogeens were once one of us 'ah. But as our age grew on, ours lifetime grew short. See, ones 'ah tried to live forever. The potion he created was 'ah to makes yous 'ah stronger then any other creature. Well, its sort of worked. The Thog put some of itselfs 'ah into the potions and made mores. More Thogs tooks 'ah the potions. Theys all become verys strong and large and all of them wouldns 'ah die of old age. We called them Thogeens, because theys used to bes Thogs 'ah. But yous 'ah see, it had one weakness."

"What was it?" Jerry asked.

"Well, yous see, the Thog was being very greedy indeed. He wanteds to bes stronger and biggers than everyone else. He only thoughts of himselfs 'ah. He poured all of his ambitious greed into the potions 'ah. Well, the ambitions went into every Thogeen. And they become mores and mores greedy, like him. Theys 'ah want to make more of them then us. They tries to destroy us's. But since they have so much greed, all wes 'ah have to do is use our strongest emotion and put it into physical form like yous 'ah did."

"But I wasn't thinking about anything," Jerry began, but the Thog cut him off.

"When yous 'ah dreamin', we looked inside yours 'ah mind with special machines to see what power yous 'ah contained. Do yous 'ah know what wes 'ah saw?"

"No, because I wasn't thinking about—"

"Wes 'ah saw jealousy," the Thog said to him. Jerry gaped at him.

"Jealousy," Jerry said. "I'm never jealous."

"Yous 'ah very jealous when yous 'ah faced these 'ah Thogeen. You were jealous that it was 'ah stronger then yous."

"Well, yeah, I guess so ..." Jerry admitted.

"Jealousy can leads yous to corruptions," the Captain said, "Yous 'ah might head downs the sames 'ah path that the first Thogeens 'ah did. Jealousy gets 'ah yous power now. Maybe a better virtues 'ah will get you more and for laters.

"I'll keep that in mind," Jerry promised. "But as long as it gets me what I want, why change?"

"Well, wes 'ah better not keep talking like dis, or wes will miss your brother's fight," the Thog replied.

"I just hope Paul can figure out how to defeat the Thogeen quicker than me," Jerry said as he watched Paul get into the field. Paul pulled out his ax from his belt and waited anxiously, but Jerry could see that there was fear in his eyes. The door at the opposite side of the field opened again. The muscular Thog was pulling hard on the chain to move a Thogeen forward. Finally, when it was on the field, the Thogeen tried to get to Paul. It advanced on Paul, who gripped his ax firmly and took aim. He swung it at the Thogeen who caught the ax by its blade and threw it aside. It charged at Paul who ran away, but the Thogeen caught up with him. It grabbed Paul and threw a punch at Paul's ribs. Paul staggered and fell over. The Thogeen went up to Paul and punched him in the face. Blood from Paul's nose splattered onto the ground.

"NOOOOOOOOO!" Jerry yelled, getting out of his seat and running down the steps to the field. When he had gotten halfway there, however, at least a dozen Thogs ran up to him.

"He wills half to fight this on his own, and nos one can help him." The nearest one said.

"Oh, so I, his oldest brother, am going to just sit in the top row of some stands, watching my brother get killed?!" Jerry said angrily. "I don't really care about the chip. I am going to save my brother and going to find another way out."

At this, he pulled out his sword, and Jerry swung it at them and half of them ducked. The ones he hit got thrown backward, into some seats. Jerry ran past the others, sword still out. He got to the end of the stadium and looked out at Paul. Paul had looked up at Jerry and so did the Thogeen. The Thogeen seemed to have had done enough damage to Paul and wanted a new victim. He ran at Jerry.

"Jerry, look out!" Paul panted, and with all the strength he could muster, flung himself at the Thogeen's neck. He grabbed its neck and pulled the Thogeen to the ground. He squeezed its neck and the Thogeen gasped for breath. A few seconds later, its head dropped to the ground and Paul released it. The crowd roared and Paul got to his feet.

"Good job, Paul," Jerry said, jumping into the field to help him.

"Yeah, but you might have been killed," Paul said, irritated. "What did you think you were doing?"

"Trying to save your life," Jerry said, pushing Paul over the stadium wall. "Come on, let's get out of here. I don't want John to do this either. We can find another way out of this world. I'll get your ax."

Paul got up into the stands. Jerry went over and got Paul's ax. They went up to the top of the stands where the Captain Thog was sitting.

"We are getting out of here," Jerry said firmly. "Where's John and Lino?"

"Hes 'ah already down in the stadium," the Thog replied, pointing. "Yous 'ah just missed him."

"It's alright."

They turned around. It was Lino.

"I watched you both," he said smiling. "I talked to your friend (referring to the captain) here and he said it would be alright. If it got too bad, they would have sent some Thogs in and save Paul. In fact, they were about to."

"But Victor said—" Jerry began.

"They only said that to see how you would handle pressure," Lino interrupted. "So, are you going to watch John or go inside and eat some of that delicious food?"

Lino licked his lips. Jerry said he would eat and made Lino promise to tell him everything that happened. Lino promised and Jerry went inside the booth. There were dozens of Thogs inside. They sat eating and talking to one another in an accent that Jerry had difficulty understanding. He went up to the counter where the Thogs were getting food. He realized that he had no money; Would they charge him? There was only one way to find out. He cleared his throat. The Thog did not look up at him as it answered.

"Yes?" it said.

"Uh, what do you have?" Jerry asked.

"Let's 'ah see here, we have the usual," it said and by its voice, Jerry guessed that it was a female.

"Uh ... well you see, I am a human," Jerry said. "I—"

"Oh, it's 'ah yous 'ah," it exclaimed suddenly, looking up at him. "The one that beat the Thogeen 'ah! Wes 'ah only have Thog food, I'ms afraid."

"Would you recommend anything I might like?" Jerry asked.

"Oh, deras 'ah lot of things you might like," she said nodding. "But I's 'ah give yous 'ah some delicious foods 'ah!"

She turned around and looked at some drawers. She opened one and Jerry almost gagged. It was the most revolting thing he ever saw. It looked like brown mashed potatoes mixed with sliced up, moldy tomatoes and mud. Jerry thought if he smelled it, he might faint. The Thog, however, took a spoon and put some on a plate and gave it to him.

"Doesn't that smell 'ah lovely?" she said smiling. Jerry thought that he would rather do anything else, even face another Thogeen, than smell the mush. But out of politeness, he nodded and gingerly smelled it. The scent was much different than he expected. The smell made him relax. It smelled almost like tulips, with a faint aroma of salt water. He immediately felt drowsy. His initial reaction toward the mush changed completely as he now longed to eat it. He walked over and sat at one of the empty tables. Taking a mouthful, Jerry immediately felt energized, but at the same time, received a peaceful calm. He could feel the strength replenish within himself. The effects were so rapid that he felt them before he received the taste. The taste was smooth in his mouth. No delicacy in the world could compare with what Jerry was eating now. It took him a minute to recover from the first bite.

"Its 'ah called 'Angel's Gift', for ete is our most powerful weapons 'ah," The female Thog explained. "It puts 'ah Thogs in our mosts strongest state 'ah. It looks terribles, we knows, but 'ah it is our disguise fors when wes 'ah need to battle 'em. Plus, ete's a good taste."

Jerry nodded and dared another bite.

He sat there for a while eating the Angel's Gift, when the door burst open. Most of the Thogs around him looked over to the door, but Jerry didn't, supposing it was just another Thog coming in. It was probably that thought that made him be surprised to hear his name being shouted. He looked up. It was Lino. *John probably defeated the Thogeen and he's come to tell me the details*, Jerry thought. But as he got a better look at the expression on Lino's face, he changed his mind. Lino's face looked pale, panic-stricken and seemed disheveled.

"You-you better come here fast, Jerry," he said, trembling. "It's John, hurry!"

Jerry jumped out of his seat and ran to the door. He went back into the stands and understood why Lino had been so shaky. John was on his back on the field with his hands on his stomach. There were at least 15 Thogs trying to control a huge Thogeen. Jerry also noticed there was more than one Thogeen, but the other one was dead. Without trying to think he said, "Where is Paul?"

"He is going to try and help the Thogs silence the Thogeen," Lino replied.

"Let's go," Jerry said, pulling out his sword once again. They ran down to the field. *Think*, Jerry thought. *What am I jealous of? Paul has a laptop and I have always wanted one.* He concentrated on the longing in his stomach for the computer as he ran up to the Thogeen. All of a sudden, someone Jerry's size jumped up next to him. Jerry realized it was John. He looked cut and bruised up a lot, but not so bad that he couldn't fight.

"Hey, Jerry, thanks for comin' down, I need some help," John said, a little dazed.

"I noticed," Jerry said. "Why did they put you up against two?"

"I don't know," John said, slowly approaching to the creature.

"What were you thinking when you were facing the other Thogeen?"

"Is that what they're called?" John asked dazedly. "Well, I was thinking about how brave I was facing two. So, well, I just killed one, and tried the same thing on the other."

"And I guess it didn't work?" Jerry asked, knowing the answer.

"Nothing I tried worked," John sighed.

"Well, we need to think about the feeling or attribute that will give you your power," Jerry said. And then it hit him. "You are the most honest person I know. Focus on your honesty."

"Come off it," John said, grinning. "You think me being honest will help me defeat this creature? What am I supposed to do, walk up to it and say, 'I'm afraid of you and I'm telling the truth' and then cut him in half?!"

"Yes, everything except that you won't say it out loud," Jerry said, putting his sword away. "Just think in your mind how honestly scared you are of this creature."

John clutched his sword tightly. He went up to the creature, running flat out. He thought hard about how much he was "honestly afraid of this creature." He leapt into the air and swung his sword with all his might. He cut the Thogeen's head off. The Thogs all cheered. Jerry ran up to him.

"I was right, wasn't I?" Jerry said, grinning. "Come on, they've got some good stuff to eat up in the stands."

The two went up to the stands where they were greeted by Lino and Paul. John told how he defeated the two creatures in detail.

"Man, you must have been pretty brave, facing two," Paul commented.

"Truthfully," John said, glancing at Jerry, "I was scared stiff."

John ordered the Angel's Gift that Jerry had recommended. Jerry and John continued to talk about defeating the Thogeens. Finally, Paul yawned and said, "What time is it?"

John looked at his watch. "Six-fifteen," he replied.

"We should look for some place to sleep before we go to the metal door," John said.

"Oh, yous 'ah won't get no chip," said a deep voice. They turned around. It was the Thog Jerry sat with in the stands.

"What do you mean?" Lino said. "They got through your stupid test."

"Sa' middle child didn't get pas' the Thogeen 'ah," he said. "Yous 'ah gots helps with the Thogs 'ah. Yous would haves been killed 'ah."

"Come on," John said angrily. "You put me up against two. What's up with that?"

"Yous 'ah had two powers," the Thog said. "No other human 'ah had two powers. What could wes 'ah do?"

"Choose one and leave the other," John said, now on his feet. "If I defeated one of them, I think that should be enough."

"Are there other chips in this world?" Paul cut in.

"Yes, theres 'ah more," the Thog said. "But you would have to search far and wide. Yous 'ah may sleep here for tonight if yous 'ah like. Tomorrow you will be trespassing. The Thog behind the counter there will show yous 'ah directions."

He pointed to the Thog who gave Jerry some food. They got up and walked over to the Thog. Suddenly, Paul got an idea. He ran back to the Thog.

"Hey, at the one room when you gave us the weapons, my Thog said that we face a creature. He didn't have the *creature* plural," he said. "So there are two possibilities: One, you both lied; two, I must have heard him wrong because of his bad accent."

"But it couldn't have been the accent, because mine said the same thing!" John said, popping in.

"So that means you lied to us, making the conditions of the challenge different," Paul stated.

The Thog looked at the pair of them. Then he smiled.

"So yous 'ah play dirty, do yous?" he said. "Very well. We didn't knows that yous 'ah would face two, but okay. Besides, the chip is meaningless to us. We will try to get yous 'ah the chip tomorrow."

Paul woke up early the next morning. He was very impatient to get back into the maze. When he awoke, however, he wasn't the only one up. John was sitting on the window sill, looking out with crossed arms. Hearing Paul waking up, he didn't look at him but started talking.

"I wondered when you'd wake up. I got some food from one Thog. She was tired, but pleased that we liked Angel's Gift."

He pointed to a bag nearby with the revolting-looking food. Paul glanced down at the bag and then back at John who still hadn't looked at him.

"Why are you up so early?" Paul asked.

John grunted.

"Why are you?"

"Well, I'm just really anxious to get back in the maze," Paul said.

John sighed.

"What's up?" Paul said, looking concerned.

"Well, yes, I'm anxious to get back into the maze, but not to get into another world and see what it's like on different planets or something. I want to get out of this maze and back home. I don't really care about Zyno's inventions anymore."

"Why?" Paul asked.

Finally, John looked at him.

"Well, it might be my imagination, but it seems like every time we enter a new world, it gets harder and harder, and it doesn't look like Zyno is doing anything to prevent this."

"Don't you think so?" Paul said. "I mean, he might think that only 'worthy' people should see his inventions. Because look, all this time in the worlds, it takes a genius to figure out this kind of stuff ("Which we have," John said, smiling a little.). He might think only people who are smart should see his inventions."

"Or something else," John said, frowning at him. At first Paul looked puzzled. Then, as if he could read minds, his eyes widened.

"You ... you couldn't think ... do you mean, he might want to k-kill someone?" Paul stammered.

"I don't know, Paul," John said, turning his head back to the window. "I don't know."

Paul paused for a second before saying "Do you have any ideas?"

"One." John replied. "Just one."

He turned back to Paul.

"Benjamin was a scientist working for some unknown boss, Uncle Dan said so. That person might just be Zyno. Because look at us now. Benjamin chased us over here. What a coincidence that Benjamin had a gas station near Zyno's lab when I thought he was still a working scientist. Another coincidence –why would Benjamin give up so easily when we locked him out? If I was a person running a gas station and someone just ran away without paying me, I would be there all night trying to get that door open if I had to. He must have known all about the maze and the worlds and how dangerous it would be. How? He probably works for Zyno. Only one question remains … why is he trying to kill us?"

"Or who," Paul said. "But these could all be very strange coincidences, couldn't they?"

"For all I know, Zyno could be a good friend of Uncle Dan and he might not even know who Benjamin is," John shrugged. "But this all fits, doesn't it?"

Paul chose not to reply. After some silence, Paul looked at John confidently.

"Even if Zyno is bad, we can take down any world he throws at us. We have made it this far, haven't we?"

John shook his head. "Paul, haven't you been listening to anything I have said? It's going to get harder and harder, and we barely got through this world."

John turned his head the opposite way. He lifted some hair off his ear and Paul gasped. A huge, thick red scar ran from above his left ear across to the left side of his forehead.

"That was from the Thogeen. The Thogs said it was pretty much permanent. If this is the third world, I'm dreading what we have to do in the sixth world, if we survive that long."

Paul sat there looking at John, wondering. Was John right? Could Zyno be evil? He looked at Jerry, still fast asleep. He checked his watch. Five o'clock in the morning.

"I'm going to wait until they get up to go and find the Thog with the chip. Go ahead and eat the Angel's Gift." John said, looking at the Thog food.

After two hours, John and Paul got so impatient waiting for Jerry and Lino to wake up, they woke them. They were very tired, but surprised when John and Paul told them their concerns.

"You really think so?" Jerry said. "I always imagined Benjamin to be a huge science nerd. I didn't think he would have time to work with someone."

"When did you start thinking this way?" Lino said.

"Since the second world. It occurred to me that this maze was very dangerous because that triceratops was really close to killing me," John responded.

"Where is he, do you think?" Paul asked, referring to the Thog.

"I think I see him," Jerry said, pointing to their left. He was running toward them, flat out.

"I was sa' looking for yous 'ah for hulf an hour," He said, breathing fast and looking frightened. "I looked for yous 'ah in yous 'ah room. Theres 'ah problem."

"What? Did you lose the chip?" John looked at him angrily.

"No, no. The chip ese fine," he said, showing it to them. "But we beg yous 'ah to stay."

"We aren't staying here if you paid-"

"There 'sa emerganzie," he said, sweating. "The Thogeens 'ah escaped. We can't control them 'sa. The Thog War has begun 'ah. We's 'ah need your help."

7) The Thog War

"The Thogeens escaped?" Paul asked, stunned.

"Yes, efrey single one," the captain said. "Wes 'ah needs your help."

"That's your problem, not ours," John said, taking the chip from him. "We are sick of this world and we are out of here."

"Please! Wes 'ah desperate," he said, jumping up, attempting to get the chip back from John. "The armies of Thogs have mostly fallen. Wes 'ah need some good leaders. Wes 'ah chose you."

"And we chose not help you guys," John said. But none of the others agreed with him.

"Of course we will help you," Paul said. "We wouldn't let our worst enemies face them without our help."

"Good," the Thog sighed. "But theys 'ah heading dis way, so let me show yous where whats 'ah left of the armies ares 'ah."

He led them to a door at the side of the stands out of which Jerry remembered his Thogeen had come. The Thog took out some keys and opened the door.

"Hang on," Jerry said, stopping. "That was the door that my Thogeen came out of. Won't they come trampling out if we try to go in there?"

"No, theres 'ah no more in theres," the Thog Captain said, shaking his head. "All of thems 'ah have escaped. Theys 'ah don't want to be locked up, sos we hid here because they won't thinks 'ah to come here."

"That does seem to be the last place they'd come," Paul admitted.

They followed him through the door down a dark, slopping path. As they walked on, it got darker and colder. John shivered.

"I wouldn't want to be a Thogeen if this is where I'd have to live," John said.

"Yes, it is like e jail," the Thog said, also shivering. "Us Thogs have a choice yous 'ah see. We have a choice to become a Thogeen. But et is illegal now, yous 'ah see. Theys are too powerful for us to control, and theys are murderous plunderses. So wes 'ah have no choiced but to put thems 'ah heres. We's 'ah catch them and bring them down here and give thems 'ah no food. Most of thems 'ah still live but are really weak. Some didn't take a lot of ta potion and die. Ta potion gives yous 'ah immortal life—excepts, of courses, for yours powers 'ah."

"How can you catch them if they are stronger than you?" Paul asked socratically.

"Wes 'ah usually outnumber them and surrounds 'ah them," the Thog Captain said.

"You mean you don't use your feelings like we do?" Jerry asked, surprised.

"It's harder for Thogs to have 'emotional' powers. You umans' 'ah have them each days 'ah. Wes 'ah occasionally 'ah have emotions 'ah that forms intos powers 'ah," the Thog replied.

"I see why you choose us then," John said. "We are the only humans here, aren't we?"

"Yes, there was another 'uman here, but he left a short time before yous 'ah came," the captain replied.

The slope was now flattening out and, through the gloom, they saw some Thogs. As they got closer, Paul was able to count how many there were – 43. They noted that only a few of them had weapons; mostly spears or small bows and arrows.

"This is all that survived?" Jerry asked.

"Yes," The Thog said sorrowfully.

"About how many Thogeens are there?" Paul asked.

The Thog swallowed.

"Five hundred."

John's mouth fell open. Jerry's eyes widened. Paul gasped. Only Lino responded.

"THAT IS TOO MUCH FOR OUR TASTES!" he growled so loudly that many Thogs shivered and recoiled. "FOURTY-SIX AGAINST 500? THAT'S INSANE! THAT'S SUICIDE! HOW ARE WE SUPPOSED TO WIN, HUH? TELL ME! TELL ME!"

"Wes 'ah sorry, but wes 'ah-"

"Excuse us, we're leaving," John said, almost as angry as Lino. He turned to leave. So did the others, obviously scared at the thought of half a thousand Thogeens.

John was so mad that he didn't see where he was going and he walked right into something hard. He took a step back and saw, in horror, a figure in a black coat with a hood. Behind the figure, there were about 100 Thogeens.

For a second, a brief second, nothing happened. No movement, not a single noise.

Then, a single arrow flew by Jerry's head from behind – the first shot of the true Thog war. A Thog must have shot an arrow at the hooded figure. But the black figure was fast. He pulled from underneath his coat a glowing sword. It was as big as Jerry's sword, but it glowed aquamarine. With amazing precision and speed, he effortlessly split the arrow in half, tip to feather. Jerry took out his sword, John his, and Paul already had his ax out. The captain Thog yelled, "CHARGE!"

The cloaked figure swung his sword at John who ducked and swung his sword back. The figure's sword countered John's. Jerry jumped in to help. Flames erupted once again from Jerry's sword. He swung. The figure deflected Jerry's attack. The figure unsheathed another glowing sword. This one was sparkling ruby colored. Fighting both of them at once, the figure proved to be an expert swordsman.

All the Thogs behind them charged forward with Paul and Lino. The Thogeens surged right back. Paul tried to discern his power, since he did not discover his power in the battle. *Well*, he thought, *I was thinking about my brother's safety when I was facing the other Thogeen, so maybe loyalty?* He went up to a Thogeen and threw his ax at his throat. It gasped for breath. Then, with no success, it fell to the ground, dead. Paul pulled out the ax from his throat and thought *one down, 99 to go.* Lino leapt onto a Thogeen's head and began mauling it. The other Thogs started rapidly firing their arrows at the Thogeens.

The dark dungeon was soon raining with arrows as Thogeens fired arrows back. Only a few Thogeens had fallen, but no Thog had been hit yet. Paul was fighting two Thogeens at once. As he repeatedly attacked and parried, he saw glimpses of familiar faces amongst the fighting Thogs: Victor, Julia, who had served them food, and Maurice, the muscular Thog that had pulled out the Thogeens at Paul, Jerry, and John's matches. The three seemed to be the most skilled Thog warriors. Victor fought with a tiny dagger and defended with a small shield. Julia rapidly shot with a bow and a small quiver of arrows. Maurice fought with two spears and was working wildly with them. Arrows constantly came at Victor, who was able to block them with his shield.

Led by those three, Thogeens started to fall faster. The Thogs were winning.

John and Jerry, however, were having no luck defeating the black-coated figure. Occasionally, the figure would deflect an inbound arrow with one of its swords and then, without losing a stride, return back to fighting.

As Thogs began to fall in battle, the fighting became desperate. John was knocked off his feet by one of the dark figure's blows. As he got up to rejoin the fight, Jerry said, "Leave me, go help Paul and the Thogs!"

With rapid effort, it looked like Jerry was fighting with a stick of fire, slashing at the figure with no mercy.

"That's it, Jerry," the figure spoke in a ghostly tone. "Fight me single-handedly. You can't beat me."

John didn't argue with Jerry; he ran to aid the Thogs.

Lino looked as if he couldn't fight any more. He was covered with blood and looked exhausted. But he kept going.

Paul, on the other hand, was fighting without tiring. He killed two Thogeens with one rapid motion. Another Thog fell, an arrow in its chest. John ran up to another Thogeen and stabbed it. An arrow headed for Victor, but he blocked it too late. It struck his arm and he staggered in pain. He ripped the arrow out of his arm. Losing the use of his fighting arm, he tossed his shield aside and switched hands, leaving him defenseless.

Victor stabbed another Thogeen, putting it to death. Julia and Maurice killed one each. Lino managed to bite the throat of another one. John was encouraged when he quickly counted the number of Thogs verses the Thogeens. But even as he counted, the Thogs were killing the Thogeens. The six other Thogs that were alive killed one each. Paul, once again, threw his ax at a Thogeen's throat. The Thogeen was gasped for breath. Paul didn't see another Thogeen advancing behind him.

"Paul! Behind you!" John yelled. Paul turned just in time to see the Thogeen lowering a great club down upon him. Paul ducked underneath, retrieved his ax and killed the Thogeen.

John thought they might have a chance to win this battle now that the number of Thogeens fell again. Even though the Captain Thog had implied this forced effort, John was surprised to see the Thogs closing their eyes when fighting, probably trying to think of an emotion.

John turned to look at Jerry. He was fighting desperately against the figure's two swords. John really wanted to help, but he also wanted to help Paul. The decision came when a stray arrow killed a Thog and Victor was shot in the side. He keeled over and, like the previous arrow, managed to pull that arrow out. John decided to help the rest of the Thogs. As Julia shot the remaining arrows and Paul killed one, another Thog was killed. There were only a couple Thogs left and around 30 Thogeens. As 20 clubbed Thogeens attacked the four Thogs, Paul ran to defend them. He jumped over the Thogs so that he was between the Thogs and Thogeens. He threw his ax at the middle Thogeen's throat. When it touched skin, emerald lightning came out of the blade. The lightning hit the six closest Thogeens and electrocuted them along with killing the one Paul hit. The Thogeens stopped and looked at what Paul's axe did to their army. That pause gave Paul enough time to recover his ax and throw it again. The same effect happened. The Thogeens were shocked (literally!) With only 10 Thogeens left, there was now hope of winning for the Thogs. Julia shot some used arrows she found on the ground. John killed two with one swipe, mimicking his brother. Paul managed to kill a couple more as well, and Lino shredded a few. Maurice threw both of his spears, impaling the last two. Paul recognized the last Thog as the captain.

"Yes! We's 'ah are victorious! We's 'ah won round two!" he said.

"Not quite," John said, breathing hard. "The round isn't over."

"What makes you say that?" Lino said.

"Because two people are missing," John said, looking a bit pale. "Jerry is gone. So is the black-coated figure."

8) Round Three Begins

Jerry was thrown to the ground inside a room. He had been unconscious, but the impact woke him suddenly. The black-coated figure advanced towards him. Jerry quickly got to his feet, but his sword was gone. He didn't know what to do.

"Who are you?" Jerry asked, confrontationally. The figure stopped walking.

"My true name I will not reveal to you," it said. "But you may call me Alvin."

"So Alvin, how do you know my name?" Jerry blustered.

"Some secrets I will keep to myself," Alvin said calmly.

"Oh, like your face?" Jerry sneered, angrily. "Why don't you show your face, you coward?"

"You're in no position to insult me," Alvin said, tapping the hilt of his sword. "But I will reveal my face."

He lifted a hand to his hood and pulled it back. Jerry saw a human, adult face. Alvin had a yellow mustache and long gold – yet messy – hair that went down to his shoulders. His face was gentle, not full of anger. Jerry could hardly believe that he had fighting him just 20 minutes ago. And he looked somewhat familiar to Jerry ...

"I am, as you can see, a human," Alvin replied. "I am also going through this maze to reach Zyno. I have already been through six lands."

"You mean these places we have been transported to?" Jerry asked.

"Yes. Zyno created this maze for one reason," Alvin said, sighing. "So that I would go through it."

"You?" Jerry asked curiously. "Why you?"

"He is jealous of my inventions. He built this maze so I would be attracted to it. So that I would go through it. So that I would come to him and he might have the chance of brain-washing me."

"Jealous? You are a scientist too?" Jerry said.

"Yes. Zyno managed to get Ben on his side, fortifying his scientist team. That leaves us with another scientist down."

"Ben? You mean Benjamin? That would mean John's predictions are right," Jerry replied. "But why would they want to capture you? The only person that Benjamin ever was jealous of was Uncle Dan."

Alvin stiffened slightly. "I ... I guess your Uncle Dan is a scientist also?"

"Yes."

"Well, both Benjamin and Zyno are jealous of me, too. I was a fool to come here. You cannot get out once you are in. I will have to face Zyno single-handedly, unless your uncle falls for the same trick of entering the maze. Well, that was my plan, but I think I will help you guys instead. I wouldn't let my worst enemy face them without my help."

Jerry's eyes widened. *"We wouldn't let our worst enemy face them without our help."* Paul had said that.

"So ... so why were you fighting me before?" Jerry asked.

Alvin grinned. "I wasn't really. I was a spy. I convinced the Thogeens that I should be on their side. After defeating one of them one-on-one, they said I was worthy to join them."

"You still haven't answered my question," Jerry said.

"Because I wanted to see how well you and your brothers fought," Alvin replied. "All-in-all, I'll say you are a fair fighter. Now, about this Thog war ... "

"Are you going to help us?" Jerry asked.

"Yes. I have also rounded up the last of the Thogs in this world. There are about 700."

Jerry's eyes lit with excitement. If they won before with less than the enemy, then with more, they would surely win.

"And I will fight with the Thogs," Alvin finished. He smiled. Suddenly the door burst open. As he turned around, he pulled out his two swords and swinging, he deflected two arrows, an axe and two spears. It was John, Paul, Lino, Victor, Julia, Maurice and the captain.

"John, it's alright," Jerry exclaimed.

"It is not alright, this guy is about to kill you," John replied, raising his sword.

"You've got it all wrong," Alvin said, lowering his swords, "I am—"

"—Here to save me," Jerry lied. "He-he isn't the same guy as the black-coated figure."

"Then ... then why does he have that same cloak on?" Lino asked.

"To pose as him," Jerry said, as Alvin opened his mouth, "so that he would get through the Thogeens around here."

"I didn't see any Thogeens in here," Paul said, looking nervous.

"Well, you didn't encounter any yet," Jerry said as Alvin looked at him.

"An why dous hes 'ah haf it's swords?" Victor asked.

"Once he defeated the figure, he took his weapons," Jerry said. "They were more useful than his, you see, and he grabbed mine which the hooded figure had stolen and he was about to return it when you came in."

Everyone looked stunned. Alvin return Jerry's sword.

"Well, then," John said. "Let's go."

"So, out of this entire story we don't know his name," Paul said, as they were walking.

"Call him Al." Jerry said, looking at Alvin. Alvin leaned over to Jerry and said, "Thanks."

"Sevun 'undred?" the Captain said, an hour later at the base. "But vere?"

"All over," Alvin said. "They are moving this way. We have to counter attack soon. The question is *how*."

Alvin and the captain were talking. Paul and Lino were playing holographic checkers. Jerry was playing a video game on Paul's computer. John was talking with Julia and Victor, though having trouble understanding what they were saying. Maurice, however, was alone, apparently doing nothing.

"So, are you sure your side is all right?" John asked. "Flaminetore said that it might still hurt—"

"I'm 'ah finey, I'm 'ah finey," Victor said.

"That was some fighting you guys did back there," John continued. "Thirty against four, you guys really—"

"Didn't does 'ah wells 'ah, thats 'ah what," Maurice finally said.

"Watza do yous 'ah mean, Mauryace?" Julia said. "Theys 'ah ten times 'ah more powerful 'ah. And we's 'ah beat thems 'ah, yes!"

"We's 'ah have four in our armys 'ah," Maurice replied. "Theys 'ah have a thousands 'ah."

"First of all, we have about 700," John said. "And they only have 400."

Maurice shook his head.

"Theys 'ah have a thousands," he said. "Even asks 'ah Al."

John looked over at Alvin, who had been listening. He nodded his head sadly to John, "the Thogs I was able to get told me that a lot of their group had joined the Thogeen side because the Thogeens had escaped. They wanted to be on the winning side."

John was amazed. They were still a smaller army. Will they ever be ahead in numbers?

"Sos 'ah," Julia said. "Does yous 'ah like 'ah my fighting 'ah?"

"Yeah, you guys were great!" John continued like there was no interruption. "Two guys with one arrow? That was amazing! And Victor, two shots didn't bring you down, huh?"

"Theys 'ah were minor 'ah," Victor said triumphantly.

"Yeah, well," John sighed. He changed the subject. "So when are we going to fight?"

"Well," Alvin replied, "we figured in about four days, we are going to encounter them if they don't encounter us first."

"Four days?" John said, amazed. "Don't you think they would find us before then?"

"Is 'ah doubt its' 'ah."

"We still haven't decided how we are going to meet them," Alvin said. "I have 600 gliders, but I think I could get more in a couple of days. Or we could go by ground; we might have a better chance that way. Or we could just hide in a building, and start shooting arrows at them. Everyone could just have a bow and seven arrows ... "

"I've got it!" Paul said, standing up from his checkers match. "We could do a little of each! John could be captain of flight—with 200 gliders—Jerry could be captain of ground—he would lead 300—and Julia captain of arrow shooters from the window!"

Alvin stood up. "That's a great idea, Paul! I could round up the best shooters of the Thogs, while—" he pointed at Jerry "—you could find the best land fighters! Find the ones that are good with spears and I think I could arrange getting some swords for them. John will teach the Thogs how to glide!"

"But I don't know how to—" John began.

"It's 'ah easy 'ah," Victor said. "I've done its 'ah before 'ah."

"Then you should be the leader and teach me how to glide," John said.

"Ok, that settles that," Alvin said. "Let's go. We only have four days to prepare."

The gliders were much different than John expected. Instead of holding onto a bar of the glider, they strap someone's shoulder to the glider itself. This way, the person could carry an object in each hand, and could turn by shifting their shoulders. Also, on the back of the gliders, there were small fans that the pilot could turn on to propel upward to the launching point.

John had gotten the hang of flying as Alvin had predicted. John could not carry anything yet, but it was only day one of four. By day two, he could carry a small bow. Alvin came up with idea of pasting arrows on the side of the wing. At the end of the day, John had managed to hit a target while flying. When day three arrived, Alvin woke them up early.

"Our spy just confirmed that the Thogeens are a couple of miles away. They may avoid us, but today we are training inside."

So, on day three, everyone tried on armor except the glider pilots. Victor reminded them that too much weight might interfere with gliding. Instead, the glider pilots made more arrows for the archers while the archers were busy with their armor. Maurice was still teaching the inexperienced Thogs how to twirl the spears and throw them at targets. In five hours, they had all mastered the skill. Each archer had 20 arrows; each glider pilot had six arrows, two stones and a dagger in case of a crash. The soldiers of the ground army each had two spears and a sword. They had the most protective gear. At the end of the day, the army was very confident.

They all woke early the next day to get their assignments. Paul was on the archery division along with Julia; Lino was on the ground team along with Alvin, Jerry and Maurice; John and Victor were head of the gliders. The gliders started on top of the tallest building. It was the same building where the archery team was hiding. The ground team was close to the building, out in the open.

There was silence for two and a half hours before the ground team felt the rumbling of feet.

"The enemy approaches!" Alvin yelled. Everyone behind him pulled out swords. They now could see the Thogeens, who bore a dark green armor.

"A at ready!" Alvin yelled. There was a *swoosh* underneath the gliders as the archery team put an arrow in their bows and pulled back on the string.

"B at ready!" Alvin yelled.

"That's us," John whispered to the gliders. They all got to the edge. Then John turned to Victor and said, "Good luck!"

"Good 'ah luck 'ah to yous 'ah too!" Victor squeaked.

The Thogeens stopped a few feet from Alvin. One of the Thogeens yelled something that had to mean "Charge!" because they ran towards Alvin.

"Fire!" Alvin yelled. Two hundred arrows came out of the building and shot many Thogeens.

"Fly!"

One hundred gliders jumped. This was the plan. Half of the gliders would stay while the first wave was out. The second wave would go off when the first came back to reload. John was among the ones that went in wave one. He managed to hit Thogeens with all of his arrows. Triumphantly, he turned and was about to go rearm himself, when he turned back and saw that some Thogs were having trouble with their gliders. He took a purposeful nosedive, pulling up at the last second, scaring away some Thogeens, making a nice path for landing. After the Thogs saw John doing this, they quickly landed in the path that John had made. Some Thogeens surrounded them, but other gliders' shots gave them protection with their arrows.

John turned on his glider. He was three feet from the ground, but he did not intend to land. He turned on the glider's booster on the back. He got up in the air again and the booster died. He landed on the building for rearming. When the rest of team one landed, team two – including Victor – jumped off.

Jerry had killed a few Thogeens already. Once again his sword was flaring. He was thinking about how much he wanted to be the head of the gliders and that he was jealous of John. Alvin had killed a couple dozen Thogeens in a short amount of time. Lino was not doing as well as he managed to kill only three. Not many Thogs had fallen yet.

Paul was not firing any arrows yet, but kept on ordering Flaminetore to build more arrows. But he was running low on batteries so they weren't very good. Sometimes Flaminetore would provide Paul with a stick and Paul would have to do the rest. But even with this inconvenience, they always had extra arrows. When his computer's batteries got extremely low, he asked Flaminetore for new batteries. When provided, he replaced the old with the new, and the computer got recharged.

Soon, Jerry became extremely tired. He had killed a few dozen Thogeens. Alvin, however, was fighting as if he just had just started, even though he had killed the same amount. The Thogs were now falling. Soon, Alvin called for some of the archers to come down to the ground and help. Even when they cut the Thogeens' number in half, they continued losing Thogs fast. Lino was on the ground, gasping for breath. Alvin told Jerry to leave him, that his life would be in more danger if he tried to help him. Jerry reluctantly agreed.

After three hours of continual fighting, the total number of Thogeens was 300 against 300 Thogs and John, Paul, Alvin, and Jerry. For the first time, Alvin looked like he could not go on any longer. He had already asked for backup twice from the gliders and archers. Jerry was okay as long as there were people to help him.

Alvin was dueling a Thogeen. The Thogeen knocked one sword away. Alvin was fighting desperately to defeat him, but the Thogeen looked like he was well-trained. Jerry tried to concentrate on his own Thogeen, but at every little millisecond that his Thogeen wasn't attacking him, he kept glancing over at Alvin. After Jerry had defeated his Thogeen, he turned completely to see how Alvin was doing. He saw him on the ground, weaponless. The Thogeen was lifting up his sword for the final blow.

"Noooooooo!" Jerry yelled, running to his aid.

The Thogeen was bringing his sword down upon Alvin before Jerry could arrive.

9) Two to the Company

Jerry quickly threw his sword to Alvin who caught it and deflected the Thogeen's attack. Jerry ran over, took the sword from Alvin and started fighting the Thogeen.

"Jerry, be careful with him!" Alvin said. "He is the first ever Thogeen, and he is the most powerful one of all! Since he created the potion, he drank it before the ambition got poured into it! Feelings don't affect him!"

Jerry's heart sank. He had heard that the only weakness of the Thogeens was to use your feelings against them, but what if they don't affect them?

"Come in, Paul," Jerry said as he deflected another attack. He was talking into the microscopic walkie-talkie Paul had given him so that all three brothers could instantly communicate with each other.

"Paul here," the walkie-talkie replied.

"Paul, get John and get down here *now*!" Jerry said. "Over-and-out."

Jerry then heard static and knew Paul's invention had broken.

"Jerry, I'm here!" Alvin said, getting up. He had recovered his two swords.

"I'm not letting you fight this thing by yourself," Jerry said as Alvin joined the fight.

"We don't have time to argue," Alvin said, sighing.

Ten minutes later, Paul was running down the last flight of steps with John at his heels.

"I don't get it, Paul," John said. "What did Jerry actually say?"

"I told you, 'Get John and get down here,'" Paul replied. "He sounded like he needed help. We have to hurry."

They got down to the battle scene where there were about 200 Thogeens and Thogs. They saw Jerry and Alvin fighting a very powerful Thogeen. They ran towards Jerry. As they were running, they pulled out their weapons.

"This Thogeen must be very powerful if Jerry is calling for help to beat it," Paul said.

"Guys! You're here!" Jerry said. His sword was dully puffing out flames. "If you are focusing really hard on your power, your weapon will unleash some type of force, as you saw from my sword earlier. Please help!"

Paul tried to think how he could be loyal. He figured that he could show loyalty by giving up his axe in order to kill the Thogeen. He was about to throw his axe when Jerry stopped him.

"John still needs to think up his!"

John thought that if *Jerry* couldn't beat the Thogeen, then he would really be scared of it. John would have to show bravery in fighting this creature.

"Three … two … one," Jerry said, pausing his fighting, "NOW!"

Jerry took a swing at the Thogeen. The Thogeen didn't have enough time to defend itself. Jerry hit it in the side and flames erupted just as Paul's axe hit the throat and lightning came out. John's sword hit the creature's leg. Instantly, all three weapons bounced off.

"John, think of something more honest or brave!" Jerry yelled as he kept sword fighting the Thogeen.

Think, John thought. He couldn't come up with anything. Then something strange came to his mind. He had always lied about it. So if he thought about it, everything he would say would be honest. He just realized it – it was his love for his family. He had denied it for years, but now he knew what he must do. He thought how much he loved them.

"Ready?" Jerry said.

"Ready," John said, smiling.

"Go!" Jerry said. Jerry hit its side again and more flames shot out of the sword then ever before. Paul threw his axe at its throat and more lightning came out of the axe than Paul had ever experienced. But John's sword had missed the Thogeen completely. When it struck the ground, the earth shook and everyone was thrown off their feet. When the Thogeen hit the ground, it didn't get up again.

"WE DID IT!" Jerry yelled.

When the rest of Thogeens saw what had happened to their leader, they all ran away from battle.

"Oh, noes yous 'ah don'ta," Victor said from his glider up above. He shot down some of them. The last charge of the Thogs finished the rest.

"WE'S 'AH WON! WE'S 'AH WON! WES 'AH BEAT THEM ALL 'AH!" The remainder of the Thogs chanted. There were about 150 Thogs left still standing.

"Well, that was 'ah most excellent 'ah!" Maurice said, six days after the war. Maurice had been elected to be the head of all Thogs. The original captain had been killed by the Thogeens. "Yous 'ah may now leave and gos to maze 'ah. Wes 'ah will escort yous 'ah to the doors 'ah."

He, Victor, Alvin and Julia went with the Quaills. They went to the side of a building where they saw a metal door. Alvin turned to them.

"I promised Jerry to protect all of you," he said. "I am coming with you."

"But 'ah," Maurice said. "Yous 'ah please stay here 'ah! Wes 'ah need yous 'ah! Theres 'ah will always be Thogeens 'ah to fights, and we needs 'ah yours helps 'ah!"

"No. I need to face your master, Zyno," Alvin said, bending down so that he was level with him. "You are a great leader, Maurice. You are the best warrior and the leader of the warriors. One day you will lead your people into battle again. You are very strong and might be the one who could end war here forever. In fact, there may be a time when our world falters, and we will call you for help first. You will never lead your people astray. You vowed to never become a Thogeen. I will hold you to that."

"I swears 'ah," Maurice said, pounding his fist to his chest. "Is'ah will answers any call you needs 'ah from us's. You saved our's way's of life's 'ah. Wes 'ah wont forget's a that."

"We won't either," Alvin said. "And we'll miss you."

"Ohs 'ah wells 'ah," Maurice sighed. "Yous 'ah visit 'ah?"

"Yes."

"Good 'ah," Maurice said. Shaking hands with Paul, Jerry and John and with a nod to Alvin, he stepped back. Julia hugged everyone unexpectedly.

"Goodbye!" she said. Everyone was amazed.

"How—" Jerry began.

"Been working on it for days now," she said, using complete English now. She concentrated hard on pronouncing each and every word correctly. "I wanted to surprise you."

Everyone was impressed.

"You are quite a perseverant Thog," Alvin said. "Even though you are less strong than the others, you push yourself further than anyone else. You care for the Thogs around you when you fight. You give them food and encouragement. In the future that encouragement will be necessary. You will fight and be strong the rest of your life. Not just in strength, but also in hope. You heal the weakened."

"Thank yous-I mean you," she said. "I will keep the work up and strengthen my people. And heal those who are wounded."

Then she stepped back. Victor stepped forward with tears in his eyes.

"Oh pleases 'ah," he said, sobbing terribly now. "May I 'ah asks 'ah favors 'ah?"

"Sure," Paul said, confused.

"Oh pleases 'ah," Victor said, "Can Isa go with yous 'ah?"

"What?" John said. He looked to the others.

"Pleases 'ah!"

Alvin took in some breath and said, "Of course not—"

"-Without a weapon," cut in Jerry.

"But-" Alvin began. But he thought about it. He nodded, and turned to Victor. "You have much courage to go with us. You will be the first Thog to see our world, and how corrupt it is. You will have to see through people to their emotions, or in your terms, to their powers. See who is good and who is bad and tell us, for you can see things we cannot. When the time comes to call the Thogs again, I promise, you will be the messenger for it."

"Ohs 'ah thank yous 'ah," Victor said, hugging Jerry. Jerry smiled, then realized something.

"Where's Lino?" he said. They all turned around. He was gone.

"Isa knows 'ah where hes 'ah is," Victor said. "Hes 'ah in the maze 'ah."

"How?" John asked. "I was the one with the-"

He reached into his pocket for the chip, but he only found his dead walkie-talkie.

"He must have taken the chip!" he exclaimed. "How are we going to get back in?"

"I think we have one more extra chip," Julia replied. "Wait! We gave it to you for defeating the Thogeen!"

She pointed at Alvin. Alvin looked at her curiously.

"No, you must have given it to someone else," Alvin replied. "Because I don't have it."

"Well, this person had something oval over his eyes and wore a purple turtle neck," Julia said. Alvin smiled.

"Zyno," He said.

"Excuse me?" Paul said.

"It was Zyno," Alvin said. "He always wears something purple. It's his symbol. I just find it very amusing that he is blind."

"He's blind?" John said amazed.

"Do you think he wore those glasses for looks?" Alvin said, laughing. "Oh, no, he's blind alright. Unless he's just changed the type of goggles he uses to see, it must be pretty sudden; I mean, since the Thogs didn't recognize him as their master ... "

"Wait," Paul said. "What if that is why he wore the glasses?!"

"What do you mean?" Alvin said. He had stopped laughing.

"If he came here, disguised," Paul began, "then the Thogs wouldn't recognize him. He would know how to defeat the Thogeens. Then all he would have to do was take the chip, the last chip, and leave!"

"That might be it," John said, "or he could be both blind and disguised."

"Both prove very good points," Alvin said. "But we haven't figured out how to get out yet."

"Sorry to interrupt, but I think we've got company," Jerry said, looking behind them. They all spun around. There they saw the sight of macaw's wings in the sky.

"Does he have to visit us in every world we go?" John said angrily.

"Who is it?" Alvin asked.

"You'll see," Paul answered.

The hyena landed a few yards from them.

"Didn't I warn you," it said, "That if you hurt any more of the pack you will regret it?"

"Actually," John said, reaching for the hilt of his sword, "you threatened to kill us."

"Well, I guess promises can be broken," the hyena chuckled. "Because I like this better. Are you guys gonna miss your little tiger friend?"

"What have you done to him, scum face?" Jerry said threateningly.

"Me?" the hyena laughed. "Oh, no, not me. I think you are talking about my master."

"What?" Paul said.

"Oh yes, he's here," the hyena grinned. "We have many parts to the pack. You killed all in one section. Any more, and slowly everyone will fall from your group. Why? Because of my master."

"Your master is a good for nothing—" Jerry began.

"Nothing? I think he is good for something," the hyena replied. "You might say he's good at brain-washing, considering the Pink Panther was!"

"No!" Paul yelled, pulling out his ax. John and Jerry had to hold him back. "He can throw us in a freezer for three hours, he can threaten to kill us, but when he takes our friend, that's when I get mad!"

The hyena burst out laughing. This seemed to make Paul angrier.

"You still think *I* brain-washed that tiger?" The hyena said, laughing harder then ever. "Do you really think I could do that?"

"You struck a really good point," John said, getting a better grip on Paul's arm, "considering you are dumber than a cow!"

The hyena stopped laughing.

"Say what you want, you are going to stay here for life!" The hyena said. "Thanks to the Pink Panther, the only chip available belongs to Zyno."

Alvin's hands clenched into fists.

"And where, may I ask is Zyno?" Alvin said in a deep voice.

The hyena suddenly looked frightened at the sight of Alvin.

"I will not tell *you* were he is," the hyena said bravely.

"You will tell me now!" Alvin said a little louder and at the same time reaching down to his sword. When the hyena saw this, it laughed.

"You gonna kill me?" it said. "Fine. Before I go, I might as well tell them your *true* identity."

Alvin flushed. Breathing hard, he put his hand down. The hyena laughed again.

"I will tell you where Zyno is," The hyena said, laughing some more. "He is in the maze at the exact location you would be if you went through that portal."

It pointed at the metal door.

"And where is this chip that Zyno has?" Alvin said.

"Ah, yes, I was thinking we would be getting to that," The hyena replied. He reached under his wing and pulled out a computer chip.

"You mean this chip?"

Everyone froze. The hyena laughed.

"Yes, Zyno told me to do this in front of you all," he said. Everyone was breathing hard. The hyena broke the chip with his teeth.

10) Revenge

That was the final straw for Paul. He pulled away from Jerry and John's grip and ran at the hyena. He pulled out his ax and jumped on the hyena. He started hitting the hyena wildly with his ax. The hyena threw him off.

"You want to face me, little baby?" the hyena said in a babyish tone. "To get revenge on your little baby friend, the Pink Panther?"

Paul couldn't remember ever in his life being so angry, but after that comment, he got angrier. He ran and jumped, bringing the ax down upon the hyena's throat. The hyena moved out of the way and Paul fell into the mud. Once again, the hyena started laughing.

"Oooooo, little baby wants to fight me single-handedly," he said. "Fine then little baby, I'll play with you!"

He picked up Paul, flew up to the highest building and dropped him on the roof.

"There you go," the hyena said. "You have your chance to get your vengeance."

Paul wasn't expecting this. He always trusted that someone would be there to look out for him. But now was different. He was all alone andabout to face a creature beyond Thogeen. He was certainly unprotected. His only weapon was his ax. He looked behind him. The building went about 100 stories down. On the ground, he could see five dots that were his friends and family. The hyena guffawed.

"Not so sure about fighting me now, huh?" the hyena said. Paul turned back to the hyena with a smile.

"Oh, I'm sure," he said. "The question is, will you run away?"

The hyena stopped laughing.

"Oh, yes," Paul continued. "When I start smashing you into the ground, *you* will fly away like a little baby. And you were the one calling me a baby, when you are the one who is a whimp."

The hyena jumped forward. Paul ducked. The hyena turned and launched again. This time Paul swung his ax at it. The ax hit the hyena in the eye. The hyena screamed.

"Not so tough now, are you?" Paul said. He had stalled too long. The hyena smacked Paul with his paw. Paul fell to the ground, but he rolled onto his back and threw the ax at the hyena's throat as he did many times when he faced a Thogeen. It hit the hyena's throat and bounced off, but the hyena staggered and Paul could see some blood on his throat. The hyena growled and kicked Paul's ax off the building. Paul leapt forward and grabbed it just before it went out of his reach. The hyena leapt again and Paul spun away from the edge. He stood up and faced the hyena again.

"You will pay for what you did to me in that freezer," Paul snarled. The hyena finally took him seriously.

"You're the same," the hyena said. "They could've put an ax into your hand, but you are still a child. You cannot fight against a creature who's friends with Zyno himself. You will die!"

He rocketed towards Paul who ducked again. The hyena turned in midair and Paul kicked it under the chin. The hyena staggered and fell to the ground. Paul got his ax close to his throat.

"I have changed," Paul said. "I have had training against you and your precious 'pack'."

The hyena twisted his body away from Paul. It stood a few yards away and then Paul had an idea. He thought of how loyal he was to Lino for fighting Lino's biggest enemy. Lightning shot out of Paul's ax, aimed for the hyena. The hyena got the full blast of it and started to screech loud. Paul stopped his lightning and the hyena fell lifeless to the ground. Paul approached it in triumph. *I finally killed it*, Paul thought. Just then, the hyena's giant wing came out and whipped at Paul's ax. Paul was taken by surprise and the strike shot his ax off the building. Paul stood back as the hyena got up and laughed.

"I am not finished that easily," it said.

The hyena ran at Paul, but Paul saw a cut on the side in its eye that his ax created. Paul punched the hyena in that eye, and the hyena stumbled again. Paul started to punch and kick it in the eye, each followed by a scream. The hyena, being defenseless, lifted up his wings and flew off.

"I told you you'd leave!" Paul yelled. "You chicken!"

Paul grinned in triumph. All of the sudden, a rope flew up to roof. A few stories down, he saw Jerry's face sticking out a window.

"Are you alright?" Jerry yelled up to him.

"Yeah," Paul said, tying the rope to a flagpole that was near the side of the roof. "Old scum face ran away before I could finish him off."

"I doubt it," Jerry said as Paul started climbing down. "We saw your ax fall off the building. I don't think you could last much longer."

Paul climbed into the window.

When he reached the ground, he didn't see Julia or Maurice. They must have left.

"Any ideas on how to get through the metal door?" Paul asked.

Jerry and John looked at each other.

"Uh … Paul? We're … uh … wondering if we really *want* to go through that door," Jerry said finally.

"What do you mean?" Paul gasped, surprised. "Of course we want to go through!"

"Paul, listen. We will have to face Zyno if we go through that door. He is more dangerous than all of these worlds put together!" John almost pleaded.

"Lands," Alvin corrected.

"While here 'ah," Victor said. "Yous 'ah will be safe 'ah."

Paul was astonished. They were right, logically at least. But he was still angry with their inconsideration of Lino. However, he kept the same tone of voice when he spoke.

"So," he said. "We are just going to leave Lino abandoned? Look, I know it's dangerous, but we can't just leave him there!"

"Paul, that's exactly what Zyno wants you to think," John said. "So that we will go into the maze to try to find him and Zyno will be right there waiting for us."

Paul went up to John and unzipped his book bag. He pulled out his computer. He put it on the ground and turned it on. Flaminetore came out.

"Noy ercomin fier howsre," Paul said. Flaminetore disappeared. In its place came a small, circular object.

"Paul, don't," Alvin said. Paul had stuck the object on the door and pressed a red button. He took a step back. There was a huge explosion and the door fell open.

"How come we can't do that for all of the doors," John laughed.

"I only supplied my computer with one," Paul said. "I was saving it, but that's beside the point."

Paul sighed.

"Look," Paul said, turning to them. "I'm going no matter what. You can either go or stay."

He took a deep breath, took off his glasses, and stepped forward through the door. John sighed.

"Paul's right," he said. "I'm going with him."

He stepped through. He fell into a blue tornado. He tried to balance himself so that he could land on his feet. He found this difficult. Before he knew it, he landed next to Paul, who had landed on his feet.

"We did it," Paul said.

"Yeah," John said. "We got out of that freaky land."

"That's not what I meant," Paul said. "I mean we actually landed on our feet. Let's be sure to tell Jerry."

"If we ever see them again," John sighed.

They glanced around.

"Where's Zyno?" John said.

"I don't know, I guess the hyena lied," Paul said.

"I don't think he lied about Lino, though," John said. "It would make sense that he was captured. Where else could he have gone? Come on, we've got to find him."

They came out of the dead end. Then John realized something.

"Paul, maybe we can catch up with Jimmy and Tyler while we are looking for Lino!" he suggested.

"Ok, but only as we are looking for Lino," Paul said. "And be on your toes. Maybe Zyno's in the maze. We have to keep quiet."

"You've got it," John replied. "So where should we go? There are 20 paths to take!"

"Actually," Paul calculated, looking down all the paths, "There are seven."

They looked down each path. All of them looked dark.

"Well," John said, "I don't think we should split up first of all."

"Right," Paul agreed. "Let's take the middle path first."

"Ok," John said, "And if we hit a dead end, let's turn back."

They went through a middle passage, Paul in the lead. Paul bumped into solid wall. Dead end. It started sucking him in.

"No, no, no!" Paul yelled. "John, I accidentally bumped into the wall! I'm getting sucked in!"

That was all that Paul said before he was sucked in.

Paul fell again into a red tornado and was thrown around. He landed face first in the mud.

"You alright there, son?" someone said from behind him. Paul felt himself being pulled up. "Here, wipe your face with this."

Something made of cloth fell into his hands. Paul could not see since mud went into his eyes. He wiped off his face, but everything still looked kind of blurry. Then he remembered that he took off his glasses in the maze. He quickly put them on. He found himself in a large, busy city with very tall skyscrapers. It was so hot; it had to be hotter than the maze. It looked a lot like the outside world today. Paul wanted to test to see if he was right. He looked at the middle-aged man who helped him up.

"Excuse me, but what year is it?" Paul asked.

"Whoa, what a nasty fall you must have taken," the man said. "Rattled your brain, probably."

"Can you please tell me?" Paul said.

"It is the year of 2009," he said. "March 28."

The man turned and left. Quickly, Paul went inside a building and looked around. He saw what he needed. He ran into the bathroom and went over to the counter near the sinks. He turned on his computer and clicked on the "date" button. It read *March 28 2009, 12:54.* Paul looked up at the clock on the wall. It read *12:55.*

"That clock must be fast," Paul concluded. *Because why would Zyno make a world that was one minute ahead of our time*, Paul thought.

Paul left the bathroom. He exited the building. *If this is the present,* Paul thought, *I wonder where I am.* He left the building. He ran into solid object on the ground.

"Hey, watch it!" said the voice from the ground. Paul looked down and saw his older brother covered in mud.

"It's about time you got here," Paul said, helping John up. "Sorry, I don't have anything to wipe you off with."

"So where are we now," John said, wiping his eyes with his shirt. "Past? Future? Saturn?"

"Actually," Paul said. "We are in the exact present."

"That's cool," John said. "It isn't as dangerous."

"But we've got a long way to go," Paul said, looking around. "How do you think we are going to find that chip in this city?"

"You got me there," John said. "And there must be thousands of metal doors."

"Well, it might help if we knew where we are," Paul said. He walked up to someone and asked, "Excuse me, my brother and I are lost. Can you please tell me where I am?"

"You are in the capital of Arizona, of course. Phoenix," the man replied hurriedly. He walked around them. Paul blinked.

"Have you ever heard of Phoenix?" Paul whispered to John.

"Nope," John said.

"Well, let's try asking people if they have seen any particular chip," Paul said.

"Yeah, maybe people might-Jimmy! Tyler! There you are!" John said recognizing his friends. Two people turned and ran towards them.

"There *you* are," Jimmy said. "We saw your friend, that pink animal by itself. What happened?"

While Paul told them the story, John started asking people if they saw any computer chip, but nobody seemed to want to help him.

"Yeah, we seemed to go through the maze and accomplished seven lands total," Tyler said. "They seemed to go past very easily. Nothing as dangerous as your's, though. By the way, we found that chip thing."

"You did?" John said, turning to him. "How long did you look for it?"

"We didn't look for it," Jimmy explained. "We had to win a motorcycle race. They said the prize was a 'rare and mysterious' computer chip. After seeing the last seven chips, we could tell it different from a regular computer chip."

"Then you won?" Paul said, impressed.

"Yeah, but the metal door?" Tyler sighed in exasperation. "We have been stuck here forever trying to find the right one. We have been staying at a hotel. We better find it fast. I am running out of money."

John laughed. Tyler's parents were billionaires.

"How fancy is this hotel?" he asked.

"Not very fancy," Tyler said. "But I didn't bring much money at all. I keep most of my money at home."

"How much money do you have?" Paul said.

"Seventy dollars," Tyler answered.

"Well, we're in luck," Paul said. "I have my money in my computer."

"But I thought you were saving your money for college, Paul," John teased, grinning.

"Well, if we don't get out of here, there won't *be* any college," Paul replied.

"Of course, we could always do this," Jimmy said. He walked up behind someone on a cell phone. There was some money sticking out of his pocket. Jimmy snatched some of his money sticking out. He came back grinning. Everyone scowled at him. Jimmy looked down at the money. He was jumped in surprise.

"Hey, guys, come here," he said to them. They gathered around. They all looked at the dollar.

"Whoa, who's he?" John said, looking at the face of a guy on the dollar. "Washington?"

"These people put people on their dollar named after washing-machines?" Jimmy said. "And look at this one! Lincoln?"

"Now they're naming them after computers!" Paul said. "What's the last one?"

"Hamilton," Tyler said, shaking his head. "Naming their money after food. This is so bizarre. And it seems like these people are stupid. Look, they put the number of its worth multiple times."

"This stuff looks like play money," John said, waving it in his hand.

"This is just great," Paul said.

"What is?" Tyler asked.

"Well, if this is the money they pay with," Paul said. "Then we have a total of 16 'dollars', or whatever they call their currency, to pay the hotel!"

Everyone stood still. Finally, John spoke.

"Couldn't ... couldn't you translate it somehow, Paul?" he said.

"How could I do that?" Paul replied.

"Flaminetore!"

"I ...he can't do that!" Paul said, looking desperately at John who looked back at him hard. Paul sighed. "I ... I'll try."

"Impossible!" Jimmy said. "No laptop computer can do that!"

"You haven't seen the complete power of Paul's computer," John said proudly. Paul smiled.

"Well, it'll be hard, and I need a place to work," he said.

"Let's go to the hotel," Jimmy said. "We can eat there."

"Room 312 ... 313 ... 314," Jimmy said, walking past doors in the hotel. "Room 315 ... 316 ... aha! Room 317."

He opened the door to reveal two beds, a TV, and a computer on the desk.

"That might help," Paul said pointing at the computer. He turned on his computer along with the other computer. When Flaminetore came out Paul said, "Throyer cabinel sord."

A cable came out of the computer. Paul plugged one end into the hotel's computer and the other end into his. Paul inserted the one-dollar bill into his computer's disk slot. He then went over to the hotel's computer and opened that disk slot. He inserted one of Tyler's one-dollar bills into the computer's slot. Then he opened the folder labeled "Disk" on both computers. A picture of a dollar came up on both of the screens, one having a big one in the middle of it, the other having Washington's face on it.

"Whoa, how did you do that?" John said, coming over to Paul.

"He created me to recognize the dollar bill," Flaminetore said. "But only because he needed a place to keep his money safe. When the cable linked computers, that computer is almost as smart as me."

"I see," John said.

"Can you please stop talking?" Paul said. "I am trying to concentrate."

Paul clicked on the "computer interaction" button. After about 30 seconds, both computers had both dollar bills on the screen. Paul looked at the dollar bill with Washington's face on it.

"Hey guys," Paul said. "I know where we are!"

"Where?" John said.

"The United States of America," Paul read. "It says so on the dollar!"

"Cool," John said, lying down. "Hey Paul, would you mind if I turn on the TV?"

"Yeah, sure, whatever," Paul said, turning back to the computer. Paul looked in between the dollar bills. He looked at Flaminetore.

"Do you think I could drag information from one dollar to the next?" He said.

"No, not without programming it into me," Flaminetore replied.

"But that could take weeks!" Paul exclaimed. He buried his face in his hands. Paul then looked back up at the screen.

"What about duplication?" Paul asked.

"No, not without programming it into me," Flaminetore replied.

"How about translating?"

"It's the same language, sir," Flaminetore said.

Paul looked at the screen again.

"There has got to be a way," he said. Paul thought a moment. Then he got an idea.

"What about editing and deleting information?" he said.

"Yes, sir," Flaminetore said after a moment's thought. "I believe that would work."

"Alright then," Paul said. "Delete the information on the length of our dollar."

Paul turned to Jimmy.

"Hey, Jimmy, give me that five you had."

Jimmy gave Paul his five-dollar bill.

"Flaminetore, a ruler please," Paul said. A hologram ruler came out. Paul measured the dollar bill.

"Ok, enter six inches for our dollar," he said. Instantly, the dollar became smaller. "Right, now delete the color of our dollar and replace it with the color of the one with Washington on it."

When he said so, it instantly changed color. Then he turned to Flaminetore.

"Can we copy and paste?" Paul asked him.

"I'll try," Flaminetore said. "It will be difficult."

Paul copied and pasted the money's value onto the other. Then he copied the face to the other dollar bill. He copied and pasted for six hours before he called out to everyone.

"Guys! I did it!"

"You did? Let me see," John said.

"You see?" Paul said, "Now, when I put a dollar where we come from, it can translate it in a blink of an eye."

"Well, it worked on the computer," Jimmy said. "How will it come out?"

Paul opened the CD drive. There where Paul put in the dollar with the huge one in the middle, stood one with Washington's face on it.

"And that's not all," Paul continued. "I also downloaded the 100 dollar bill in their language. The face that is on it is Franklin."

"Isn't that the guy that who invented the hot dog?" Tyler asked.

"I deleted the information of the value and face of the one dollar bill," Paul said, opening the CD drive on the hotel computer, "And replaced it with … "

He pulled out a dollar with Franklin's face.

"And now that I did that, when I enter a dollar (our dollar that is), it will turn into the other dollar, but since the information is deleted, there is only one dollar left … the one hundred dollar bill!"

"I am confused," John said, shaking his head.

"Do you mean when you put one of our one dollar bills in," Jimmy began, "it comes out as one of their one hundred dollar bills?"

"Precisely," Paul said. "And since I keep $205 in here, I could get them into ones, and then change them into one hundreds!"

"So you mean to say," Tyler said, "that you will have to multiply $205 by one hundred and that's how much you have?"

"Yes, a total of $20,500," Paul said. "And if you change your money into ones, you would get $70,000 which would give us a total of almost $100,000!"

"I think that might just give us enough to pay off the hotel's price," Tyler said sarcastically in awe.

"What's even better is that we could do more exploring on the Internet trying to find the one thousand dollar bill and then download it onto your computer," Jimmy suggested.

"Nope," Paul said. "I looked everywhere for it until I saw a site that said it was out of the money system."

"Man," Jimmy said.

"Wait ..." John glanced at Paul in the eye. "Isn't this whole process ... er ... kind of illegal?"

Everyone looked at him without emotion. John bit his lip and said nothing more.

"Let's all get some rest," Tyler said. "It's late."

"But I am hungry," Jimmy repeated, frustrated.

"Ok, then," Paul said, giving Tyler a one hundred. "Go buy us all some food."

Tyler turned and left. Paul played solitaire on his computer. Jimmy played one of his video games. John opened up his bag but found only dinosaur skin and a few bags of Thog food. He dug underneath it and found what he was looking for. He pulled out a thick-spined book that was labeled *Wars of the Century*. Paul looked over his shoulder at him.

"Why do you always read that?" He asked.

"Well, it is about our history," John said. "I am almost done reading the end of this war. It's awesome."

"Fine then," Paul said, turning back to his game. Tyler came in with a half a gallon of milk and some ham. Jimmy looked up from his game.

"You know," Jimmy said. "I am lactose intolerant."

"Then get water from the sink," Tyler said with a scowl.

"Geez, somebody's grumpy," Jimmy said, heading for the bathroom. Tyler poured milk for everyone (except Jimmy) and cut some ham off angrily.

"What's up?" Paul said.

"I asked the person at the cash register why they name people after washing machines and put them on their money," Tyler replied.

"YOU *WHAT*?!" Paul said, choking.

"Yeah," Tyler shrugged, "she threw the ham at me and said 'Get out!'"

"Geez, I'd do that to," Paul said. "Why did you do it?"

"I couldn't help myself," Tyler said. "I was so curious."

John took a slug of his milk and started to read again. Then he spit out the milk and gagged.

"What?" Jimmy said, turning to him.

"Lis ... listen to this," John said. *"In 1959-"*

"Oh be quiet," Paul said. "We don't want to learn about some stupid war."

"No, it's not that," John said. *"In 1959 a war stretched across the country. On one side, there were three divisions with three leaders: James Stone, Richard Yeller, and Grant Wayne!"*

"Wayne?" Paul said. "That's Zyno's last name!"

"Keep reading!" Tyler ordered.

"After the three leaders fell," John continued. *"The war looked like it was over. Then the other side came over and surrendered. They came with half their army, for a huge bomb killed the majority. Recent studies stay that some of the army might have been brain washed, but there is no evidence of this. Later, the surrendering army attacked again. Grant's son rose against them and defeated them. The war ended in 1995. The war had been won because of Zyno, Grant's son."*

"Zyno?" Paul said. "He fought in a war? What side was he on?"

"This book said that this war was fought in our country," John said, scanning the page. "And it was fought as a civil war. One side wanted to surrender to Australia. You know about that war. The Thousand-Year-War was going badly with Australia so one side gave up and talked things over with Australia. The other side fought for things to stay the same, keeping our country – Locombony – peaceful and free. Zyno was on the side of keeping it free!"

John looked at them.

"Ninety-five," Paul said. "That was the year Jerry was born."

"And that was the same year Benjamin threatened to our Uncle Dan that he would kill Jerry," John said. "But he waited seven years to make a move. Why do you think he did that?"

"I'm not sure," Paul responded. "Unless … unless he was busy with something extremely important!"

"What would be more important to them than making Uncle Dan join their side?" John said.

"Maybe something that would be the finishing touch *for* Uncle Dan to join their side," Paul replied.

"What would that be?" John asked.

"The *Maze*!" Paul exclaimed. "Don't you get it? Zyno made Benjamin ask Uncle Dan to join their side. When he refused, Benjamin made his threat and told Zyno that Dan had refused. Zyno got the idea of building a maze, sticking it an ad in a magazine that Uncle Dan would surely read, and Uncle Dan would be attracted to it. The only trouble was that they had to build it. It would have taken *years*!"

"Seven years, in fact," Jimmy said. "Then he would go to your house, shoot Jerry, and leave. Then your uncle would want to get revenge on Zyno, so he would go through the maze and be killed by these lands. Or, if he reached Zyno, he would get brain-washed!"

"But still one question remains," John said. "What does he want with Uncle Dan?"

"I think we need to talk with someone," Paul said.

"Who?" John said.

"Alvin," Paul replied.

"Who?" Jimmy asked.

"A scientist who Zyno is also jealous of," John replied. "Somewhere inside me, however, I don't trust him. Remember what the hyena said? 'Fine, go ahead and kill me. Before I go, I will tell them your true identity.' What does he have to hide?"

"So you're going to trust the hyena more than Alvin?" Paul said. "Come on, I know it's a little suspicious, but he is our friend, right?"

"We need to talk with him alright," John said. "Ask him if he saw or was a friend of Uncle Dan."

"Yeah, maybe he and Uncle Dan were work buddies," Paul said.

"Only one problem," Jimmy said.

"What?" John asked.

"The maze," Tyler said. "How are we supposed to go back with all those metal doors?"

"We've got to try," John said. "Let's try to find a door with a slot for the chip in the morning. I am beat."

The next day, they left the hotel and paid for the room. When they were outside, they decided to ask someone. Paul went up to someone.

"Excuse me," he said. "But have you seen a metal door with a strange slot on it?"

The woman turned to him. Most of them prepared themselves for the obvious answer

"Yes, I have," she said. She pointed to the left. "Over there."

They walked over to the building she pointed at. There, undoubtedly, stood the metal door. John turned to Paul in impressed surprise.

"That was simple," he said. Paul took the chip from Jimmy, and put it in the slot. There was some humming and the slot spit out the chip, but the door opened. Instead of complete blackness swirling, it looked like they had opened a closet. There stood what looked like something that should have come out of a child's Jack-in-the-Box toy. It was a tall jester with a four-pointed red, black and white colored hat. He had a huge grin on his face and, at the sight of them, started laughing with a laugh that made their neck hairs stand on end. He handed them a piece of paper with a huge number five on it colored in red paint. The door slammed shut.

"What was that all about?" Tyler said. All of a sudden, Paul felt a ton of pain in his left arm. It felt like someone had pulled his arm into fire. He fell to his knees, screaming and holding his arm. The pain became more and more extreme.

"Paul, what is it?!" John yelled. Then suddenly, the pain stopped. Paul got up, shaking.

"I-I-I felt a lot of pain in-in-in my arm," Paul said, barely able to speak. He held his arm and noticed that there was a total numbness about it.

"Are you ok?" Jimmy asked.

"Now-now I am," Paul said. "The paper."

"What about it?" John said.

"What does it say?"

"It just says the number five," Tyler said. He touched the ink. "In red, sticky ink."

Paul examined it. He touched it as well.

"That's not ink," Paul whispered. "It's blood."

"What?" Jimmy said. Paul got out his computer and turned it on. Paul opened the start menu. He clicked on search. He typed in DNA.

When a screen came up, Paul opened the CD drive. He wiped some of the ink on the disk drive. Paul pushed it back in. Seeing the results, Paul gasped.

"It is bl-blood," Paul said, breathing hard. "M-my blood."

11) Only Five Chances

"Your blood? How do you know?" John interrogated.

"It says on my computer," Paul said.

"But you touched it," John said. "Your DNA should show up if you touched it."

"That's what I thought too, but Tyler touched it too! It refers to the blood, not fingerprints," Paul said.

"I did touch it," Tyler admitted.

"I just don't get why we couldn't get into the maze," Jimmy said.

"Maybe we got the wrong door," John said.

"Look," Paul exclaimed, "another door!"

Paul ran up to it with the chip in hand. He put it in the slot. It opened again and another joker stood there. He took the sheet from Paul and laughed. He ripped the sheet and handed Paul a new sheet, this time with a red four on it. The door slammed shut and spit out the chip. Paul's right arm burned as bad as his left one, and, again, this took Paul by surprise. He fell to the ground and started squirming. After five seconds, it stopped.

"This is terrible," John said. "It keeps hurting Paul, gives us a number, and won't let us back into the maze!"

"I don't know how much more I can take of this, guys," Paul said.

"What do these numbers mean?" Jimmy said.

"Maybe," John said. "It means we have four more doors until we get into the maze. To see if you can take the pain."

"I don't think so," Paul said.

"What do you think it means then?" John said.

"Maybe," Paul said, looking around. "It means we have four more chances to get the door right. Look how many there are!"

They all looked around. There were at least a hundred metal doors with slots in them.

"We need to choose our doors carefully," Paul continued. "Because if we run out of numbers, I might-might-"

Paul couldn't say the last word. Paul could barely move his hands.

"It's alright, Paul," John said. "We can get the right one. Remember what happened in the freezer? We beat the odds. We'll do it again."

Paul nodded.

"I will take pain as long we can get out of this maze and back home," Paul said.

"Well, home's no picnic either," John said.

"You've got that right," Jimmy rolled his eyes.

"Well, which door should we try?" Tyler said.

Paul felt the world freeze. Everything and everyone stopped moving

"What happened?" Paul said. No one answered. He looked around. Everyone looked like someone had pressed the "pause" button on their life.

"Hello … anybody home?" Paul said, waving his hand in their faces. Nobody answered.

"CAN … YOU … HEAR … ME!" Paul yelled.

"They can't hear you," said a voice behind Paul. "And yelling won't help."

Paul spun around. The person who had said that was six feet tall with gray hair and unusual shaped shoes. He also had a purple vest and wore white, oval-shaped goggles that prevented Paul from seeing his eyes. Paul was looking at the face he had been dreading to see since the third world.

"I see you have a big choice on your hands," Zyno said. "Four more chances until you die. But which door to choose?"

He walked closer to Paul who didn't take a step back.

"And as creator, I know perfectly well which door leads back to the maze," Zyno continued. "And you don't have a chance to get it right. Without my help …"

Paul didn't know what to say.

"What do you want?" Paul finally said, fiercely.

"Want?" Zyno said. "Who said anything about me wanting something?"

"Oh, cut the false humbleness," Paul snarled with no respect. "I don't think you made this maze for child's leisure. You want something. What is it? My Uncle Dan?"

Zyno stopped walking for a second and gave just the shadow of a twitch.

"Not just your uncle, entirely," Zyno said. "But some brilliant minds to help me."

"I will never help you," Paul snarled.

"Never?" Zyno said. "Even when you are close to death? You see, if I help you, then you should help me."

"What exactly do you need help with?" Paul asked.

"There is one of my inventions that doesn't quite work right," Zyno replied. "I need it to be finished. I need some brilliant people."

"Are you saying that *you* need *me* to help you with one of your inventions?" Paul said, almost laughing.

"It is very important to me," Zyno said. "I saw what you could do with that laptop. Only a pure genius could design something like that. I will be willing to give you anything you like. First, to prove it, I will give you the correct door."

Zyno snapped his fingers and a red outline surrounded a door they hadn't tried yet.

"Second, I will give you a chip so that you can pass the next land you go through," Zyno continued. He handed Paul a chip.

"Third, when you go back to the maze, you will find your friend Lino there," he said. "I know that you are very frustrated with me now, after whatever someone has told you, but I have done nothing wrong. That is why I am letting you decide after you make it through the maze. But I must warn you, the other lands are more dangerous and *keep* getting more and more dangerous, and I will not be there to help you. I will now send you back to the present, and you have the choice of trusting me or not. But I think you will trust me in the end. I hope you make the right choice! If you want to know about me, *he* might know."

He pointed at John. He laughed and disappeared. Everything started moving again. The outline of the right door disappeared, but Paul still knew what door Zyno had outlined.

"Let's try that door," John said, pointing to a door next to the correct one.

"No!" Paul said. He had made his decision. "Let's try that one."

Paul put the chip Zyno had given him into his pocket. He took out the other chip. He went over to the door. He took a deep breath and put it in the slot. The door opened and twisting blackness appeared. Zyno was telling the truth! Paul jumped in, slowly followed by John, Jimmy, and Tyler. Paul hit the ground inside the maze, face first. John followed behind him. Then Jimmy and Tyler.

Paul got up and saw a pink tiger in front of him.

"Hello, Lino," Paul said, hugging him. "Are you ok?"

"Am I ok?" Lino said. "I'm fine. Are you ok?"

"Yeah, we all are," John said. "Thanks to Paul."

John slapped Paul on his back.

"Good job back there, Paul," John said. "We wouldn't have got out if it wasn't for you."

"Yeah," Paul said, sighing. "Lucky guess."

"Where is Jerry?" Lino said, noticing that he wasn't here.

John looked at Paul.

"He's … uh, in the maze somewhere," John lied.

"Well, there's no time to lose," Lino said. "Quickly, let's find him so we can move onward."

He ran ahead of them. Paul couldn't stop thinking about what Zyno said. *I haven't done anything wrong.* And now that he said it, they don't actually have any proof he had done anything wrong. Nobody said that Benjamin was on Zyno's side. *Ah!* said a little voice inside Paul's head, *but he did say he was jealous of Uncle Dan.*

But jealousy is a common thing, another voice said. *I am jealous of Jerry and John all the time. A ton of other scientists could be jealous of Uncle Dan's inventions.* Yes, Zyno *could* be good. But what about Alvin? He said that Benjamin *was* working for Zyno.

But John is right, he is *kind of suspicious. He didn't tell us his name.*

But he helped us, said another voice. *He helped us go through a world. But so did Zyno.*

Paul was so confused. All in all, Zyno was right: Paul did need more time to think about it.

"I think we should split up," Lino said. "If we find a dead end, we'll yell."

They all agreed. Paul went down a path, very slowly. He heard some voices.

"He's here! He's here! I saw him!" said one voice. Paul recognized it to be the hyena's.

"I knew Daniel got in here since the second he stepped into this building," Said another Paul also recognized as Zyno's. Paul gulped. His uncle was here.

"No, no, no," the hyena said. "He's in the maze now! He's near us!"

"Good, the closer the better," Zyno said. "I need to ask you something. Why did you try to kill the young one?"

The hyena didn't say anything. Paul got closer. He peered around the corner. He saw Zyno with his arms crossed, looking at the hyena who was on the ground whimpering.

"I am sorry, sir," the hyena replied.

"I need you to make sure that the little one stays safe," Zyno said. "You lay one finger on the boy and I'll kill you."

"Yes, sir," the hyena whimpered. "But what about the others? What about the little one's brothers?"

Paul held his breath. *This was it.*

"I don't care what you do to them," Zyno said. "But they will be surprised that there will be holograms amongst them. It's the last people that they would expect them to be!"

Paul froze. Holograms? Who was it?

"Yes, sir," The hyena said, forcing a fake laugh. "You are a genius."

"The little one has only two more lands to go through before he gets to me," Zyno said. "Do you think you can protect him?"

"Yes, sir," the hyena said. "I will never fail you again."

"Good," Zyno said. "*Shrinky* is almost ready. Maybe Daniel and his nephew will help me. After all, I don't exactly want to make trouble, but if I have to, I will."

"Sir, there is one more thing that is the most important information of all!" the hyena said, voice lowering to a whisper. Paul leaned in closer. "The magician … is here."

Zyno's arms dropped to his side and his whole body gave an involuntary shiver.

"W-where?" Zyno asked, stuttering. "My-my cameras must have-have missed him …"

"He's only a world away!" the hyena screeched. "And-and he's angry with you, master!"

"There's no time to lose," Zyno said, glancing over his shoulder. "We need to start moving."

Zyno turned and left. The hyena ran head first into a wall and disappeared.

"So he wants me to help him on a machine called *Shrinky*, eh?" Paul said. "We'll see about that!"

"I found one!" yelled a voice. Paul recognized it to be Lino's. He ran towards the voice. He saw him there along with John. They waited a few moments before Tyler and Jimmy joined them.

"Ready, guys?" Lino said.

"Yeah," They all said. They pushed the wall. They were suddenly sucked up into the wall. They were falling into a green tornado. Then they hit the ground. When they got up, it looked like they had hit the ground in a desert. While everyone was looking around, Paul pulled out the chip that Zyno had given him. Zyno had fulfilled his promise so far; so he might not be lying on this either. Paul couldn't tell the others. He dropped the chip on the ground.

"Hey guys," Paul said, picking up the chip. "Look what I found!"

"Geez," John said when he saw the chip. "That was easy."

"Yeah," Paul said, shrugging convincingly.

"Look! Could it be?" Jimmy said. "It is! It's an airplane."

They all looked the direction that Jimmy was looking. In the distance, they all saw a parked airplane. There was no one or nothing in sight besides that airplane.

"Well, I guess we have no choice," Lino said. "Quick, let's talk with the pilot."

They ran towards the plane. The steps were down when they reached it. John looked at Paul.

"Boy, we have all the luck," he said. Paul nodded. He knew exactly why, too. Paul went up the steps. When he reached the top and turned, he looked into the most unlikely face Paul expected to see.

"Hello Victor," Paul said. Paul also saw Alvin and Jerry.

"Hi's 'ah!" Victor said, hugging Paul. "You's 'ah are heres 'ah! Jerry! Yours 'ah brother is heres 'ah!"

"Paul!" Jerry said, turning around. "You're here! We waited here forever! Alvin is gonna fly this baby."

"How did you get here?" John said after he, Lino, Jimmy and Tyler got on.

"We followed after you when you left the maze," Alvin said. "Dang! The engine is out of fuel."

Paul was thinking about what Zyno had said. So his uncle *was* in the maze, there were holograms that they thought were their friends or family, and the hyena is going to protect him. He had to tell John or Jerry.

"John, can I talk to you for a second?" Paul said.

"Sure," he and Paul went to the back of the plane.

"John," Paul said. "Uncle Dan's in the maze."

"He is?!" John said eyes widening. "How do you know?"

I can't lie, Paul told himself. He took a deep breath.

"Because I heard Zyno talking to the hyena in the maze," Paul said.

"How did you know it was Zyno?" John asked. "Did anybody else see it?"

"No," Paul said choosing to answer only the second question. John noticed this.

"So how do you know that it was him?" John asked curiously.

"He was, uh, wearing a purple vest," Paul lied. John sensed the lie.

"Alright, you don't have to tell the truth, whatever the reason," John said. "But at least tell me what he said."

Paul told John what he heard Zyno tell the hyena. When he ended, John was pacing up and down the aisle.

"Ok, so, it can't be as if he just entered the maze," John said slowly. "Because Zyno said he 'knew Uncle Dan was in the maze the second he stepped into this place'. And if the hyena had just heard from him and we just saw the hyena, he could be very close to us."

"Yes, in the same world," Paul said. "There's something else, too. Uh, he said you had all the answers about him."

"I do? But I don't carry anything," John said. "Except …"

"That one book!" Paul said. "It already said something about Zyno saving our country. Maybe there's more …"

But John was already digging through his book bag. He pulled out *Wars of the Century*. He had stuck a bookmark in the place that contained information about Zyno and his father.

"We need to talk to someone," Paul said.

"Who?" John said, flipping through the pages of the book around the area of the bookmark.

"Alvin, I already told you," Paul said. "He'd go berserk if we'd tell him that we saw Zyno, so better not speak to him about that. On second thought—" Paul said when he saw John was barely listening, "—I'll speak to him, and you stay here and look for clues."

Paul walked back up the plane. John stopped him.

"Ok, what's going on? I know you know something I don't. What is it?" John said angrily. This took Paul by surprise. Then Paul got angry too.

"I don't have anything else to tell you," Paul said coolly. "You want more information? Go read that stupid book of yours!"

John moved in front of Paul, fuming.

"Look, *genius*," John said with sarcasm. "You are going to tell me every bit of detail you know. Have you seen him before? Did Lino tell you about him? Tell me!"

"I can have my own secrets you know," Paul said, temper rising.

"Your life is in danger if you don't tell me," John said, nearly yelling. "So is all of ours."

"Your life is not in danger," Paul snarled. "And my life is not in danger either. I know the facts. I know the details. And you don't!"

"Well, you might want to give them to me," John said. "Or I might force it out of you."

John wanted these facts really badly. Paul stepped up to him. He was pretty tall for his age, just a foot smaller then John.

"What do you want to know?" Paul asked angrily.

"Everything," John replied.

"That might be pretty difficult," Paul said, smirking, "considering I don't know everything."

"Very funny," John said. He shoved Paul a little. "Tell me everything you know."

"That would be difficult too," Paul said. "It might take hours to tell you everything I know. Plus, I don't think you could take it all in, since your brain is so small ..."

John threw a punch at him. Paul ducked and kicked him. John staggered. Paul jumped back up and pulled out his ax. John took a good look at the ax and smiled.

"You really want to hurt me?" he said grinning. "Fine."

John pulled out his sword.

"Come and get me."

Paul stood where he was. He couldn't believe John would actually want to fight him. Perhaps John thought that he would heal himself with Flaminetore. Paul didn't think so. But Paul knew that if they did fight, they wouldn't fight to the death. Or so he hoped.

Before Paul knew it, John had struck. Paul shot his blade at John's sword. John threw Paul's ax away by the blade. It cut his hand, but John didn't seem to notice. He took a swing at Paul's side. It had his hand and Paul felt the sword go in pretty far. Paul screamed, dropped his ax, and fell to the floor. Suddenly, John's sword flew out of his hands and fly against the side of the plane. John turned to see Alvin and Jerry coming towards them. Alvin was in the lead. He looked much different – he had his hand out which was glowing red, his hair and cloak were blowing back as if there were wind, his eyes were wide and completely blood red. Then, like John's sword, Paul's ax flew against the wall. Paul felt another sharp pain in his side where John's sword had struck him. Paul looked down and saw his skin healing, coming back together. Paul was amazed.

Alvin lowered his hand and his red eyes came back to normal, his hand changed to normal color, and his coat and hair stopped swooshing. He looked angry.

"What-were-you-two-doing?" he yelled as if each word was a sentence. "Trying-to-kill-each-other?"

"I—how did you do that?" Paul said.

"I have that power," Alvin said. "I was born with it. It takes a lot of my strength. I use it only in an emergency. But that is beside the point. What was going on?"

"I-I-I don't know," John said, breathing hard. "One minute I was right here and a second later I was in the Thog land and I was facing a really tough Thogeen. I pulled out my sword and the Thogeen ran towards me. I put up my sword to stop him from biting my head off. I pushed back his head from my sword, and he bit my hand. That's why my hand is bleeding. The next second, I was back here."

"Well, you were still here," Paul said to him, afraid.

"I was?" John said. "But, how?"

"You were fighting me!" Paul said.

"All I remember is being mad at you for leaving the talking to you and leaving me back here," John said. "I sat down when it happened."

They all turned back to the seat where John had been sitting. The book lay on the seat, still open. John ran over and grabbed it. Alvin went in front of John after he had retrieved the book. He pulled out one of his swords and stabbed the seat.

"Just in case," he said. They all headed up to the front. Paul pulled Alvin back and pushed him into a seat.

"We have got to talk now," Paul said. Alvin looked at Paul boredly. He yawned.

"What do you want to know?" Alvin asked.

"Do you know my Uncle Dan?" Paul said. The sound of Uncle Dan's name made him straighten up.

"Yes," he said.

"Do you know him as a rival scientist, an enemy, a friend or even a lab partner?" Paul said.

For a split second, Paul thought he saw a look of amusement on Alvin's face.

"Well, all scientists are rivals to each other, aren't they?" Alvin said. "Even if they are good friends!"

"Answer my question," Paul said. "My patience is leaving me."

"You know who you remind me of?" Alvin said.

"Who?!" Paul said, eyes closed in frustration.

"Zyno," Alvin said.

Paul opened his eyes.

"You know him?" he asked.

"Yes, didn't I tell you?" Alvin said. "He was really jealous of me and my inventions. But before all that, we knew each other as friends. Same goes for Benjamin. But they both hate me now. So to answer your question, I did know your uncle as a good friend. But now I don't even know what to consider him."

"What is your name?" Paul said.

"Alvin," Alvin replied.

"That's not your true name," Paul said, smiling. "You can't pull that one on me. The hyena said that was a fake name."

Alvin sat there blankly.

"You really think if I didn't tell you my true identity before, I would tell you now?" Alvin asked, smiling.

Paul put his hand to his belt. His ax had fallen a few seats behind them.

"I don't trust you," Paul said. "What if right now you pulled out your sword and killed me? I am completely unarmed."

Alvin folded his arms.

"Look, I would tell you my name if you tell me all of your secrets," Alvin said.

Paul thought about it. Making a deal with Zyno would be a secret he wouldn't tell anyone. Maybe Alvin's name was something like that.

"We will both know both of our secrets in time," Alvin said. "I heard John yelling at you for not telling him some information. Well, I will know what it is after we leave the maze. You will know my name after we leave the maze."

Paul got closer to him.

"I need to know now," Paul said, firmly. He was really close to him now. "Will it make a difference to you if I know now or later?"

"Yes, it actually makes a very big difference," Alvin replied. Paul saw the hilt of Alvin's sword. Paul reached down and pulled it out. At the same time, Alvin stood up, and pulled out his other sword. The colors of his eyes started to darken. Paul knew what would happen next. Paul held firmly on to his sword. He felt an invisible force tugging on the sword. Paul took a swing at Alvin, but the blade started to bend in a different direction. The sword flew out of Paul's hand. Alvin went back to normal. Exhausted, he fell to his knees, breathing hard.

"Well, can you explain that?" Paul said angrily. Alvin looked up at him, unsure. He then made up his mind.

"Alright," Alvin said. "I will tell you something but I must ask you to keep it secret from everyone else."

Paul glanced up to the front of the plane. Everyone seemed to be preoccupied with something.

"Alright," Paul said, lowering his voice.

"I am a magician," Alvin replied, clutching his chest. Paul just stood there.

"I am not surprised," Paul said. "After what you did to the sword and my ax. Even though there is no logical evidence that magicians actually exist."

"Some vocabulary you have there," Alvin said, impressed. "How do you know all these words? Early school?"

"Actually," Paul said, "I am a genius. My mother gave the test to me and it proved it."

"Indeed," Alvin said, nodding. "But that is not the only thing you are. You see, you also have a great power."

"You mean like what I had at the Thog land?" Paul asked.

"No," Alvin replied. "This is actually your physical power. More like what you are."

Paul looked surprised. He *was* something.

"You mean besides a mammal?" Paul said, "And a vertebrate?"

"Actually," Alvin said humorously. "You are neither of those things."

Paul was shocked. *That was a joke*, he thought.

"No, it wasn't," said Alvin smiling. Paul took a step back. *Did he just read my mind?*

"Yes, I did," Alvin replied lazily.

"You mean," Paul said, breathing slowly. "That you can read minds? And thoughts? And memories?"

"Yes, yes, and no," Alvin said, sitting down. "I cannot read memories."

"So-so what were you saying about me? What I was?" Paul asked, attention completely on him.

"Yes," Alvin said. "You are—"

The plane gave a jerk. It started to move.

"What the—"

It gained speed. Alvin glanced at Paul.

"I thought it was out of fuel," Paul said.

"It was," Alvin said slowly. They both ran up to the front. John was in the pilot seat and Tyler was in the co-pilot.

"How did you get this thing to start without gas?" Alvin asked them.

"I'm not sure, but apparently we do have fuel because it says so here," Tyler said. *It was the hyena*, Paul thought. He looked at Alvin, who looked back at him. Paul remembered that he could read minds, so he quickly cleared it and sat down.

Tyler pointed to one of the gauges on the dashboard that a red line was pointing to the right side. Alvin looked impressed.

"How did you know that that showed the fuel?" Alvin said. There were at least 30 gauges.

"My father is a pilot," Tyler answered. "He taught me all about flying. I am still learning, though." He added when Alvin looked surprised.

"And what are you," Alvin asked. He glanced at John and then back at Tyler, "Twelve? Thirteen?"

"Fifteen," Tyler said. "Anyway, we are about to take off."

"All right, John take a seat back there, I'm flying," Alvin said. John got up sadly and went back to a seat. He passed Jerry and Jimmy, talking about their favorite video games.

"Mine is defiantly *Kyle: The Main Sector*, I am so far on it," Jimmy said. "I also really like *Jukiliia*, too, but it's really hard to defeat Tex and Euon 2000. Anyway what's your favorite arena?"

"I've never played it," Jerry replied, sadly. "But what about *Hurrak Galaxies*? I managed to defeat a few levels but I am stuck on this one level, I can't defeat ..."

John tried not to laugh at this discussion. *Who really cares about this stuff?*

John also saw Lino and Paul playing checkers. Paul had just opened his laptop and a hologram of a checkers board was on the seat. He also saw Victor eating Angel's gift and was reading a book called *Venemay: The Planet of Snakes, Dragons and Other Creatures*.

"What is Venemay?" John asked. Victor looked up. He smiled.

"Why, sirs 'ah," Victor said. "That was 'ah the planet 'ah that wes 'ah live on 'ah"

"Oh," John said. "Good book?"

"Oh yes sirs 'ah," Victor said nodding very fast. "It talks 'ah about Thogs, Thogeens, snakes, dragons, watersnogges, dinosaurs, wiggle-trans, floppingyens, green horenslings and more 'ah!"

"Sounds interesting," John said. John tried to understand if Victor's speech was that bad or if these were creatures he just hadn't heard of.

"Oh yes 'ah," Victor said. "It even talks about our captain, Maurice 'ah!"

"Co—hold on," John shook his head. "But he wasn't captain when this was written, was it?"

The plane had left the ground. The desert was speeding away from them very fast.

"Sirs 'ah," Victor answered as though someone had asked him what one plus one was, "Wes 'ah have technology that programs 'ah us to be able to change the statistics 'ah."

"That's really cool," John said. He explained to Victor that their books remain the same. When he finished, Victor had huge eyes.

"Yous 'ah mean that theys 'ah don't have chips 'ah inside the paper 'ah?"

"No, we don't actually," John finished. "But what I don't understand is why don't you have better weapons than swords and axes?"

"Sirs 'ah," Victor said, visibly offended. "Its 'ah take a lot of technologies 'ah to build those weapons 'ah!"

"Oh," John said. He reached into his book bag and pulled out Thog food and *The Wars of the Century*. He flipped through the index looking for something.

"Yous 'ah mean a book that thick 'ah doesn't have chips 'ah in it?" Victor asked as he examined the book.

"Nope," John answered scanning the names. "It just has so much information about stuff, the pages take up a lot of space."

As Victor exclaimed something, John was running his finger down the long list of names. *Yes*, he thought, *this was a thick book*. It had over 5,000 pages. It had a section for almost every man fought in any Locombonian war.

"Warring, Steve, Wayne, Grant," John was saying the names. "Wayne, Zyno! Page 345."

John flipped to the page. He read:

ZYNO WAYNE

Zyno Wayne, Trust Side of Freedom (TSF), was a three-star entry level general who joined the war after his father Grant (Page 343) died. He helped the TSF by developing a triple atom bomb and providing the entire army with armor made of redlined adamant (the strongest substance in the world but lighter than a feather). Zyno was a prestigious medic. He was thrown out of the war because he became interested in science, and in rule # 361 (page 713), it says that anyone with a job in chemistry, physics, or geography must not participate in any type of war (they were meant to go under different types of war efforts that held no chance of being killed) . Zyno then forfeited, but he illegally helped save the freedom of the country. He made a potion that no other scientist has been known to make. It somehow changes the personality of a human being. Researchers have no further information on the potion.

And that was it. That was all the information on Zyno. John didn't know how that would help them at all. So Zyno had been good at one point. Big deal. John had read enough comic books to know that each bad guy had been good initially. John then looked at Victor, who was still eating. He was getting really bored. He put his book down and went up toward the front. Paul was still playing checkers with Lino, but Jimmy was looking out the window and Jerry was asleep. He went up to the front where Tyler was flying the plane while Alvin was supervising. He turned back and found Paul done with the match.

"Who won?" John asked lazily.

"Lino," Paul said coolly.

"Three times," Lino grinned.

"Yeah, well, I'm better at chess any way," Paul said.

"Hey Paul," John said, having an idea. "Why don't we practice fighting?"

"What?" Paul blinked. "How are we going to keep it from being dangerous?"

"Well, I don't know about it being safe," John said. "But it's not like we've been away from danger this entire trip, have we?"

"Yeah," Paul said slowly, "but what are we going to do about there being no room?"

"Well," John said. "Couldn't we use Flaminetore or something? I mean, you store money in it all the time, couldn't we just store some chairs or something?"

"I don't think there's enough space for that on my computer," Paul replied.

Something came out of Paul's back bag. It was Flaminetore.

"Sure there is," he reassured. "Come on, I'll lead you through it."

So after about 20 minutes of instructions, Paul managed to get a good open space. Paul turned to John.

"We could hurt each other though," Paul said nervously.

"We won't go fast," John said. "We'll just go fast enough to work on the technique."

Paul nodded, snatching his ax from his belt. John pulled out his sword. John quickly went for a low swipe that Paul barely blocked. John swung around and went for Paul's other side. Paul, not being able to block it, fell to the ground, avoiding it. (From a few feet away, Jimmy, Lino, Victor and Jerry turned to watch the commotion.) Paul got up, but John put his foot on the dull side of Paul's blade, preventing him from pulling it up.

"John, I thought you said—" Paul began straightening up. John threw his sword at Paul.

What Paul did, he couldn't explain. He turned his body away from the sword, but Paul felt his entire body stretch and very suddenly his right side felt weird. He looked down at it and gasped. It was stretching to the left, making it thinner than the rest of his body and he was able to dodge the sword. John very suddenly fell to the ground. He had his hands in his face.

"It happened again," John said. "I was in the Thog world again, facing a Thogeen."

"I could tell," Paul said. "I cannot see your eyes when it happens."

"I don't know why, though," John said. "I have to remember I am still here."

Paul glanced at the others. They were all shocked. Paul understood why too. He had bent his body so far to the left, it looked like he was a cartoon. He didn't know what to say. He just started walking toward the front of the plane. When they saw that he was coming toward them, they backed away. He kept walking, ignoring them. When he got close to them, they backed into the edge of the plane as if he had some kind of contagious disease. He went right up to the pilot seat where Alvin was working very hard to keep the plane in the right direction because of the wind. Paul took a deep breath.

"Alvin, do you have a moment?" Paul said. Alvin looked up quickly. He looked very calm, but was sweaty.

"Not really, Paul," Alvin answered. "It's really hard to control right now and I don't think Tyler can manage."

"Well, then just stay here and supervise," Paul said impatiently. "And then, well, just listen."

Alvin raised an eyebrow.

"You didn't want to see me in private?" he said.

"Well," Paul said. He thought a moment. *Yes, I did want to see him in private.* Then he thought of something.

"Well you could just," Paul began. He finished by thinking: *Read my mind.* Alvin nodded.

"Go ahead then," Alvin said. Paul (by thinking) told him the story. When he finished, Alvin thought a moment.

"Ah, yes," Alvin said. "This cannot wait. Tyler, do you think you could take over for a few minutes?"

Tyler looked reluctant, but nodded saying, "I'll call if I need help."

Paul and Alvin found a seat away from everyone else.

"Paul, let's just get this over with," Alvin said. He took a deep breath and whispered. "You are not a human. You are a genie."

12) Weather

Paul stared at him. He must not have heard him correctly. He must be joking. *And yet,* Paul thought, *how could I have avoided that sword John threw at me?*

"You can't tell anyone this," Alvin said. "And I am going to tell you something else that you must promise not to tell anyone."

Paul nodded. His brain was so full he thought it must explode.

"Your brother, John," Alvin said, "is a magician like me. Your other brother, Jerry, is psychic which is like half magician, half human. After we get out of this maze, I will teach you all how to use your power in an amazingly good way."

Paul glanced at John, who was trying to explain to the others about what had happened. *John was a magician as well. What powers did he have? Would he be as powerful as Alvin?*

"How do you know all this?" Paul asked.

"I have paid a visit to a fortune teller," Alvin said. "I know you would think a fortune teller as someone who 'tells you your fortune.' That's not true. Actually, what they do is tell someone their past, future or about someone else."

"But why me?" Paul asked. "Why am I a genie? Was my dad a magician or something?"

"Yes," Alvin said. "He was a great magician. Unfortunately, he is lost and we cannot find him, as you may well know. There are not many magicians left. The genies are almost extinct. People that are psychic, however, are not uncommon at all. This is because people can be born psychic or can learn it."

"What about my mother?" Paul asked. "Was she magical too?"

Alvin thought a moment. Then he shook his head.

"No," he said. "Your mom was not familiar with anything about magicians and other magical people. She never knew about your father being a magician. She only knew about those stupid acts on TV. You know, the ones with the bunnies? That's all fake."

"Did you know my dad?" Paul asked him.

"Very well," Alvin said. "He was a member of a magician council called *The Ring* council. It was for the preservation of the magical races and to protect the weak. Your father was sent on a mission to stop a rebellious magician, but never returned."

"Who was the rebel?" Paul asked.

"Alvin! Quick, get up here!" called a voice from the front of the plane. Alvin quickly got up and strode up to the front of the plane. Paul got up and joined him. He grabbed his laptop on the way.

"What is it?" Paul asked as he got up to the plane.

"Hurricane," Alvin replied frightenly. "We don't know how fast."

"How is there a hurricane in a desert with no ocean?" Paul asked skeptically.

"This is Zyno's lands, he can do whatever he wants," Alvin said.

Paul opened his laptop.

"What's the speed of the hurricane out there?" he asked Flaminetore as he came out. Flaminetore glanced out the window. He frowned.

"It's 172 MPH," He replied. "Good luck getting out of this."

At that, he left. Paul looked at the bottom of the screen. The batteries had died. He growled in a Lino-like way and closed the computer. He felt the plane turn.

"Paul, get everyone one to sit and buckle," Alvin commanded. "And yes, that means you too, Tyler."

Tyler left the co-pilot seat, sat down on a different seat, and strapped himself in. Paul ran down the plane looking for the others, slipping because the plane kept on flipping. He found Jerry asleep on the empty floor. Paul managed to drag him into a seat and buckle him in. *How can you sleep through this,* Paul thought. He ran down the aisle and found John and Victor already strapped in. Lino couldn't put on his seat belt, and Paul doubted that it mattered. That left Jimmy. Jimmy came out of the bathroom angrily.

"Can't even go to the bathroom without getting flipped over, can I? Geez … "

Paul saw a wing that looked like it belonged to a macaw behind the bathroom. He ran over to it, pulling out his ax as he went. He turned the corner. Here stood, unsurprisingly, the hyena. It had his face to the wall and was working with some circuits. Paul quickly jumped on it, wrapped his arms around its neck, and held his ax up to its throat.

"Alright," Paul said. "Slowly set down those wires now!"

The hyena whimpered and dropped them.

"Alright, ugly," Paul said. "I want some answers from you now! Where is my uncle?"

The hyena whimpered again. Paul held on tighter.

"I'm waiting."

The hyena spoke softly.

"He's outside your control," it breathed.

"And that means what?" Paul asked, moving his ax closer to the hyena's throat. Still, the hyena didn't speak. The plane flipped and Paul let go of him and fell toward the ceiling. When it rightened it self, Paul jumped back on the hyena.

"Alright, fine," Paul said. "Then tell Zyno to stop the hurricane."

Finally the hyena spoke, but in a frightened, high pitch voice.

"I can't tell him," he said. "He can't hear me."

"Oh, sure, like he doesn't now that I am threatening you right now," Paul said sarcastically. "Let's get talken' or else. Tell Zyno now."

The hyena didn't do anything. Paul swung his ax down on one of the hyena's wings. It cut some of the flesh off and the hyena screamed.

"A little test," Paul said. "Want to go for the real pain?"

Paul couldn't think of what could be more painful at the moment, but the hyena looked terrified when he had finished speaking. It began to cry. Then the hyena yelled: "Master! Master! Please help me!"

First, nothing happened. Then the plane stopped shaking. The hurricane must have stopped. Paul noticed this change, for he loosened his grip. The hyena turned his head and bit Paul. Hard. Paul yelled and pulled back his hand. The hyena wrenched free from his clutches and turned the corner. As he turned, three arrows hit him in the wing. The hyena fell on his stomach in agony.

"Got ya'," Paul said, jumping on him again. "Let's tie him up."

He looked up and saw Victor with a bow in his hand, running towards him. He had a rope around his shoulder. Victor went over and tied the hyena up.

"You'll be sitting there for a while," Paul said, getting off. "Then sooner or later we will kill you."

The hyena whimpered frightenly. Paul started walking up to the front.

"Thanks," he said to Victor. Victor nodded.

"Is 'ah heard the hyena cries 'ah," Victor explained. "Is 'ah came over there to investigate 'ah."

They both sat down in a seat. Paul remembered something as he looked at Victor. *"They will be surprised that there will be holograms amongst them. It's the last people they would expect!"* Paul hadn't given that a thought. Maybe he should tell someone. Just then, Alvin, Tyler and John walked by. Paul did a double-take.

"Hey Alvin," Paul called. Alvin turned. "Who's flying the plane?"

"It's on auto-pilot," Alvin said. "I had it set to travel some hundred miles. I wanted a break."

"You're not the only one with an advanced laptop," John said winking as Paul open his mouth. Paul nodded.

"Hey guys," Paul said. "I need to tell you something."

He told them about what Zyno had said about the holograms. Tyler and Alvin were surprised.

"So it could be any of us," Tyler said. "Right now."

Victor was listening too. He nodded in agreement.

"Its 'ah very well planned out 'ah," He said. "All hes 'ah would hafta dos 'ah is kidnap one of us 'ah and replace it with a hologram 'ah! So it 'ah could be anyones 'ah!"

"John, I need to read that book of yours," Paul said.

"I've read it through, Paul, there's nothing in it," John said. Paul kept on asking until he agreed.

"Don't say I didn't warn you," John said as Paul flicked threw the pages. "Hey, look who it is! It's old scum face. I should pay him a visit."

Paul glanced to the back. The hyena was still struggling with the cords to free himself. Paul glanced back to the book. He looked in the index. He looked up Zyno's name and turned to the page. Paul read through. Then, after reading it twice more, he gasped, got up and strode to the back quickly. John was punching the hyena, Alvin and Tyler watching. Paul ran up to John and smacked him in the back.

"You-you didn't ... you should of ... 'Nothing in it'?!" Paul said, trying to find the right words. "There was something important in there!"

"What? There was noth—" John began, turning to him.

"Nothing? Read the last sentence aloud," Paul said.

John glanced at the hyena on the ground before clearing his throat.

"Researchers haven't had any further information on the potion," John read. "So what?"

"So? If we drank anything of his, he could control us," Paul said. "This is an unknown substance. He could have invented something more powerful now. If he could make something at the age of, oh let's say, 20 that could control people, imagine what he could do 20 years later!"

"Good point," John said.

The plane gave a sudden lurch and everyone was thrown to the floor. Then the plane turned upside-down into a complete nose-dive. Alvin got to his feet and ran up to the front. Everyone started sliding down the plane. Paul glanced angrily to where the hyena had once lain. It was gone!

"That hyena got away," he said to John and Tyler as they ran up to the front. "Ran off."

"Yeah, I figured he might," Tyler shrugged, frustrated.

The plane pulled up from its nose dive. They began to walk casually up to the front when Alvin screamed in frustration.

"What is it?" Paul asked loudly.

"It's a tornado," Alvin replied. "Out of the blizzard and into the freezer, huh?"

"Wait ... doesn't it go—"

"Yeah, but he can make up his own," Paul interrupted. He wasn't as scared as he was when the hurricane hit, but was still a bit worried.

"Oh my goodnesses 'ah," Victor said a few seats away. "Look at it's 'ah!"

Paul, Tyler and John ran over to the window. They could hear it now. It was making a low, sucking noise. When they all looked out, Tyler said something, but John didn't catch it. He was gasping at what he was seeing. It was a 7.6, the third biggest windstorm ever. Over a mile and a half wide, the tornado could usually wipe out an entire island and more. It was all black and was ripping cactuses off and throwing them about 300 yards. John knew there was only one thing to do. He ran up to the front.

"Alvin," he said reaching the pilot seat, "Land the plane now!"

"I can't," Alvin said. "The landing gear is out."

John slapped his hand over his forehead. He was very tired and hot.

"Do we have any parachutes?" John asked.

"Yes, but it might be dangerous to jump out," Alvin replied.

"Let's drive as far away from the tornado as possible then jump," John said hurriedly.

"That really can't be done," Alvin sighed. "A 7.6 can go to a range of 600 and 1000 miles per—"

"I don't care, just try," John said. He could hear that the tornado was getting much closer. "We just need to find a hole or something."

Alvin gritted his teeth but nodded.

"The parachutes are in the back," he said, "Near where the hyena was."

John ran to the back, beckoning everyone with him. He went to the back and saw a compartment filled with backpacks. There were only a few. Then it hit him what a large party was with him: Victor, Lino, Alvin, Paul, Jerry, Tyler, and Jimmy. When they had entered the maze, they only had three, but then everyone else came. *But it was worth it*, he thought. *Lino helped us with finding the first metal door; Jimmy and Tyler saved us from the freezer; Alvin helped us in the Thog war; and Victor saved Paul from the hyena just now.*

He counted the backpacks: six. They needed eight.

"I can't wear a parachute," Lino said, reading his mind (not like Alvin did, just very carefully guessing what he was thinking).

"Good, I can carry you then," Jerry said.

"And that means I will carry Paul," John said, handing them out to everyone. Then he looked at his own parachute. "But this means we leave all our possessions behind."

Only Paul argued. John agreed for him to take his laptop and they unanimously agreed that weapons were a necessity.

Alvin was ready. He opened the latch to the airplane and jumped. Jimmy was about to go next when he glanced back to where he was sitting.

"Well there goes my chance of ever beating *Pussiche: The Great Return*," he said.

"You play that?" Jerry said, almost laughing.

"No," Jimmy said, going a little red and then jumped out.

"Bet he does," Jerry said, laughing. "I'll go check his backpack-"

Lino shot him an angry look and said, "You can find humor in any situation. I actually *want* to live, ok?"

Jerry sighed and picked Lino up. He staggered.

"Geez, how much to you weigh?" he asked.

"10,000 pounds," Lino said. Jerry yelped. "I'm kidding."

John pushed them both out. Next, Victor went, then Tyler. John looked at Paul who was clutching his laptop.

"Ready?" He asked. Paul nodded. John picked him up. He jumped. He felt like he was in one of Zyno's transporters. He looked down and saw the others running for what looked like a big cave. He heard a crunching behind him. They looked back and saw the plane getting destroyed by the tornado. The tornado was now 30 feet away. John was far from the ground. He turned himself around to face the tornado. Paul pulled the string on the backpack and a parachute spat out. The tornado was sucking them in like some huge vacuum cleaner. John felt himself separate from the parachute. Paul hung onto the arm of the bag, but John was falling and getting sucked in at the same time. John completely left the parachute, pushing his brother away from danger. John was now in total freefall. He felt his hand being raised. *I am going to stop the tornado.*

Why did I just think that? John thought. But another thought came up– *Because you can. You are. You are about to stop a natural disaster.*

He gained confidence, but he just thought it was insanity. His hand was very tense. It was about 10 feet away. *Stop it,* he thought. *Stop the tornado now.* His veins were showing in his left, raised arm. He thought really hard about stopping it. He saw himself escaping from the clutches of the tornado. His hand suddenly started to turn a different color …

It hit him really hard. He concentrated hard on wanting to get to the ground. The tornado spun him fast. Metal parts of the plane started to come towards him, but they suddenly missed him. He opened his eyes. This was difficult because he could feel the tornado put real pressure on them. He looked at his hand. It had become red like Alvin's. But that was impossible. Alvin was a magician, he saw him do that magic thing. But John couldn't do it. Unless …

John shook his head. He couldn't think properly inside of a tornado. He saw a white barrier around him forming a sphere. He was spinning, but it wasn't that terrible. It felt like a hard rollercoaster ride. He started to fall, but the barrier remained around him. *If only I had a camera,* John thought. It was actually a beautiful sight, in a dangerous sort of way. He saw big pieces of metal flying around inside of the tornado, and he could only see partly outside. Pieces of junk were bouncing off John's barrier and it protected him from anything that got near to him.

Then John thought with another problem. How was he going to survive the fall without a parachute? Would his barrier save him from that too? Quite suddenly, the tornado spewed him out. The barrier disappeared and he was falling faster now. He held out his hand. *Parachute,* he thought. He was 20 yards from the ground. *Barrier,* John thought. Nothing happened. He was now 10 yards. *Anything,* John thought, desperately thinking hard. Something appeared in his hand. He looked at it. It was a battery.

WHAM! John felt many bones crack, one John swore was his spine. The tornado barely missed him. *Great,* John thought.

Zyno is going to let me die right here instead of finishing me off with the tornado. What a cruel man.

"John? John? John! Are you ok?"

John tried to lift himself up to see who it was. But he couldn't. Even when he tried, it hurt. He saw Paul and Victor looking at him.

"He looks bad," Paul said. "Can you hear me?"

Of course I can hear you, idiot, John tried to say, but nothing came. Victor, with great strength lifted John up on his back. This hurt John even more.

"Wes 'ah got to help the misters 'ah. The tornadoes 'ah is coming back," Victor said, beginning to walk. He was only about three feet tall, so John's legs dragged on the ground. *This hurts*, John thought. He didn't even bother trying to say it. They pulled him into a dark cave. John couldn't see where anyone was, but Jerry said, "John? Are you ok?"

"Course he isn't Jerry; we all saw him fall from the tornado. What was that, 500 feet?" Lino said.

"Lino," Paul said. "He's not talking or moving or even blinking. Do you think … "

"No," Lino said. "He-he couldn't be …dead?"

Everyone gasped. *I'm blinking!* John tried to say. But that moment he felt water go down his face. It must have been tears. He wasn't blinking so the water fell from his eyes. *Well, I'm breathing, guys, can't you tell?* John thought. But even breathing – one of the easiest things – was painful on John. They were such shallow breaths, they could pass for nothing.

"Maybe he isn't," Jimmy said. "Start up that one hologram."

"Oh yeah," Paul said. He turned it on but it was still black. "Man, I forgot that it's out of batteries."

"What does he take?" asked Jimmy.

"Double—A's," Paul replied.

"Well," Jimmy said apologetically, "I kinda …well I really liked … uh … well … "

"Spit it out!" Paul said.

"Well, I liked this *N-Box* game, so I uh … brought it in my pocket before we jumped off."

"You did?" Paul asked.

"Yeah, and it's double—A," Jimmy said taking out a game player. He took out two batteries and handed it over to him. Paul looked at them and shook his head.

"Jimmy," Paul said patiently, "This is the best computer in the world. Do you think it runs on two double—A's?"

"Yes?" Jimmy asked hopefully.

"No," Paul said. "It runs on three."

Even in this kind of situation, Lino tried not to laugh at this comment.

I have one! John tried once again. Nothing came out. *Look at my hand! Please!*

"It's no use," Paul continued. Just then Alvin walked over to where John was. Concern was on his face, even though he could barely see him. More concern then a friend would usually have.

"And I didn't get a chance to tell him," Alvin said in a whisper that only John heard. John was so depressed that he might not have done what he was about to do. He tried with all the remaining strength left inside him to say it.

Look in my left hand.

Nothing came out. Alvin leapt back.

"He's alive! I saw him think!" he exclaimed. Everyone else ran over, "something about his hand."

John thought hard. *Look in my left hand.*

"'Look in my left hand,'" Alvin quoted. Alvin reached down and opened John's palm. Everyone saw a battery.

"It's a double—A!" Paul exclaimed. He grabbed it and put all the batteries into his computer battery slot. The computer started up. Flaminetore came out. He looked at John.

"Another healing job for me, I suppose?" Flaminetore said. He looked at John carefully. Then he shook his head. "Not much I can do for him, master. He looks paralyzed. It's very hard for me to heal something like that."

"I can't just leave him like that," Paul said. "He won't be able to survive like that. I have to program it."

"But that'll take weeks!" Jerry cried. "The batteries will die!"

"Not if I program an outlet into this cave," Paul said. "And that I can do in a few hours. With the help of Flaminetore, of course. Flaminetore, give us some candles."

Immediately, seven holographic candles appeared in the cave, lighting the entire cave.

"And give my friends and family some entertainment while I work on the outlet," Paul requested. Two checker boards, five lemons, and some video games showed up in the cave. Paul immediately got to work. He knew time was everything. He grabbed a lemon.

"Cup."

A holographic cup came out of the computer.

"Will this work?" Paul asked, referring to the cup. "Won't the lemon juice spill out?"

"No," Flaminetore said. "And don't you have work to do?"

Paul squeezed the lemon so that the juice spilled into the cup.

"Sugar."

Paul asked for wires, circuits, batteries, more lemons and more electronic devices. While he was working, he noticed nobody was doing anything.

"Paul, if we don't help it could be ages until you finish," Lino said.

"Let useses 'ah help 'ah," Victor said.

"I know a lot about computers," Alvin said.

"We can help!" Jerry said. Paul agreed. After all, they were right. Paul suddenly felt his stomach lurch. He was being transported, he could feel it. He landed on the ground. He looked up. The place was tropical. It was really hot. There were palm trees everywhere, big ponds and also big trees with huge trunks. It all seemed so familiar …

Paul got up and smelled … moist. The landscape was very plain. No buildings, no houses, no nothing.

"Well that was weird," Paul said. After a second, he realized he was talking to himself. "Jerry? Lino? Alvin? *Any*body?"

Then he felt something—the sensation of being watched. He turned around. There was no one was there. Paul got worried. He could still feel it. He started to walk. Then he started to hear something: A cold intake and exhaling of breath. He could hear, but it was no human breathing. Something bigger. Much bigger. He started to run. Something big fell in front of him. He saw that it was water. A big pile of it. He bent down to examine it. After looking at it closely, he could tell it was saliva. Not human saliva, though. He looked up. As he did he could see a monstrous, strong, fierce creature that had been extinct for over 500 million years. The giant Tyrannosaurus Rex lifted its foot and was about to stomp Paul.

13) Healings

Paul tried to turn to run but the T-Rex already stomped his foot. Strangely, Paul felt no pain. *Probably because I'm dead,* Paul thought. But he felt the feeling before. It was a sudden loss of stomach. *I'm going back,* Paul thought jubilantly. He went back to the cave. Nobody seemed to notice his disappearance.

"Guys," Paul said, turning to them. "I'm back!"

"What?" Jerry said. "You were right here."

"No!" Paul said. "I'm back! Didn't you see me leave?"

"No," Lino said. "Where did you go?"

Paul explained it to them.

That's exactly what happened to me on the plane, John thought. Alvin nodded.

"John says that was exactly what happened to him on the plane," He replied.

John thought it was really cool how Alvin could translate to them. He could finally communicate to them.

"He felt like he was being transported like going through a metal door," Alvin said, still staring at John's head.

"That's how it felt for me, too," Paul said.

"Then that must be the answer," Lino said. "The goal you have to accomplish during this land is to try to fight off these transporting things."

"Most likely," Jimmy said. "How did you get back?"

"Well, the T-Rex stomped me and I got transported back," Paul said. Then he snapped his fingers. "I got it! When get pain or do pain, you get transported back. John was about to attack a Thogeen, twice, and he came back a second after he did damage. I was about to get hurt from the *T-Rex,* but I got away before I got hurt."

"John says 'good thinking'," Alvin said, glancing at John again.

"Well, let's keep working on this outlet," Paul said. "Flaminetore, give them the run down on how to help."

Paul started digging out the wall of the cave.

After three hours, they had dug to the outside. Paul yawned and looked at his computer's time. It was very late. But he didn't stop. He fed the wires through the hole.

"Well, a quarter of the job is done," Paul said to his tired crew. "We still need the energy source. What should it be, solar powered? That's probably our best bet since we're in the middle of a desert."

Nobody cared.

"Paul, what can we do?" Jerry said. "We don't have anything left to put together. We didn't bring anything else with us when we left the plane."

Paul thought a moment. *Come on*, Paul thought. It was just too late. He must get some sleep. But John could be dead by tomorrow. Then it hit Paul.

"Well, using the ultra powerful satellite waves, I could shoot out a signal to completely connect with the satellite E-RT-74 in space, reversing the satellite waves 70 degrees southwest, so that the rays might hit the computer at our house (of course I would only hope it was on), hook into it, sending waves through the electrical system, sending a message at the control center, make a loop in the system, shooting out extra electricity, firing it at light speed, going through John's computer, flying back up to the satellite and back down to us sending off lots of electricity. Of course, tons of things could go wrong, especially the looping part, so I would ... "

Jerry interrupted.

"You know, Paul?" he said. "You might be the smartest person in the universe, but of course we are not. If you could rephrase that in a way that we could understand, please do, or else we will fall asleep from you explaining physics or technology and other junk like that."

Paul nodded.

"Anytime, Jerry," he said. "I-ii-ii-ii-sss-ssss thiii-iiii-ssss sloo-ooo-ooo-ooww-ww enooooughhh fooooor yooooooou?"

"Fine, do what ever you want Paul, we will help, but don't even bother explaining it to us," Jerry said. "What do you want us to do?"

"Well, I need the rays to hit the satellite in space, so I would need to create something to reach the satellite," Paul said. "This means I'll need to use my computer's batteries for a while, but soon I won't need them. Then I would need some metal, aluminum if possible."

"How about your ax's blade?" Lino said. "We could cut a few pieces off and use that … "

"Yeah, but I need a lot, and I like my ax," Paul said. "Unless I could save it on the hard drive of my computer, I could do that …

"Then I would have to have some support to hold it up, then make an outlet on it and fire up a laser to hook with E-RT-74. But that's the hard part. I would need a laser beam from a gun, or something really fast, maybe very close to the speed of light. Like … "

"Lightning," Alvin said. "From your ax. Remember? The power from it. Of course, you would need to use your power while the machine is working, so we could hook you up to it. We also need to use your ax to get the panels."

"And wes 'ah could use 'ah Zyno's own land against hims 'ah!" Victor said. "We could somehows 'ah transport you to a different lands 'ah and you could use yours 'ah power against a fierce creatures 'ah!"

"Yeah, while your mind stays here and uses the power to get to the satellite," Tyler said. "Come on, let's get to work."

Paul couldn't believe it was going to be that easy. It wasn't either. Paul uploaded an exact replica of his ax into his computer. This took tons of time. Then, Jerry had to carve square pieces of metal out of Paul's ax, which took more time. Paul became really impatient. They made a long metal board that Paul hooked up wires around the three batteries and 17 more that Flaminetore provided. Next, Paul, with the help of Alvin, hooked some wires up to his head and wrist. Then they hooked some more wires to Paul's ax's blade. Now all they had to do was wait. They waited two hours plus the five hours spent on building the satellite. It was now 5:45 in the morning and all of them except Lino and Paul couldn't help but sleep.

"Us tigers can stay up for a long a mount of time, maybe about three days tops," Lino explained in a voice close to gloating.

"So … tired … can't … stay … awake," Paul muttered, nodding almost to sleep. He felt his stomach lurch. *Finally.* He got transported to a big lab. Zyno was sitting there waiting for him.

"Ah, Paul, I see you have built a station to try and hack into the Satellite E-RT-74," He said approvingly. "Very difficult. Yet you did manage to have only one problem."

"What's that?" Paul asked, reaching down to his belt, which hung his ax.

"You hooked up the wires to your brain and your body," Zyno replied. "You see, when the extra electricity flies through your brother's computer, it'll fly back to the satellite and that will overload having no choice but to send it back to you."

"Which is what I'm trying to do," Paul said.

"But you don't catch it – it will be so much electricity that if you are hooked up to it, you will be electrocuted," Zyno said. "So I decided to help you. Take some of this potion and give it to your brother. He will instantly be healed."

"Yeah, right," Paul said, almost laughing. "How do I know that's not one of your potions that take control of a person's mind?"

"You'll have to trust me," Zyno said calmly. "I really need you and I am impatient. I'm not willing to take this risk for your brother's heath. Give him this."

"No," Paul said, taking out his ax. "There is only one way. I'm sorry, but *I'll* have to take the risk."

He ran up to Zyno. He cut him on his side. Distantly, he could hear Lino's voice.

"No good, Paul," he said. "Needs more batteries."

"I got some from my walkie-talkies," he also distantly heard Jimmy's voice. Jimmy had obviously woke up.

Paul transported back to the cave. He still had the potion that Zyno had thrust into his hand.

"I hooked up the other batteries to the station," Jimmy explained. "After I woke up, that is."

Everyone else was awake as well.

"What do you have there?" Alvin said, referring to the potion.

"Its-um … well … you see-"

"Zyno's potion?" Alvin asked suspiciously.

"Yes," Paul said, surrendering.

"Destroy it immediately," Alvin said.

"Hold on," Paul said. He took out the wires carefully from his head and wrist. "Look, wait until the power on my computer comes on. Then we can just look at the ingredients and what it can do."

In less then six seconds, Paul's computer came on.

"Flaminetore," Paul said. "Study this potion. What does it do?"

Flaminetore picked up the beaker and poured a drop of the green potion onto his hand.

"Pretty hard to interpret," Flaminetore said.

"You mean you can't do it?" Paul said, sighing.

"Did I ever say that?" Flaminetore snapped. "I'm the best computer in the world, but I'm not that fast."

"Ok, but we are not that patient, so hurry," Paul snapped back. "I have had no sleep for about 24 hours and I need some."

Flaminetore glared at him for a second. Then he said.

"One percent … two percent … three percent … "

"I know you can go faster than that," Paul yelled. "What percent is it really?"

" … Eight percent … nine percent … master it really is taking me this long, this is a very complex potion. Twelve percent … 13 percent … "

"You know," Paul said, through clenched teeth. "I think I do have my ax repaired. Do you want me to test it out?"

"Ok, ok, ok, 87 percent, 89 percent, 94 percent, 97 percent … fully uploaded. The potion contains 14 percent hydrogen and 86 percent pure genius." Flaminetore said.

"Flemena!" Paul yelled in Neptune's language. "Howerly lere fensed dwinces!"

"Fine," Flaminetore said. "It contains 30 percent hydrogen, 10 percent lostwell—"

"Lostwell?" Jerry asked.

"Type of liquid only Zyno has discovered yet," Alvin said. "He told me once."

"When?" Jerry asked curiously.

"Before we were enemies," Alvin explained. "He made some medicine out of it once."

"Zyno comes up with the stupidest names," Lino shook his head.

" … 50 percent bone plasma, and 10 percent human electricity. Looks fine to me, master."

"Yes, I would think so," Paul said, smiling a little. "Zyno has technology inside it preventing any access to any snooping people looking for the ingredients. He underestimates me."

"I see," Alvin said. "Maybe not."

"What do you mean?" Paul said

"Well, if he needs you, which I bet he does, he will know that you are going to stay here until John is well," Alvin said. "Believe me, he is not a patient man. He would want you to get out of the maze ASAP. He doesn't want you to be delayed by certain injuries. If you used Flaminetore, it would take weeks to install it, and might even longer to heal John. If he gave you a potion to heal John, it would take seconds. Trust me."

Paul looked at him carefully. He knew it. Alvin *was* one of the holograms made by Zyno. He couldn't tell anyone though. But of course, Zyno and Alvin might not be lying.

"Alright," Paul said. He poured some of the liquid on John's lips. John felt something warm go down his throat. Nothing happened. They waited for a long time. After half an hour, Paul shook his head.

"It's no use guys," he said. "I'll start working on programming how to heal John tomorrow."

They laid down and closed their eyes. John felt his eyes preventing the tears from falling. He blinked. It worked! He could use his fingers a bit now, but couldn't lift his legs yet.

After 10 minutes he was completely healed. He was about to wake them when he thought better of it. He lay back down and slept.

John woke up with everyone looking at him. He got up and stretched.

"Yous 'ah ok! Yous 'ah ok!" Victor said happily.

"Yep, the potion worked," John said.

"Flaminetore, save the ingredients," Paul ordered happily. "I want to sell this to a hospital for 10 billion dollars."

Jerry wasn't that happy though.

"Uh...Paul?" Jerry asked. "Can I ... er... borrow your computer for a second? John and I need to play a quick game. In a private room, if you please."

"Sure," Paul said happily. "But make it quick, we need to find the metal door."

Paul turned on the computer and Flaminetore came out.

"Romese aprovet gema," Paul said to him. A square room came around John, Jerry and Flaminetore.

"John," Jerry said. "I have a theory. I can't tell you, just in case we are being watched by Zyno."

"What is it?" John asked.

"I can't tell you," Jerry repeated. "But you have to trust me on this. For starters, I am not in a different land, I'm doing this on purpose."

Jerry took out his sword. John looked at it uneasily.

"Jerry, what are you doing?" John asked.

"Please John," Jerry said. "I still don't trust Zyno's potion, whatever other people think. If he works with Benjamin, he is more dangerous than what he claims to be. Think about what Alvin said."

"Alvin can't be trusted," John argued. "He won't tell us his true name. What if he was Zyno himself?"

"How could you say that?" Jerry said angrily. "Alvin is a friend; you have got to know that."

"Look," John said, frustrated, "Did you ever ask him about Uncle Dan? I did. He is so afraid of the name. Why? Because his rival must be Uncle Dan!"

"But that still doesn't say he's in league with Zyno!" Jerry said.

"Did he look familiar to you when you first saw him?" John said slowly.

Jerry thought back. After a few moments he admitted, "Yes, he did. Why?"

"Because he might have been friends with Benjamin," John said. "You remembered Benjamin's face, didn't you? The night when he attacked you all those years ago? Could he not have been *alone*?!"

"He might not have been, yes," Jerry said slowly.

"And what excuse did he have when he kidnapped you?" John asked.

"He said—wait, he didn't kidnap me!" Jerry said quickly.

"Jerry, I know he did. I know he was the black-coated figure that I, personally, fought. Now, he kidnapped you for one reason," John said. "To draw us all to him so that we may be used as blackmail for our uncle. Then he would transport it back to Zyno."

"All the evidence points that way," Jerry said. "But there is one thing that blocks that theory."

"What?" John asked.

"Look at his face," Jerry said. "He is so trustworthy. He is so gentle. When I first met him, I knew. He was not a villain, but someone we knew before. As a friend."

"Fine," John said, shaking his head. "But we must save our uncle. He is in the maze somewhere. We must save him from the clutches of Zyno. If Alvin is evil, then that's one off our side. Then, there are the two holograms and that's three off our side. Do you know what this means? We could be five-on-five against Zyno. But that's to say if Zyno doesn't have any more followers on his side."

"You're right," Jerry said. "Let's quickly go through with my plan, though."

"So what is your plan?" John asked.

"I have to repeat this how many times?" Jerry asked frustrated. "I-can't-tell-you!"

"Then what's the point?" John asked.

"It might help us in the battle with Zyno," Jerry said.

"Geez, what's taking them so long?" Jimmy asked.

"Well, when Jerry starts to play a game, he won't show his face until the next millennium," Paul answered.

"I see," Alvin said. "But we have to get going soon. The metal door could be anywhere in this desert. We have to start looking immediately."

"Yes," Lino said. "Did we ever find out what happened to the hyena?"

"No," Paul said, sadly. "He got away."

"Looks 'ah out for hims in the next land," Victor said.

"Victor, your speech has gotten better," Lino said.

"Thank yous," Victor said, bowing.

"I need to tell John," Alvin muttered.

"Tell him what?" Paul asked.

"About his situation," Alvin replied, flexing his hand. Paul nodded.

"What situation?" Tyler asked.

"Nothing," Alvin said.

"And Jerry's his," Paul added, "We can't keep it a secret from him if everyone else knows their power."

"What power?" Jimmy asked looking at them both.

"Mind your own business," Paul said. Tyler and Jimmy looked completely confused.

"Flaminetore, are you ready to heal?" Jerry asked Flaminetore who had been silent during the conversation. "And *not* with that potion, got it?"

"Yes, Jerry," he replied.

"Good," Jerry said. "John, there is no other way, I'm sorry."

Before John could respond, Jerry slashed John's arm off.

14) The Final Land

John howled in pain.

"Flaminetore, now!" Jerry said. Flaminetore touched John's arm and it reappeared on his shoulder.

"What was that for?" John asked, breathing hard. "I just got healed!"

"That's the point," Jerry whispered. "You'll thank me later."

They came out of the holographic room.

"You will not repeat anything that went on in that room to your master, understood?" Jerry whispered to Flaminetore.

"Of course, Jerry," Flaminetore said.

"What took you guys so long?" Paul asked. "You were in there 10 minutes!"

"Somebody's impatient," John mumbled. They left the cave. Alvin beckoned John away from the group. They spoke at the same time.

"Look, we need to talk about what happened last night," They said at the same time.

"About what had happened with the tornado," They said again.

"Fine, you go first," Alvin said smiling.

"I know you are a magician or wizard or something," John said, "and I saw your hand turn red when you performed magic. My hand turned a different color when I hit the tornado and a barrier kept me safe from the tornado's mighty winds. That is the only reason I survived. I need to ask you, did you form that barrier around me?"

"No," Alvin said, smiling still. "I was too far away to perform it without my wand. You created it yourself."

"But," John said slowly, "that would mean that I am … "

" … a magician," Alvin finished. "Paul is a genie. Jerry is a psychic."

"I thought about how I could stop the natural disaster," John said. "Instead, a barrier came around me. I guess I am a weak magician."

"To stop a tornado," Alvin laughed, "is a power that even I can't do, even with my wand. Only the most powerful magicians can do that, and I know six that can … "

At this, Alvin shivered. But John still had questions.

"Isn't a genie a creature that lives in a lamp and grants wishes?" John asked, still surprised.

"Yes on the lamp part," Alvin said. "No on the wishes. He cannot live in a house now that he knows he's a genie. He must now live in what you might call an oil lamp. Well, now I must tell Jerry."

John ran back to the group and told Jerry that Alvin wanted to see him. Paul had Flaminetore out.

"Any sign of it?" Paul asked.

"Yes, it's over there!" Flaminetore said. When he looked at Jimmy, he said, "Strange."

"What?" Paul said, looking at him. Jimmy shrugged.

"Nothing," Flaminetore said. "Due east. Fifty feet."

They ran straight forward. They found the door.

"Please do the honors," John said to Paul. Paul nodded and put the chip in. The door opened. Jerry and Alvin joined the group again. Jerry looked excited.

"I'm psychic!" He rejoiced, hugging John. John struggled free.

"Get in the door already," he said. Everyone now was in. They all felt like going through a tornado (except for John who thought it was not like one at all). They all landed on their feet, except for Victor.

"We're getting kind of used to that," Paul said. There were no alternate paths. They walked down the path. They came to a dead-end. On the wall was a message:

You made it!
You have made it through the best of my lands and will now go through the last land. I, as a great man, have given you the chip for the next land. This time, you are timed. If you do not get out in time, your chip will disappear. You have one hour after you're done reading this note. Good luck!

" 'Great man', my foot," Alvin snorted. He picked up the chip from the ground. "Well, let's go. We have no alterative."

They pushed the wall and went through. No tornado, though. They just went straight to the land. The land was filled with lava, volcanoes and other creatures they had met in previous lands.

"Good to see familiar faces," John said sarcastically as a small dinosaur came running past them.

"Yeah, the sooner we get out of here the better," Jerry said. "The only way to get out here is to find the metal door. The biggest thing that might stop us is the time limit."

They stood on an island surrounded by lava. There were a few bridges connecting the islands together. The volcanoes were spewing out lava and smoke constantly.

"I don't know what to do," Paul said.

"What?" Alvin asked.

"About being a genie," Paul replied. "It sounds hard. Do we have magic like you guys?"

Alvin nodded.

"Only some, I'm afraid," He said. "But we can't talk about this right now. But I swear, we will when we get out of the maze."

Paul bumped into something. He looked down and saw a big egg. It was about two feet long. He picked it up with difficulty.

"Geez, what is this thing?" Paul said staggering.

"Is it one of those dinosaur eggs?" John asked. "If so, drop it. We already talked about this."

"Quite the contrary, John," Alvin said. "Try to collect as many things as possible. It might help us on the way. Try to imagine what happened with me in my third land – I hatched an egg of a dinosaur and, using my computer, I was able to grow it into an adult. That made it easy to travel, for I could just hop on its back, and it could reach speeds up to 40 miles per hour."

"But this isn't a dinosaur egg," Paul said.

"How can you tell?" John asked.

"Well," Paul replied, "The dinosaur egg was much bigger than this."

"Well, I guess we can take it with us for a little while," Lino said. "As long as when it hatches, whatever it is, it doesn't attack us at all."

"Hey Jerry," Paul said, "can you start your watch?"

"Way ahead of you, man," Jerry said, holding up his watch. It read 54:37.

"Come on, let's hurry," John urged. He ran across one of the bridges to the next island. Paul had his computer out.

"Where is there any metal object?" Paul asked his computer. After about three seconds, the computer replied:

"There is no steel object beyond a 12-foot radius of this computer."

"You mean the only metal things are what we have on us right now?" Paul said.

"Correct."

"That's great," Alvin said.

"Hurry up, guys!" John shouted. Paul turned off his computer and handed it to Alvin. He took back the egg that Jerry was holding for him. They crossed the bridge. Alvin suddenly pulled out his two swords. They all turned to him.

"Whats is it?" Victor said, turning to him.

"I feel danger," Alvin said. "I just can."

"How?" Jerry said, taking the computer from him.

"No, no," John said. "I feel it too."

The group pulled out their weapons, if they had one. Tyler had a small sword that he had gotten in his third land. Alvin lent Jimmy one of his swords.

"Where is it coming from?" Jerry asked.

"Over there," John and Alvin said at the same time, pointing behind them.

"Come on, let's keep moving," Paul said, moving to another bridge. After they all crossed it, it broke and fell into the lava.

"There," Paul said. "Now that'll throw anyone off who was following us."

"What if they have wings?" Jerry asked, looking above them.

"Don't tell me ... " John began.

"Yep," Jerry said. "We get to meet him for the last time."

They all looked up. The hyena looked down upon them. He landed on the island.

"Well, well, well, if it's not the unstoppable crew," he said sneering. "Hello to you all."

"What do you want now, scum face?" Tyler asked.

"What? No 'hello'? No 'how are you'?" the hyena said mockingly. "We became almost *friends* in this un-ending journey."

"We have better business to do," Paul said, "than to talk to you. We don't want to waste any time."

"Well, once again, you have hurt one of the pack," the hyena continue. "So—"

"For *The Ring*'s sake!" Alvin yelled. "What is this stupid pack you keep talking about?"

The hyena grinned.

"Why, it's all the animals you have met!" he said. "In fact, do you wish to meet them all? Fine by me."

Suddenly, creatures started to come onto the island from the many wooden bridges of other islands. When all of them were there, Paul saw that there were Thogeens, T-Rexes, hyenas that looked almost like the one in front of them, saber-tooth tigers, crocodiles, alligators, triceratops, pterodactyls, and tigers that looked like Lino, only they were gray, not pink. There were about 200 creatures in all.

"Yes, yes, now you know who the pack is," the hyena said laughing at the terrified look on everyone's face. "Now it's time to see if they want you to live. Everyone in favor of killing them all, make a noise."

Every creature yelled, growled, roared and made some type of sound.

"Now you see why you shouldn't have killed any of the pack?" The hyena yelled triumphantly. "The cost is your lives."

Even though Paul was scared, he thought of something. If Zyno wanted him and Alvin, he won't kill them. But he remembered something else Zyno had said: "*I don't care what you do them.*" The hyena would kill the rest of them. He had made up his mind. If Zyno was good, he wouldn't let this thing happen. Paul decided then and there not to go with Zyno. He would defend his brothers and friends. He set the egg down and prepared to fight.

"You'll never defeat us!" he yelled, lightning coming out of his ax. The Thogeens backed away, frightened. The hyena laughed his hardest yet. When he stopped, he wiped a tear from his eye.

"Please excuse me," he said, giggling, "But I believe you can't beat us. Two hundred creatures against—"

He counted the group.

"—Eight? Please, you don't have a chance!" he finished.

"We beat all of thems at least once, wes can do it agains!" Victor replied angrily.

"Look," said the hyena, rolling his eyes, "I understand you might be good enough to get past some of these creatures *separately*, but come on, have you taken down five T-Rexes at once? No, you could only destroy one."

"Did we have our weapons then?" John asked, shoving his sword into the ground. The island shook violently and some creatures (including all the Thogeens) fell to the ground. They all got up, however.

"So you think that now that you have your weapons," the hyena said menacingly, "you're home free? You'll win?"

"That's correct," Alvin said, "for you have not seen or felt the power of my weapon! The great *FANG* and *SABER*, the two most powerful swords in the universe!"

The Thogeens – the big, strong, powerful Thogeens were shaking and whimpering.

"Yes," Alvin continued, holding his sword above his head. "If you thought those brothers' weapons are powerful, then you are going to experience something worse than your worst nightmare. May all the horrors of the universe come into this one sword in which the mighty kings on the *Ring* call *FANG*! May he blow away every creature that threatens my friends! Oh great *FANG*, reveal your great powers to the fools around us!"

Alvin swung his sword in the air and in its path flew huge piles of snow, water and ice. The lava cooled a little as the snow covered the island. The kids shivered. Some of the creatures got caught in some of it and fell into the lava. The hyena merely continued to laugh.

"So you say you are powerful now that you have your weapons?" he said.

"That's right," Lino said, growling. "So, now you're history. We'll kill all of you."

"Well, we can arrange something, Pink Panther," the hyena said. He stood up on his hind legs clapped his two front paws together. All of their weapons suddenly started to melt to nothing.

15) Sheen

As if they had dipped them in lava, the weapons melted down.

"Not so tough now, huh?" the hyena said laughing. It was true. No one knew what to do. John had a desperate idea. He reached into his pocket, but couldn't find it.

"Where is it?!" he yelled.

"What, John?" Jerry asked.

"My pocket knife! It's gone!" John replied.

The hyena just couldn't stop laughing.

"It took you this long to figure that out?" He said.

"When did I lose it?" he asked himself. Then he remembered. On Venemay, he looked in his pocket for the chip, but could only feel his walkie-talkie.

"Now do you realize you can't win?" the hyena said. "Give up now, and we won't kill all of you—just two of you so it's even because you killed two parts of the pack."

"You'll have to take us all down," Paul said, grabbing his computer. One of the flying hyenas flew over and took Paul's computer. He held it over the lava.

"Should I even cough, this thing might fall," he said, grinning at the look of horror on Paul's face. "So give up."

Paul put his hands in his face. Zyno couldn't kill him, but he could do tons of things to him. Paul remembered something. He wasn't sure if it would work, but it was worth a try. For the lives of his brothers.

"You will have to kill us all," Paul repeated. The hyena with the computer shrugged.

"Fine by me," he said, dropping the computer into the lava. Victor yelled.

"NOOOOOOOOOOOOOOOOOOOOO!"

He pulled from behind his empty quiver a dagger he used on Venemay against the Thogeens. It was amazing how high he leapt. He jumped up to the height of the hyena that destroyed Paul's computer. He cut part of his wing off, and the hyena fell into the lava. When Victor landed, he ran to a Thogeen and cut his arm off. Suddenly, the dagger melted away like the others.

"It's all over," the hyena said, impatience building. "Let's finish this. ATTACK!"

Every creature on the island bellowed out a noise and they charged. The animals came really close when suddenly they heard a tapping sound.

Everyone and everything stood still. The tapping came from near Paul's feet. Everyone looked down and saw that the egg was hatching. Alvin pulled John close to him.

"Listen, John," Alvin whispered. "You may not trust me, but here is a good time to start. You have to concentrate on the word when you say it. Grab Paul and say with me the word *Lankto ... lance.*"

Instantly, John touched Paul. The tapping continued.

"One ... two ... three!" Alvin said. John and Alvin said together: "*Lanktolance!*"

The world froze. Paul, John and Alvin could still move.

"Alright, Paul," Alvin said. "This will take tons of time, but we might have to make a new computer for you."

"No, you don't," Paul said, grinning. He went over to the side of the island. They followed. There, floating in the lava, was Paul's computer.

"How did it still survive?" Alvin said.

"I told John this at the beginning of the second land, it's everything-proof except if a blast of lightning hits it."

"Amazing," Alvin said, carefully picking it up out of the lava.

"So why did you stop time?" Paul asked. "And couldn't we just keep it this way and try to find the metal door?"

"Because I need to install something onto your computer," Alvin said starting up the computer. "And it's hard to do it with more than one person, so I needed John's help. I can't hold the connection for long."

"What are you going to install?" John asked curiously.

"Time flier," Alvin replied as Flaminetore came out. "It makes time go faster on a certain object. Remember about what I said about the dino? Whatever is in that egg, I'm growing it."

"How long will it take to install?" Paul asked.

"Maybe five minutes," Alvin said. But he was wrong. It was two minutes.

"Finished. Now focus it on that one area where the egg is," Alvin said. "Ready John? Repeat what we said before. One … two … three-"

"*Lanktolance.*"

Everything came back to normal. The egg started to crack open. When it was fully hatched, everyone got to see what it was.

It was a dragon. It was about three feet long and green. It was also slimy. It had two wings that were as long as its body. It had teeth that were being bared, showing sharp piercing fangs. It opened its mouth and roared a deafening roar, which was a surprise to everyone, since it was still a baby. Alvin pressed a button on the laptop, and it instantly began to grow to an adult. In 30 seconds, it was 60 feet tall. Even though the *T-Rexes* were ninety, the dragon looked much fiercer.

"Now save us all from certain death … Sheen!" Paul said.

"Sheen?" Jerry asked incredulously.

"Well, yeah, I guess," John shrugged. "He has to be called by something, you know."

The dragon roared again and whipped his tail around, which was about 40 feet long. It knocked, with huge force, all of the T-Rexes off the island. He bit the pterodactyls' heads off. He stomped on the hyenas and tigers except for the original hyena, which escaped. With one breath, he blew off both the alligator and crocodiles. At the sight of their comrades' deaths, they Thogeens committed suicide by jumping into the lava. Sheen rammed into the triceratops, one by one, until they all passed out. Last, he knocked out the saber-tooth tigers off except for one, who dodged it.

"Knock that one off too, Sheen," Jimmy said impatiently.

"No, wait," Lino said, smiling. "I remember that one. He's the one I fought before."

The two tigers advanced on each other. They both pounced.

"I have been training, unlike you," Lino said on top of it, ripping it to shreds. "You are going down."

The saber-tooth tiger couldn't understand him, but he didn't show any sign off weakness, either. He scratched Lino on his face, but Lino didn't care.

"Do you know how close I was to killing my own friend, just because you attacked me?" Lino asked, biting him. The tiger roared. "Very close, that's how much."

The helpless saber-tooth tiger scratched Lino one more time and then stopped struggling, but Lino kept on biting and slashing until he was satisfied that it was dead. He looked up and saw the hyena gone.

"Dang him," Tyler said, also noticing. "We just can't kill him, can we?"

"No," Paul said, shaking his head, "I don't think we can. Maybe we were just not meant to."

"Obviously Paul, or else we would have killed him by now," John said, rolling his eyes. "Hey Jerry, what's your watch say?"

Jerry checked it.

"Forty minutes, 20 seconds," He replied. Then suddenly Sheen began to shrink. He didn't go back to his baby stage, but he shrunk about to 20 feet.

"Did you see that?" Jimmy asked pointing up to one of the volcanoes. "I saw something in the smoke made by a volcano."

"I don't see anything," Paul said, looking up to the place he pointed to.

"Because the smoke went away," Jimmy said. "Maybe it'll be there when the smoke reappears."

"I'm not waiting that long," Paul said. "Remember, we have to get out of here in a certain amount of time. We can't risk being any later than we already are."

"Ok, ok," Jimmy said. "How are we going to find the metal door? If there is one, anyway."

"Well," Paul said, looking at Sheen and Sheen looked back. "We could ride on Sheen."

They got on Sheen and Sheen took off.

"Paul," John whispered. "I know who one of the holograms is."

"Me too," Paul said. "Alvin."

"Why Alvin?" John whispered.

"Well, the obvious of him being so secretive," Paul said, "And he was the one who tried to persuade me the most to let you have that potion, which I still think has some defects in it. Hopefully, we can get rid of Alvin before we reach Zyno."

"The one I know is Jerry," John said. "The real Jerry has been kidnapped. We can't trust them."

"How do you know about Jerry?" Paul asked.

"He sliced my arm off while we were in that room," John answered, "for no reason at all. He defended Alvin too, so if you're sure Alvin is one, so is Jerry."

"Right," Paul said. He climbed up to the neck of Sheen. "Fly around the place ok?"

Sheen roared.

"There it is again!" Jimmy said pointing. This time, everyone saw it. They couldn't tell what it was, though.

"Sheen, fly over to that volcano," Paul said. He turned and headed that way.

"Hey, Als," Victor said. "How comes Sheens shrunk?"

"Because I only had two minutes to install it, so after about five minutes, he would shrink back to an adolescence," Alvin replied.

"So you mean it could shrink into a baby right now?" Jerry gasped. Alvin laughed.

"No, I didn't do it *that* quick," He said.

"Right," Lino said, looking over the edge. "So it just depends on how long it takes to install? Just great."

He looked sick. Just then, everyone felt something on their hips. They looked down. Their weapons were back!

"I feel safer now," Lino said sarcastically as they all looked jubilant. "Any sign of that thing in the smoke yet?"

"Nope," Paul said, but John exclaimed …

"Look, in the other volcano," He said, "There it is!"

"There what is?" Alvin asked.

"I don't know," John replied. "But it's something."

They got really close to the volcano now. So close, that they could feel the heat.

"Well, the smoke is gone," Jerry said. "Let's wait—"

The volcano erupted. The lava came close to them.

"Jerry what time is it?" John asked.

"Thirty minutes and 10 seconds," Jerry replied. Then he gasped.

"Whats 'ah is it?" Victor said.

"The temperature in here is 115," Jerry replied. "I guess we kind of get used to the heat inside the maze. Whoa!"

Some lava got on Jerry's leg.

"AHHHHHHHH! GET IT OFF! GET IT OFF!" He yelled.

"Hold on Jerry!" John said. Even though he *thought* this Jerry was a hologram, didn't mean he was one for sure. "I'll get it off!"

The lava was quickly going through his leg. John tried to get it off with his hand, but it burned his hand.

"PAUL! GET FLAMINETORE, IT HURTS," Jerry screamed.

"Getting it," Paul said, glancing around for his computer. Just then, more lava splashed on Jerry's face. This made him scream louder. Paul opened the computer and found, to everyone's horror that the batteries had died. Alvin's hand began to glow. His eyes turned blood red and a sudden breeze was blowing his hair and cloak back. Some of the lava started to disappear, but it wasn't enough—they saw the lava burning Jerry's face. Sheen turned his head around and roared.

"Not now," Paul said to him.

Sheen spit on Jerry's face. Slowly, the lava disappeared from his face and he was completely healed. Not only his face, but also the huge burn that he had on his leg had gone, too.

"Wow," Jerry said, breathing hard. "How did that happen? That was crazy. I almost died!"

"I know," Alvin said, clutching his chest. "I wish I had my wand. Doing magic by hand is so hard."

"What happened to it?" Jimmy asked.

"It disappeared the second I entered the building," Alvin replied. "Probably another of Zyno's tricks."

"I really wish I had my batteries," Paul said.

"Well, once you used mine in the cave," Jimmy said, taking his game out of his pocket, "I took the batteries back. You can use them again if you want. But that would still mean that we are one battery short."

"No problem," John said. He thought really hard about a double A battery. Instantly, one appeared in his hand. He handed the battery to Paul. "You know, I kind of like being a magician."

"Yeah," Paul said, putting them in his computer. "I can't wait to live in a lamp."

He started it up. Flaminetore came out.

"How may I be of service—hopefully not another healing job, is it?" He asked.

"Nope," Paul said. Then he turned to face Sheen. He put out his hand. "Sheen, spit."

Sheen licked his hand. Paul looked disgusted.

"Good enough," He said. "Flaminetore, save the contents of everything on my hand."

Flaminetore made a face. Then he wiped his finger on Paul's.

"Saved, master," Flaminetore said.

"And if we ever need another healing, please give us this saliva," Paul said. "It somehow gives us some healing power."

"Do you know what this reminds me of?" Jerry asked.

"No," Paul said. "What?"

"Lino's healing ability," Jerry replied. Lino looked up at him from the side of the dragon.

"I guess we might have something in common," Lino said. He looked down again. "But what we don't have in common is our likes of heights. Please, can we hurry up and find this stupid metal door?"

"Do you think I am in charge of finding it?" Paul snapped. "I can't find it either, and I am equally frustrated."

"Fine," Lino said, transfixed on the sight below him. "I am not much of a fearing kind of guy … but I hate this."

"You will fear this," said a voice behind them. "I'm back. And not a moment to soon, either."

They turned around. In horror, they saw the hyena again. But he wasn't alone. Behind him was an entire army of winged horses with fiery wings.

16) Inside the Smoke

"You really think I was out just because you took down creatures you had already faced before?" The hyena laughed. "No, no, I can use the creatures on this world, too. I also have dragons and horenslings.

"Nots horenslings!" Victor yelled. Nobody seemed very frightened by the name except Victor. The hyena smiled.

"Yes, meet the horenslings!" he yelled. Below them spits of lava came flying up. Creatures were coming out of the volcanoes, huge monsters with one eye. They had teeth like vampires and had three fingers. They were half the size of the volcano themselves. They were completely red with some black spots on them.

These horrendous creatures reached out to get the group. Paul got out his ax.

"Back you fiends, back!" he yelled. Lightning shot out of his ax right at them. The snow and ice hit one, but had no effect.

"I'll handle this," Alvin said. He swung his mighty magical sword and snow shot at them. It hit one in the eye, but it only looked mad.

"Yeah … " John said. "We better find those doors quickly."

Sheen grew. He grew to be sixty feet again. Fifteen dragons, each forty feet tall, rose out from the lava. They each spewed lava at Sheen. Sheen dove out of the way. He grabbed one by the neck and threw it into the lava. It hit the lava with a big splash, but came right back up.

Meanwhile, the four hundred Pegasus flew at them. Paul shot lightning at them, killing seven. Alvin shot some snow at them, but it almost immediately melted into water because of the intense heat. Forty fell when that happened. Jerry's sword didn't seem to affect any creature, because any creature could take the heat. John's sword also didn't work, for they were in the air. Alvin's sword looked like it had become a fire hose, since water was spraying all of the Pegasus. The hyena's face fell as he saw what was happening. He charged at Alvin. Jerry jumped to his aid, (having someone he could actually defeat), swinging his sword. He struck the hyena in the head with the fiery sword. The hyena yelled and fell. Jerry saw him smash into an island. A Pegasus came close to Alvin, but Alvin didn't see it. John quickly jumped onto its back. He stabbed his sword into its neck. It turned with sharp teeth and bit him. He couldn't jump off, for Sheen had moved. The horse threw him off and he fell screaming. He was about to hit the lava when something caught him underneath. It was a pegasus, only a different one that he had seen: this horse had a different colored coat. John yelped for joy.

"Now, let's go take down the rest!" John said, steering it upward. He was very scared, but since he had a horse at home, he knew how to control one. He saw one of the dragons fall, dead. Then, right on top of it, slammed down two more. Sheen was winning!

John, sword in hand, killed over thirty pegasus. The one he was riding didn't try to stop him. On the contrary, it seemed to help him. Paul killed some with his ax and Alvin killed the rest. By then, there were only three dragons left. Sheen killed those in a matter of minutes.

"Whats about the horenslings?" Victor asked. A big hand knocked all of them off the back of Sheen. The five horensling had finally attacked. Sheen turned around smacked one of the horenslings. He bit its arm off. It growled and slid under the lava. He bit the others and they also sunk beneath the lava. Sheen turned just in time to see Paul and everyone falling, about to hit the lava. He quickly dove and caught them.

"That was close," Jerry caught his breath. The others nodded in frightened relief.

"Hey, where's John?" Jimmy asked.

"I's 'ah saw hims riding a pegasus," Victor said.

Just then, John rode the red-striped Pegasus next to Sheen. He got off it a little shaky and teeth chattering. He managed to say to the creature: "Thanks again! You really helped me!"

Then it flew off.

"How…" Alvin began.

"I don't know," John said, reading his mind. "It just…joined my side."

"Really amazing," Alvin said, shaking his head.

"Look," Lino said, looking at the smoke. "Can it be?"

"Yes!" Paul said. "It's the metal door! Only, it's not metal, it's not even solid, it's...it's..."

"In the smoke," Jerry said. "Quickly before it goes away!"

They flew towards it, but it disappeared.

"How are we going to get the chip in it if it won't even stay in the same place?" John asked.

"There it is near another volcano!" Jerry said, pointing. Then his eyes widened. "No...it can't be..."

"What?" Paul asked.

Jerry took out a piece of paper with a red three on it.

"Remember this land?" He said.

"Yes," Paul said.

"Well, I just saw another door in different smoke. Maybe it's this thing all over again."

Everyone gasped.

"How many more minutes do we have, Jerry?" Jimmy asked.

Jerry checked his watch.

"Under five minutes," He replied. "We have to find a way to get the chip into the door."

"I've got an idea," Paul replied. "How about we wait over a volcano for the smoke to rise?"

"Sounds dangerous," Alvin replied, "Let's do it."

They had waited for three minutes before smoke came out. It was so hot, however, that they couldn't reach the door.

"Jerry," Alvin said desperately, "It's up to you! Try to use your psychic power to move the chip into the slot!"

"Me?" Jerry yelled, "Why me? Why can't you use your magic to do it? I am not even trained to float a feather or anything!"

"Try, Jerry," John said, "Quick!"

Jerry concentrated really hard on trying to lift it into the slot. Paul put out the chip. He let go. It floated! Then it dropped. It was falling into the volcano.

"No!" Alvin yelled. "No!"

Jerry tried with all his might to bring it back, but couldn't. Lava erupted from the volcano, spewing out the chip. Jerry reached out and grabbed it.

"How did it survive?" Paul exclaimed. "The chances of it surviving are one in one hundred million!"

"Well, it did," John said. "But the smoke is gone."

Paul swore.

"How can we get out of here?" He yelled. "We have almost a minute left and we can't do it!"

Jerry received a strange sensation. A strong urge to walk off the dragon. Why should he argue? He got up and walked off. He could still walk... on air!

"Jerry—whoa," John said, "How did you do that?"

Jerry didn't answer. He had the chip in his hand. He saw some smoke and he walked up to the door. He put the chip in the slot and it opened. The jester was there again and he laughed hard and gave him a number: three.

"Jerry, get out of there!" He heard Paul yell. The chip came back to him and he walked up to a different door.

"Jerry, get back here now!" Alvin cried.

Jerry ignored them and walked up to a different door. He was about to put it in when Sheen got in front of him.

"Jerry, that's enough," John said, pulling him on. He checked Jerry's watch: 00:35.

"Well, gang," Jimmy said, sighing. "It was worth a try. Now it's over."

Jerry put the chip into the other door's slot. It opened and the jester gave him a number two. Jerry ran on air to the last door.

"Jerry, no!!!!" John yelled.

"Don't Jerry," Paul cried.

"Pleases!" Victor said.

"Jerry, stop!" Alvin said as Jerry checked his watch: 00:20. He kept on running.

"Stop, friend!" Tyler yelled.

"No!!!!" Jimmy yelled.

Jerry ignored them all. He reached out to put it in. 00:10. He had to make it...

A hand smashed into his, causing the chip to shoot out of his hands. It was one of the horenslings. Jerry tried to grab it, but it went too high up. He glanced at his watch: 00:04, 00:03, 00:02. He grabbed it as it came down.

00:01, 00:00.

Their time was up.

17) Ending the Maze

Jerry had grabbed the chip when his watch said 00:01. He could feel it disappearing while he was putting the chip into the slot. The door opened. There was swirling blackness inside and no jester. It was the right door! He then started to fall. He was going to touch the lava inside the volcano.

But there were still the horenslings. The one that knocked the chip away was right underneath him. Jerry landed right on top of its eye. Then, to Jerry's horror, it blinked. The eyelid slammed against Jerry, throwing him off his eye. Jerry was disgusted by it, for he was covered with water from his eye. He caught onto the horensling's arm. He held on tight, not wanting to face the horrors below. The horensling tried to throw him off, but Jerry was glued to its arm. Then suddenly, Jerry saw Sheen nearby. He leapt off it on an upward swing.

"Grab hold, Jerry," John cried. "Sheen! Go faster! Go faster! Hurry! Jerry, reach out!"

Jerry stretched out his hand and barely grabbed onto Sheen's wing.

"Whew, that was a close one, guys," Jerry said, breathing hard. "I put the chip in the right door just in time, too. It was a milliseconds difference. The door's … still …"

He looked up. The "metal" door was closing. Jerry swore. He couldn't let that door shut. After all the things they did in the maze, after all the dangerous worlds that they went through, after all the injuries they had gotten didn't matter anymore, for their only escaping route was through that closing door. It was 30 yards from them.

"Guys, quick, let's grab it," Jerry yelled. "Sheen, fly up there!"

"You heard my brother," Paul exclaimed to Sheen, "hurry up and fly to that door!"

It was nearly closed now. Alvin got on top of Sheen's head and reached up. It was almost shut but Alvin was almost there …

Alvin put his fingers between the door and the doorway. He had stopped it! It was smashing his hand, but he could care less.

"Wes are safe!" Victor yelled happily as he saw what Alvin had done.

"Well, we certainly aren't out of the woods yet," Alvin said trying to pull open the door. "One, I can't get this thing to open and it's smashing my fingers. Two, even if we do get out of here, we would still have to face Zyno, and he is harder then all the lands combined … twice!"

Victor tried to help Alvin, but he couldn't pull it open either, for it was still pulling shut. Everyone helped now. Then Victor had an idea. He got his rope from his shoulder and tied it to the door. He then tied the other end to Sheen. Paul saw what he was doing and nodded.

"Alright, Sheen," Paul said, "fly that way."

Sheen roared its ok. He flew for about one foot before the rope snapped.

"Well that sure didn't work," John said, fingers sore. "We have to try something stronger. Do you have anything on your computer, Paul?"

"Let me check," Paul said, letting go of the door and getting his computer off Sheen's back. "Mmmmmm—" Paul said as he started it up, "—well, I have wires and rope, and that's the only thing that can tie a knot around the door."

"How thick are the wires?" Tyler asked in agony.

"Two … three inches thick," Paul said. Flaminetore came out with a beaker of water in hand.

"Healing job?" He asked. Paul shook his head.

"Nope, we need some of those big wires," Paul said, taking the beaker and putting it on his belt, "We need to pry open the door. The wires are the strongest things. Unless you can recommend anything."

"Nope, some wires will do the trick," Flaminetore said. Immediately, the wires appeared in his hand.

"Ok, just tie that end to Sheen," Paul ordered, tying one side to the metal door. Flaminetore tied it to Sheen's neck.

"Ok, Sheen," Alvin said. "Pull hard on the door."

Sheen flew hard. Pulling with all his might. Jerry kept on urging him on.

"That's it, big fella, keep pulling," he would say.

"Oh, man, hurry up!" Lino said in Sheen's ear. Lino couldn't help at all. Paul noticed the wire was starting to break into two. He leapt onto Sheen, abandoning the door. He pulled on either side of the breaking part, towards it. He managed to keep *that* part from breaking, but other sides of the wire were ripping as well.

"Come on," Jerry said, pulling really hard on the door. "Why won't this stupid door open?"

"I don't know," Alvin said. "But I won't be able to use this hand, except for magic, again. Well, on the silver lining of a cloud, at least it's not shut or we would be here for life."

"Well, staying here forever doesn't sound that bad," Jimmy said his hand turning a little purple.

"Come on, Sheen!" Paul yelled. Sheen tugged one more time, and the door came off the hinges.

"Well, that's one way to do it," Jerry said, examining the doorway. "The smoke didn't disappear at any time, that's good."

"Yeah," Tyler said. Quite suddenly, Sheen shrank back down to 10 feet. "Whoa, I didn't know it could do that whenever it wants."

"Obviously," Alvin said. "Which still leaves the question of whether to bring him with us or not."

"Why nots?" Victor said, "He might help usses defeat my master, I mean Zynos."

"Yeah," Lino said. "It's nice to have a dragon on your side."

"Ok, ok, I guess we can bring him with us," Alvin said, looking between the pair of them. "He'd just better stay on our side, though."

"Yeah," Jerry said. "Well, come on guys, last one into the maze is a leopard!"

At this, Lino immediately jumped in. Jerry went after him and then Paul and John. They were flying into a purple tornado. Quite suddenly, Jerry caught something in the face. He peeled it off and saw it was a piece of paper. He couldn't read it, but he knew there were letters on it. He landed on his feet next to Lino. Everybody else landed on their feet next to Jerry. Jerry could read the note now:

Final Land Accomplished

You have finished all the lands in the maze. Now when you get to a dead end, you must turn around and go back. When you find a metal door, you will know I am through it. Do whatever it says on the door and you can enter it. You will not need a chip. I wish you good luck:
                    -Zyno Wayne

"Well that's good," Jerry said. "No more worlds. And we can go through it like a normal maze."

He gave the note to everyone and they read it.

"That's very good news," Alvin said. "So let's hurry up through this part of the maze. First, let's see if we can exit the maze through the way I came in. Does anybody have a compass or something?"

"I do," Jerry said. He looked at his watch. Then he muttered, "Just what I expected."

"What?" John asked.

"Nothing," Jerry said, quickly looking around. "That way—" he pointed in front of them "—is south."

"Ok," Alvin said. "I entered in here from the south, so we have to go north to get out the way we came in."

They turned north to see that there was a wall. There were no other routes, either.

"So I guess we have to face Zyno," Lino said in a final tone. "Not that I want to, it's just that I want to see the outside world. After being inside a world that doesn't even exist yet, it will be cool to see what it was like eons ago."

"Yeah, but didn't you already?" Paul asked. "You got to see those dinosaurs, and that to us is eons ago."

"Not eons eons ago, but just one eons ago," Lino said.

"Which makes no sense at all," Paul said shaking his head. "… Eons eons … please …"

John walked ahead of the group. He knocked on the walls. It was hard. *Wait a minute*, he thought. *This isn't right. I remember the walls feeling soft when we leaned against it.* This wasn't soft; these were harder—like it was made of the steel that felt like a metal door. The walls he felt before felt like a soft plant.

"Guys have you noticed the difference in the walls?" he asked. "Feel this. It feels different."

"I guess my idea of burning the walls down isn't going to work then," Jerry said, feeling it. "How about Sheen? Can't he knock them down or something? Or do we have to go through the maze the hard way?"

"Hard way," Paul said, also feeling it. "This is so hard, I doubt if a bulldozer could do it. Do you know what's strange though? It's the same color as the last one we went through."

"Yeah, I noticed that," John said, still rubbing it. "Hold on a second, feel this spot."

John beckoned everyone around him. They felt the area. It was a little softer.

"So this part of the wall is a little less dense," Paul said shrugging his shoulders. "So what?"

"No, no, wait," Alvin said. "Sheen, please punch this spot."

Sheen roared and swung his claw into the spot Alvin pointed at. It went right through. He had trouble getting it out, for it went very deeply in.

"Whoa," Paul said, taking a step back. "Sheen, punch some more."

Sheen kept on punching until there was a hole big enough to squeeze John through. John, Paul and Victor went into it, being the only ones able to fit. They didn't make Sheen punch any more because his hand was very red. They saw a machine that was obviously in the middle of being worked on. Paul walked around it. It looked like a big ray gun on a stand. There were oranges a few feet from the gun. John looked on the machine. It said "0.20 m". There was a knob next to this number.

"I wonder …" John said. He turned the knob. The number went down. He turned it the other way and the number went up. He looked at the scribbled name on the front: *Shrinky.*

"*Shrinky?* What's *Shrinky?*" John asked.

"Where?!" Paul yelped. He was shuffling through some notes on the table. He remembered the name coming from Zyno's own mouth … this was the machine he couldn't get quite right.

"Right here, what Zyno's obviously working on," John said. "Wonder what it does."

"Kinds of self-explanatory isn't its?" Victor said. "Its shrinks."

"That's right," Paul said, walking around the machine. "I wonder how you turn it on."

"Well, if this is what Zyno wants Uncle Dan, you, and Alvin for, for heaven's sake, let's destroy it," John said. "It's this machine that's going to put all our lives in jeopardy."

"That would be even more dangerous," Paul said. He glanced back at the notes for a minute, then back at the broken machine. "It says that this starts it."

He pressed a button. The machine made tons of noise. First humming, then banging. Paul heard a voice outside.

"What's going on in there?" it was Alvin.

"Nothing, just hold on a second," John said.

"And this ones shoots the laser," Victor said, also looking at the notes. He pressed a red button. A laser shot out to one of the oranges. It did nothing but slowly wear away the orange into nothing.

"Well, that was interesting," Paul said, still studying the notes. "I see what he did wrong, too. Laser booster went up too high. Also, it can only shrink if the batteries are smaller. If it's too big, then it one, couldn't fit into the machine, or two, small X small = small. It's just common knowledge. Geez, I don't know why he needs my help. Any two-year-old could figure that out. There are other problems, too. I could solve them in about a day, however."

"Wells, I guess we should leaves," Victor said, exiting out of the hole. Paul left too. John was about to leave when he had an idea. He went over to the notes that Paul had set back down. There was a pen near by. John grinned. He picked up the pen and shuffled to the last page of Zyno's notes. He wrote on it:

"*Laser capacity is too low. Turn up switches. Make the batteries bigger, because big – big = small. Here's a thanks to Paul Quaill.*"

"Hurry up, John, what's taking you so long?" yelled Jerry.

"I'm coming, I'm coming," John said, setting the paper and pen down. He left the room.

They began walking down the path. They came to a fork.
"Let's take the right path," Paul said.
"Yeah, let's not take the wrong path," Lino said. Paul
scowled. "Ok, ok, ok, let's take the right path."
They walked down the path a little and found out it was a
dead end. They turned and went back. They hit five more dead
ends and then the path started to straighten out and there were a
lot less forks.
"Where in the world is that door?" John panted.
"I don't know," Paul said. "But I have a feeling that when
we get to it, there is going to be an obstacle."
"Yeah, what if it was a riddle?" Jimmy said. "I hate
riddles."
"Nah, I doubt it," Jerry said.
"Then what do you think it is?" Tyler asked.
"Probably another world," Jerry said.
"Land," Alvin corrected.
"Yeah, but he said there aren't going to be anymore," John
said. "But of course, he could change his mind."
"Or cover it ups with loopholes," Victor said.
"Yeah, you're probably right," Alvin said. "That's Zyno
alright. Trying to weasel his way out of everything."
"Let's go, we don't have enough time for this guessing,"
Lino said, way ahead of them. "We have to find that metal door
now!"
"Yes," Jimmy said, sighing. "Let's."

They walked for a long time. Jerry said, however, that it was
only forty minutes.
"How can that watch be right?" Lino panted. "We had to
have been walking for at least four hours. We really need a
break."
"Yes," Alvin said, slamming into the ground. "I need water
now. This place has to be over one hundred."
"It's only ninety-eight," Jerry said, checking his watch.
Everyone groaned. "At least it isn't like that oven land we were
in not that long ago. Come on, this is great compared to that!"
"Wes weren't hanging on a horensling when we left," Victor
exclaimed, also falling to the ground. "A horensling is a creature

that sleeps in a volcano all day. It would be very hot. When you got off its, anything would feel cool to yous."

"I was on it for fifteen seconds," Jerry said in a disbelieving tone. "It couldn't have affected me *that* bad."

"And weren't you the one who got his face soaked in lava?" John asked. "And also your leg?"

"Once again, it wasn't that long of a period," Jerry said, shaking his head. "Geez…"

"Look!" Jimmy gasped from the floor. "It's the metal door! And there's a note on it…"

They ran over to it. Yes, there was a note on it. It said the words:

Touch this note

Jerry reached over and touched it. The note suddenly began to change. First the word went away and was replaced by a name:

Jerry Vincent Quaill
Others touch this note.

Everyone touched it and their names appeared on it too. Alvin didn't touch it. Then something else appeared on the note:
> *I am two and six's constant mean,*
> *I can go into 12 and 20 but not 18,*
> *Also I am a letter that isn't in 'gland',*
> *Because it rates a movie for who can,*
> *Third I am something that is childish,*
> *A letter that's a part of a two-letter delish,*
> *I'm a sound made by something creepy,*
> *A snake, or something that's weepy,*
> *Put them together, you'll know without a doubt,*
> *Something you cannot drive without.*

"See? I told you," Jimmy said. "It's a riddle. Now how are we going to solve it?"

"Step-by-step," Paul said. "It's a step-by-step riddle. Ok first, what's two and six's constant mean?"

"Pardon the pun," Jerry asked. "But what does 'mean' mean?"

"It's the average of multiple numbers," Paul replied.

"It's four," Alvin said.

"How?" Paul asked.

"The only numbers that multiply to twenty," Alvin replied, "are ten, two, five and four. Ten and five aren't it because they aren't multiples of twelve. This says this number cannot go into eighteen, so it can't be two. That only leaves four. Plus, the average of two and six is four."

"I'm confused," Tyler said.

"It's math really," Alvin responded. "What's it next say?"

They read it.

"'Rates a movie for who can'...'" Paul said. "Like PG! Or G!"

"But the letter isn't in the word 'gland'," John said. "So how about 'R'!"

"That's right!" Alvin said. "What's next?"

"Part of a delish with two letters," John said. "What's this?"

"I am guessing 'delish' means a dessert or a candy," Alvin replied, "but I am not sure."

Jerry smiled, announcing, "*M&M's*."

"M!" Paul said. "That's letter in a candy. Good thinking Jerry."

"Ok, then there's the last lines," Victor said. "And I think I can use English now, my accent has gotten better. A snake..."

"Makes a hissing noise," Jimmy said. "But how would you say that?"

"Ssssssss," Tyler said. "Like that."

"So it makes what ever we are trying to say, plural," Alvin said. "So what are they combined?"

"Something you can't drive without," Paul said.

"A license?" Jerry guessed.

"No, no, it can't be," Tyler said.

"That wouldn't make sense," Alvin reprimanded.

"We also would have guessed that first," John said.

"Alright, alright," Jerry defensively interrupted, "I admit I was wrong, but it's not as if something went wrong, right?"

"Yeah, but you better watch it," Paul said. "Or it might be bad if we get it wrong. I won't be surprised if Zyno has one more trick up his sleeve."

"Add them together," John continued.

"Four...R...M...sss—four... rms, I know! Forearms!"

"Yes," Jerry said. "But how do we write it in?"

Immediately, a pen appeared in Jerry's hand. He took a deep breath.

"This is it, guys," Jerry said. "We accomplished every obstacle, every riddle, and every test that the greatest scientist in the world could present to us. Now we finally get to meet him."

"The dead ends..." Lino suddenly said.

"What?" Paul asked.

"Just something I noticed," Lino said. "We head towards the dead ends in this maze. We usually try to avoid dead ends. We try to not face our problems. Zyno, regardless of which side he is on, has taught us something: we can try to get through the journey by avoiding these dead ends...but to accomplish the journey correctly...we have to accept all feats...learn from them, and use them to our advantage. Without using this philosophy, we would have failed. We can carry this on...for the rest of our lives."

"Thank you, Socrates," Paul said, rolling his eyes. "But I think the more important thing is getting this whole dang thing over with. We need to capture him before our uncle gets here. You all ready to take this guy down?"

"Since the beginning," Lino growled.

"It will be my absolute pleasure," John said, rolling up his sleeves.

"He is my master...no more," Victor said.

"I want his body to rot in prison for the rest of his life," Jimmy commented.

"I am a force to be reckoned with," Tyler snarled.

"As for Benjamin, let me introduce him to my sword," Jerry said courageously.

Sheen roared in anticipation. Everyone turned to Alvin.

"Wait," Alvin said. "Before we enter into Zyno's lab, brace yourself. When the doors open, pull out your weapons. Also, my name will be revealed. You will understand later."

They nodded. Jerry wrote "forearms" on the paper. The door slowly opened. They ran in and pulled out their weapons. Zyno was sitting in a chair with something in his hand. He pressed a button on it and said:

"Ten hours, two minutes and 43 seconds. I expected better from you, all of you. Especially you," he grinned, tossed his stop watch over his shoulder, and looked at Alvin dead in the eyes, "Daniel Quaill."

18) Answers

John, Paul and Jerry looked at Alvin.

"U-uncle Dan?" John stuttered. Alvin nodded his head.

"But, why? How?"

"What's this?" Zyno said, looking between the pair of them. "You didn't even tell your own nephews you were their uncle? My, my … "

"They could have been the holograms you know," Dan snapped. "When I heard you did have spies on me, I couldn't tell my own nephews, for they might have been the spies."

"I see," Zyno sneered. He turned to the three Quaills, "And none of you recognized your own uncle?"

"The last time I saw him," Jerry answered, "was when I was seven."

"I saw him a long time ago, I don't even remember when," John said.

Paul gazed at Dan and said, "I have never seen my uncle in my life. I was always too young. I only heard stories … "

"Amazing stories, I am sure," Zyno said seriously. Two figures appeared behind him. One, was obviously Benjamin, the other was hooded. "But you still don't know who the holograms are? Let me show you who they are."

He snapped his fingers. John and Paul quickly looked at Jerry, but he remained still.

"Then," John began, "Who—"

Something hard hit him and Paul in the back and pulled them up to the wall. Paul turned and saw who it was: Jimmy and Tyler.

"No," John said. "How could it be you?"

"Very easily," Tyler said smiling. "Zyno captured the real Tyler and Jimmy while they were making a call on their walkie-talkie. He stopped them immediately and replaced them with us."

"I thought the batteries died," John moaned.

"No," Jimmy laughed. "Don't you remember? We used the same batteries to help with your brother's station. If they were dead, it wouldn't have worked."

"I didn't catch that," John said, defeated.

"You had it wrong when you said that you were 15," Paul said angrily. "Tyler isn't 15; he's 12. I just thought you said that to make yourself more proud to our uncle."

"Isn't it convenient," Tyler said, pushing harder on them, "That I had learned to fly a plane?"

"Yeah, your dad is a pilot," John said, "Wait, that's not true … your dad moves wood … a carpenter. You told me."

"But you didn't catch that either," Tyler laughed.

"Your computer figured it out, though," Jimmy said. "In the fifth world, he noticed something strange about us."

"I noticed it," Paul said. "But I didn't think anything of it."

"Obviously, genius," Jimmy said, pushing harder. Lino jumped into the air and tried to tackle Jimmy, but he went through him.

"Ah yes, about the tiger and Thog," Zyno said. "You are both my creations. I have control over you, so goodbye to you both."

He snapped his fingers. Victor disappeared, but Lino didn't. Lino got up and smiled.

"What?" Zyno said, frustrated, "What happened?"

"Duh, don't you remember?" Lino laughed, shaking his fur. "I was the first tiger you brought into the world, so I actually exist. You had brought me back from scarce DNA. I couldn't remember it myself until I walked in here. You must have put a memory device into me. Victor was not the original one, you had created him."

Zyno smiled.

"Oh well, can't have things the easy way, can we?" he said. The hyena came back out of the shadows. "Hyena, finish him."

It pounced at Lino and Lino pounced back. Zyno looked at Sheen, who was growling.

"Hatching dragons, Dan? Well, since I only created the egg, you made him. I can only turn him back into a baby," Zyno said. He typed on something behind him and Sheen shrunk back to a baby dragon. Zyno turned towards Dan and Jerry. "Well I guess we can't leave you guys out, can we? Finish them, Benjamin and Zach."

Benjamin pulled out a sword and headed toward Jerry.

"You owe me $7.43," he said, taking a slash at Jerry. Jerry pulled out his sword and deflected it, "for gas."

"Ah, my dear Daniel, we meet again," Said the hooded figure.

"Yes," Dan said. "I'm terribly sorry that you left the *Ring*. You were a powerful sorcerer."

"Were?!" Zach said. "What do you mean, were?! I am still alive, aren't I?"

"Yes," Dan said. "The owner of the great Ring of Death. Sorry to say this, but I also have a ring. The Ring of Fate!"

"I can control who dies and who doesn't," Zach said fiercely.

"While I can control what the outcome is," Daniel said, lying.

"I guess we can't settle this with rings," Zach said reaching into his pocket. "We can only settle this by wands!"

He pulled out an instrument half a foot long. Then Zach laughed.

"That's right; you can't work your magic."

"You're not the only one with a wand," Dan said, pulling out his sword angrily. The sword transfigured into a wand. Dan shot a spell at Zach, but Zach countered it with a different spell. They shot magic spells at each other until Dan's spell hit Zach in the gut and knocked him to the ground.

"Give in," Dan said, breathing hard. "And rejoin the *Ring*. It is not completely without mercy."

"I know that," Zach said, pointing his wand at himself. "But I stay loyal to Zyno. Goodbye, one who I had once called a friend."

"No," Dan said, about to conjure a spell. Zach immediately said, "*Quarellent!*"

With that, he disappeared. John, seeing all this felt a sharp stab in his stomach. It had no explanation (but he would learn in three years). He then saw Paul's computer on the ground. He stretched his foot down and kicked it open. Flaminetore came out.

"That's enough," Flaminetore said, punching the hologram forms of Jimmy and Tyler. He fought both at once and started to win.

John's mind was suddenly covered in blackness. He felt strings on his arms and legs. He was a puppet. Zyno was making him move. He swung John's arms up and grabbed something John couldn't see. But he could fight; he could feel it. He pulled off the strings and attacked Zyno. He went back to the present, where he was holding Paul.

"Whoa," John said. "Something weird happened. Sorry Paul."

Flaminetore stopped Zyno's holograms from attacking John or Paul again. Jerry was battling furiously against Benjamin.

"You failed to kill me once, you'll fail again," Jerry cried.

"Sure, what are you going to do about it?" Benjamin asked sneering. Jerry saw a crowbar on a desk. He tried to use his powerful psychic powers to lift it. He saw it rise up.

"I'm going to take you down," Jerry said, grinning.

"How?" Benjamin asked.

"Just like this," Jerry said. He used the power to smash it against Benjamin's head. Benjamin fell to the ground, unconscious. "Now for old scum face."

Lino had beat up the hyena so badly that the hyena could barely lift its wing. Lino jumped off it and it got up again.

"Well, now you know the better one of the two of us," Lino said. The hyena just looked at him.

"You might have beaten me," he said. "But my descendents will torture you and your entire family. You may kill me now, but you know deep inside you that you're nothing but a Pink Leopard!"

Lino became mad and was about to rip him to nothing but shreds of skin, but the hyena ran to Zyno's aid. Everyone looked at Zyno, who knew he was outnumbered. He pressed a button and a cage went over them all.

"See you later!" he called. He ran out the door riding on the hyena. Paul squeezed through his bars and flew over to the door (being a genie, this was easy). He freed everyone, and John followed Paul outside through the back door.

"Man, if only we had known about that back door before," John groaned. "Come on! We have to get Zyno!"

John felt a powerful gust of wind as he put his hand up in the air to where Zyno was escaping. His hand turned dark red and a powerful ball of lightning shot at Zyno. Zyno became immobile in a magical sphere and John pulled him back. Paul stretched his arm very high up and caught Zyno. He knocked Zyno to the ground. Paul got down and put pressure on Zyno's neck.

"Give up," Paul said. "The game is over. We're done here. Give up."

"It's never over!" the hyena screamed. John shot lightning at him, too, but the hyena dodged it.

Zyno stopped struggling. Then he bowed his head.

"Yes," He said. Then he looked up at the hyena and nodded.

"NO!" The hyena said, coming to the ground. "We can't give up now, master! Unleash the Thogeens! Release the pack! Do something!"

Pivoting on his foot to face the hyena, John removed his sword from his belt.

"I have waited a long time for this," John said, almost growling at him. "You have messed with me and my brothers for the last time!"

"I will die for you, master," The hyena said, angrier than ever before. "There's no way I am going to give up this easily. After all that has happened, I am not giving this up now."

John spun his sword forward and went towards the hyena. The hyena opened its wings and shot towards him. With a powerful kick, it kicked the sword out of John's hand. It did, however, cut the hyena's foot... enough for the hyena to fall to the ground in pain. John got up and reached back.

"Paul, give me your ax!" He shouted. Paul moved his hand from Zyno's throat to throw the ax to John. That was enough for Zyno to roll from under him and start running towards a bike ... the bike that had rockets on the back.

"I'll get him, you worry about the hyena!" Paul said, stretching his arm to get John's sword. He grabbed it and ran towards Zyno. Suddenly, Zach appeared out of nowhere in his black cloak and clotheslined him. Paul fell to the ground.

"*I've* got Zyno, you get the hyena," John yelled to Paul. They swapped weapons. John ran at Zach. Zach reached for his belt, which had a sword. Zach removed the long sword that had a weird looking symbol on the hilt. Zach swept the sword hard at John who barely deflected it in time. When he did, it was so powerful that it knocked him to the ground. The unknown pain in the stomach region burned John again. John glanced at Zyno, who he saw was very close to the bike.

Paul approached the hyena again. The hyena stayed his distance. Paul stretched his foot behind him where the hyena wasn't looking. The hyena took a step forward, enough for Paul to swing his kick. The now stretched foot went into the hyena's side, knocking him to the ground. Paul charged and jumped at him. The hyena got up and ran to Zach's aid.

Zach noticed him coming, giving John enough time to run past him. He ran flat out at Zyno, who mounted the bike and was beginning to fire it up. John felt an invisible force pulling him back and noticed that Zach was using his magic on him.

Paul saw what was happening and shot his ax at Zach's risen arm. The ax hit his hand and Zach clasped it with his other hand in pain. John broke free and sliced a rocket off Zyno's bike. Zyno pulled the gas, but it was broken.

Paul went forward to finish off Zach, but Zach turned to him first.

"You'll be the first one to experience true pain, Quaill," Zach said. "You are dealing with something much bigger than you know. You will suffer. You mark my words."

At that, Zach shot magic at Paul as he raised his ax. Paul was unready and was knocked to the ground. Zach grabbed the hyena and disappeared. Zyno saw he was outnumbered yet again when everyone else started to come outside. Even though John was closer, Paul got to Zyno first.

"You wanted me to be at your mercy," Paul said, gripping Zyno's throat. "Truth is, we're better than you ... we always will be. You think that you can just steal our minds for yourself, but we will always be smarter than you. So I give you the same offer I did before. Are you going to give up?"

"I ... guess," Zyno gasped, "that ... this ... means ... that ... you ... are ... turning ... down ... my offer ... to ... give you ...glory ... strength ... power ... something ... no one ... will...ever ... offer?"

"I have that," Paul snarled, triumphant. "You never did ... you never will. I promise you that. But this game is over. The maze is over. The journey is over. Give—up!"

Zyno stopped struggling. He glared up at Paul with pure hatred in his eyes. Yet he smiled and said the three words, "I give up."

"Thank you again for capturing these two," an officer said an hour later, "we have been looking for this Benjamin guy for seven years. Attempted murder and other charges. This Zyno character we will do a thorough investigation on. Please accept our thank you."

"I think we can accept it," John said, counting his thousands he had been given. They were putting Zyno and Benjamin into a car. After fifteen minutes of explaining what happened, John asked Dan, "What happened with the puppet thing? Zyno was controlling me. What happened?"

"I can answer that," Jerry said. "The potion you took in the land not only healed you, but also contained the potion Paul said it contained. And yes, it did have something in it that hid some of the ingredients. Al—I mean Uncle Dan—said Zyno had given it to you because Zyno was impatient and he wanted you 'out of that land ASAP'… which I knew was wrong, because no time passed when we went into the land and when we exited the land. I knew this because I checked my watch before we entered the first land and checked it when we left it because Paul wanted to know how hot it was in there. So I had part of good inside you when Flaminetore healed you. That's why I cut off you arm, because a bad part of your body was removed and then he healed it, removing the bad stuff."

"I see," John said smiling. "That's genius work I tell you."

The officer came running back towards them with Jimmy and Tyler at hand.

"Here are your friends," He said. "And Zyno said that someone named Paul could keep his lab. He said he didn't need it anymore."

"Cool," Paul said. "I get to keep the maze? That's awesome."

The officer scratched his head.

"I didn't say anything about any maze, son," he said. "But this building is so big, someone could consider it a maze."

"It's ok," Paul said, pocketing his money. "This sure will cover college."

Jerry then thought of something.

"Uh, officer?" He said. "Could I ask the scientist something?"

"Sure," the officer said. "Just hurry up, they are about to leave."

Jerry ran over to the car. He told the other officers that he needed to see him.

"Ok, hurry, we are about to leave," Said the chief. Jerry got in the back of the suburban and saw Zyno and Ben tied up, Ben now conscious.

"What do you want?" Zyno said.

"I didn't want to talk to you," he said, sneering at Zyno. He looked at Ben, "I wanted to talk to someone I had an argument within the lab, my dear friend Ben."

"What is it?"

"Well, I needed to give you something," Jerry said, reaching into his pocket.

"What?" Ben said, looking hopeful as Jerry was rummaging through his pocket. "Something I could use in jail?"

"Do you really think I am really thick enough to give you something to break out of jail, and then let you hunt us down and kill us?"

"I don't know, just give it to me all ready," Ben yelled so hard that spit flew on Jerry's face. Jerry shook his head.

"You shouldn't treat me that way, Ben," Jerry said, taking out a 10-dollar bill. He thrusted it at Ben. "For five gallons of gas. Go crazy."

Zyno looked angry as he looked at what Jerry had given them.

"You think you have gotten away with this?" Zyno said. "We planned something ahead of time, and you better hope to your God that Zach didn't do it."

"What was it?" Jerry asked skeptically.

"I have a right to remain silent," Zyno said. "But you haven't heard the last of us. We will break out in no time. You cannot stop Zach. You and all the Quaills will pay!"

"Yeah right," Jerry said.

"You don't believe us?" Ben said. "Here, take this ticket. Maybe you can figure it out."

Jerry looked at the ticket Ben had given him. It read: *Phoenix, Arizona, USA.*

Jerry looked at them.

"Still don't understand?" Zyno said. "Well just think about this … why do you think we were defeated so easily?"

"Wishful thinking, Zyno, Jerry said. "I hope the jail mates treat you well."

Jerry sneered and left the vehicle. He thanked the chief.

"I'll take you guys home," Daniel told the three Quaills. They all stuffed inside Daniel's small car. John looked out the window at the large lab.

"It's hard to imagine we only spent a few hours in there. Zyno really is amazing in the ways of controlling time," John muttered.

"Indeed," Daniel sighed. "He has always been a threat, even to the magical race."

"That Zach … " Paul whispered. "Was that the rebellious magician you were referring to?"

Daniel nodded.

"So … so that man … could have killed our dad?" Paul questioned.

"I think so," Daniel sighed.

They pulled into their driveway … to find a horrific sight. Their house was on fire.

Daniel leapt out of the driver's seat and looked about. The flames completely consumed the house.

"Stay in the vehicle," Daniel commanded as Jerry was about to get out. In the dead of night, nothing could be seen beside what the fire revealed.

But there was a lone figure standing in front of the inferno. He was hooded.

"Zach," Jerry whispered. Before the others could move, John leapt out of the car and raced up to his uncle. Daniel made no attempts to stop him. They both approached the arsonist.

Nobody spoke. They stood for a few minutes with daggers in their eyes.

"Was my sister-in-law in there?" Daniel asked, barely audible.

Zach flashed a grin. He whipped his snake-like hair off of his face. His skin was almost as white as his horrible teeth that bore like a demon.

"You single-handedly made my nephews orphans," Daniel growled.

"Don't go that far, Danny-boy," Zach hissed. "Soon you too will have to yield under my blade."

John made to grab his sword, but Daniel stopped him.

"You do realize that there will be a war? You have openly defied every living magician," Daniel snarled at Zach.

"I have many, many plans," Zach laughed in a way that made John recoil. "I'll give you very fair warning … should you worry about Zyno or me?"

With that, and a puff of black smoke, Zach disappeared.

"Uncle Dan," John shook. His house was almost completely destroyed. His mother … was dead.

His uncle turned to face him. The other two slowly joined them.

"I am sorry you have become involved in this," Daniel began.

"You mean 'were involved', right?" Paul corrected in a hopeful breath.

"No," Daniel sighed. "Because of this journey, I believe you will now have to live in a new world. A world of magic, a world of danger, a world of war, a world where happy endings are not promised. We have impossible goals, higher expectations, and greater responsibilities."

"But you are never alone," A growl came from behind them. They turned to see Lino walking in a prowl-like way. "We will always have each other. Meet our dead-ends head on, with each other."

All the Quaills held a hopeful smile. They didn't know what was going to happen next, all that they knew was that they had merely opened the door to the labyrinth called "Life."

Epilogue

Dan spent the night and told them this was their last night together. Paul, not being able to go inside the house at night, slept outdoors and was very uncomfortable. The next day, John was flown to Ransville where he would be trained as a magician. Paul was sent to Billington where he would be trained to be a genie. Jerry was sent out to the borderline of Australia and Locomony, where the two continued the Thousand-Year War. Dan went with him. As they were all flying in different directions, all of them had mixed feelings. John was mad his uncle didn't tell them his name, Jerry was sad about leaving his brothers and Paul thought he was too young to know how to become a genie. But as they all boarded their planes, one thing was very clear: Zach was still at large, and they would have to capture him before he gained too much power. They would all miss each other but they would all have one thing in common— they made it through their first journey together. They would also accomplish more journeys in the next few years.

For the Maze was only the first of their Perpetual Journeys.

The Quaill Brothers

Introduction

Three years have passed since the Quaills had accomplished the journey through the maze. After three years of mystical training, John, Paul and Jerry were unrecognizable in their magical powers. Paul, coming to the age of nine, had an unthinkable IQ. He had already finished his studies with doctorates in philosophy, astronomy, geology, mathematics and paleontology. He also graduated from mythical school, which had helped him train in his genie powers. John, at 14, had graduated from his magician school with flying colors. He would be able to get his "wand"—or magic license— at the age of 16. Jerry, who just turned 17, had been fighting in the War of Locombony for three years; it had made him strong and tall. He was a psychic, and his magic could do unbelievable things. They had not been together or seen their uncle for the three years they had been apart.

All three were legendary in their wealth and in their defeat of the most dangerous scientists in the world: Zyno Wayne and Benjamin Xeronin. Still, they were unable to catch the third and perhaps most dangerous of the trio – Zach. All but John had last seen him heading for the jail, but fortunately, he had not been able to free Zyno or Ben. Paul sent a message to all the Quaills to come together to plan an attack against this archenemy. Zach gathered some followers to try and free Zyno so that Zyno's unknown plan for world destruction would be carried out. However Zyno is still imprisoned, yet Zach has done nothing – he is planning global annihilation.

It is the silence before the storm. The small island of Locombony and the world now turn to the Quaills to stop the evil trio from carrying this horrible plan out ... this is where the Journey begins ...

Prologue

Zach waited impatiently. His men were supposed to be
here hours ago. He checked his watch again and grumbled. He
walked into an open field and still saw nobody. He reached into
his pocket and pulled out his wand and an atlas map.

"Number one? Is that you?" said a voice from the forest.

"Who enters this place?" Zach asked, pointing his wand in
the direction of the voice.

"Number eleven," He replied, walking out of the forested
area. He was completely hooded so that Zach couldn't see his
face. "Why did we have to meet here so early?"

"Because," Zach said, trying to be patient. "We needed to
avoid searching eyes."

"Right," Eleven said. "So why are we supposed to meet
here?"

"Eleven," Zach said, holding his temper by a thread. It was
just too early to get on Zach's bad side. "I needed some
magician followers to help me so we can get to the ship."

"Ship?" Eleven asked.

"MY GOD, ELEVEN," Zach yelled angrily. "Do you ever
pay attention? We are heading to Phoenix!"

"I know that," Eleven said quickly. "But I was just
wondering why we were going by ship instead of by plane. It
would be easier."

"They are about to shut down plane travel, you know that,"
Zach said. "And there are no other methods of getting there.
Now do you understand why we destroyed almost all of those
ships?"

"No," Eleven said.

"It feels like I am trying to teach a baby how to write,"
Zach said. "If we wipe out those ships we can get to the island
and Phoenix without any interference."

"Right," Eleven said. "Should we wait for the others?"

"No," Zach said hurriedly. "I only have room for one more. We have to go."

"Hold on," Eleven said nervously. "What if the Quaills show up?"

"Then we'll give them what they deserve, those brats," Zach said. "Still, one is almost an adult now, right?"

"Seventeen, I believe," Eleven said. "And quite rich."

"Yeah, that's another factor," Zach said, turning to him, "Hopefully, when this is all said and done, money will no longer be an issue. I will own everything. But the nuclear power costs were ridiculous—"

"You used nuclear power?" Eleven asked.

Zach clenched his fists together. He was almost cool-tempered until now.

"Yes," he said through his teeth. "We needed it for Roboblast. Just in case this plan of mine fails, the world will pay."

"What's Roboblast?" Eleven asked again.

"WHY DIDN'T SOMEONE ELSE COME?!" Zach yelled. "WHY DID AN IDIOT HAVE TO SHOW UP?!"

"Sorry, One," Eleven said quietly. "I am not thinking clearly at two in the morning."

"Neither am I," Zach said angrily. "And do you know what happens when I am tired?"

Eleven said nothing.

"I—" Zach pulled out his wand, "—get—" grabbed Eleven, " —very—" put his wand at Eleven's chest, over his heart, "—ANGRY!"

Eleven swallowed. Zach, realizing what he was doing, let go.

"Come on," Zach said. "It's about time."

They both walked across the field in silence to the other side of the forest. They had to avoid a dead log in the middle of the field. When they got there they heard a rustling of the bushes. Zach stuck up his wand.

"Who goes there?" He said.

"Number Eleven," A voice said.

"Nice try, fraud," Zach's eyes widening. "Show yourself!"

"No, it's really me – One," A person said coming out of the bushes. He was also hooded.

"Fraud!" Zach yelled, pointing his wand at him. "Number Eleven is right next to me. Time to die!"

He was about to cast a spell when the first Number Eleven stepped in front of him.

"Let him go, Zach," He said. "You've killed enough innocent people, and in the near future you will be killing much more. At least kill someone for a reason. He's just obeying your orders."

Zach took a step back at being addressed by his name. Then he realized what the statement meant.

"Daniel! How dare you stand in my presence!" Zach said as the fake Number Eleven unhooded himself. The true Number Eleven stepped back.

"You told me all your plans and that's all I need to know," Daniel said. Number Eleven unhooded himself as well. "Now I understand why you didn't free Zyno before."

"Not for long you won't," Number Eleven said. "Soon the rest of us will come, and you'll be outnumbered and dead!"

"Why? Can you raise people from the dead?" Daniel asked Zach. "You lost your Ring of Fate … and the Ring of Death."

"Raise … wait, what?" Zach said.

"Why don't you think anyone else showed up Zach?" Daniel said.

"You killed them?!" Zach yelled.

"And I hope to do the same thing to you," Daniel said in a fierce voice, "considering what you did to my brother! I'll let you go this time, Zach. But be warned: the Quaills are coming for you."

Daniel – for the first time – made eye contact with Number Eleven.

"Now that I know the truth."

Daniel clapped his hands and disappeared.

"NO!" Zach screamed. "I WILL KILL YOU ALL DAN! YOU CANNOT STOP ME NOW!"

"He had the nerve to show up," Number Eleven said, almost as angrily as Daniel. "Are we leaving?"

"Yes," Zach said, staring hard at a dead log lying on the ground. "But there is a change of plans. We are no longer taking the Northern route."

Eleven understood perfectly.

"Let's go."

1.) The Legends

John Quaill pulled his cloak tighter as he walked under a full moon. He heard wolves in the forest howl as the grass crunched under his feet. It was a little into December and the darkness surrounding him was creepy. It was no help that it was midnight and he was walking alone. John looked around as he crossed a small cliff heading off into the sea. The waves crashed onto shore and John wondered how he had gotten here. He looked back upon the past few years...

Three years previously, Zach left an imprint on John: a second soul and personality. With it, Zach attempted to control him, which explained the "sharp pain" in his gut when Zach had escaped. But until this past year, it had no effect on him.

In the last 12 months, John had finished a journey of his own. Zach had attempted to steal the power of the *Ring* council, which stored their power in rings. Zach managed to get nearly all of them, and because of that, he had almost complete control. The only reason he didn't have absolute power was he was missing the mysterious Ring of Life, which was hidden away from even the *Ring* council.

The spirit inserted into John slowed down his process of stopping Zach. Eventually, he found himself having to fight a mental battle with the creature. He barely survived.

By himself, John built up an army to face Zach and all his creations: zombies, imps and other horrible monsters. A large battle ensued, and John's army barely prevailed against them. But when the time came to face Zach himself, Zach exterminated all John's army. John and his uncle had to stand up to Zach in the end. Zach countered every shot they fired, and easily took them out of commission. With his last breath, John was able to transform himself into a werewolf, or Morphelellist in magician's terms. He reached the "last stage" of Morphelellism, which was never accomplished anyone before (furthering his reputation within the magical world). As a werewolf, he became immune to the powers of the Rings. John ripped off the rings from Zach's own hand. Weakened, Zach disappeared. Now, John's morph – because it was complete – was nearly impossible to reverse. He could not maintain control of his body, and his mind was trapped due to the power of the morph. In the theories about a complete morph, it was thought to be impossible to stop by exterior or interior force. This werewolf had stopped the most powerful creature in the universe, and was now out of control and unstoppable. The only way to survive its wrath was to evade it until such time that the overload of power caused it to self destruct.

But John was a special case – being made of two persons – thanks to Zach. He forced the evil spirit that Zach had put into him into the Morphelellist … which, in turn, died from the power overload. John barely survived the mental and physical trauma.

Now as John looked at his hands, he could see in the moonlight the black claws at the tips of his fingers – permanent remnant and constant reminder of his morph.

"I will never forget those days," John said. "And if my family reunites, I will never leave them again. They are the only thing I have left."

All of John's friends had been killed in the battle, including Jimmy, Tyler, but most painfully, his girlfriend, whom he loved very much. John vowed he would kill Zach for all the death he had caused.

John had spent all of his money on the war. His brother, Paul, who now owned a business, sold his inventions every month and was no doubt the richest child in the world. Paul didn't own a house because there was no need for it; he was a genie and lived in a lamp. After the war, Paul had kindly given John money to support his house and land. But because of the large debts, John was forced to sell his property.

John gazed out at the wavy ocean and wondered if he might someday go back to his brother's lab and travel through his maze again.

Suddenly John heard a rumbling above him. He turned quickly and saw a dark shape high in the air. John immediately reached for his belt where his sword hung. John vividly remembered where he had gotten his sword: when he was in the maze he had to fight a war on an unknown planet – called Venemay – for unknown creatures called Thogs.

John thought he might have to face another unknown creature as the monster in the air landed on the ground. He let go of his hilt and put his hand over his arm. He thought "Shield. I need a shield." Instantly, a metal kite-shield appeared on his arm. He pulled out the sword and began to prepare for an attack. As the creature got closer, John saw how big it truly was. It was as large as a dinosaur. But once it unrolled wings from its back, John understood that it was no dinosaur; it was a dragon.

"Come on, Sheen," John said, referring to a dragon he had met. "Where are you when I need you?"

The dragon got closer to him. John realized he had no way of defeating it. True, he had a little magic, but he couldn't take down a dragon on his own. It came within 10 feet of him. John was about to run away when the dragon bent its head down so that John could look directly into the eyes of the dragon. John breathed heavily and dropped his weapons. It *was* Sheen.

"Sheen," John said. "You shouldn't scare me like that. I thought you were going to kill me."

John smiled, but then thought a moment. It was foolish of him to jump to conclusions like that. True, he was a little shaken from the two life-threatening journeys he had to endure in a stretch of three years, but John knew now he would have to get over it. If he jumped at objects in the sky or people he didn't know, he might end up in the same place Zyno was.

"Well I guess it doesn't matter now," John said. "But what are you doing here?"

Sheen lowered his head further and John saw a note tied to its ear. John quickly removed it and read it carefully, knowing it had to be important if someone used Sheen to carry it to him.

Dear John,

I am glad you got this letter without any interference. My dragon should hopefully get it to you without interruption, and now I can relax from using my pseudonym. I am sorry to say that I was requested by Jerry to fight in the war against Australia; our reunion will have to be put off until later. To keep you updated, my lab has been under attack many times by Zach and I almost lost the maze. My Thog army is just barely holding out. The ways of communication are thin now and I was forced to use Sheen. On his back – if you don't already see them – are some items you might find useful.

John quickly looked onto Sheen's back and found Paul's laptop, his ax, a sack of something and a small wooden box.

I have seen Uncle Dan recently and he said something about stopping Zach's plan, but he was in a hurry. He also mentioned being near you, so I hope you guys can get together without us. Zyno isn't even close to breaking out; he is under such a tight guard. Good luck catching Zach, and I hope to be fighting with you soon.

Best wishes,

Dr. Paul M. Quaill

John quickly gazed over the many letters corresponding to the numerous terminal degrees of education Paul had included under his name.

P.S. Lino is also traveling from my lab in secret and hopefully will get to you soon.

John grinned happily as he thought of the idea of catching up with his friend Lino, who he had not seen in a long time. But as he reread the letter, he frowned. Even his brother had to fight against Zach.

He had read up on the war Paul was talking about. It seemed to be enduring since the beginning of time. It was fought between the small and independent island of Locombony and the empire of Australia.

John looked at the items and wondered why Paul had sent them to him. Paul's laptop had been one of his most precious possessions and John felt Paul needed it more than he did. John opened Paul's laptop and a familiar hologram sprung out of it. The hologram looked around and – once it saw John – jumped back.

"Who are you?" It said. "Where is my master?"

"Calm down, Flaminetore," John said. "I am your master's brother, don't you remember me?"

Flaminetore looked John up and down and sighed.

"Yes, I do," Flaminetore said. "But I haven't seen you in three years. I have to say that this computer isn't capable of immediately recognizing people's identity."

"You mean Paul hasn't upgraded you by now?" John asked curiously.

"Sadly, no," Flaminetore sighed. "He built a new one and forgot about me."

"That's sad," John said. "You were so much help in the maze that I thought Paul would perfect you."

"He did," Flaminetore muttered. "But just on another computer."

"I'll talk to him about it," John reassured. "You saved our lives; that's got to count for something. But for now, can you explain what he sent?"

"Certainly," Flaminetore said. He picked up the bag. "This is pure gold that can be used in any country. My master figured you might be heading out of the country for a while, so he gave you the gold for money. It's a lot easier than trying to 'translate' ours into theirs."

"That's a good idea," John agreed. "What else is there again?"

"There's the ax," Flaminetore commented, "which has a large amount of upgrades. My master can now grip his ax tight and lightning will come out; he doesn't have to use his emotions anymore."

"That sort of loses its point, though," John teased. "But why is he giving it to me?"

"I am not sure," Flaminetore admitted. "I think by now, he doesn't need it."

"And what about this box," John asked, picking up the box that was the length of a finger.

"That contains some of my master's best medicine," Flaminetore explained, taking the box and opening it. The inside contained many small tablets. "They can heal you of any injury. It is made of dragon's saliva."

John remembered when Sheen spit on Jerry when he almost died of a lava eruption. Jerry was instantly healed.

"One more question," John asked.

"Sure," Flaminetore said indifferently.

"What does 'pseudonym' mean?" John asked.

Flaminetore laughed.

"It means pen name or alias," Flaminetore explained. "He kept using a pseudonym with his other letters because he hoped when someone else read it, he wouldn't be discovered."

"He had the pen name for a reason?" John said. "I thought he chose to sign letters 'Peter' just to be funny. Who else that would read his letters could be dangerous?"

"Zach would," Flaminetore said, and that was all John needed. John didn't need to be reminded about how they were constantly looking for the evil sorcerer or how many lives Zach had cost them.

"Besides, you're a legend," Flaminetore added. "You and your brothers are all legends. Anyone would want to be you. They could kill you to get your fame."

"So even if Zach is killed or arrested, people would still want to kill me?" John said angrily. "I am going to move to China."

"No, you won't," Flaminetore laughed. "How are you going to get there?"

"By plane, I don't care," John said, facing the ocean again. "Or by dragon."

Sheen snarled.

"Or by ship," John whispered.

"Your brothers need you," Flaminetore said softly. "You can't betray them."

"My brothers ... " John said, staring at the ground. "I haven't seen them in three years. My life has fallen apart."

John fell to the ground and shut off the laptop so he wouldn't hear Flaminetore speak. He put his face into his hands. Sheen reached down and nudged him lovingly, which nearly knocked John onto his stomach.

"It's confusing, Sheen," John lamented, looking up at the dragon. "Zach killed my mother, my friends, and split my family away from each other. I would still be back home, my mom still alive, my brothers with me and I wouldn't have met some of my now dead friends if I ... if we had decided to stay home instead of going into that maze. And who knows? Uncle Dan might not have needed us. He might have defeated Zyno by himself."

John marveled at the sea as he saw it calm down into small waves. He sighed and thought how beautiful it would be, standing up on Sheen, if his uncle and brothers were beside him as they flew over the ocean, free of all problems. He could see

Paul, sitting on Sheen's head, explaining how Sheen's saliva had a healing ability. He could see Jerry laying back and talking about the war he had been through. He could see Dan standing up, smiling as he talked about the inventions he recently created and how the *Ring* council was holding up.

John realized that he would never see this picture in real life. But he couldn't help looking at the waves and wondering if he could ever ride on a ship in such calm waters. He knew what his dream ship would look like and imagined a beautiful ship on the sea, speeding away from them …

John blinked. There *was* a ship out there. It had its sails up and was flying through the water. The wind suddenly picked up as it passed, as if the captain could control the wind. There was something about this boat, however, that made John uneasy. Sheen obviously felt the same way, because he straightened up. John looked back at the ship and realized that was going too fast for a ship like that. John glanced back at Sheen. Sheen stared back at him, as if awaiting instructions.

"God knows what's on that ship," John said. "And now, we will too."

John summoned up a backpack with his magic and threw Paul's items in it. He tossed it on his back and jumped on Sheen.

"Let's go," John said hurriedly. "Let's get out there now!"

As Sheen lifted its wings, John thought of something else. He remembered what he had said to himself when Sheen appeared.

"No, wait Sheen," John said, ashamed. "It's probably nothing. I am just jumping to conclusions. The captain is probably some medieval freak who loves those ships."

Sheen gave an angry roar and continued to flap its wings.

"Sheen, get down!" John cried. "We can't take that chance! If anyone saw you, they'd freak out! We can't do that!"

Sheen ignored him and headed for the ship. John didn't know what to do, but his curiosity kept him from continuing to try and stop Sheen. When Sheen stopped a few feet short of the boat, John gasped at what he saw. Maybe his life *would* fall apart.

"Ah, the Quaill," Zach said, looking straight into his eyes. "And a mythical beast as well. We shall see how long you last against me. And you won't escape me like your uncle did.

2.) The First Stand

John stared in awe for a moment. He didn't know if he should urge Sheen away or attack Zach. He came to his senses. He grabbed his sword – which he had put on his belt – and his shield, which he had put over his shoulder, behind his backpack. He hopped off Sheen and held his weapons fiercely.

"You won't escape me this time, Zach. You can't get past both me and Sheen."

Zach laughed hard and yelled, "Crew! Get up here."

John's eyes widened as a small army marched from a lower level up to where Zach and John were standing. Zach smiled and turned back to the wheel of the ship.

"Too bad I am not the one to finish you," Zach said. He nodded to his crew, "Kill him."

John closed his eyes, hoping for the last time that he was dreaming. He opened them to find Zach's crew with their weapons pointed right at him. They suddenly charged, yelling at the top of their lungs. John retreated to the very edge of the ship in fear. Sheen, still flying behind the ship, kicked the ship. John grabbed hold of the side for support, but the crew fell backwards. John jumped on Sheen and put his land weapons away. He opened his palm and thought hard about a bow. A bow and a quiver immediately appeared. He aimed an arrow directly at Zach's back. He fired, but a red beam appeared around Zach and the arrow bounced off of it.

Sheen roared in anger and, with one swipe of his hand, shoved nearly all Zach's crew into the sea. Zach turned around, equally as angry as Sheen, and pulled out his wand. John readied his shield.

"I should have known," Zach said as his crew screamed and ran to the bottom of the ship. "A dragon isn't anything to play with. Very well. Get ready to meet my true soldiers … my true army!"

Zach shot lightning into the air, just as Paul's ax would do. There was total and complete silence.

Then a bone-chilling horn echoed out into the air. John cringed at the sound. The horn was soon followed by enormous chants made by beasts. John looked at where they were coming from and saw – to his horror – 20 long, black ships coming from the horizon. The sun, which was just beginning to rise, seemed to set again as the dark ships approached them at high speeds. The loud horn was blown again and John understood that it was the battle horn for war.

Zach was going to wage war with the world.

The ships stopped slowly right behind Zach's ship and John saw what the creatures really were. They looked human-like, but they had dead skin and black eye sockets, as if they were creatures that had been dead for many years. Their bodies were much stronger than that of a human, but the skin was rotted away. John could only think of one creature that was more fearsome, and they were the demons that would haunt him in his nightmares … that John swore were real. Even Sheen shivered when he gazed upon them, about 500 per ship.

"My devils," Zach said, grinning. "Annihilate these fools."

All of the creatures roared in delight and prepared for an assault.

"They can't hurt us," John whispered hopefully. "We are at sea, so they can't march at us."

But John saw how wrong he was. They couldn't march towards them, but they all pulled out bows, crossbows and prepared the cannons. Sheen swallowed. One of the creatures stood up on the edge of the ship and aimed an arrow right at John. John scrambled for his shield but it was too late. The creature fired his shot at John. The sound almost killed John by itself. The buzz it made as it flew at John was enough for him to drop his shield and cover his ears.

The arrow came within a foot of John when an object came out of the sky and deflected it.

It was a hooded man with two swords in his hands. He fell onto Zach's ship. He rolled to a standing position and walked up to Zach, both swords clenched tensely. Zach was not surprised at all. On the contrary, he looked at the hooded man as if he was a watching the same play run for the fifth time.

"Surrender, Zach," he said in a deep voice.

"Oh heavens above, of course," Zach said in a falsely defeated tone. "I can't beat you three. Come on body guards, we must surrender."

The creatures growled in a horrible laughter.

"I am sorry, I guess they don't agree with me," Zach pronounced sarcastically.

"Zach, no more jesting," The hooded man snarled. He whipped his two swords quickly so they stopped at Zach's throat. "Give up or die."

"Kill me, and I'll kill your nephew," Zach said in one motion, whipping his wand, pointing it right at John. "Daniel, it's inevitable. If you kill me, you will face the wrath of my army. You'll never defeat me by yourself."

The man unhooded himself and replied, "Zach, I am never alone."

The army of creatures growled again, but they were suddenly drowned out by another, louder roar. Sheen and John turned towards the forest from which it came. Suddenly, about 30 gray dragons larger than Sheen rose up from the forest. On their backs – hanging by the spikes – were fifty men per dragon. They flew above Zach's ship and jumped onto the army's ships. As they fell, they pulled out their wands … magicians. Zach watched this and turned back to Daniel.

"You are still highly out-numbered," he said. "Sorry to mention the obvious."

"No worries, old friend," Daniel added sarcastically. "But remember, our dragons will rip through your ships."

John listened and thought they were talking about a video game instead of a war. John grabbed his sword and shield and ordered to Sheen, "Head for that ship!"

The magicians hit the ships and the creatures attacked at once. John looked in horror as one by one, the half-dead creatures murdered the magicians. As the dragons swooped low to knock the ships over, the creatures fired their cannon balls at their wings. After they punctured the wing, the dragons screeched and fell into the water. John knew that he would need more of a miracle than this to survive.

Gripping his sword tightly, he jumped onto the ship, screaming. Some attempted to shoot arrows at him, but John knew they would have to do better than that to defeat a famous war hero. John had fought in the Thog war when he was 11, the Thousand Year War at the age of 13, and in a war against Zach a couple months previous.

John kicked two off the ship as he landed. Five more shot arrows at him but he used his magical barrier to deflect them back at the creatures. Now ready for battle, he charged at the demons without any fear. John took swipes left and right with his sword, killing many. He looked at the ship triumphantly as he and the magicians killed the others. The monsters were able to kill about 400 magicians.

Now having a place to form up, John's confidence in the army rose. The 19 other ships headed for the lone magician ship. The magicians quickly formed into a box-shaped formation as the ships surrounded them. All the magicians pointed their wands at the nearest enemy ship. Since John had no wand, he stood behind them. The magicians shot red fire balls into the air, above the enemy ship. At a certain amount, it formed into one gigantic fireball. One of the remaining dragons flew above and pushed it down upon the enemy ship. It hit about half the devils and killed them. Along with that it set the ship on fire, a promise of a sunken ship.

The other ships prepared harpoons. They shot many of them at the magician's ship's mast. They started to swing over to the magician's ship. John swallowed and once again, lost hope of living through this experience. However, as the creatures started to swing over, the other dragons flew by and cut the ropes before they could reach the boat. John breathed a sigh of relief and looked over at Dan and Zach. They were still arguing, but Zach was out of the reach of Dan's swords.

The magicians were powerful. They battled with the creatures fiercely. As the creatures shot over arrows and cannon balls, the magicians blocked them with their magic and shot right back at them. One ship tried to ram the magician ship. The magicians and the dragons couldn't stop it and it smashed into the side of the ship. Immediately, the magicians and creatures clashed. John was amongst them. He cut through one side so that he could squeeze onto the opposing ship. He went up to one of the enemy's cannons and killed the monster that was there. He pointed the cannon at another ship. He lowered it so it would hit right at the lowest point of the ship. He fired and the cannon ball hit the ship in the side, causing water to flow through. The creatures on that ship screeched and tried to get onto another ship before it sank. But the other ships were so full, there was no room for them.

"That'll teach Zach not to over-stack his ships," John said, smiling as the ship started to sink. He turned just in time to see a blade coming right at him. He ducked and thrusted his sword into the stomach of the creature. The magicians helped him out and they were able to wipe out the rest of the creatures on their boat. John relaxed as he grew in confidence. They had destroyed five out of the twenty boats so far. But now the other 15 all headed for the two magician ships. They came at once and their sheer numbers overwhelmed the magicians.

The creatures started to slaughter them. John realized he was nearly alone and quickly looked up to the dragons for help. They were too busy with the other ships. John jumped off the boat onto Sheen right as the last of the magicians were crushed. Daniel finally turned to John and, giving up, jumped onto Sheen with John. The couple of magicians still alive called over the last dragon, which they left upon.

"Is this enough to prove that you people can't win?" Zach said tirelessly.

"We'll be back with a lot more than this, Zach," Daniel said. "And your reign will be short!"

"Try me," Zach said and he laughed.

John urged Sheen to go. Daniel sheathed his two swords and fell back against Sheen's back. He then looked at John and smiled.

"I guess I didn't get to say hello again," he said.

John couldn't take it.

"What was that all about?!" He said angrily. "You killed many innocent lives by leading them to a battle with no hope at victory. Why did you attempt to defeat him?"

"I must admit, I miscalculated how strong the army is that Zach had around him," Daniel said, sighing. "But I did not mean to overtake Zach's 'body guard' with 1,500 magicians. We meant to slow him down and they came willingly to put their lives at risk."

"Risk?!" John sputtered. "There was absolutely no chance at survival!"

"You should thank me," Daniel said calmly, "and not argue about war and its tactics. I saved your life."

"I'd rather die," John said, "than see well-trained magicians fall without any success."

"You do not understand," Daniel said. "We needed more time. We sent out this wave to delay them. And we did take out a lot … I would guess about 2,500 of the enemy, and crippled most of their ships. Zach will have to stop for repairs, which will give us more time."

"Time for what?" John asked exasperated. "And who are 'we'? We have no army to face Zach's."

"That's where you're always wrong, John," Daniel said gently. "We have an army. You always think you're alone, John, but you're never alone, just like I said to Zach."

John said nothing. He stared at the long land below him and knew another journey was about to take form.

"What do we have left to count on?" John asked. "We depended on magicians, genies and animals in the last war, but they all fell."

"Not all of them," Daniel replied. "Paul is calling the last of the genies to battle while the *Ring* council's new mission is to recruit every magician in the world and prepare them for war. Jerry, however, can't help like he did last time. He sent us some of his troops in the last battle with Zach, and now he's paying for it. That was his big mistake in the Thousand Year War and he is required to stay to 'work it off', if you will."

"Who cares about Locombony?" John asked indifferently. "Isn't the war of the world more important?"

"It is, yes," Daniel replied patiently. "But if Australia takes over our small country, it would never allow us to build an army for fear we would use it for a rebellion."

"It seems as if we do not have many options," John said quietly.

"Exactly," Daniel said. "If Zach gets to the U.S. before we can assemble our army, we're finished."

"What happens once he gets there?" John asked nervously.

"Do you remember the Thog land in the maze?" Daniel asked him.

"Vividly," John replied.

"And you remember the original Thogeen that took all three of your weapons to beat?" Daniel said.

"Yes ... " John said with a little bit of fear in his voice.

"That was fake," Daniel said. "Most of the lands were. Zyno proved it at the end when he snapped his fingers and Victor disappeared. However, the Thog planet does exist and there is a real Thogeen master. He is much different than the one we fought, however."

"Do you mean to say," John asked, "that Zyno let us off easy?"

"Yes," Daniel said, "for his own reasons. The real Thogeen is much more powerful than that. There is one more thing. This Thogeen has an orb that Zach is planning to get his hands on."

"What does the orb do?" John asked.

"That's what we can't figure out," Daniel rubbed his eyelids. "It's obviously magical, but I don't see why Zach needs it."

John looked sadly at Sheen's scales and knew they had no chance of fulfilling these high hopes.

"Where do we go?" John asked.

"We have to wait until Paul and Lino come," Daniel said, "and then leave by ship."

"Why can't we ride by Sheen?" John asked.

"The way of traveling is watched because of the war in Locombony," Daniel said. "They will shut down the planes soon and if their radar picks up something big in the air, they could delay us. No, we go by ship."

"Alright," John said. "But it just seems so hopeless."

Daniel nodded.

"It will take a miracle to pull this off and we haven't had much luck with Zach," Daniel said. John knew he was talking about the previous war.

"Well, if what you're saying is true, then we're better prepared than last time," John said reassuringly. But he was kidding himself. He saw the armies Zach had. If that was just his guard, then he shivered at the thought of what his real army was.

"He will, no doubt, have the greatest army in the world," Daniel said sadly. "Nobody will be able to match it. Not even us."

"Is there no hope at all?" John asked, lying against Sheen's head.

"Of course, or else we wouldn't try and make a stand," Daniel replied, sitting up. "I have a plan. If we destroy the orb before Zach gets it, we could delay him from building up his army. What I don't get is why Zach has to build up such a large army to defeat us. We're no threat."

"Remember, he wants to take over the world," John said. "With a conquest like that, he might need hundreds of thousands, maybe even millions."

Daniel laughed.

"John, we can beat millions, and Zach knows that," Daniel said. "He will have more than that."

"Impossible," John almost laughed at the idea. "There's no way he could have more than millions. Even if he recruited those soldiers, all of them on this earth, he probably wouldn't be able to do it."

"Bare in mind, John," Daniel cautioned. "Zach is older than you think. Those creatures can live a long time. He could have been recruiting throughout the ages."

"Uncle Dan, how old is Zach?" John asked.

Uncle Dan only smiled. John steered Sheen down to his home. A black cave was all that he was able to live in.

"You're one of the richest kids in the world," Daniel said. "And you have to live in a cave?"

"*Was*," John corrected. "I had to pay off that war debt out of my own pocket. That cost me a ton."

"I never thought of that," Daniel said.

"Maybe with Flaminetore in here we can make it more livable," John said, jumping off Sheen.

"This is sad," Daniel said.

"Yeah, but it could be worse," John said, trying to put it in perspective. "I guess Zyno has bad living conditions as well."

"But he deserved it," Daniel said.

"And you do too," said a voice from the mouth of the cave. "And you also deserve what you are going to get. Say goodbye, Quaills."

3.) Reunion

Daniel jumped off Sheen and pulled out his swords. John touched his arm and once again, a shield appeared. He pulled out his sword, which he had sheathed. John looked at his uncle as Daniel came closer to the cave.

"That's right, Daniel," the voice said. "Come closer and prepare to experience your worst nightmare."

"Show yourself, whoever you are," Daniel called. John was a bit more cautious. He lowered himself behind the shield and prepared for an attack. Then suddenly a fast streak slammed into Daniel and he was thrown to the ground. John held his sword out in front of the shield and gripped them both tightly. The object hit John's shield, and they both fell to the ground. Quickly, John looked up and saw a small creature with long ears – cat-like yellow eyes – and hair that almost went down to his nose.

"Victor!" John said, getting up.

"How are you?" the creature said, standing. "New master sent me over with the liger to see his brother."

"Liger?" John said, looking back to cave.

"Surprise, surprise," the deep voice called. It walked out of the cave and John saw a pink leopard. It laughed.

"Lino!" John nearly shouted, running to him. The leopard jumped onto his hind legs and put his front paws on John's shoulders. "Why did you scare us like that?"

"John, you always jumped to conclusions now," Daniel partially reprimanded.

"You pulled out your swords," Lino defended John. Lino looked back and smiled, "Just keeping you on your toes."

"You came early," John said, putting his sword away. "How did you do it so fast?"

"We left as soon as we could," Victor said. "But we were attacked as soon as Sheen left. We defended the maze while our master was away. Hopefully Maurice will be able to hold them off until the master returns. Anyway, we headed to you in the fastest way possible."

"Which was?" Daniel asked cautiously.

"A straight line," Lino replied. "We headed directly from Paul's lab to your cave. Nice home, by the way."

"Har har," John said. "Come on, let's head inside. We should talk over our plans."

They headed into the cave and John turned on Flaminetore. The hologram appeared and it lit up the cave.

"Now, let's talk war," Lino said, taking off the collar that was around his neck. He pulled out a piece of paper. "Paul gave us a map of our island and we see there are two smaller islands off the coast. Paul said that *that* one was the place where Zyno had been working on his chemical healing potion and war materials."

"And the other one is where the location of the *Ring* council usually has its meetings," Daniel said. "And the big island is our country, Locombony. Australia attacks from the east near the Zynon River, which ironically is named after Zyno's great-grandfather … "

"Thanks, but we'll talk history later," Lino interrupted.

"So," John continued, picking up a few pebbles on the floor. "We have Jerry's army right here—" he set a pebble on the river "—facing Australia, and our magician army here—" he set another pebble on the western island "—and a genie army … where?"

"Right here," Victor said, pointing near John's old hometown. "Plus once the attacks stop, we'll have the Thog army."

"You do?" John asked. "How many?"

"Forty thousand strong," Lino said triumphantly. "Plus I gathered up some of the Thog's enemies and now they are our allies."

"As in the Thogeens?" Daniel asked curiously.

"Oh boy, no," Lino whistled. "It would take years to do that. However, we did get the horenslings and the fire-winged Pegasus. We got some more dragons for the magicians and dinosaurs for psychics."

"Oh yeah, *do* we have an army of psychics?" asked John, who had been waiting for this topic to come up.

"Not exactly an army," Victor replied, concentrating on pronouncing each word correctly. "You could call them skirmishers. There really aren't a large amount of them."

"Then why didn't we send the psychics instead of the magicians to delay Zach?" John asked, anger returning.

"They wouldn't last a second," Daniel explained. "Besides, the dinosaurs can't fly; how would they reach the ships? Our dragons had the advantage."

"Alright, so the armies are spread out pretty much as far as they could possibly be," John announced, staring at the map. "Zach's army is on the move to the U.S. to grab an orb from the *real* head Thogeen. So ... "

"We must head after him," Daniel said. "But the thing is, like I told John, we can't reach him because planes will be shut down soon. We can't use Sheen or any other dragon because of radar. We can't even use a large boat with any type of electric motor because it can be picked up by Locombony's sonar system."

"Can't we use a medieval type of ship?" Lino asked.

"With that we might have a chance," Daniel said, pulling a hand-held computer out of his pocket. "According to my research on the technology, I believe the radar might have a more difficult time tracking down something with no electricity. Plus, the radar needs metal to bounce the signal back. Yes, they could spot us, but it is less likely to happen. That's probably why Zach went medieval. We must follow suit."

"So Paul and Jerry aren't coming?" John asked.

"No," Lino replied. "They were not able to get free in time. Plus, we should leave immediately."

"When's 'immediately'?" Victor asked.

"Soon," Daniel said, pressing a few more buttons on his computer. "Very soon."

"I'll prepare my weapons then," John said. "Who else are we traveling with?"

"About a few miles out to sea, we will meet with the magician and psychic armies," Daniel replied. "But the genie army is traveling alone to delay the damned army."

"Right," Lino agreed. Then John realized something.

"What about the Thog army?" He asked.

They all looked at each other.

"They might not get the chance to come if Zach's army keeps attacking them," Lino announced sadly.

"How is Zach attacking the maze if his army is at sea?" Victor asked.

"He split his army," Daniel answered. "One to stop us in Locombony and one to travel with him by sea. He is attacking Paul's lab because he wants to stop us from building more of an army."

"Well, hopefully we can escape with a decent amount of soldiers to help you guys," Victor said.

"Thank you," Daniel sighed. "We need all the help we can get. If my numbers are correct, the great army on the sea with him is merely his body guard. He could have so much more."

John whistled.

"I need to get this hopeless war off my mind," he whispered, picking up his sword. He began to clean off the blood when he remembered Paul's gift. He took out the ax.

"Paul didn't explain to me why he gave me his weapon," he said, turning to Lino. "Do you know?"

"Yes," Lino nodded. "Like his computers, he perfected his new weapons so that he doesn't need *those* weapons anymore.

All he has to do with the new ax is twist the handle instead of focusing on loyalty and lightning shoots out."

Daniel sharpened his swords.

"That's kind of cheating," he said.

"I agree, but it is great technology," Victor commented. "I can't believe we didn't think of it."

"Let me just review our journey quickly," John said, pondering. "We are taking an old ship to chase Zach while our other armies try to catch him to delay him so we can get the orb first?"

"Right," Lino said, sharpening his claws, "But I think we should connect with Paul and Jerry anyways. If Jerry gets a chance, he could join us."

"He is not exactly on the way," John said. "I mean, we have to travel away from him, don't we?"

"Yeah," Victor said.

"And what about Paul?" John asked, "No chance that he may come either?"

"There's every chance I might come," said a voice from behind them. They spun around and John saw his brother, Paul, standing proudly in front of them.

"Paul!" Lino yelled.

"Master!" Victor cheered.

"What are you doing here?" John asked, running to and embracing him.

"Jerry sent me a message and told me I should head here to help you guys out," Paul said. "And I think he was right – just look where you live!"

"Let's talk about that later," John interrupted. "Come on, we can tell you the plans briefly … "

"I *know* the plans," Paul announced. "I pretty much created them."

"So I guess I was the only one not clear on this," John said, sighing.

"Pretty much," Lino shrugged. "Well, that makes almost everybody."

John turned away from the group and wiped his eyes. He was overjoyed that he was finally seeing his family again. True, Victor and Lino weren't exactly related, but John would always consider them family. He turned back and saw that Paul had tears in his eyes as well.

"I am really sorry I couldn't come before," Paul said. "I think Zach is really trying to keep us apart."

"He'll pay for what he did to me," John said confidently. "I vow that his life will be in my hands one day and … and … I'LL KILL HIM!"

"John," Daniel began gently.

"There's more than what meets the eye with him and I," John said angrily. "He didn't just kill my friends and my mom; my life has been a living hell because of him. I live in a cave for the *Ring*'s sake! He separated me from my brothers and changed my life forever. I have already fought in a war against him and saw … I saw him. Inside me, he was there. He took control of my body many times! His evil lived inside me. I have felt his soul inside me. Yes, he hates you guys, but he has something more for me. I don't why, but it's true."

"I know," Daniel said. "I know that he has a special case for you, and I know why."

"Why?" John asked quickly.

"Because you're a magician," John saw Daniel think (magicians have a special power to communicate to each other through thought). *"He hates me the same way. The only things he really fears, in this world, are the magicians. Genies don't scare him at all, or men, no matter how big in number they are. When he wipes out the entire magician race, there will be nothing that can potentially stop him."*

John understood and nodded. Then – as if a person smacked him over the head with a frying pan – John had an amazing revelation.

"*That's it!*" John thought triumphantly to Daniel. "*The orb that he wants must have a special power to destroy magicians! If nothing can stop him besides magicians, then that has to be the answer!*"

Daniel's eyes widened when he saw John's thought.

"We must get going *now!*" He said, standing up. "Paul gather your stuff, we're heading out!"

"Now?" Lino asked surprised.

"Now," John said firmly, now afraid of what Daniel's thoughts might tell him. Almost nothing scared his uncle, even when faced with the certain chance of death.

Paul immediately grabbed his backpack and threw it to Victor who quickly put it on. He pulled out an identical ax to the one he gave John and tested the sharpness. He put it back and turned to Sheen.

"Is he able to come?" he asked Daniel.

"He can come for now," Daniel hurried, straightening his cloak. "Do you have your lamp, Paul?"

"Every day," Paul replied, pulling an oil lamp from his pocket. "I need it."

"Come on," Lino said to Paul and Paul leapt onto Lino's back. John gave Lino a skeptical look. Lino explained, "I've been a bit more lenient about treating me as if I were an animal."

John laughed as he tightened his cloak and grabbed his shield to strap onto his back.

"Where's the ship?" Victor asked.

"Fifteen miles from here," Daniel said. "I would transport there, but you guys can't."

Daniel squinted into the distance.

"I have some bad news for you guys," Daniel continued. "Zach must have spread some of his terrible creatures in the forest directly in our path."

"We can take them," Lino said confidently. John grinned.

"Bring it on," Paul snarled. "There is nothing I haven't faced before."

"It's time for some pay back," John said.

Sheen roared in anticipation. John jumped onto one of his spikes. Daniel couldn't help but smile as well. Even though they knew what they would soon have to face would be treacherous, they grinned. They were together again, and to Paul and John, that meant everything. Both of them knew their journey was now going to start, but they didn't know that evil was literally behind the closest tree.

4.) The Thousand-Year War

Jerry avoided a bullet that was shot directly at him. He swung his sword against a rifle to knock it off course. He looked at his exhausted troops and knew it was only a matter of time before they would all fall. The enemy seemed to have great insight to what they were doing. He had no choice. He leapt onto the horse that he had fallen off during battle.

"Retreat!" Jerry yelled. He and his men sprinted back into the forest, away from the river. After a while, he pulled back on the reigns of the horse and breathed heavily. After sheathing his sword, he fell off his horse in exhaustion. He had been fighting for two days straight without any rest.

"That's another battle we lost, sir," a general said riding over to him. "If we lose another one, we could just consider The Thousand-Year War over. We have no reinforcements, and the capital is 20 miles away."

"I am aware of that," Jerry said, rolling onto his back. "I guess we have no choice. I must bring in William's army."

William told Jerry once that he held the allegiance with Locombony. He was a rebellious general with an army of 25,000 men, and told Jerry that if he needed help to just call him for aid. Jerry didn't want to use his army because the army was all barbarians. They slaughtered their opponents and tortured their prisoners. They would never listen to or follow war ethics. But now that Jerry was so frustrated with the opponent, he honestly didn't care what happened to them. Besides, he needed to get with his brothers.

"Your army needs you," the general said, reading his mind. "You can't betray them in the highest time of need."

"My brothers need me more," Jerry said, taking out his cell phone. He dialed William's number. "William? Yeah, I need back up desperately. When can you come? ONE WEEK AT THE EARLIEST? Dang it! Oh well, I'll try to hold them off until then. Yes, I appreciate it. Yes, thank you man, you're a lifesaver. Can you bring all six legions? Great, thanks. See you."

"So?" the general asked.

"He said he'll come as soon as he can but that it might take about seven days at minimum," Jerry said standing up, drained of strength. He pulled his sword out fearlessly. "I guess that means we'll have to hold them off until then."

"Sir, you and your men are both courageous," the general said. "But there is no hope for victory without reinforcements. If you count carefully, you can see that we only have about 200 men."

"We must go," Jerry said. "The country, no the WORLD depends on our victory."

"You're the captain," the general said.

Jerry leapt onto his horse. He breathed hard. He turned to his men.

"FORM RANKS!" He yelled. His men formed into two sentries (a box formation that holds between 80 and 100 men). He pointed at his two generals, "YOU, THAT SENTRY, YOU, THAT SENTRY! WE WILL NOT GIVE UP THIS WAR!"

He remembered his role model, a Scotland general who defeated the oppressive English army. He learned how he had beaten the English army while they were highly outnumbered. This inspired him.

"THIS MAY SEEM TO BE A BATTLE TO DEFEND OUR SMALL ISLAND, BUT YOU'RE WRONG," Jerry hollered at the top of his lungs. "OUR ARMY MUST DEFEND THE WORLD. I CANNOT TELL YOU HOW, BUT THIS BATTLE WILL DETERMINE HOW OUR DESCENDANTS LIVE THEIR VERY LIVES. BUT I CAN TELL YOU THIS! IMAGINE YOUR CHILDREN FORCED TO LABOR FOR A GREAT KING AND BEING TORTURED BY THE VERY WORST WAY POSSIBLE. IMAGINE YOUR LIVE

DEVOTED TO HONORING THE DEVIL HIMSELF! IMAGINE A WORLD IN WHICH THERE IS NO RHYME OR REASON. IMAGINE SOMETHING 20 TIMES WORSE THAN THAT! YOU CAN'T, CAN YOU? LET ME TELL YOU THIS, MEN. IF WE LOSE LOCOMBONY, THERE WILL BE NOTHING STOPPING THE DEVIL FROM TAKING OVER. YOU MUST WIN THIS BATTLE GENTLEMEN."

The army looked at each other in fear.

"YOU THINK IT'S GOING TO BE EASY TO WIN THE BATTLE FOR THE WORLD? DID YOU THINK SUPER COUNTRIES WOULD WIN THE WORLD? DO YOU THINK YOUR LIFE DOESN'T MATTER? MEN! YOUR LIFE MIGHT BE LOST TODAY IN A POWERFUL WAY. WE WILL NEVER FORGET EACH OTHER!"

Jerry said all this trying to hold his tears as he gazed upon his men. They had been through a lot in three years. He considered each and every one of them family. He sighed.

"BUT DO YOU ALSO THINK WE WILL LOSE THIS BATTLE?" Jerry cried. "NO! TODAY, WE WILL BE VICTORIOUS. THERE IS HOPE. OUR STRENGTH WILL NOT FAIL US. FRIENDS MAY FAIL US. HOPE MAY SEEM TO FAIL US. IT MIGHT SEEM LIKE EVERYTHING FAILS YOU, BUT IT WON'T. THERE IS ALWAYS SOMETHING."

Jerry looked up to the sky and then back to his troops.

"WHENEVER THERE IS A DEMON, THERE IS AN ANGEL," he said. "THERE IS A DIVINE POWER OUT THERE SOMEWHERE. HE WILL NEVER LET THIS DEMON TAKE OVER, BUT WE MUST TRUST HIM. HE WILL NEVER FAIL US. WHATEVER SPIRIT IS UP THERE, MAY HE HELP US."

Jerry turned to the river with his army behind him.

"WE FIGHT TOGETHER NOW!" Jerry yelled as loud as he could, putting his sword in the air.

That was his army's signal to charge. The army, now full of hope and high morale, yelled and charged behind Jerry, making thundering noises from their feet. The Australian army was surprised, and tried quickly to form up. As Jerry came closer to them, he saw the thing he was desperately hoping for – the fear in the whites of their eyes. As Jerry struck the first man, he knew what he said was correct; they would win, no matter how outnumbered they were.

Jerry kept riding on his horse, which he called "Black Melody." He hit men left and right while his horse trampled over men in front of them. He turned back to his troops and saw the Australian army didn't have enough time to reload their guns. They had to settle for using their guns like bats and try to whack their enemy. The Locombony army was able to swing their swords and block the attacks, so the Australian army was helpless. Jerry laughed as his men started to wipe out the Australians. Then something Jerry didn't expect happened. There was a loud cry from the forest ahead; 10,000 armed Australians charged down at them. Seeing this sudden change of events, the Locombony army turned and ran back into the forest. Jerry was about to call them back before he thought about it. He turned his horse around and charged back with them. They could always come back out, Jerry thought. As he and his men entered the trees again, Jerry realized they had been lucky, not powerful. Just when Jerry was beginning to lose hope, he heard a voice behind them.

"Looks like you could use a hand, Jerry," it said. Jerry turned quickly on his horse and saw something amazing. A man no older than Jerry stood there.

"Who are you?" Jerry asked reaching for his sword.

"I am Shiach," the man said. "I lead the mythological army. I was supposed to travel to the lab when Alvin said you needed help. I see now that he was right."

Jerry sighed, relieved. "Alvin" was his Uncle Dan's alias to people he didn't trust yet.

"Do you know Alvin well?" Jerry asked.

"Yes," Shiach said. "Now let us be as we easily take out these men. Move your army aside, please, and we'll show you how it's done."

Jerry hastily moved his troops and in amazement, saw the creatures behind Shiach – black unicorns, fire-winged Pegasus, many-headed dogs, horenslings (large volcanic creatures that Jerry had only seen once) and some other types of creatures. There was so many of each that Jerry thought victory was inevitable. Jerry turned and peered out of the trees and saw his opponents form into lines and reload their weapons. He knew they would easily fall with the element of surprise on their side.

"CHARGE!" Shiach yelled as he ran out of the forest. The mythical army followed him. Jerry thought for a second and then signaled for his men to follow. He laughed as he saw the look on the Australian faces. The unicorns reached them first. Their black horns drilled through the Australian's first rank while the Pegasuses attacked the rear so that they were sandwiched. Shiach gave Jerry the signal to attack at their right and everything else attacked from the left. This left the Australians completely surrounded and helpless. They quickly ran out of ammunition. After losing 1,000 men and not being able to kill 10 of either Shiach or Jerry's army, they surrendered.

Jerry turned to Shiach.

"How can we ever thank you?" Jerry said, breathing hard.

"By giving me the authorization to force these men into war," Shiach said, pointing to the Australians. Surprised, Jerry looked at the mud-splattered Australians.

"In … uh … what way?" he asked.

"We need to train them so they can help in the battle against Zach," Shiach said.

"You're aware of the war against Zach?" Jerry said, surprised again.

"Of course," Shiach said. "I need to train them with swords because a lot of the modern weapons, such as guns, don't affect magicians too well."

"I guess … " Jerry was kind of hesitant. He wanted to obey the rules of war but he also wanted to remain as united with the army against Zach as he could. "Yeah, go ahead."

"Thank you," Shiach said, nodding to the unicorns. "Call again if you need help."

"Again?" Jerry said as they turned to leave. Shiach winked at him. They quickly departed. Jerry turned to one of his generals.

"You heard him," Jerry said. "If you need help, call me and I'll call him. I need to catch up to my brothers."

"But sir … " the general said.

"No," Jerry said, sheathing his sword. "I must go."

He turned his horse around.

"ON BLACK MELODY!" He shouted to his horse. Black Melody neighed and swiftly started to gallop. Jerry loved the wind in his face as the horse flew across the ground. Trees passed in a blur. Black Melody panted, not in exhaustion, but in proof of power.

Black Melody was known all around as one of the fastest horses ever to walk the earth. Thought to have a heart five times the normal size, it was built for endurance and strength. Jerry knew there must be magic in her blood, perhaps a descendent of a Pegasus or unicorn. Wherever Jerry needed to ride, his horse could handle a fast-paced journey.

He then wondered where he would go. He would most likely miss the ship his brothers were taking. He could go with the other psychics down south and try to catch up with them later. No, Jerry thought, I have to try and make it to my brothers first.

Jerry suddenly stopped his horse. He heard voices. They were growling voices that made Jerry shiver. He kicked the side of Black Melody to command her to slowly walk toward the sound. Jerry kept his hand on the hilt of his sword. Then he saw two figures by a gray gate. Quickly, Jerry hopped off his horse and tied it to a tree. He snuck carefully to the two figures and heard low voices that made Jerry concentrate hard on what they were saying.

"The magician says we might come in later if he needs us," one of the creatures said. When Jerry got within 10 feet of them, he stopped behind a tree. He peered out to see them. The look of them petrified Jerry. Their skin was gray and dying and they had no eyes in their sockets. Their teeth were as sharp as daggers. They were heavily armored and had a jagged sword at their side. Jerry saw pictures of them in his book of parapsychology. They were the archrivals of the magicians and genies in ancient times: ogres. "He's going to pull the second army from the lab to head to the base in Phoenix. We might be able to prove ourselves great there!"

"Who are we kidding?" The other ogre growled. "There's no way the magician will ever recognize our power. Remember what he is … "

The first ogre growled and punched the other to the ground.

"Take that back!" The first one yelled. "HE'S OUR MASTER!"

Jerry heard enough to know what was going to happen if he didn't tell someone. He turned to go back to his horse when a crazy idea came into his head. He pulled out his sword carefully.

"No one will stand a chance against the magician," one of the ogres said.

"Unless he's a very powerful psychic," Jerry said loud enough for the ogres to hear. He jumped out from behind the tree and charged at them.

"SOUND THE ALARM!" one of them said. The other one quickly pulled out a horn and blew into it to make a roar so horrifying, that Jerry dropped his sword and covered his ears. The ogre stopped blowing and they both charged at him. Jerry quickly got up and used his psychic power. An invisible force pushed them straight to the ground. Jerry ran at them and stabbed both of them.

"Nice try, pals," Jerry said, but he knew the damage was done. He turned to the gate and saw many ogres coming toward him. He reached behind him and pulled out 20 arrows out of his quiver. He threw them near the gate, but stopped them with his psychic powers. He turned them so they faced the ground. The gate slid open and 30 ogres came charging out. Jerry quickly shot the arrows straight down at the ogres. It hit most of them, but Jerry was forced to fight the rest. CLANG, CLANG, stab, CLANG, stab, stab, CLANG, CLANG, CLANG, CLANG, stab. The ogres kept coming at him. Slice, Slice, CLANG, Slice. Jerry went faster. He used his psychic power again, knocking a few off their feet. Jerry slowly started to advance into the base. He sliced the ogres, one by two by one (he killed some with one swipe of his sword). Finally, one knocked him down to the ground. Jerry looked up at him angrily and clenched his sword tight. Suddenly, flames appeared around the sword. Jerry looked at it and grinned. He hadn't had that happen in about three years. He swung it around, getting up and the creatures backed away. Suddenly, an arrow shot from one of the ogres went sipping towards him. The arrow made a noise so terrifying that, once again, Jerry dropped his weapon to cover his ears. The arrow struck his arm and he fell to the ground in agony. The ogres quickly surrounded him and two of them grabbed his arms and pulled them behind him. Another ogre ran up to him with a

large club. He swung it over its head and brought it down upon
Jerry's. Jerry saw stars, and then passed out.

    What seemed to be days later, he woke up.

    An ogre stepped up in front of him.

    "So you were the one who tried to stop us, eh?" it growled.
"Not for long … give him his sword back and take him to
MAROWLOG!"

5.) Marowlog

Jerry gasped at what he heard. The two ogres that were dragging him pulled him slowly across the ground.

"Who's Marowlog?" Jerry asked.

"Be quiet, human!" one of the ogres said.

Jerry sighed and knew he wouldn't get much more out of them. At least he'll have a chance to fight this "Marowlog", whoever he is. Or *what*ever he is.

They dragged him towards another gate, this time very large and black. The two ogres waited as the gates slowly opened. Jerry braced himself as they took him inside.

At first, Jerry only saw the long, black walls coming off the gate that formed a circle around an empty patch of land. Then he noticed what looked like a large pile of rocks in the middle.

The ogres threw Jerry near the rocks. They quickly ran out of the gate and started to close it.

"Wait!" Jerry called. "What about my weapon?"

As the door was just to close, the ogre threw Jerry's sword at him. Jerry caught it and looked around. It didn't seem like there was anything here. Then the horn blew out its horrid sound again and Jerry, this time holding onto his sword, plugged his ears. When the horn stopped, there was a loud growl from behind the rocks. Jerry carefully made his way around them and peered around. There was nothing. Jerry's eyes widened as he heard something above him. He looked up and saw to his horror a red dragon. Jerry swallowed. He only remembered one dragon in his life and that was Sheen. Jerry took many steps back as it landed. It gave out a deafening roar and slowly started to approach Jerry. Jerry yelled and attempted to attack one of its feet. The dragon swung its foot at Jerry and kicked him across the land all the way to the black gate. He smashed into the gate and slid to the ground. Had he been a normal human being, the kick would have killed him or at least knocked him out. Jerry, however, was a powerful human and psychic as well (psychic people were naturally stronger). He got up and felt blood from his head drip down his neck.

"You think you can get rid of me that easily?" Jerry said, bringing his sword to his chest. "I have faced creatures worse than you. Bring it on!"

The dragon roared again and blew fire at Jerry. Jerry was ready. He put an invisible barrier around himself and the fire only reached a certain point before the barrier stopped it short of hitting him. Jerry grinned and Marowlog looked frustrated. He took another swing at Jerry with his tail, but Jerry was able to dodge this one. Jerry threw his sword as hard as he could at Marowlog's foot. It bounced off the strong scales. As he ran to pick up his sword, he had a sudden flash back from about three years ago …

They all dove away from the T-rex, but John wasn't so lucky. John got caught in the back by the T-rex's jaws. It dragged him upwards. He was screaming wildly. Jerry talked to Tyler and asked him if he knew how to beat a dinosaur.

"Course' I do," Tyler said. "I actually pay attention in science class. You hit it in the only soft part of the body."

"Oh I get it," Jerry said. "You hit it in the eye!"

Jerry brought himself back to the present. A dragon was close to a dinosaur … would it work? Jerry also ran into the same problem he had three years ago – how could he reach the eye of a dragon?

Jerry paused too long. Marowlog blew flames again and Jerry barely dodged the worst of it. Some of his body got too close, though, and got a little scorched.

Jerry comprehended what he had to do. He concentrated hard on lifting his shoes. He started to rise to the dragon's height. Jerry used all his psychic power to lift a rock from the pile. Marowlog sucked in some breath to blow fire. Jerry tried to lift the rock towards him at a faster rate, but the dragon was faster. Marowlog blew fire at him, but Jerry was ready. He dropped the rock and focused his psychic energy to protect himself before Marowlog's fire hit him. The blast shot Jerry over the wall, even with the protection of the sphere. His sword went flying. When he hit the ground, many ogres came running to him. In pain and not able to get up, Jerry just shoved them with his psychic power. He got up carefully. More ogres. He cautiously pulled out two knives from his boots. Having weapons seemed to awake some adrenaline inside him. Remembering what Maurice had taught him three years ago, he spun his knives making them twice as deadly. He threw them at the ogres with such power that they went straight through the ogres' necks and hit the ogres behind them. As a quick, last resort, he pulled out two arrows out of his quiver and stabbed the two remaining.

His cell phone then rang. Hoping it was just the psychic army, he answered it with gritted teeth.

"What?!" he said, hoping that no ogres heard him. "William? You WHAT?! Where? That's awesome. Alright, I'll see you, and hurry."

William had told Jerry there was a break-through and his army was very close to the base.

"I have to find my sword first," Jerry said to himself. Grabbing his bow off his shoulder and throwing an arrow into his quiver, he headed stealthily around to the walls. Pulling back on the string, he peered around the curve.

He saw at least 50 ogres coming towards him. Jerry closed his eyes and immediately his mind wandered to a fictional elf that was a superb warrior, especially with the bow. He concentrated hard and ran out to face them. He shot the nearest one right between the armor so it killed him. Quickly pulling another arrow, he shot the next one.

Jerry woke up from his fictional-character-daze with horror. He couldn't take down 50 ogres with just arrows because his situation wasn't fictional.

He heard a loud neigh behind him and he quickly spun around. It was Black Melody. Jerry exhaled in relief and ran towards her. He leapt onto her and simultaneously loaded his bow. As Black Melody charged and trampled the ogres, Jerry shot arrows at them. He saw his red-orange sword in the hands of one of the larger ogres.

"That's mine, bub," Jerry said, shooting the ogre with an arrow. He leapt off his horse and retrieved his sword. He jumped back on Black Melody and turned her toward the gate.

After he exited the gate, he found to his surprise William and his six legions of cavalry perfectly lined up. Jerry quickly rode over to them.

"We're ready for the devil himself," William said, fiercely.

"Good," Jerry said, trying not to grin at the irony. "Let me scare them up a bit."

Jerry turned his horse around again and headed for the black gate. He stopped a few feet from it.

"PREPARE FOR BATTLE, YOU DEVILS!" Jerry yelled. "WILLIAM AND JERRY'S ARMY IS ABOUT TO OVERTAKE THE OGRE RACE! PREPARE FOR DEATH!"

Jerry rode up and stopped parallel with William.

"That'll get 'em out," William said. And then to his men, "Prepare to charge!"

They all heard scattered marching inside the walls. Jerry hoped William's men wouldn't fail. Jerry heard a loud roar and looked up in horror to find Marowlog rising above the trees. The gate rattled open and many ogres came charging out. The barbarian army charged ahead of Jerry at the ogres. Jerry realized he was delaying, so he stormed ahead with the rest of them. It was hard, however, for the cavalry to sprint because they were in a forest full of trees.

Jerry had no idea how they were going to defeat Marowlog, but he knew that non-army trained ogres would fall to William.

The ogre guards tried to stop William from entering inside the camp, but, having swords in each hand, William took them out one by one. The first line of ogres fell easily. Jerry was with them, but he wanted to wipe out Marowlog before the dragon really entered the fray. Marowlog, however, was still swooping around the trees.

Jerry turned his attention back to the ogres. The ogres were easily getting slaughtered. Left and right, two by two, Jerry was killing so many of them that the ground looked like a floor made of ogre corpses.

Suddenly, Marowlog dove down at the barbarian army. Marowlog opened its mighty red claws and brought them down upon many of the cavalry and then squeezed. Jerry heard screams from the men and then the dragon roared. The army turned in fear to its new opponent. With a screech, the dragon blew fire, scorched and killed about 100 men. The army charged at the dragon, some shooting arrows at it. The arrows bounced off its powerful scales. Marowlog swiped his hand and sent the first line of cavalry flying. William ordered all his men to head towards the dragon. Jerry quickly rode over to him.

"I'll handle him," Jerry said loudly. "You take care of the ogres. Call your men back!"

William nodded and signaled for his army to come back. Jerry dramatically turned to face Marowlog as many men passed him.

"For my brothers," Jerry said.

He put his sword high in the air. Marowlog roared in acceptance to his challenge. Then, for a brief moment, they looked at each other in the eye.

Jerry urged Black Melody forward to meet the dragon. Marowlog blew fire, but Jerry avoided it by turning left. The dragon then swiped his hand, but Jerry ducked and headed right.

Jerry avoided the stomping of Marowlog's feet and rode underneath him. He quickly rode back into the forest, hoping Marowlog would follow him. He did. Jerry hoped his plan would work.

"Come on," Jerry said, urging his horse faster. But Jerry knew it was going as fast as it could. He kept slashing his reigns and kicking the side of his horse. He heard a giant mouth open behind him. Quickly, he shot his horse to the right, making the dragon continue to fly forward. He turned left so he was parallel with the dragon. Nothing stood between Jerry and Marowlog except a couple of trees. There was a huge blast of fire behind Jerry which was caught by the trees. They were scorched to ashes. Marowlog flew through the opening and started to approach Jerry again.

"I'm being chased by a dragon!" Jerry yelled.

The dragon roared again and opened his mouth to blow fire. Jerry sensed it and crouched down to the horse's mane.

They came to an opening where Jerry's plan was executed. Thousands of Pegasus flew out and rammed into the dragon, stopping it. Jerry let his horse slow down, turned around and whooped. Jerry looked back and saw Shiach and the mythological army. The black unicorns and the Pegasus then did something amazing. They merged together so that the Pegasus now had horns.

"Whoa, how did they do that?" Jerry asked.

"Magic," Shiach replied. "Now they can attack it in the only soft spot. Watch."

Marowlog tried to blow fire, but they were too fast for him. A Pegasus charged at one of its eyes. Its horn punctured it and the dragon roared just like the dinosaur did three years ago. Jerry knew that now the skin was uncovered, they would have no problem beating it. He no longer needed to watch.

"Thanks, Shiach," Jerry said, riding away. He rode back to the ogre camp where he found William circling it, barking orders.

"Surround the walls," William said. "Let not one escape for they wouldn't let us! Force them into a circle. Kill them all!"

"Good job," Jerry said. "Anything you want here is yours. You don't know how much I needed you. How did you get here in time?"

William just glanced at him and said, "God willed it."

"Is it ok if I head out to meet my brothers?" Jerry asked. "And I need someone to watch the river while I'm gone. Can you do that for me?"

William paused in his orders.

"Depends," William said. "Where are you heading?"

Jerry pulled a three-year-old ticket out of his pocket.

"Phoenix," Jerry said. "But I must leave now. Good luck."

Jerry rode quickly past William to the gate. He tried to do the math in his head. *Almost 180 miles*, he thought. *Black Melody can do 30 miles per hour, but then he needed rest and trees would be in the way.* Jerry's heart sank. It would take him a day to get there. Jerry thought of some other options. He turned his horse north.

"I can still head for Zyno's former lab," Jerry said. "And I can meet them by sea."

Black Melody snorted in disagreement.

"You're right," Jerry said. "We have to meet them on land."

He turned his horse again.

"Can you ride for six hours straight through anything that comes in our way and without any rest?" Jerry asked his horse. He neighed and leapt onto two feet.

"Then to the ocean we head," Jerry said. He kicked and Black Melody charged forward. Jerry grinned at their victory. Maybe there was hope after all.

Then Jerry's idea was crushed as he heard a noise. They had been traveling for about an hour now. He turned Black Melody towards the noise. He kicked, hoping this noise wouldn't be too much trouble. The horse was very reluctant, but did as Jerry commanded. Jerry's horse came to a cliff, which gave Jerry an enormous view. He gasped. In front of him was an army, and Jerry was certain that William's, Shiach's or even Daniel's army couldn't defeat this new foe.

6.) The Ship

John leapt off Sheen and headed out of the forest. There, waiting for him, were a few creatures Daniel had mentioned. John took his sword out and shoved it into the ground. The ground shook because of John's sword's magic power. He yanked his sword from the ground and started to run again. He led the group. They came to a swampy area. John started to make his way carefully through it when more creatures came out. The swampy substance slowed his attacks down. Daniel leapt above John to the other side of the swamp. With two swipes of his sword, the creatures fell to the ground. John hoisted himself out.

"Careful of that swamp," John warned the others.

John knew they had to keep moving.

"How much longer now?" Lino asked.

"Another few miles," Daniel said. "Come on."

They came to another open field.

"This is where I stopped Zach's men from coming to him," Daniel replied. "I took down 10 of them but the eleventh showed up late. Now Zach only has one partner."

Paul nodded.

"I ran through this field once as a child," Paul said. "I mean, younger than I am now."

"This is where I built the rebellion against Zach," John said. "Where the genies, the animals, and some magicians came to my aid. I guess this is a pretty memorable spot."

There was a fallen tree in the middle of the field. Daniel took out one his swords and shoved the sword into the trunk. He took a step back.

"And thus the spot was officially a memorial," Daniel prophesized. "The place where many people tried to stop the evil sorcerer."

John bowed his head. Then he quickly looked up.

"Can we go now?" Victor asked.

"Yes," Daniel said, looking one more time at the sword. "Let's."

He pulled out his other sword and ran to the opposite side of the field.

More creatures came after them. John ran ahead and clashed with one of them. John was amazed at his instincts. He was always one step ahead of his opponent. That was the same with Paul. It was easier for Paul, however, because all he would have to do was shoot lightning at his opponent.

John ran ahead again as Daniel slew the rest. As he reached one tree, however, a creature leapt out and took John by surprise. It swung its jagged sword at John's leg. It struck and John fell to his knees in agony. John's strong will forced him to launch an attack at the creature. John swung his sword quickly at the creature's waist. The sword sliced the monster in two.

John pulled from his pocket a brown box. He took out one of the tablets and swallowed it. His leg miraculously healed. John got to his feet again and started to run. He wanted to stop Zach at all costs and he wouldn't let minor injuries to get in the way (even though he could still feel the pain vibrating in his leg). Running from tree to tree, he came to another opening. There, in the opening, were about a hundred devil creatures.

"How does Zach produce so many?" John asked when the others caught up with him.

"No idea," Daniel exhaled. "I don't even know where these creatures came from. If I had to guess, though, I would say from Zyno's lab. They prepared this army just in case."

"Nice," Lino said when he saw them. "And how are we supposed to get through all this?"

"Sheen, fly above and see where the ship is. Let's see," Paul said. "There are about a hundred of them and five of us, not including Sheen. And I guess the rest of us will each take down 20. How does that sound?"

"Insane," Lino said.

"Let's do it," Victor added.

"Logically," Daniel said quietly, "it would be easier if we formed up into a phalanx. That's where we two or three will stand in the front and fight off enemies who approach while people in the back can fire arrows or projectile attacks at them. Let's see … John, Lino and I will go in a front line and Paul and Victor will take the second line. You guys shoot your attacks from range while we fight with our swords, or in Lino's case, with his paws."

"I like that better," John said.

"Sounds safer," Paul agreed. "Let's form up."

Paul got behind John and John crouched down. Victor got behind Lino.

"Let's go," Daniel commanded. They moved into the open. John grabbed his shield he had swung over his shoulder. Some of the creatures noticed and ran towards them.

"Fire!" John said, and Paul and Victor fired their ranged attacks. Paul's ax's lightning shot down a couple creatures at a time and Victor was able to string his arrows very fast. Now all of the enemies saw them. They charged in a scattered way.

"Hold them!" Daniel shouted to Lino and John. Two creatures ran at John. They tried to get to John, but he held his sword out and they ran into it. John quickly pulled it out and looked at Lino. Lino couldn't hold so many from one side without a weapon. John realized that he should have taken the wing, and Lino taken the middle.

"We've got to retreat, this is too much," John said, stabbing another.

"I am running out of arrows," Victor gasped.

"We can hold it for a bit longer," Daniel sputtered, slashing with his two swords.

"Are you insane?" Paul said, blasting three apart with lightning. "We must get rid of this formation or we're all done."

"Pull back!" John yelled before Daniel could answer. They turned around to go back to the trees only to find to their horror the creatures had surrounded them.

"Form a circle!" Paul said. "Shoulder to shoulder!"

They quickly formed into a circle facing out in all directions. John was not afraid at all. He knew that eventually they would be able to kill all of the remaining creatures; they weren't very smart.

One of them roared and blew a horn. The deafening sound rattled the field, but they all stood their ground, no matter how terrifying it sounded. The enemy charged. John swung his sword a few times, stopping the ones charging at him. Paul used his ax to swipe at the creature's necks. If he got the chance, he would shoot them with lightning.

"We must break through!" Daniel said, sword fighting one. "Where is it weak?"

"Thirteen, fourteen…" Paul said, counting as he killed them. "Here! There's few!"

"Head there!" Lino said, charging in that direction.

"I'll cover the back!" John said, taking Paul's idea in counting. "Ten … Eleven… "

Daniel, Paul, Victor and Lino easily broke through the 10 that were blocking them. The five ran into the forest, followed closely by the creatures.

"Up the tree!" Victor said, swinging quickly up. Using his magical powers to support him, Daniel leapt onto a branch. Likewise, Paul used his genie power to stretch himself up the tree. And of course Lino, being a tiger, climbed up. John, however, stayed on the ground.

"John!" Paul whispered to him. "Get up here!"

John gripped his sword tightly.

"You guys better hold onto those braches," John said as a few creatures headed towards him.

"John," Lino said. John took his sword and swung it into the ground. The earth shook and the creatures fell to the ground. John went by and stabbed each of the closest fallen enemy. Most of them got up, however. John, once again, swung his sword into the ground. The same result happened. John ran out into the opening to find Sheen there.

"Sheen, get them!" John yelled, swinging his sword at a few others and killing them. "Eighteen … nineteen… hurry!"

Sheen roared and came to his aid. He swung his tail around and sent many flying. One creature turned toward Sheen and pulled out a crossbow. Sheen shot out his hand, but the creature shot Sheen before he could hit any of them. The arrow shot his eye.

"NO!" John yelled, running towards the creature. He knocked down the ones in his way. The creature reloaded and pointed the crossbow at John. John stopped when it was shot and defended himself with his shield. He ran towards the creature again. With his first swipe, he chopped the crossbow in half and with another, he took out the creature. He turned and saw the other 60 creatures charge at him. They all suddenly stopped. John turned to see what they were staring at. He saw a man riding on a sprinting black horse come out of the trees. The man was heavily armored. The knight yelled at the top of his lungs and headed in the direction of the creatures.

John turned and fought with the stranger. Out of the forest came Paul and the rest. Daniel gripped his sword hard and swung it. Ice flew off and the icicles went into the creatures' necks. Daniel turned to Paul.

"There's my 20 He said, laughing. Lino leapt into the crowd of creatures and tore them apart. The rest of the creatures ran toward the sea.

"Don't start what you can't finish!" Daniel said, putting out his hand. A magical ball started to form in his hand. His eyes turned red. He shot the ball at them. It hit one and exploded, killing the others.

John turned toward the mysterious warrior.

"Once again, you're late," John said, trying to keep a straight face. "And once again, you embarrassed yourself by thinking we have no idea who you are. Next time you better paint your horse a different color, Jerry."

The warrior shook his head, laughing. He removed his helmet.

"Jerry!" Victor said. "Nice to see you again."

"And I you," Jerry said, leaping from his horse. "Nice to see you, John."

He grasped his brothers' hands. He nodded to Daniel.

"Where's the ship?"

They turned to the wounded Sheen.

"Open, Sheen," John said, taking out his box. The dragon opened its mouth and John threw in a pill. The eye of the creature healed.

"So, even his spit works on himself?" John questioned.

"No, it's not that," Paul replied. "It's a combination of Zyno's potion as well ... minus the controlling part, that is. It seems to work on dragons too."

Sheen pointed to the other side of the opening, referencing to where he found the ship.

"Alright, I guess we're in a hurry?" Jerry said.

"Yeah, we can explain on the way," John said. He leapt onto Sheen's back. "Come on, it's easier than fighting these skirmishes."

Everyone except Jerry got on Sheen. Jerry rode under Sheen as they took off. Sheen flew over the trees to the dock. He landed, closely followed by Black Melody out of the trees.

"That *was* easier," Victor said. They all gazed at the parked ship. It was medieval looking – large and brown with a large wheel.

"Come on," John said, heading towards the ship. Jerry threw out a hand to stop him.

"Wait," Jerry said. "That might be an ambush. Ogres are everywhere."

"Good call," Daniel said. John realized the demon creature's name was "ogres". Daniel ran onto the dock, pulling out his two swords. Victor pointed his arrow at the ship. Suddenly, a row of ogres jumped out of the ship.

"Ambush!" Daniel yelled, kicking some into the water. Victor shot arrows at the creatures, which kept leaping out of the boat. Paul and John ran to Daniel's aid while Jerry pulled out his bow. John leapt into the ship to see how many there were. There were, at most, 20. John sliced the ones in the ship and Paul leapt in.

"Easy enough," Daniel said as he kicked the last one into the water. "But let's get out of here before more show up."

Black Melody sprang into the boat. Paul ran up to the controls.

"Whose boat is this?" John asked.

"The *Ring*'s," Daniel replied. "We're picking up some magicians and the others will travel behind us."

"I desperately need some sleep," Jerry said. "But when I wake up, remind me with the word 'punishments.'"

Jerry opened a door leading down to the lower area. John took out Paul's ax replica and sat down with it. He started to sharpen his sword with it. Sheen roared and shrunk down to six feet tall (it had that ability to shrink and grow at will). Victor sat down next to both of them. John looked up without stopping.

"Tell me about Venemay," John asked Victor. "Has it turned out ok after the large war we had on the planet?"

This was merely a hypothetical question; he had learned that Maurice was a hologram three years earlier and the planet was fake. But he was genuinely curious how the story went.

"Sadly, there are still Thogs out there who wish to be stronger and become Thogeens," Victor said, sighing. "So war continues. Maurice battles with the rest of the Thogs to stop the Thogeens from overpowering us again."

"How is Julia?" John asked, remembering the kind Thog that had helped them. Victor's ears dropped.

"She was an excellent fighter," Victor said. John gasped. "But she went down like a heroine."

"How'd she die?" John asked sadly.

"Fifteen Thogeens surprised her at night," Victor replied. "She killed five, but by the time Maurice got there, it was too late. The cowards. She would have killed them all if they had attacked her in the daylight. But caught by surprise … "

John stopped sharpening his sword. Again, he knew it was all fake, but he could nevertheless feel a bit empty to hear she had fallen.

"I'm sorry," he said.

"You didn't do anything," Victor said. "In fact, you saved our lives when you helped in our war."

John smiled.

"I didn't have a choice," John said. "Your leader made us fight in the war or else we couldn't leave."

John sheathed his sword and put his ax on his belt.

"So now what?" Victor asked the pacing Daniel.

"Now we make sure we have cannons and ammunition," Daniel replied. "Check in that closet to see if we have arrows. John? You check to see if we have cannon balls."

Victor opened the closet and gasped in delight. The room was filled with arrows, more than he could count.

"Feel free to reload," Daniel said to Victor, but Victor was already stuffing his quiver full of arrows.

"There are 10 cannon balls for each cannon," John said, coming back. "And 10 cannons. Five on each side."

Daniel nodded.

"And hopefully we don't use them until we pick up the magicians," Daniel said. John glanced at his watch. It was noon.

"Actually, Uncle Dan," John said. "I need some rest too. I have been up all night."

John headed to the lower levels of the ship. He saw Jerry sleeping on one of the cots. John leapt onto one and fell asleep.

As if a dream was sitting on the cot waiting for him, he dreamt. He saw fire, everywhere. There was a large castle with black and red dragons flying around it. He saw ogres running around, destroying everything, living or dead. Then he saw himself, alone, with only a sword for protection. He looked up at the castle and saw Zach laughing. He then saw Paul next to him.

"Paul, they'll kill us," John yelled.

Paul didn't move. He just grinned.

"Paul?" John asked afraid. Paul raised his ax at him. "Paul! It's me, your brother!"

Finally Paul spoke.

"I have no brother," he said in a voice quite unlike his own. John then noticed that his skin was dead and rotten. His clothes were ripped. "I only have Zach!"

John realized with horror that his brother was now an ogre. Then, just before Paul swung, John had a revelation.

"John!" a voice called to him from far away. "John, wake up, you're dreaming!"

John opened his eyes and breathed. He looked up and saw Jerry above him.

"You really shouldn't think about Zach before you rest," Jerry said. "Here, have a cup of water."

Jerry handed him a glass and John slugged it down. John looked at his watch.

"Eight o'clock," John muttered. "When did you wake up?"

"After you started shouting," Jerry replied. "Oh well, I need to talk to Uncle Dan about the army."

Jerry headed up the ladder. John hesitated, then threw the glass at the floor and followed him.

"Dan?" Jerry said, approaching his uncle.

"Punishments," Paul said, coming down from the controls. At John's worried look, he explained, "I have Flaminetore driving."

"I remember, thanks anyway," Jerry said. "I need to call a war meeting because of what I saw on my way up here."

They all sat down.

"On my way here I saw, approaching from the south," Jerry breathed, "an army."

"What kind of an army?" Paul asked.

"It was a variety," Jerry said. "Partly war mammoths. Part goblins."

"Wait, wait," John interrupted. "Now, what's the difference between a goblin and an ogre?"

"Ogres are strong, human–like creatures," Jerry replied. "A goblin is a creature that is sort of bat-like and looks nothing like a human."

"But this army," Paul said, getting back on track, "it doesn't – besides the mammoths – seem too difficult."

"But here is the crucial part," Jerry said, eyes widening. "The last part is made of … phantoms."

Daniel gasped standing up.

"Are you serious?" Daniel said.

"I never joke anymore," Jerry said.

"Which makes you no fun," John laughed.

"Do you know what this means, John?" Jerry said, looking impatiently at him.

"Honestly," John said lightly, "no."

"A phantom is a creature that died, but didn't deserve an afterlife," Jerry explained. "The phantom never dies or even gets injured. It is only judged properly when it accomplishes the mission it was sent to do after its death. It's a punishment, you see, to become a phantom. It separates you from the afterlife and you can only go to the next world after you completely finish your mission."

"Wow," John replied.

"Now imagine an army of phantoms," Jerry said.

John leapt to his feet.

"Are you serious?" John asked.

"Enough," Jerry said, standing as well. "We cannot stop these foul creatures unless each of them succeeds their goal. I don't see how, though."

"Wait one second."

Paul stood.

"Living things can't hurt phantoms I am guessing, but what about other dead beings?" He asked.

"I am positive a living thing can't hurt a dead thing," Jerry replied, raising an eyebrow. "But I am not sure about a dead thing versus a dead thing."

Paul grinned.

"There's really no chance of getting a phantom on our side," Daniel said.

"Have all of you forgotten," Paul said, "that I am the greatest scientist in the universe?"

"What does science have to do with this?" John asked.

"Everything," Paul said. "There is a creature, I think, that can defeat a phantom."

"What's that?" Jerry asked, excitement mounting.

"First, let me give some history," Paul replied. They settled themselves as they listened to the boy-genius speak. "Legend has it that there was, long ago in the eighth century, a war. We're not sure it actually existed, but it was a war with dead people – ghosts. A ghost war. Now ghosts include phantoms, but they also include two other types – specters and ghouls. The three types of ghosts battled each other. The war secretly existed, according to legend, for a thousand years. No one knows if the ghosts 'died' or if they were unable to be killed. But near the 1700s, the war ended. No one knows the victor, no one knows anything. But one thing is for certain, the specters never returned. They live somewhere in Ireland, I think. But the ghouls are still enemies of the phantoms."

"How can you tell the difference between the three?" John said.

"Phantoms look like gray humans," Paul said. "And ghouls look like they were ripped to shreds and then assembled again. Specters, well, they are white skeletons. All of them can go through solid objects and vice versa."

"Scary," Victor whispered, shaking.

"But if I could convince ghouls to join our cause … " Paul planned. "I don't know how they became ghouls. Is it the same as the phantoms? Do they have to reach a goal? Either way I can, somehow, create them."

"Create the dead," Daniel said.

"Sounds impossible, I know," Paul said. "The other option is to head to Ireland."

"Ok, ok," Daniel said. "I mean, it can't be that hard. All we need is one ghoul and the rest should be easy."

"I wonder if you could make ghostly weapons," Jerry asked. "Imagine how you could do that."

"I think they took the idea and called it 'air'," Paul replied. "It would be kind of pointless, weapons that would go through opponents."

"Then what are we afraid of?" John asked. "I mean, if they go right through us, we don't need to worry about their attacks, do we?"

"Yes, we do," Paul replied. "I guess I should take that back. Phantoms can choose to be solid, but they still can't be killed."

"I see," Victor said.

"What I'd like to know is how many there are," Daniel said

"An army's worth," Jerry replied. "I estimate of 18,000."

"Even if we could build a ghoul, it would be impossible to create more than 10,000," Daniel said, sighing.

"Never say 'impossible' in front of me," Paul said, eyeing him. "It makes me want to prove you wrong."

Daniel laughed.

"How did Zach convince the phantoms to work for him anyway?" John asked.

"My guess would be he somehow convinced them they'd come to rest if they helped him," Daniel pondered. "Maybe their mission is evil. Maybe by joining him, they are fulfilling the mission. Or perhaps Zach is just manipulating them like he is everyone else."

"That's horrible," John thought. "It seems, either way, the phantoms don't really want to kill us, but they have no choice either way."

"I wouldn't sympathize with the phantoms," Jerry shook his head. "They must be horrible to get into that state. They deserve an everlasting Limbo. And ghouls can provide that for us."

"So our first mission," Paul said. "Find a ghoul."

"No need," a deep voice from behind them said. "A ghoul is here. No promises that I'll work for or even help you while Zach is still out there."

7.) Ghouls

Jerry turned around and threw his sword at the same time. The ghoul just floated in the air and the sword went right through him. Jerry used his psychic power to pull it back to him. Jerry knew now that weapons would be useless. Daniel, however, put his wand out and magically made a purple magic sphere.

"Who are you and what do you want?" Daniel said menacingly.

The ghoul looked at the sphere and laughed.

"You cannot hurt me," it said.

"You want to test your luck?" Daniel said. "I know that phantoms aren't affected by magic, but ghouls ... well ... "

The ghoul suddenly looked angry.

"Are you saying we're weaker?" it growled.

"Well," Daniel said, pretending to think. "I could spell it out for you if you didn't want—"

The ghoul lunged. Daniel staged a strong standoff. The ghoul paused in midair, pondering. Daniel held a steady gaze, and the others wanted to see if the ghoul would push its luck. But deep down, they were wondering, *is Dan bluffing?*

"Are you willing to negotiate a few things?" Jerry asked.

The ghoul stared at the ball but replied, "Yes."

"Alright," Paul said. "First off, who are you?"

The ghoul finally turned to Paul.

"Just call me Sire, for now," the ghoul replied. "I am the leader of the ghoul colony. We have heard that a magician made a deal with the phantoms. This really is to the annoyance of us ghouls, for no ghost has been in battle for over 300 years. But the ghouls know that when there is a battle involving ghosts, the ghouls must win. We must. So we quickly built a militia to fight against the army. But now we are ready to attack. All we need to know is who is leading this army."

"First off, I need your allegiance," Daniel said, destroying the ball. "I can give you the location of the enemy and who is leading them in return if you help us in a simple battle."

"If it's simple, why do you need our help?" Sire asked.

"Simple for you, Sire," Daniel answered, bowing. "The army we need you to defeat is not magical, let alone magicians.

We will have a problem because they are large in number. But one of your ghouls could take them out, so let's say 50 of your finest would do."

Sire thought for a moment.

"Fifty?" he asked. John was surprised.

"Actually," he said. "How many do you have?"

"A thousand, no less," Sire said. "Though low in number, I am positive we will succeed."

John, as he sometimes does when he has a dream or adrenaline pumping through him, had another revelation.

"The orb," he whispered.

"What?" Daniel said, turning to him. John turned to Jerry.

"You're wrong, Jerry," John said. "There is something that can destroy the dead."

"The dead," Paul replied. Sire nodded.

"No, not that," John said grinning. He looked back at Sire. "Jerry said there were about, what was it? Thirty thousand?"

"Less than that, no more than 20," Jerry said, nodding.

"A thousand ghouls cannot defeat an army that is greater in number and, no offense, stronger," John explained. "But we can help each other. We both agree that we need to destroy the phantoms – you, as a matter of pride; us, as a matter for life. Are you with me so far?"

"So far," Sire pondered cautiously.

"But the dead can only be blocked by the dead," John said. "It would be pointless for the living to face them if we needed a diversion, which is what we need. If the phantoms reach any part of our army before we can eliminate them, we will surely lose. We need a dead army to delay them."

Sire liked the idea so far. He nodded.

"Now, if you were to recruit every ghoul possible, how many do you think it would be?" John asked.

"I am not sure," Sire replied thoughtfully. "Maybe 4,000."

"Now Paul, here's where you come in," John said, turning to him. "Can your super-computer clone?"

"I could clone some of the living," Paul said. "The cloning of the dead is a complex theory that requires much needed analysis. However, the internals of such creatures are a lot easier. I hypothesize that it could be done, but I do not know where to start on the ectoplasmic layer of skin."

"Wow," John said. "I honestly don't have a clue what you said, but just get it done. We need at least 10,000."

"ARE YOU INSANE?!" Paul yelled, hands pulling out his hair. "Do you know how long it takes to clone someone?!"

"An hour? Half?" John guessed.

"ABOUT A WEEK!" Paul said.

"A week?!" John yelled back. "We don't have weeks, we have days! I thought your computer was more advanced, Paul. Seems like the same old unreliable one I am used to."

"John, think logically," Jerry said. "This earth, filled with its best scientists, could only clone a sheep. That took long periods of time and cost a fortune. Only for a sheep. Now a ghost is much different than a sheep and a ghost army would take, in modern ways, probably a century to clone. You have to cut Paul some slack, I mean, producing one in a week is miraculous."

"That is wonderful you can produce *a* ghoul. But it just isn't enough," John said. "We need more."

"It is just impossible," Jerry said. Paul turned to him, glaring. He turned back to John angrily.

"How much time will you give me?" He asked.

"One day," John said. "No later."

"Paul," Jerry said, awestruck.

"Not this time, Jerry," Paul said, squinting hard at his computer. "You know my policy – never say impossible. One day, and you will have no room to put your amazing army."

John fell back onto the ground and laughed. Jerry joined in, and then everyone else. It was hilarious that they actually thought that they could stop Zach. It was hilarious that they thought they could create the dead. It was hilarious that they saw themselves arguing about war when most of them were still children. They laughed for quite some time. They ate what they could find in the ship, inviting Sire along (Victor stayed at his lookout position). They told stories about when they were away, Jerry having the most exiting. Sire told them about his life in the 1740s and they laughed and clapped when he told them of his journeys. They all went to sleep pleasantly that night, knowing that they were with each other and could count on each other once again.

A few days passed. John got up early to talk to Sire. He went up on deck where the ghost was awake.

"Do you sleep?" John asked him.

"No, no ghosts do," Sire replied.

"So how do you become a ghost?" John asked him.

"Well, that depends," Sire answered. "Phantoms, as you might know, are sent here as punishment. Ghouls are sent here as a second life if they had a terrible one before."

"Oh, so like a reincarnation?" John said.

"Exactly," the ghoul responded. "And I believe a specter comes back because they weren't ready to die. An example is if a person was cooking something, but then had a heart attack. They weren't thinking about death or weren't ready to die. This doesn't include those whose death is quick but not sudden, for they think that they are going to die just before they do. So some, not all, come back as a specter."

"Right," John said. "Well that's good, maybe my friends will come back as specters."

"I doubt it," Sire shook his head sadly. "I might have seen them. Anyway, why did you want to talk to me?"

"I need you as a distraction," John said. "My family is convinced that they can have you as an ally and you can defeat the ghost part of the army and we beat the living part of the army. Well, I know that won't work because you have a thousand strong while they have about three legions. It would be a fantasy for you to beat them."

"I see," Sire said. "But you think by distracting them you would be able to defeat them in the end? How do you plan to do that?"

"This whole war is a distraction," John said. "We try to distract the enemy while we try to reach Phoenix."

"So what's in it for us if there's no hope for victory?" Sire asked.

"Well, a couple nights ago, I figured something out," John began. "You see ... we're after this ... orb. This orb has the power to destroy all the magicians. If it has the power to wipe out the magicians, it might have enough power to destroy the phantoms. That way, all phantoms will be killed. The ghouls will be the dominant ghost power."

"And if the distraction isn't long enough and the enemy gets to the orb first?" Sire asked.

"I don't know," John replied sadly. "We have nothing to offer you except allegiance … if we are to die and come back as a ghost of some sort."

"That's not good enough, I'm afraid," the ghoul said. He looked at John's disappointed face. "But I'm sure you'll find a way."

Sire turned around and sort of floated away from John. John had an idea.

"Wait a minute."

Sire turned to him.

"Can just humans become ghosts?" John asked.

"I am not sure if any other creature has the emotions needed to fulfill the requirements."

"I think it can," John said, smiling. "What if we traded you a few dragons or horses if you were to distract them?"

Sire's eyes widened.

"Dragons?" he said disbelievingly.

"Yes, that would be harder, but imagine your army on the backs of horses," John said. "Imagine instead of 'Ghoul Army,' it's the 'Ghoul Cavalry'."

"Mr. Quaill, you have yourself a deal," Sire said, holding out a hand. John paused, and then reached for it, but then Sire put it down, "Ah, yes, I forgot … "

John laughed.

"I'll wake my brother," John said. "It can't be too hard, naturally creating horse ghouls as opposed to an artificial process."

John ran down to the lower levels and woke his brother. He told him his idea of horses.

"Excellent," Paul said. "You're right, it is much easier, I can explain why after you wake everyone else up."

John hastily woke everyone. They all ran up onto the deck. Paul pulled out from his pack bag a laptop. He opened it and turned it on. John expected a hologram to come out, but none came.

"Alright," Paul said to his family. "I need to create a ghoul horse and I have an idea how. I have saved on my computer the genetics of a horse that I tried to clone. I was successful, of course. Now all I have to do is combine some genes … "

Paul typed something on his computer. Suddenly, a horse appeared out of the computer.

"Now, Sire said something about animals not having the proper emotions to become a ghoul," Paul said. "But my computer is so advanced, it can create emotions. Which emotion do we need? Oh yes, despair."

"Why despair?" Jerry asked him.

"If it has a terrible life, it comes back as a ghost, according to Sire," Paul replied, typing. "Now I must hook up these wires to the horse's head."

Wires came forth from the end of the computer and Paul grabbed them. He reached for the horse but the horse snorted and snapped its mouth at him.

"I'll do it," Jerry laughed. He took the wires from Paul. "Whoa now, pretty, calm down. Whoa … "

The horse calmed down. Jerry stroked its head and carefully pressed the wires above its eyes.

"Very good, Jerry," Paul said as if he personally had taught Jerry how to calm a wild horse. "Now, just step away."

Paul pressed a button on his computer and a humming noise came from the wires. The horse froze.

"Alright, he is not thinking about his death or defending himself. And he feels he has had a terrible life," Paul said, taking out his ax. He stepped up next to the horse's neck. He raised his ax, but didn't bring it down. The horse looked at him with a strange look on its face.

"Paul?" John asked him.

"I can kill a hundred ogres," Paul said, not taking his eyes off the horse. "But I can't kill a defenseless horse."

"I'll do it," Daniel said, stepping up. He pulled out one of his sharp swords and brought it to the horse neck, next to the ax. With swiftness, he chopped off the head. The body of the horse slumpt to the floor. Suddenly, a white shadow appeared out of the horse. It rose up to the height of Sire. Sire looked at them.

"Is this … mine?" he asked in a whisper.

"Yes," John said. Shaking, Sire put his foot over the horse's body. He then mounted the horse.

"This is the first time I've been on a horse in three and a half centuries years," Sire said, grinning.

"That's great," Paul said impatiently. "But the thing is, I need the horse's new DNA and stuff to clone it."

"Yes, yes, of course," Sire said, riding towards him. "Go ahead."

"I honestly don't know how to save something that's not a fluid or solid," Paul laughed. "But why not try? F2, scan and save."

"F2?" Jerry asked him.

"Flaminetore II," Paul explained. A red beam came out of the computer and went up and down the ghoul horse, scanning it. The beam went away and a computerized voice said, "Scan complete, Data saved."

"Good," Paul said, reading what he was typing. "Wow, this is easier than I imagined. There is nothing inside them internally so that it's simple and the layer of skin is thin—I guess that was the easiest for F2. Now create the saved data. Amount? One thousand. Ok."

A large blast came from Paul's computer. Ghoul horses flew out of the computer by the hundreds. When they finally stopped coming out, Paul's computer overheated and shut down.

"Wow!" Sire said happily, looking around. "I think this will be enough. I will make a grand distraction with these babies! John, the deal has started; I'll bring these horses to our men to make them cavalry! Now I must go."

With that, and a flash of green light, he disappeared with the thousand of horses.

"What deal?" Daniel said, turning to John angrily.

"I told him we needed them to hold off the phantoms while we fight Zach," John said.

"We could have used them to our advantage," Jerry said, "besides distraction."

"And I didn't get to capture some of the ectoplasm that is needed for cloning the ghouls," Paul muttered.

"But you guys are forgetting the orb," John said. "I believe this orb can wipe out every thing in a certain species. If we are able to get this orb, we will be able to, yes Jerry, kill all the phantoms in the world—no, the universe!"

"Ha," Jerry snorted.

"*You think?*" Paul asked him. "*You think* you know what it is? Nobody but Zach knows. And what if you're wrong?"

"What do we have to lose?" John asked. "This war is a big distraction anyway, right?"

That quieted them down.

"Uncle Dan, you had no problem leading tons of magicians to their deaths," John said, "only to delay Zach for a few hours at most. These guys actually might defeat the phantoms with horses."

"True," Jerry said.

"It'll just make things more complicated," Daniel said.

"We still have the mammoths to worry about," Paul pronounced, grimacing. "They aren't picnics; we will have trouble with them too."

"I bet I will slay 15 of them," John spat arrogantly, "by myself."

"Are you dead serious?" Paul said, smirking.

"Name your price," John replied confidently.

"Loser states that the winner is a better warrior," Jerry said. "Those things are huge, I think even I could only beat two at most."

"Fifteen," John repeated.

"You're on," Jerry and Paul said at the same time.

"Land!" Victor yelled from the crow's nest. They all turned.

"We're at the island already," Daniel said, sighing. "Now we can pick up the *Ring* and the rest of the magicians."

They hit shore and saw many ships lined up ready to head off. Each was packed with magicians.

"I've never seen so many magicians," Paul said in awe.

Daniel leapt over board to the shore. He headed for one of the ships.

"Should we follow?" Paul asked.

"No," Jerry said. "I think he is talking with one of the council members."

"Alright," John said. And as Jerry predicted, a few magicians followed him. John looked at the forest on the island. Suddenly, pain struck through his heart like fire. John let out a scream with instinct. Jerry and Paul turned to him in surprise.

"What's wrong with you, John?" Paul yelled.

The pain stopped.

"It's not me," John said, looking back at the forest. "It's the enemy."

John stood up.

"There's something bad in that forest," he said. Suddenly, Daniel and the other magicians turned to the forest. "We have to get out of here."

Another burning thing shot through John, this time in his head. He fell to his knees. John then knew why.

"Oh no," he muttered. "Not again."

He looked up to his brothers.

"He's back," John breathed, panic in his eyes. "I thought he was dead, but he's back. And he's back for my mind. I can't help you in this battle without putting you at a greater risk. Here they come!"

Jerry and Paul at first didn't know what John was talking about. All of a sudden, a loud horn was heard from the forest and the trees came crashing down as something enormous smashed into them. It was the first of many mammoths. Behind them were at least 10,000 ogres and goblins.

8.) The Second Stand

Jerry and Paul leapt out of the boat. The leading mammoth proceeded towards them. The magicians started to jump out of the ships and line up in formations. All of the magicians fired blasts of magic at the mammoths, but none of the mammoths fell.

Jerry and Paul ran to the front of the army, waiting for impact. One of the mammoths charged into the lines. All of the magicians focused their power on that mammoth. Their shots bounced off the creature's skin and fur.

"I'm going in," Paul announced, taking a deep breath. He ran up to the mammoth. Using his genie powers, he stretched himself up to the mammoth. He smashed his ax into its side, but the mammoth kept charging over magicians. Paul twisted as hard as he could on the ax's handle. Lightning shot out and Paul aimed for its side. It shocked it, but the mammoth kept moving. *How am I supposed to kill this thing*, Paul thought. Paul crawled up to the head of the mammoth where a goblin was controlling the mammoth. Paul leapt forward to kill the creature, but the creature was exceptionally fast and had good hearing. The goblin swiftly turned around, dropping the reigns, and stopped Paul with his knife. The goblin had reddish gray skin. It was much friskier, in an evil way, than an ogre. It leapt over Paul and took a swung at his neck. Paul stretched away from him and grabbed the reigns and pulled to the left sharply. The mammoth jerked his head and body to the left so fast that the goblin flew off it.

"The magicians can deal with it now," Paul said, turning towards the ogre army. "Let's give them a taste of their own medicine."

He whacked the reigns and the mammoth went. He headed towards another mammoth. It was almost a game of "chicken," only the stakes were higher. The other mammoth tried to turn first. Paul aimed directly at the side of the other mammoth. Just before he hit, the mammoth trampled over a couple dozen ogres. Paul's mammoth hit the back leg of the other mammoth and knocked it down. This shot Paul's mammoth backwards onto its backend. Paul held onto the reigns, just barely preventing his fall. The mammoth began to roll onto his back and was about to smash Paul. Paul carefully leapt off the creature. The mammoth fell onto its back, helpless. It smashed fifty ogres in the process. There were 40 or so mammoths left.

Jerry had pulled out his sword and thought of jealousy. His sword turned very red and the sword's blade caught fire. A magician next to him looked at the sword with a strange expression.

"May I?" The magician asked, pointing at the weapon.

"In the middle of battle?" Jerry said in awe.

"They haven't reached us yet," the magician replied, raising an eyebrow. He gave Jerry a strange look.

"Sure," Jerry answered, still unsure. The magician took the sword from him and his eyes turned blood red. The eyes reminded Jerry of something ... but he couldn't remember what. A big wind picked up, blowing on his face, his hair pushed out of his eyes. Then Jerry remembered his uncle doing the same when he healed Jerry and Paul three years before: his eyes were blood red as well as his hand ...

Jerry quickly looked at the man's right hand and recognized the shade of color. The magician waved his hand over the sword's blade and the fire came off it onto the ground. The wind swept around it and it formed a dust devil. The tornado caught the fire and it formed a small "fire devil." The magician shot both hands into the air, expanding the small tornado until it was an enormous cyclone. All the magicians forced the tornado towards the approaching army. Jerry realized something.

"My brother's over there!" Jerry yelled, but nobody heard over the wind. He grabbed his sword from the man. He ran past the tornado, which was moving very fast. He saw scattered ogres and goblins heading towards him. "I don't have time for THIS!"

He put his hands to his chest and concentrated as hard as he could on his psychic power. He concentrated all the psychic power he had and formed it in a sphere around him to deflect the attacks and the tornado. He ran as fast as his feet could take him (and maybe even faster). Ogres bounced off his new psychic shield. Panicking, Jerry looked for his brother. Already, ogres and goblins were getting sucked into the fire devil and Jerry knew his brother would be next.

John fell onto his back on the deck of the ship, sweating. He was fighting hard for his body against an evil spirit inside of him. It was the same spirit that he had fought against a few months previous, the presence that Zach forced into him – the spirit John had forced to take the blast of the Morphelellist.

"No … not … again," John muttered in agony. "I will … not … "

"You will," came the response in his head. "You will surrender to me, your master … "

"Never … "

"NOW!"

"NEVER!" John yelled. He opened his eyes widely.

"Then I will force myself into you, just like you did to me," It laughed. Another jab like a knife and John let out a screech. He finally had to give in. He closed his eyes. Someone else inside him opened them and made him smile.

"I'm back," John said in a voice not his own. "But I need to kill his family to complete Zach's plans."

John's new spirit leapt up in John's body, pulling out his sword.

He said, "He couldn't hold me off this long. Not when Zach is so close. Obey me, servant."

Paul looked up to see the tornado of fire. Paul ran towards the magicians. He had killed only one more mammoth, using constant lightning, but he lost count how many ogres he killed. On his way, he saw a large, purple sphere. He ran towards it to find it was his brother.

"Paul, are you ok?" Jerry asked.

"Yes," Paul panted. The tornado hit the first rank of ogres, sucking them in and destroying them.

Then, suddenly, an abnormal feeling went through Paul's and Jerry's skin. They looked in the path of the tornado. The ogres parted and there was a large man in the path.

This, beyond all else, carried the aurora of hell.

The man, or creature, had a black cloak on, darker than Daniel's or Zach's. It was blacker than the pitch-blackness of the night. He had a dark hood that covered nearly his entire face, except his eyes. The bystanders could see white eyes shining out of the hood. The ogres seemed to fear to even look at him and Jerry now knew that he and they had something common.

The cloaked man raised his hand at the tornado and Jerry and Paul saw what its hand looked like. They were redder than the dragon Jerry faced, deader than the skin of the ogres, more scary than his white eyes, and the claws on his fingers were thicker and redder than the devil's hate.

Jerry and Paul ran.

John's possessed body leapt out of the ship, but caught sight of the man dressed in black. He let out another scream.

Jerry and Paul ran to Daniel.

"Uncle Dan," Jerry said. He pointed to the tornado. "There's a man ... he's evil ... and ..."

The tornado stopped. The top of the cyclone stopped spinning and slowly, all the way down, the tornado stopped spinning. The fire hit the ground, but it just turned into embers. Daniel spotted the man, the one who stopped the tornado. He turned to Paul.

"Well," he said. "Time to go."

"What?" Paul asked confused.

"RUN!" he yelled. He turned to the magicians. "Retreat to the boats! Run! RETREAT!"

Paul and Jerry ran towards their ship. All of the other magicians jumped into random ships, not the ones they were originally in. Daniel saw John lying on the ground, unconscious.

"Someone get him!" he yelled. Jerry picked him up and dove into the ship. "Unroll the sails! Hurry! We must move!"

Paul stretched up to the crows' nest.

"Victor, come help me unroll these," Paul called to Victor.

In 10 seconds flat, all the ships left the island. John awoke.

"Are you ok?" Jerry asked him.

"Yes, except..." John whispered, dazed, "I can't remember anything. I remember landing on an island and that's it."

"We were ambushed," Daniel explained, crouching down next to him, "by the ogre army."

"How does Zach do it?" Jerry asked Daniel. "I mean, where do ogres come from?"

"They are transformed," John replied. "They were originally genies that were turned insane and lost all of their powers."

Daniel and Jerry both turned to him in amazement.

"How'd you know that?" Daniel gasped.

"I have revelations or dreams that make my brain work extra hard," John replied. "I dreamt Paul had turned into one, one time."

"So that would explain why the genie population has dropped over this past century," Daniel said. "There used to be millions of genies, but now they are nearly extinct."

"Wait, Zach's not 100 years old though, is he?" John almost laughed.

Daniel looked at him quickly.

"He's ... a bit older than you think," Daniel whispered.

"And this also explains why Zach has so many," Jerry added, not catching the last part of the conversation. "He could have millions. I don't think genies are the only way to create ogres, though. There's got to be another way."

"Maybe," John said. He then turned to Daniel. "I remember one thing from the island and that's before I fainted. It was this black man. The black sort of 'shown through' the darkness. Who was he ... or it?"

Daniel focused on the floor. He didn't look up when he answered John's question.

"There are things in this world," Daniel whispered in reply, "that have attributes. People might call these attributes stances or sides. We are considered the 'good' side. Zach is on the 'bad' side. Most people stop there. However, magical and intelligent people conclude there are two more categories: evil and pure. I can explain. Zach doesn't go around killing squirrels because they're living. However, Zach would kill the squirrel if it meant killing you. An evil person would kill anything in its path that's living. A 'bad' person doesn't care about the living, but evil goes farther and makes sure that anything living is dead."

"And pure?" John asked.

"Ah," Daniel sighed, "there are so few that exist, or ever existed for that matter, that few people count them. Pure care about living. They hate sin. Sin and evil is the only things pures hate. They don't go to war unless it is against evils. They love life and hate sin so much, they would give up their lives to save lives and get rid of sin and have everyone live forever. In fact, one pure did die—"

"Wait, what does this have to do with the black cloaked man?" John asked.

"Anyway," Daniel continued, "they're the only thing that keeps sin in existence, evils. So pures and evils both want to be rid of the other. However, pure people are the only ones that can kill an evil. Pures cannot be killed unless they choose to die. That black cloaked man, he is an evil, one of the first I have ever seen."

"So we can't defeat him without the strength of a pure?" John asked.

"Correct," Daniel said, "but I highly doubt there is a pure now. They usually appear bi-century."

"Bi … you mean every 200 years?" John asked in amazement.

"At the most," Daniel said. "Evils become evils under much dedication and choice. Pures must have the strongest dedication to become one. In fact, sometimes it isn't their choice."

"What do you mean it's not their choice?" John asked.

"Sir," a magician ran up to Daniel. "The ogres have ships and are gaining on us!"

"Hold on, this is important," Daniel said. "I'll hurry. This evil bares the mark of the Kraskull."

"Kraskull?" John asked.

"It's a part of the evil category that makes up the most vicious or all evils," Daniel replied. He stood up. "But now we must face the naval ogres."

"I have heard of the Kraskull," Jerry said. "I thought they were called the Soulhaunts."

"Different names, I guess," John shivered. "I don't think I have heard of anything more scary."

"Prepare the cannons!" Daniel yelled. He glanced up at the many black ships that were quickly approaching. "All ranged weapons to the side, prepare for The Second Stand! Sound the horn of war."

Victor jumped out of the crow's nest and ran towards the bow of the ship where a giant horn was. He blew it loud; the ogres answered with a fearful blow of their own. They were catching up. John ran to the side where everyone was going. He pulled his bow off his shoulder and pulled back on the string. The ogre ships pulled parallel to the magician ships. There were 12 magician ships and 18 ogre ships.

Once the ships were completely parallel, they each shot their ranged weapons at the nearest ship. The ogres pulled out a long board and slammed it between the two ships so it made a bridge between them. John leapt onto the plank.

"Knock it off the ship or we'll be overrun!" Daniel yelled at him.

"It's too late," John called back. "They nailed it into their ship! I'll hold them off and you cut the board off!"

He ran toward the other ship and kicked two ogres overboard who had attempted to come across. He leapt onto the ship and heard a growl that signaled the arrival of Lino. John grinned at him and they turned towards their opponent.

"Let's clear it out," John said, swiping the heads off a couple ogres. John noticed there was a hole in the middle of the ship where ogres were coming out.

"I'll go under and stop them," Lino said, courageously jumping in. John had not choice but to stay above.

Jerry and Paul were at the other side of their ship, stopping the ogres who tried to come over using harpoon lines. Paul's ax was so accurate, it hit the harpoons while they were still in the air. Few made it across, and if they did, Jerry took care of them.

"You guys stay over there and stop the attacks," Daniel commanded, impressed.

"That's what we're doing," Paul said aiming his ax high.

"Well, continue doing it," Daniel said. "I'll go to John's aid. Ah, there's the signal! Only 17 left to go."

"I think we were extremely lucky when we were on that island," Paul spat, blasting an ogre apart. "I don't know who John's kidding—he couldn't take down more than three of those mammoths."

"Not only are we lucky not to have mammoths," Jerry breathed. "Those Kraskulls, we're lucky they haven't showed up yet. Maybe they left them behind."

"It's going to take a miracle to beat him," Paul agreed. "Literally."

"Another signal!" Daniel called to John. "That's the third one. They're plan is backfiring!"

"I just want to get to the lower levels," John yelled, slaying one. "Lino must be exhausted. More are still coming!"

"Then you head down there if you have to," Daniel answered, destroying two.

John nodded and ran to the hole. He threw himself down it. It was only a 10 foot drop. John hit the ground running. He saw Lino still jumping around an ogre to avoid his attacks, but John knew he was tired. He leapt up and killed the ogre that almost took the finishing swipe to Lino. John saw goblins there as well.

"I'd head upstairs, buddy," John advised to Lino. "This could get very bad, very quickly."

"I'll take my chances," Lino said. He leapt up and tackled a goblin that had charged at John. John chopped the head off another. He saw another hole.

"How many levels are there?!" he said in exasperation. Lino tackled two and clawed them until they stopped moving. John saw that the goblins were harder to kill than the ogres because they were much swifter. John conjured up a shield like he did many times before. The goblin's strange shaped weapons bounced off the shield. John turned and saw that Lino was in trouble. He was battling a strong ogre. John moved to aid him.

Suddenly, about 15 more ogres came out of the hole and surrounded John. John's superhero-type adrenaline kicked in; he yelled and swung his sword wildly. He used magic and sucked the life out of some of the ogres. There was a gap big enough for him to squeeze through. John ran through it to Lino, but it was too late. Lino was struck by the side of the ogre's sword.

Blood splattered everywhere. Lino fell to the ground.

"NO!" John bellowed. He ran and in one vicious swipe, knocked the sword out of the strong hands of the ogre. Pivoting on his foot, he threw his strength into the second strike, killing the ogre. John withheld the impulse to continue striking at the dead corpse.

John knelt down to Lino to feel his pulse. John's own heart was pounding, but he could not feel Lino's.

John closed his eyes for a second. Deep down inside, John knew that a war without the death of his friends was a miracle. John, however, had hoped that he wasn't there to witness it. He thought it might be—though hoped it wasn't—his young, inexperienced brother. One of the last ones he thought would die would be Lino.

John felt tears roll down his face. Even the goblins behind him stopped as they saw the fierce creature dead.

John felt a jab like a knife in his stomach. John got up. *Not this time*, he thought. *This spirit isn't going to control me; I'm going to control him.*

"I am in control," John said in anger. More than anger – hate. It was the 'evil' way of thinking. He turned to the goblins with a terrible grin on his face. "You killed my friends, you killed many magicians, and you are responsible for my friend Lino. However, you are also the one to mess with John Quaill's life. There is no other terror than to see John in an evil mode. Prepare for death, and no, I am not using my sword."

John threw his sword at the side of the ship.

"I am a Morphelellist, and you will feel my wrath!"

John looked up the hole and saw it was a still a full moon. He laughed. The claws on his fingers started to grow. His nose and mouth stretched into a snout. He began to grow fur. His teeth grew as long as knives. His eyes turned from blue to black. In a human's eyes he just turned into a werewolf. But in magician's language, he was now a Morphelellist in complete morph. In this stage, not even Zach and all the power of the rings could stop him—at the cost of perpetual destruction.

John let out an earth, or in this case, sea-shaking roar. He charged at the running goblins and devoured them all. The Morphelellist made sure that the dead ogres' corpses were unrecognizable. He killed all of them. The Morphelellist jumped to the upper levels of the ship.

Daniel killed a total of 200 ogres and goblins. He couldn't take much more at his age.

The left side of the ship suddenly split open near him and sent him flying through the air. He jumped to his feet. He saw a monstrous creature come out of the hole and destroyed everything in its path.

"Oh no," Daniel said, breathing hard. "Not again. Not now."

The creature came aboard and spotted Daniel. For a second, Daniel thought there was hope. Then the creature ran at him as well. Daniel brought his sword to the Morphelellist's arm. It bounced off. The creature smacked its large paw at Daniel and he went flying to the bow of the ship and almost into the sea. Daniel ran to the plank. The Morphelellist was distracted by the ogres. Daniel ran across to Paul and Jerry.

"Any luck?" he said quickly. They were just able to nod before Daniel said, "John's gone Morph."

Jerry's eyes widened.

"How can we change him back?" Paul asked.

"In complete morph," Daniel said. "Nothing. There has nothing so far that was able to beat it except a strange occurrence that stopped him, but it was a miracle, never to happen again. Only a pure could kill him in this stage."

"You mean ... " Paul gasped.

"Yes," Daniel sighed, turning. "He is now evil."

"We must beat him," Jerry whispered, taking out his sword. "There has to be a way."

Daniel shook his head.

"So we're going to surrender this early?" Paul said angrily. "If this is how we treat our second stand, we will never beat Zach."

"Even if we could overcome a Morphelellist," Daniel said, "we would probably kill John in the process."

"So are we going to let ourselves be devoured by a werewolf or are we going to go out like heroes?" Paul asked.

"This will be embarrassing if Zach hears," Jerry said. "Defeated by our own men."

They all laughed.

"Jerry, you are the only one to make me laugh in the time of danger," Daniel said. "Alright, one more stand. For the world."

"For Locombony," Jerry put in his hand into the circle. Daniel put in his.

"For John," Paul said, "who would have wanted us to do this."

He put in his hand.

They yelled as if it was a basketball game. They all stood up and pulled out their swords. They lined up and walked the plank, in Daniel's mind, of death. In that short time, the monster had destroyed all of the ogres on that ship. He now turned to his new opponents. Daniel sent out a red signal, meaning all help to this ship. Paul made the first move. He shot all the lightning his ax could produce at it. It rebounded back at him in a ball of lightning. Jerry leapt in front of Paul and swung his sword. He rebounded it back at the Morphelellist. The monster pushed it into the ground and made a blast in the ship large enough to fit 30 people. The large werewolf looked up at Jerry.

"Come at me," Jerry growled, raising his sword. "I have never been knocked down."

The werewolf rampaged at Jerry. Daniel blasted a magic ball at it. It had no affect at all. Jerry swung his magical sword at the chest of the Morphelellist. Fire shot out of it. Still, the only affect it did was to throw Jerry backwards. True to his word, he didn't fall to the ground, but slammed into the edge of the ship. He slid to his feet.

The other magicians came to the ship, followed by the other ogre ships. The first leapt off and started to blast him.

"Give it up," Daniel said to Paul, who was shooting lightning at it still. "Maybe we can escape this ship and leave it here. I don't mind dying, saving these magicians' lives, but don't pull other victims into it."

"That's my brother!" Paul yelled. "I'M NOT LEAVING!"

"He's my nephew," Daniel said. "But we can't beat him or turn him back."

John was thrown into a black room in his mind. He saw the evil spirit being forced into a Morphelellist. He laughed.

"I have no downside," he said. "When the morph gets stronger and stronger, he will eventually die. And then I'll be with Lino."

He watched ogres getting slaughtered everywhere.

"Plus, Zach will have his power used against him. The spirit will finally die," John said. He watched himself go above and slaughter everyone in his sight. He saw his uncle thrown to the edge of the ship.

"Who cares? He dragged me into this war; he's the main cause of this tragedy. Let him die as well."

John realized something that if he hadn't, the world would be lost. It wasn't his uncle's fault; it was his. He shouldn't have let Lino go below without him.

"No," John said, putting his hands into his face. "What have I done?! I have put my brothers in danger. I must kill this spirit before this causes my death along with my brother's."

John opened the door to the room of his mind and saw the spirit squirming on the floor.

"*Let me go!*" it said, no longer low and fierce.

"I did before, yet you came back," John said laughing.

"*I swear I won't,*" it said. "*I feel every blast that is fired at me!*"

"Let me hear you say an oath of magic you won't ever bother me or anyone else again," John smirked.

"*I swear ...*" he said, and then he screamed. "*No ... I'm ... sorry... he ... beat ... me ...*"

"Not this time," Zach's voice cried out in John's head. John trembled. "My servant, as you see, Quaill, has failed me again. You got lucky again, Quaill. Don't worry, we will meet in the real world again and it'll take more than your wolf to beat me again. But I am feeling awfully kind today and destroying my servant will save you as well. Goodbye, Quaill."

Daniel commanded the magicians back on their ships against Paul's will.

"We'll defeat the ogres later at sea," he yelled. "Let's get as far as we can away from this ship!"

"If John dies," Paul snorted. "I'll die next to him."

Ogres were leaping onto the ship of the Morphelellist, thinking it was on the magicians' team. They were destroyed on an average of two seconds after they boarded.

"Come on John," Paul said. "I believe in you. You're the only one that can help us all now."

Jerry hustled everyone onto their ships. He regretted leaving John, but he just couldn't put all the magicians at risk. John wouldn't have wanted that.

"Paul," Jerry whispered. "John wouldn't have wanted for you to stay …"

"You better watch it," Paul said. "I might turn into a Morph just from anger."

Already the monster had wiped out two and a half ship's worth of ogres and goblins.

Paul turned one more time to John. He focused all his loyalty on his ax, along with all his genie powers. He squeezed with all his strength.

If there were satellites watching the sea they were in, they would be able to see a green spot for three seconds where Paul was standing.

Paul's blast was so monstrous, the furthest magician from the blast could feel the heat. Paul aimed the blast right at the creature. It hit it and the Morphelellist fell over.

It was at that moment the spirit of Zach left the Morphelellist.

The creature slumpt to the ground. Its features changed back to a human. It was John, and his body was limp, dead.

9.) The Breaking of the Union

Paul ran up to John. He shook him, saying, "John! Wake up!"

"The ship is sinking!" Jerry called. "The blast was too much! It blasted everything apart!"

With all his strength, Paul picked up John's body. He ran to the ship's edge and leapt onto Jerry's ship. Jerry turned to the group.

"Is everyone here?" he asked.

"Where's the liger?" Victor asked.

Jerry turned to the nearly sunk ship.

"He must still be below," he answered. "Someone has to get him."

There wasn't much caring in his voice—he was obviously more concerned with the magicians. Daniel dove into the water. He swam to the hole John made in the ship. He swam inside looking frantically for the pink tiger. He spotted it floating near by. Daniel picked him up with one hand and swam with the other. Daniel broke the surface of the water with a gasp.

"I got him," he spat. He lifted him up to Jerry.

"Satisfied?" Jerry asked Paul. "Can we stop gambling the world over a couple skirmishes?"

"One problem," Daniel panted, getting back into the ship. "There are still ogre ships. And they just blockaded us."

Jerry turned to where they were heading and saw 14 ogre ships in the way.

"Then I guess we can face them," Jerry said. "Paul, can you see? Does the bow run low?"

But Paul was trying to revive John. Pushing against his chest and giving him some breaths, Paul felt for John's pulse. There was a steady beat. Paul slumped to the ground next to him.

"He needs to be taking care of," he said. "Same with Lino, they both look dead."

"We can't worry about that now," one of the magicians said. "Our ships are coming within 20 feet. Should we prepare the cannons?"

John felt his body coming back into his control. He breathed deeply. He opened his eyes and saw Paul hovering above him. Lino was to his side.

"Are you ok?" Paul said, sighing.

"Yes," John breathed. "Paul, there's no point in keeping Lino like that. He's dead."

"He has a light heart beat," Paul corrected. John's heart skipped. "We're in the lower levels of the ship. We decided to land on a small island and battle there. What happened?"

"I saw Lino get injured and I felt for his pulse; I couldn't feel it. I got angry and I felt the evil spirit come inside me again. I forced him to morph so that he would die and I could get my vengeance. Then I fought for my body back, but by the time I was about to take over, Zach pulled his spirit filled with the morph out of me."

Paul's jaw dropped.

"Well, that's what happened," John said. "I saw your lightning, but that wasn't the real cause of the Morphelellist being defeated."

"Wow ..." Paul said. "You mean that the only way to control or defeat a Morphelellist is to have two spirits?"

"Yes," John said. "Zach, if you remember, had pretty much the power of the entire universe with all the rings. That didn't matter if he did or did not have that last ring—not all the magic in the universe could knock me down. The only way I could be defeated is if my soul can control the morph and transform it back...or if I had two spirits. The other spirit was pulled out of my body before it died, and somehow, Zach saved him. He came back and I tried the same trip. I can't be killed in the Morph state. Well, I guess a pure could beat me."

"You were pure," Paul said. "If no magic can kill you, than you're a pure."

"I was evil," John corrected. "Evil becomes evil, don't you remember? I wasn't just made a pure."

"True," Paul said.

John grabbed his sword.

"But now I am ready for the battle at hand," he said. He also picked up his shield. "Can you take care of Lino?"

"I'll try," Paul said cautiously. "Are you sure you're all right?"

" 'Good enough to hold a sword, good enough to fight'," John recited Jerry's battle motto. "I'll be fine, Paul."

He turned to head the ladder. Paul gasped. John turned quickly.

"What's wrong?" John asked.

"Your ... ears ..."

John felt his ears. They were more pointed, like a wolf.

"And your nails!" Paul exclaimed.

John looked at his hands which had big black claws.

"I know about the claws," John said, feeling his ears again. "Every time I morph, something else becomes more like a wolf. The claws I had for quite some time now. But the ears must be from that last morph."

"John, are sure you know what you're doing?" Paul said.

John got annoyed.

"I was just possessed, Paul," John said. "I don't have cancer or something."

"Well, be careful," Paul cautioned. John laughed.

He ran up the ladder. He looked out onto the land and saw a horrific sight. A horrific sight, that is, to someone other than John. He saw magicians having to use their swords to fight approaching ogres. There were ogres, goblins, and magicians scattered everywhere. Blood was the main battleground, bodies everywhere. John grinned when most people would scream. He let out a whoop and hopped out of the ship. He ran to the aid of his brother who grinned as a greeting to him. After Jerry had beaten the ogre he was battling, they punched knuckles.

"Nice to see you as a human again," Jerry said.

"Ha-ha," John mocked. "How's battle?"

"We took out, thanks to you, seven of their ships on the sea. The Kraskull were stuck on the island along with the mammoths, from what we've gathered. Now we're beating the stuffing out of these guys. They don't stand a chance."

Sheen roared from above; he was at his actual size, not shrunk.

"Is Sheen helping at all?" John asked.

"Yes, watch," Jerry said. "He's using the same tactic that Marowlog used on me."

Sheen swooped down on the enemy when they tried to form a line. It smashed all of them into the ground and knocked many off their feet with is gigantic wings.

"So that's why they're so scattered," John said. "To avoid being attacked in numbers."

"Which is a disadvantage, too," Jerry said. "We attack as a group but they attack individually."

"Excellent," John said. "So should I prepare the ships?"

"Yes, however," Jerry sighed, "I'm afraid—"

There was a roar from above. They looked up but it wasn't Sheen that made the noise. An apparition appeared out of the sky. It wasn't a ghoul; it was a phantom. With multiple roars, many more suddenly appeared. Jerry gasped but turned to John.

"Can you make a blast of green fire that pops three times?" He asked him hurriedly.

"What?!" John asked surprised.

"It's a signal for a ghost to come to aid," Jerry said, impatiently. "I learned it from one of my mentors. Can you do it?"

John focused his hand into the air.

"Yeah, I think I can," John pondered.

"Then do it!" Jerry yelled.

Jerry looked up and saw a flame come out of John's hand and make a fiery cracking noise three times. Ghouls appeared out of the water, only now on horse back. John grinned and turned back to Jerry.

"Aren't you glad I made a deal with them?" John laughed. The cavalry stopped the phantoms before they could hit the magicians. They fought in midair. "Now that's what I called fighting for life."

Jerry laughed.

"WAHAHOOO!" John yelled in encouragement. Jerry laughed at this as well. With no back-up from the phantoms, the ogres tried to flee to their boats; but the magicians stopped them. Closed in, the ogres had no chance. The army was destroyed. John and Jerry yelled, "VICTORY!"

"I think I am a good luck charm," Jerry said to John as the magicians were running into the ships. The ghost battle was still going on above them and they were worried about the outcome. "But sadly, I think I have to go."

"Go where?" John asked, amazed. "You just got here!"

"I know," Jerry whispered to him as the boat left the shore. "But the good side counts on it. I am not sure these ghouls can handle it."

"Stop speaking in riddles," John said, annoyed. "You did this to me before and I thought you were a hologram. I'll start accusing you again if you don't tell me."

Jerry looked into his eyes.

"Are you positive the spirit left you?" Jerry asked him.

"Is that what this is about?!" John said, angry. "Yes, I am sure. The spirit died when I turned into a Morphelellist."

"Well," Jerry said, smiling. "I can tell you this. *I promise you before the eighth day of the orb's destruction, before the great King Phoenix flies, and before the world turned in its final hour of day, I will return. It will be just on time.*"

"What?" John asked. "What are you talking about?"

Jerry leaned to his brother and whispered, "*Just call on the great one and he will return.*"

He pointed to Uncle Dan.

"Did you ..." John said, turning back to him. Jerry was gone. John looked everywhere; then he looked up. Jerry was riding on a large, gray dragon.

"Call on the great one!" Jerry yelled back to him.

John looked amazed in Jerry's direction. Did his brother just make a prophecy?

"Where's Jerry?" Daniel said to John.

"Gone again," John sighed. "On the back of that dragon."

Daniel sighed as well. He turned to talk to one of the Ring's men when John came to his senses.

"Hey, Uncle Dan," John said. "What is the King Phoenix?"

"The Scarlet Phoenix?" Daniel asked. "The Scarlet Phoenix is a mythical beast that, as legend has it, is a pure existing from the dawn of time. It was the creature that was first made and will exist until the end of the world. The King Phoenix is a pure that, if killed, reborns and flies again. The

Soulhaunts hate it. No matter how hard they try, for centuries they battled it and lost. Some say it is an angel."

"But is it real?" John asked.

"I am not sure," Daniel said. "I would believe that nothing can live that long. Why do you ask?"

"Jerry mentioned it," He said. "I think … I think he made a prophecy about the final stand."

"Really?" Daniel asked. "What did he say?"

John recited it.

"Interesting," Daniel said. "So he predicted we will win, huh?"

"Yeah, I guess so," John shrugged. " 'Eighth Day of the Orb's destruction.' That means it'll be destroyed, but we won't kill Zach then? Maybe … maybe we can get to the orb first!"

"Funny you should say that, John," Daniel said. "I was discussing the orb with the Ring council and they agreed that someone has to destroy it. Zach knows how we operate, so if we attempted to destroy it, we might not be successful. That and the fact that taking an army across the ocean will take awhile. We need an individual to go ahead of us and beat Zach to it."

"… And?" John said. Then it hit him. "Do you need me to do it?"

"Yes," Daniel said. "But of course, you wouldn't go alone. We'll send Paul, Victor, and Lino with you. Oh, and maybe someone with a wand. Can you do it again, Sir Quaill?"

John mocked him by saluting him.

"Yes, sir," John said. "We will destroy that orb and meet with you in the last stand."

"Go now then," Daniel said. "I'll find some-oh, Michael, you would like to?"

John looked behind Daniel and saw a cloaked, hooded man.

"Yes, I am ready," he said.

"Very well," Daniel said, turning to John. "Get Paul and the others and I'll prepare a boat for you. You'll have to go the hard way, I'm afraid."

"Oh, no you don't," John said, looking at the small life boats on the ship. "We'll take one of the ogre ships. We don't need them anymore."

"Good idea," Michael said. John ran to the hole before Daniel could answer. He ran down the ladder to Paul. He was sitting next to a conscious Lino. Lino smiled at him.

"I heard you got kind of angry after I was knocked out," he noted innocently.

"Very funny, Lino," John said. "You're lucky I didn't destroy the earth because of it. Are you feeling well?"

"I'm fine," Lino replied. "Where's Jerry?"

"He left," John said quickly. "Listen, guys, I got bad news. We're going to have to split up with Daniel because someone needs to destroy the orb."

"We have to?" Paul sighed. "Who's going?"

"Victor, Lino, you, me," John said, counting on his fingers, "and some guy named Michael who is going to watch over us. We will take one of the abandon ogre ships. Hopefully we won't have any interference with Zach's army."

"With the luck of the Quaills," Lino laughed, "we're bound to run into at least eight ships."

"Don't jinx it!" Paul warned him.

"Ha," Lino said. "Like it will matter."

"Come on," Daniel's voice came from above. "Let's hurry. Every second counts."

"Alright," Paul called. "Are you ready, Lino?"

Lino jumped to his feet and stretched.

"I'm always ready," he yawned.

"I'll get Victor," John said, running joyfully to the ladder.

He went up the ladder again and Daniel pulled John aside.

"Just wanted to tell you," Daniel whispered. "Michael's new to the *Ring* council. Barely a year. He replaced Zach. He doesn't talk much. I've never seen his face. Be careful of him…but he volunteered. No one else was willing."

The five characters turned their ship away from the magician navy. Paul waved to his uncle, who was on the crow's nest.

"Do you think we'll see them again?" Paul asked his brother.

"It's a guarantee," John promised.

"So I hear you two are quite accomplished fighters," Michael said in a raspy voice. He still didn't remove his hood.

"Now, who would tell you that?" Paul said coolly.

"The media," Michael responded. "You are one of the last living genies, Paul. And John, this is the fourth war you have fought in and survived, correct?"

"Yes," John answered.

"Not to mention that you both accomplished the maze—"

"—three years earlier," John finished. "You don't how many times we have heard that one."

"True," Michael said, turning under its hood towards John's face. "And you stopped Zyno and Benjamin, which I doubt many can."

"It isn't as hard as it sounds," Paul said curtly. "He almost seemed happy to be defeated."

"That's a laugh," said Michael. "Zyno has and never will be defeated. I am sorry to say this, kids, but no one can out smart Zyno. If he wanted to, he could have stopped you in that maze. He had a reason to let you defeat him."

Paul vividly remembered the time when he captured Zyno. He had smiled like he wanted to kill anyone in his path. Paul didn't realize it then, but that smile would come back to haunt him.

"Will he break out?" John asked him.

"Of course," Michael said. "This is what Zach is planning. We are pulling everything we can out of Locombony and then Zach will free Zyno."

"Then why are we falling for his trick?!" Paul asked in amazement.

"Because if we don't," Michael whispered, "all the magicians will be wiped out. We can't have that. We must risk it."

"I see," John sighed. "So it's a lose-lose proposition?"

"Yes," Michael replied. "Which do you want, the world about to be taken over with or without magicians?"

"You make it seem so hopeful," Lino said, striding over. "Why don't we just finish them off all at once?"

"Ah, my naïve tiger," the magician rasped. "Your heart is wide as well as your strength, but you are no match for a well-trained scientist."

"Then how come my species will last longer than yours?" Lino asked quizzically.

"We'll never know if that is the true future," John replied patiently. "So to change subjects, where is this orb located?"

"Phoenix, Arizona, U.S.A.," Michael responded. There was a weird way that in which he answered the question.

"How ironic," John said. "And that supposedly, is where the King Phoenix is ..."

Michael straightened up.

"Who told you about the Scarlet Phoenix?" He asked them quickly.

"My brother and my uncle," John replied. "Why?"

"And they said it was in Phoenix?" he asked them.

"They didn't tell me where it was," John answered, surprised. "They also said it was a legend of the magicians and unknown to normal humans. Why do you ask about the King Phoenix?"

They could all sense that Michael had a troubling idea. He was scared about it, whatever it was.

"Now I know what this orb means," He said, standing up, "after all these years, it finally makes sense."

10.) The Kraskull and the Mages

John looked at him.

"How?" he asked him.

"It is not of your concern," Michael said, striding to the wheel of the ship. John moved in front of him.

"Actually," John said in a matter-of-fact tone, "it is. This mission was 'entrusted', if you will, to me, and it is precisely my concern about how to destroy this orb."

Michael moved around him.

"This mission was sent to you," Michael replied, "however, there are secrets in which you must not know about."

"Enough of these stupid secrets!" Paul yelled, feeling his brother's pain. "I've hated this ever since the Maze! Why can't you tell us?!"

"Because I am not sure that it is true," Michael chuckled. The hair on the back of John's neck rose. "I don't want to give you ideas unless I'm completely sure it's true."

"What's the worse that can happen," Lino said, gritting his teeth, "if you tell us all about this legend?"

"You have no idea," Michael said, turning the wheel of the ship.

"We would if you told us," Paul muttered.

Victor interrupted Paul by charging up to Michael.

"Another ship approaches," he said. They looked at each other in horror. If it was a friendly ship, they would see it was an ogre ship and attack. If it was an enemy's ship, then they would hail them.

"Where?" Michael said. "Paul, take the wheel."

"Twelve o'clock," Victor said, pointing in front of them. It was dark red ship, the color of blood.

"Hard Starboard!" Michael commanded, running to the edge of the ship. "Force all sails starboard. We'll miss them if we hurry!"

"John, you take the wheel," Paul said, running to the main mast. "I'll take down the other sails."

John spun the wheel as hard as he could so that it made five complete rotations. He then held it steady.

"Victor, prepare the cannons on the port side," John yelled as Paul jumped onto the pole. He was able to climb the mast with ease. John saw Victor prepare the cannons and Michael run to the bow to look out at the ship. He felt the ship move a little. Paul was climbing the pole without breaking a sweat. With one swift and strong stretch of his hand, he turned the sail around to face the blowing wind. The ship moved a little more. Michael noticed this and looked back at the ship.

"Hurry up!" he yelled at the ship. "I don't want them to escape!"

"I am hurrying!" Victor yelled. Michael turned to them.

"*I meant them,*" he said laughing. Suddenly his voice turned lower and there was thundering up above.

"Is a storm coming?" Lino asked John.

"Forget that," John said in an undertone, taking his hands off the wheel. "Do you know what he just said?"

"Something about hurrying," Lino replied.

"No," John whispered, drawing his sword. "He said he is going to take us down. And I have a hunch who is on that ship. I hope it isn't though ..."

"Who?" Lino asked, turning to the fast approaching ship.

"*The Kraskull,*" Michael said in a low voice. It was lower pitch than a thunderstorm. Paul heard him too and he never heard any voice so low. The eyes suddenly opened, shining through its hood. "*I joined the Ring council to learn more of you and your uncle. It sounds like you did a lot, but you cannot defeat the Kraskull!*"

"Be gone, Soulhaunt!" Paul said, leaping down to the floor. "Victor, retreat!"

"*You can not kill the Kraskull,*" it repeated. The Kraskull ship landed and five more leapt out. "*We are the Six, the malevolent number; the most purely evil.*"

John got in front of his brother. Paul pulled out his ax and Victor pulled out his knife and shield.

"There are only four of us," Victor whispered to Paul, "and six of them."

John set his backpack down and pulled out Flaminetore's computer. He opened it and he came out. Obviously, he overheard what was happening because he was suited with armor and a mace.

"Five on the Six," John said, grinning. "This should be interesting."

"*Do you have no respect for evil?*" The Head Kraskull rasped. "*That hologram can't kill us. We will destroy it!*"

"Bring it!" John said with both hands on his sword. There was a sifting of cloaks and a clink of swords being drawn. The Kraskull pulled out completely black swords with the exception of a strange, red symbol near the hilt of the sword. It looked like two sideways "Y"s stuck at the ends and a dot above and below it. John remembered his uncle talking about them bearing the sign of the Kraskull. This must be the sign. John recalled something about this sign … had he seen it somewhere before?

The Kraskull took long strides towards them. John was first, followed by Victor and Paul and then by Flaminetore and Lino. The imposter struck John's blade. The force was unbelievable; it knocked John to the ground. Paul leapt over his fallen brother and shot his ax at the side of the lead Soulhaunt. It deflected Paul's ax and sent it flying off the ship. Victor and Flaminetore attacked a different Soulhaunt. The Kraskull avoided Victor's knife and cut his hand off. Victor fell to his knees in agony and wailed. The lead Soulhaunt went up to Victor and stabbed him in the chest. Victor's wail's stopped and his eyes grew very wide. He then screamed at the top of his lungs. The Soulhaunt removed his sword and Victor slumped to the floor of the ship.

John stared at his lifeless friend. His eyes filled with tears, even though his friend happened to be a hologram.

Lino backed away from the Soulhaunt. Flaminetore was battling the same Soulhaunt that had cut Victor's hand off. It stabbed him and there was short circuiting and Flaminetore disappeared. John looked from the dead Victor to the evil Kraskull. He got angry and stood. Paul got up as well, though weaponless.

"*The tiger doesn't need to live,*" one of the Kraskull said. "*Zach only wanted the two Quaills.*"

"Run, Lino!" John yelled. John ran past the Kraskull to the bow of the ship. Lino was with him. Paul tried to go around the opposite way, but a rotting hand seized him by the neck. The Soulhaunt had a firm grip on his prisoner. The other Kraskull turned and headed towards John. John and Lino dove into the water. They looked around, but found no island. They had been traveling in open water for so long. The only other thing in sight was the Kraskull ship. Then they found a drifting log. John swam to it.

"Where's Paul?" Lino asked, after noticing Paul hadn't jump in. John turned and looked up to the ship. He sighed.

"He's still up there," he said. "But I can't do anything about it. They're going to take him to Zach and God knows what's waiting for him there."

"Nothing?" Lino asked desperately. "We can't do anything for him?"

"There's only one thing to do," John said, as Lino put his front paws onto the log. "We desperately need to head to Phoenix. There we can destroy the orb and get the Scarlet Phoenix to fight the Kraskull."

Lino shook his head.

"We have to get away from these ships," John said. He started to kick his legs, moving, inch by inch, through the water. John began to cry again. "This is so hopeless! My uncle's gone. My brother's on a dragon. Paul is captured and could be tortured at any minute. Victor's dead. We are paddling away from the only transportation for miles and we have no supplies!"

"At least we're alive," Lino said, but he was feeling morbid as well.

"That's the worse part," John said. "We're still alive. I wish I were dead. I wish that this was someone else's problem."

Lino nodded. The Kraskull ship turned and fired cannons at the ogre ship. The ogre ship then sank. John looked back and saw they were about four hundred yards away.

"And I wish my brother was here and I was there," John said. "I wish my brother made it."

"Let's not wish anymore," Lino looked up, determined. *One of us*, he thought, *has to be courageous.* "We need to worry about what's ahead. Do you really think 'Michael' knew the significance of the orb, or was he just worried about the Scarlet Phoenix?"

"Not now, Lino," John breathed. "I just need to rest for now. I have been through too much. You think for a while. When you're tired of kicking, wake me up."

The Soulhaunts took Paul into their ship. One of them carried him down to the lower level. Paul didn't get to see the top part of the ship, but he saw the bottom. It was a cell, with chains hanging from the ceiling. There was a black cauldron sitting in the corner with chemicals in it. A single rat was near the chains, but the Kraskull stepped on it and killed it. The ship made a low, moaning noise as it moved through the water and Paul could tell that the coming process wasn't going to be good.

The Soulhaunt hooked up Paul's wrists to the chains. He let go and Paul hung from the ceiling. The Soulhaunt moved the black cauldron underneath him and then attached something to it. It was a long piece of steel and it went under the bottom of it. The way it was built, Paul could tell (even though probably no else could) that it was a heater. The Soulhaunt left and almost instantaneously, the cauldron began to boil. Paul looked about the cell.

Then he thought of something: he was a genie and could stretch out of the chains. He tried to stretch his hand out, but a gold glow came upon the chain and Paul realized that the chains were magical.

"It could be worse," Paul muttered to himself. Suddenly, however, something proved that he wasn't mistaken. The chains holding him began to lower. Paul looked up and saw that the chains weren't connected to the ceiling, as he thought. There was a hole and the chains were coming out of the hole. The Soulhaunts could lower or raise him as much as they pleased. They lowered him down slowly towards the cauldron. Paul looked down at his bare feet. He gasped and started to breathe hard as he could feel the heat from the boiling cauldron. He looked down and then the chain movement stopped. His feet were no more than a centimeter away! The fear of the heat almost killed him. He breathed harder and harder.

"They're trying to drive me insane!" Paul realized. Triumphantly, he remembered ways to prevent going insane. He had to remember something about his life, maybe a happy feeling, and concentrate on that thought, as they tortured him. That way, he keeps his mind safe and the worst they could do is to destroy his body. Paul rummaged through his mind and found a jubilant thought – the time he made his first laptop. He was five and had Flaminetore as a new friend.

"Concentrate," Paul told himself. The Kraskull lowered him quickly into the chemicals so that he was knee deep. The heated liquid pierced his skin in a pain beyond Paul's comprehension. Paul screamed, but he tried with all his might to keep the image in his head. The pain hurt as much as before, but Paul was able to block out the pain by focusing his mind on something else. The Soulhaunts didn't raise him out of the cauldron. Instead, they lowered him more, to his waist. Paul's screams decreased as his mind filled up with joy of his computer. The Soulhaunts lifted him out. Paul gasped for oxygen again.

John woke with a start. Yesterday was one of the most action-packed days he has ever experienced. He glanced over at Lino, who was weary and tired.

"I told you to wake me up if you were tired," John yawned.

"You had a rough day yesterday," Lino panted. "Killing a hundred ogres, defeating Zach's spirit again, facing the Kraskull …"

"Still, I could have paddled for a bit," John said. "Where do you suppose we are?"

"You have the map in your pocket, don't you?"

John reached into his pocket and felt a wet piece of paper.

"It would be ruined by now," John said, taking it out. He looked at the soggy ink on the page. John waved his hand over the paper and it dried, but the ink was still spread out. He looked closely at it.

"I believe our island is here," He said pointing on the map. "And we need to get here."

He looked at his two fingers. The gap between them was about the size of South America. John swore.

"How are we supposed to beat Zach there?" John asked angrily. Then he calmed down and looked at Lino. "How long do you think we traveled in the night?"

"Twenty miles," Lino guessed. "But I pushed on, I wasn't measuring."

They both sighed. John looked behind him.

"Do you think the Kraskull will follow us?" He asked. Lino shook his head.

"No, I think they're satisfied with Paul," Lino said. "Maybe that was all that Zach wanted, a genie."

Another ogre for his army, John realized with horror.

"Zach is amazing," John pronounced in admiration. "I mean, he came up with this plan and our counter-attack is feeble. I don't think he could have planned better."

Lino nodded. John looked at him.

"Lino," John gently sighed, "you must be hungry."

"Not much we can do now, unless you can conjure up some food," Lino replied unpleasantly.

"No, my magic has limits in some areas," John sighed. "However, I wonder if we could catch a fish … "

"Highly doubtful," Lino said. "No net and no bait and we have to keep traveling? Nope."

"Good point."

"What's that up ahead?" Lino asked, pointing to their left. John looked beyond Lino to a fast approaching ship. John reached for his quiver and bow.

"When you can tell if it's enemy or friend, tell me," John said, stringing an arrow. "And move."

Lino squinted.

"There's a strange sign on the sail," Lino said. John's heart sunk.

"Is it two y's stuck on end?" He asked Lino.

"No," Lino answered, confused. "It's a black cross with swiggily lines around it."

John looked at the sky. *It had to be a good ship if the weather didn't change*, John thought half-humorously. John lowered his bow, but had a firm hold on his arrow. It would be just like Zach to arrive disguised as an ally.

"It's coming fast," Lino said. "Faster than any ship I have ever seen, and I have seen a lot of ships."

John nodded. He felt around in his pockets to see if he had anything to trade with these people. He had only his sword, which he was fond of.

"Let's hope we get lucky again," John hoped, "I am in no position to fight."

The ship passed them, but John didn't get to see who was on it. He breathed, braced himself, and yelled, "Men of the seas, do you not see the stranded two in the water?"

The ship stopped and someone threw an anchor down into the depths. A person (John or Lino couldn't see who, because the person had a battle helmet on) came to the edge of the ship.

"Man over board!" came a yell, and by the voice, Lino and John could tell it was a woman.

A couple of other people came to the edge and threw a rope into the water. John swam over to it and glanced at Lino.

"One of us is a tiger," John called awkwardly. "He doesn't climb ropes well."

"Indeed not," the female said. "We'll send down a raft for you."

The same person, who dropped the rope, ran away. She came back with a long raft with ropes on its four corners. John swam over to it with Lino right behind them. A couple of people pulled it up as if it were an elevator.

John hopped on board, followed by Lino. John looked around the ship and saw many people working with haste at each control. John looked at the woman with the battle helmet. She took it off an extended a hand to John.

"Welcome to the *Piranha*. I am captain of this ship. Just call me captain."

John shook her hand with confusion.

"What … " John started, but then stopped. He glanced at the crew and noticed that all of the workers were female. One of the workers pulled a wand out to use on a stubborn sail. John turned back to her. "Who or what are you? I believed that only men could be magicians."

"Of course only men are magicians," the captain said impatiently. "We are not magicians. We are mages."

"There's a difference?" John asked.

One of the idle women stepped forward.

"Yes," she clarified with an air of arrogance. "The difference is that magic men are called magicians and magic women are called mages."

"I sort of figured that out," John said shortly, gazing at her. She had brown eyes (the same as the captain) and straight, dark black hair. She was shorter than John by about an inch but was about his age. She dressed in a red, hooded cloak that went down to her thighs and tan pants that went all the way down onto her silver boots. "May I have anyone's name on this ship? Or do you people have no names?"

"You must be of the Kraskull's servants," the woman shot back, "to go insulting a mage."

John took a step back. He felt so heated at that ridiculous statement, he couldn't think of a proper retort.

"Excuse my daughter," the captain said, eyes darting at the teenager.

"No, excuse me," John said, taking a breath, "I am weary from constant battling with Zach's ogres that I can hardly concentrate. I did not mean to insult you or … "

John glanced at the teenager.

"I am Joan," said the teenager, "named after my ancestor, Joan of Arc, a pure who led the French army to end the Hundred Year's War."

"Impressive," Lino lied.

"But what about yours?" Joan asked.

"I am John Quaill and this is my friend, Lino," John answered. "My uncle is part of the *Ring* council."

"Yes, I recognize the name," the captain nodded. "I knew your father briefly—I am sorry to hear that he was still missing, the last time I checked. But I am glad to hear you are against Zach. We were called by the *Ring* council to fight in this war. The last of the mages come to the aid of the magicians. But how did you come to be stranded on a log?"

"We were attacked and betrayed by the Kraskull … " John began.

"Betrayed?" Joan interrupted.

"One disguised themselves as a member of the Ring council," Lino explained. "And attacked us."

Joan nodded, but unconvinced. John told the story of how his brother was captured and then went back to the story before that, when he and a lot of magicians attacked Zach and so on. After he had finished, it was almost dusk. Joan and the captain had been listening carefully.

"Tell me, John," the captain said. "Have you ever heard of someone named Shiach?"

"No," John responded.

"He was quite an adventurer, just like you too," the captain replied, "and I think you two would have been great friends with him. He would've thought very highly of you, at the very least. He was my husband, and he gave me two beautiful children. My son, last I heard, was in Eastern Locombony. I don't know where he is right now. But never mind that. There is only one thing not clear to us: why did you separate from your uncle?"

John turned to Lino. Lino nodded.

"We are in search of the enemy's greatest weapon, or would be weapon if they catch it before us."

"And what is it?" Joan asked.

John paused. He saw these women as allies, so he could probably trust them with the facts. *Plus,* he had to admit, *who couldn't trust those eyes?*

"The magical orb," John replied. "And we are also looking for information on the Scarlet Phoenix."

John and Lino half expected them to gasp. However, they gave them puzzled looks.

"Also known as the King Phoenix," John explained, "it is the only enemy of the Kraskull."

"The King Phoenix," Joan pondered. "I don't think I've ever heard of it."

"In all honesty, I hadn't either up until a few hours ago," Lino shrugged. Joan couldn't help but laugh.

"Well, thank you for your hospitality," John said, standing up. "But, I think we should go. I need to leave as quickly as possible. However, I need a guide to help us on our trip. My map is ruined. Does anyone know the way to Phoenix, Arizona in America?"

The captain shook her head, but Joan said, "I do. I went there on one occasion. I actually know America moderately."

"I did not know this?" the captain rounded on her. "Why not?"

"Because I wanted to see what people call 'The Perfect Country,'" Joan replied, rolling her eyes. "It isn't what it's cracked up to be. However, I will guide you to Phoenix, if permitted … "

"I will not hear of it!" The captain retorted. "You are on my ship to attack the enemy and I need every mage available."

"Look," Joan folded her arms, "these two have already proven their worth. And by the sound of it, their mission is quite crucial not only to our race, but to the world."

John was amazed at her courage to dispute her mother, her wisdom in the matter, and John could sense something else – trust?

"No, that is my final answer," the captain said shortly. She turned and John gave a half glance at Joan. She stared at him with pleading eyes. For some reason, John thought she wished to go to America again. The captain started to walk away …

"Wait," John stopped her. The female captain turned around. "I desperately need a guide. The fate of the world *does* depend on this. Your people will be wiped out if you don't let one of your people guide me. Joan seems to be capable. Why can't she lead me? She is a very good candidate."

The captain turned and looked into John's eyes, raising her eyebrows. John glanced at Joan, who was biting her lip, trying not to laugh.

"He *meant*," Lino spat impatiently, "that she'd be a great escort."

John blushed as he realized how his words came out, but looking back at Joan, he saw she was blushing as well.

The captain was searching for something in her mind. She then turned to her daughter's eyes and searched. She looked one more time at John and then smiled.

"Very well," she said. "I cannot stop you if I tried. You may have one of our canoes and I will give you my daughter as security and as a guide."

"Security?" Lino asked incredulously. "He can take care of himself!"

"You may be surprised," the captain laughed. "I do not talk about protection from any outside force. Sometimes the thing we need protection against comes from within us."

"That doesn't even make sense," Lino rolled his eyes.

"My naive tiger," the captain said. "So wise but cannot comprehend what these two are feeling."

"What?!" Joan and John said together.

"Prepare the canoe," the captain ordered one of the women, "for these two and their tiger."

John and Joan laughed at how the captain was referring to them. John ran to help the woman with the boat.

In about 10 minutes, John and Joan were paddling away with Lino in between them.

"You're mother is quite funny, is she always like that?" John asked Joan.

"Not that way," Joan said. "Of course, she hasn't been around males much."

John grimaced as he thought were the conversation might go.

"Let's change the subject," Joan suggested.

"Yeah," John concurred. "Where do you live? Certainly not in Locombony?"

"Yes," Joan said. "I grew up on the Dividing River. I used to watch the battles of The Thousand-Year War. In fact, I saw one not too long ago. But then I got drafted into the mages."

"My brother led the army starting three years ago," John said quietly.

"He's been having trouble with Australia."

Joan started to get interested.

"He wrote a long journal about each battle," John continued, "and most of the battles they lost. He is a good leader, but Locombony didn't have many men."

"Did he ever try drafting women?" Joan asked.

"Well, my thinking is," John replied, "he didn't want the men in the war to be distracted … "

He cut himself off. *How did I get myself back into this conversation*, John thought, kicking himself.

"You don't have to be embarrassed," Joan said quickly. "Besides, many of his generals wouldn't approve of women being in the war because of … well … they might get the impression men are stronger than women."

"Well, yes, I guess I haven't really seen many women in the army, any army for that matter," John pondered. "I don't think the gender matters. Of course, I've never seen a woman fight, really."

"Have you ever seen America?" Joan argued coldly.

"No," John answered quickly.

"Then how do you know there are Americans?" Joan asked.

"Well … I don't know … my Uncle—"

"You are just going off of what some else said," Joan said, calming down. "Yet you are questioning the formula about female fighters."

"I also go off of what I know about the subject at hand," John continued. "And I had a girlfriend who was an amazing mage … I didn't even know that's what she was, but not much of a fighter. She was brutally murdered by Zach. I hate him for it. But I know that there are women who could have escaped that death. Just looking at your physique, you might have survived if he attacked you. I do not stereotype. In my mind, everything has to be proven though, not accepted without showing."

"Such a shame then, to not be able to believe in pures," Joan answered, looking up. "You never saw their power. I guess you can't accept that fact since you never saw them use their power."

John struggled to find an argument against this one. He stared at her face, annoyed. *She doesn't even know anything*, he snarled inside himself. *Why was she being so difficult?*

She looked down from the sky and caught him staring at her. John kicked himself. He forgot that magicians can read minds, apparently mages can too. But it wasn't anger she looked at him with; it was pity.

"I am sorry about your girlfriend," she said. "I guess it was wrong of me to assume."

John shook his head.

"I need to watch my words so that doesn't happen again," he said. She looked at him with a bit of gratitude. John looked down. "You're a pretty girl."

John blinked. Did he just say that?

Joan's eyebrow raised a fraction. She looked at his head for a bit, perhaps trying to see if he lied or if that wasn't all he wanted to say.

"Thank you," she smiled finally. "I would say that you're a handsome guy, but I think I'll wait until you clean yourself up before I say that. You're kind of a mess."

Lino burst out laughing. John and Joan had temporarily forgotten that they were not alone. Lino rolled around on the floor of the boat, paws on his stomach. John blushed a little. Finally, Lino got up and wiped a tear out of his eye.

"Joan, I will remember that forever," Lino said, hiccupping. "Thanks a ton for that."

They paddled in silence for a bit.

Joan broke the silence, "So you never told me how your brother was able to come out of the war to help you guys."

John thought, trying to remember what his brother had said over dinner on the ship. "Oh, yeah, I remember…he had another army come, William and his legions."

Joan stopped paddling.

"William?" Joan asked, eye's widening. "Do you know if his army is full of barbarians?"

"Yes, they are," John asked, turning to face her. "Why?"

"We … we saw William," Joan said, head dropping. "He … he left by ship. There will be nobody defending Locombony. He … he bore the mark of Zach … and the Kraskull …"

Joan reached into her pocket and pulled out a long piece of silk.

"This was on one of their uniforms," she said sobbing. "I didn't know he was the one defending the river."

John took the piece of silk and looked at it. On the silk, there was a black circle and a crescent moon inside it.

"Is this the mark of Zach?" Lino asked. Joan nodded.

"What is that mark on your sail?" John asked.

"The mark of the mages," Joan replied. "And you know the mark of the magicians."

John visualized two crossing wands and a star outside it.

"Yes," John answered. "So we use four marks then."

Joan nodded. John threw the cloth as hard as he could into the water. John turned to her.

"Why are you upset? You didn't fight them, did you?" John asked.

"I am upset because my country is in ruins by now," Joan answered sharply. "What are we doing going to America? We need to head to Locombony!"

"No!" John said. "Listen to me, Joan, if there's one thing I learned in the past three years, it's this."

Joan had started back paddling, but then stopped and looked John in the eyes.

"Perhaps you haven't heard of me before," John said, turning completely around. "I am John Quaill, one of the three Quaills to overcome the labyrinth made by the infamous Zyno and supported by Zach and Benjamin. After I defeated Zyno, our family was split and I was sent away. I made new friends at a new school filled with new teachers. Zach came back and murdered my friends and destroyed my life. I could have been stupid because of what Zach did. I could have tried to attack Zach alone. But by then, I knew he had the power of all of the rings in the *Ring* council. I had to raise an army and be patient. I had to learn, from mistakes, that I couldn't let the grief of the deaths make me act irrational."

"But you don't understand," Joan growled fiercely. "My father was killed by the Australians."

"My mother was killed by Zach," John countered. "But I had to wait to get my vengeance. And I swear this – before this world comes to an end, we will both have had our revenge."

Joan shook her head and looked down.

"There is hope, Joan," John said gently. *Ugh, what is making me act this way*, John thought. "If I get this orb, well, I haven't explained to the fullest what this orb can do. Would you like me to explain?"

Joan looked up and pushed her hair out of her eyes.

"This orb," John said, words getting caught in his throat, "can … can destroy anything in a certain group. For example, let's say I didn't like ogres; I can kill all ogres with this orb.

Let's say I don't like Australians; I can kill all of the Australians.
Let's say …"

"… you didn't like life," Joan gasped, finally realizing what
John meant, "a Soulhaunt could destroy life itself!"

"See what I mean?" John said, choosing his words
carefully. "Australia takes over Locombony. Well, if we head
back and try to fight them, we will be over-whelmed by the size
of their force and our mission will be for naught. But if we get
the orb, destroy Zach's army, and head back, then we would
have nothing to lose, but our lives."

Joan nodded. She smiled at John which made his heart
throb. He began to paddle again. Lino leaned forward and said,
"Good job, John. You saved the world and won the heart of a
girl at the same time."

Lino soon found himself being thrown into the water.

11.) The Third Stand

Paul panted very fast. The Soulhaunts had been torturing him all day. After the boiling incident, there was defleshing, whipping, intense heat and finally, the process of starving. Paul was then hooked up to the chains again to rest, but Paul knew he would never rest the same again. The defleshing was the worst; the Kraskull took a long knife and cut pieces out of his flesh at random and Paul's genie power made it grow back. The Kraskull kept cutting until it really left a mark on his leg. Now drained of power, Paul wondered what they would do next.

He had only 20 minutes of uneasy sleep when he woke to the burning of his feet. The Soulhaunts lowered him once again into the cauldron. Paul screamed and struggled. After about 10 minutes of constant pain, he was lifted up. A Soulhaunt came down to Paul and unhooked him. He was then taken to the top of the ship where the other Kraskull were waiting. One of them (Paul guessed it was the leader) held a strong chain on a ferocious creature. It looked a little like a warthog, only it was stronger with a thin layer of hair. Paul thought it looked like a cross between a bull and a massive boar.

"Let's see how our prisoner faces the gladiator challenge," a Soulhaunt said. Paul looked in horror at the creature. It was lunging against the rope to attack Paul. It growled and kicked its feet. The monster was like a storm, looking like it could destroy an entire village.

A member of the Kraskull shoved Paul a small dagger that bore the mark of the Kraskull on it. The handle was heated to a scorching white hot, but it also had a sticky substance that made Paul unable to release it. The burning almost permanently destroyed his hand. But the genie powers helped him again and didn't leave a mark.

The Kraskull surrounded Paul and the hog so that neither could escape. One Soulhaunt lifted its hand to the air above Paul and a sphere came around all of them, large enough for two people to duel. Paul watched as the Soulhaunt lowered his hand and nodded to the one holding the creature. The Soulhaunt dropped the chain and the creature bounded at Paul.

Paul leapt out of the way, but hit the barrier and was thrown to the ground. The boar charged back at Paul and Paul defended himself with the knife. Paul then realized that the dagger was no sharper than his hand. The boar's horn clanged off Paul's blunt knife, but the tusk cut his arm. Blood rushed out freely. Paul realized his genie powers were wearing out. He quickly kicked the creature away and thought fast. He put his foot underneath the dagger and stood up, jerking it off of his hand. The creature charged at Paul again and Paul didn't know what to do. He leapt upward and the creature hit the barrier.

Because Paul was a genie and his powers were immune to the barrier's power for a minute, Paul didn't know how bad the shock was. The boar hit it straight on a full force. The shock shot it back at Paul, who grabbed one of its horns. With enormous strength, Paul slammed it to the ground with all his might. The ship rocked. Paul looked at the face of the creature and saw it was dead. Paul thought fast, realizing this was the only time he would get without the Kraskull holding him. He didn't know if they saw it or not, but the boar had landed on his dagger. Paul fell to his knees as if inspecting the dead creature, but he pulled the knife from under it and secretly hid it underneath his shirt. A Soulhaunt picked him up from behind and carried him to his chains below.

"*That battle proved that you can have something to eat,*" it said menacingly. "*But only because Zach wants you alive. If he didn't, I would have crucified you to the back of the ship.*"

The Soulhaunt threw him to the ground. It left, but then returned with a bowl of grey material.

"*Eat,*" it said. "*It's the only thing you'll get for about two days.*"

It left, and Paul knew it would know if he tried to escape. But Paul had other plans. Within five seconds, Paul had eaten the something that looked like oatmeal that stayed out for a century or two. Paul then took the old spoon that was in the bowl. He took out his dagger and then, with spoon in the other hand, sharpened the dagger. It made a small rubbing noise that sounded like hands sliding together rather than a sharpening of a tool. Paul sat and sharpened the knife for about 10 more minutes before he heard the sound of a Soulhaunt reappearing. He shoved the spoon in his pocket and his knife in his shirt. He hastily tucked it in before the Soulhaunt came in view.

"Good news for you," it said. *"We're going to skip to whipping you today!"*

John woke up early in his side of the canoe and looked around. Lino and Joan were still asleep. John grabbed his paddle. He began to paddle by himself. He looked quickly around and saw with relief that Joan had a bag, probably filled with supplies. John then looked up at Joan and let out a breath. She was at peace when she slept. This made John smile again. Lino woke with a start. He looked up at John and relaxed.

"I had a horrible dream," Lino whispered. "I dreamt Zach had ambushed us with his fleet and we were killed."

"That's the first logical nightmare I have ever heard you say," John laughed quietly.

"It's the only nightmare you have heard me repeat," Lino snapped. "But I am starving now. I think Joan has something to eat in her bag."

John looked over at Joan's bag which was on the other side of her. John crawled over Lino and said to him, "Balance the weight; go to the other side."

Lino crawled under him. John reached Joan and stretched over her. He couldn't quite get to her bag. Carefully, he climbed on the seat and reached over her.

It was at that moment that Joan awoke to find John almost on top of her trying to get the bag.

John looked at her. She gasped, but then looked where he was reaching and laughed. John chuckled too, but Lino laughed the hardest. John grabbed the bag and threw it at him. Lino searched through it and John climbed back to the middle of the canoe. Joan sat up and stretched.

"How far do you think we got?" Joan asked John.

John shook his head.

"I don't have a clue," he replied. "My guess would have to be that we traveled 60 miles."

"That's no where near where we have to be," Joan frowned, shaking her head. "By this pace, we might as well turn around, head back to Locombony and buy some duct tape."

John glanced at her to make sure she wasn't serious. She wasn't.

"Just remember what I said," John said, "about revenge."

"Don't worry, I'll remember," Joan nodded. "I was just saying that we're getting no where this way. And I really did think about revenge—do you seriously think it's the way to live?"

"Why not?" John shrugged. "Life is all about things staying in balance. Zach kills one, someone kills Zach. Isn't that the way of life?"

"But is that the only reason you're here, for revenge?" Joan asked him. "Or are you here to stop him?"

"I am definitely here to stop him," John emitted. "That's my reason."

"But you're pretty passionate about revenge," Joan warned. "I know—I am a bit like that too. But I try my best to set my personal feelings aside and make the best decision for others."

"Like turning back to Locombony?" John tested.

"I was wrong," Joan admitted. "Stopping Zach, preventing the world to be over-run, is justice."

"Justice and revenge can happen simultaneously," John pointed out.

Lino whipped his head out of Joan's bag.

"Please, *please*, do not get into a philosophical discussion," Lino begged.

Joan and John laughed, cooling the mood a little bit.

"Is there any food?" Lino asked in agony.

"No," Joan smirked. "I figured since we needed to travel light, I only brought what is necessary. Mages don't need food to live."

John's mouth dropped and Lino's eye widened.

"Guys, I was just kidding," the mage laughed, lifting up her hand to her other hand. She mumbled something and three pieces of bread appeared in her hand. She handed one to each of them and kept one for herself. Lino swallowed his bread in five seconds and looked up at Joan.

"Is that all?" Lino asked pleadingly.

"Excuse us," John said, turning once again to her. "We haven't eaten in about two days so we're desperately hungry, mostly because we have spent all of our energy."

"Understandable," Joan said approvingly. "Actually, I am impressed that you had energy to keep fighting without eating."

She summoned up two loaves and they both devoured them.

"So what did you bring?" John asked lightly, now that he could think clearly.

Joan looked through her bag.

"Not much," Joan said, "a potion for healing, a knife, a map of Arizona, and spare set of clothes."

"Talk about traveling light," Lino muttered. "If we're going to travel in a scorching land, we might need a water bottle."

"That can be summoned," John explained. "And I am glad you brought a potion. All the stuff my brother sent me? I had to leave it on the ogre ship. All I have left that he gave me is the ax; I had forgotten about it until now."

John glanced at it.

"Always nice to have a back-up," John said, "plus this will help me remember what I'm fighting for."

"I am glad you have siblings to help out and have for encouragement," Joan said sadly. "I haven't seen my brother for quite some time now. I was just a little kid when he went off with my dad."

John felt his heart sink for her. Joan thought for a moment.

"You know," she continued, "going by sea is pretty dangerous, maybe we should go by land."

"That would take twice as long and be tiring," John refused. "I just wish we had Sheen with us now; it would make the trip very fast and we would be out of range of Locombony's radar."

"Yes," Joan contemplated, "however, at least we would know where we would be going."

"You are our guide," John said sighing. "But at least wait until nightfall. I want to travel the quickest way."

Joan promised they would.

At nightfall, true to his word, John let them head for shore. He leapt out and smiled as he saw it was forested.

"It'll give us cover," John explained to Lino. "We'll head out immediately tomorrow."

"Right," Joan said, pushing the boat to the sea. "Well, I hope I made the right decision on this."

"I am sure you did," Lino said. "I was getting bored on the canoe anyway."

Joan smiled.

"I am tired," she said. "However, I just want to jump into the sea for a while to wash off."

"You do that," John said modestly. "I'll go and start a fire. I'll go in after you're done."

Joan nodded. John and Lino turned and headed deep into the forest. When they found a good place, John cut a tree down with his sword and started the fire with his magic. John then realized that he had nothing to sleep upon. Therefore, he just sat next to the fire to wait for Joan.

"Good job with Joan, man," Lino said. "She's just like you – fierce, perseverant, sarcastic ..."

"One more word out of your mouth about her and me and you will be as much wanted on my list as Zach," John glared at him angrily. "She's our guide and I have to live with her."

Lino tilted his head as if he didn't understand. John stared at the flames for a few moments and then looked at Lino.

"You actually think so?" he whispered with no expression.

"If you are putting on a charm, good job," Lino said, grinning again. "If not, even better. All it takes is a couple more moments and it'll be all set."

John smiled weakly.

"You sound like a professional, Lino," John laughed. "I mean, Dr. Lino."

"I like the sound of that," Lino laughed. "'Dr. Lino'... I wish ..."

Joan returned and John ran out to swim a bit to get off the for-two-days-I-was-fighting-ogres stench.

John got out in his soaked clothes and headed back to the fire where Lino was fast asleep already, but Joan was still awake. She smiled as she saw him. John waved his hand over his body and his clothes dried, but his long hair was still a little wet so it looked silky.

"Now I can say you're handsome," Joan whispered. John smiled sheepishly, swiping the long hair out of his face. He looked around.

"I have nowhere to sleep," John said. "I guess I'll just lean against this tree."

Joan looked at him concerned.

"Are you sure you'll be alright?" she asked.

"Yeah," John sighed, sitting against the tree. "Where are you going to sleep?"

"I'll be ok, too," Joan yawned. "Are you staying up late?"

"A little," John muttered, removing his sword. "I need to sharpen my sword."

"What for?" Joan asked, looking at the sword. "It's plenty sharp."

John set his weapon down. Joan crawled over next to him.

"It's either one of two things," John replied softly. "I am either depressed, which is understandable, or I am afraid. I feel like something bad is about to happen. Worse than ever, I feel it."

Joan nodded, looking away.

"I feel something too," she blurted out. "I didn't want to worry you before, but I feel it. Something's going to happen to us soon."

"Maybe I shouldn't sleep," John said. "Or at least sleep in shifts."

"What could it be?" Joan said quietly. "The Soulhaunts are way behind us. Who could hurt us now?"

John looked at her. He looked directly into her eyes and saw a fear in them. John, without knowing what he was doing, grabbed her hand lightly. She twitched, but that was it.

"Go to sleep," John said to her. "I can stay up. If anything happens ..."

"You wake us up and we'll run like hell," Joan said. John smiled and saw that her eyes were watering again.

"Don't worry," John said, sheathing his sword. Joan nodded and crawled to another tree and bowed her head. In a few minutes, she was asleep. John breathed. "What did I just do?! I am such a—"

"Would you like me to fill in that blank for you?" a voice behind him said. John spun around, up onto his feet, removing his sword. A shadow of a person arrived out of the trees; he was unhooded. John didn't recognize him at first, but then saw on the back of his hand a circle and inside it was a crescent moon: the sign of Zach. John thought he was having a hallucination and he fell to the ground. Zach circled around the fire until he was across from John and then sat down. John sat up and looked up into the eyes of his enemy. John laughed.

"What's so funny?" Zach snapped.

"For three years straight I have done nothing but look for you to kill you," John said, grinning, "yet you walk leisurely into my camp and sit down."

"You want to kill me?" Zach said, standing. "Kill me!"

John didn't move.

"It isn't the time to kill you," John explained curtly. "I will find the time when you will walk up to me reluctantly."

"Which will never come. The reason you don't kill me is that I can not be killed. Fate is on my side," Zach said. He did not sit. He instead walked over to Joan. "Is this your *new* girlfriend?

"You have a lot of nerve, Zach," John snarled, grabbing the hilt of his sword again. "And I use that term lightly."

Zach had killed his previous girlfriend at the magician school right before the War for the Rings began.

"Yes," Zach said, "I believe I have touched a nerve. You're weak, Mr. Quaill, weak. You cannot make friends this way."

"At least I have friends," John said, "and not some crazed old man who's only hopeless goal in life is to take over the world."

Zach just smirked and sat down.

"Hopeless?" he finally said. "I think there is a 99 percent chance of victory. Maybe even more than that!"

John cracked his neck and looked at Zach.

"What are you doing here, Zach?" John said. "If you wish to murder us, tell me as a last request. If not, get out."

Zach tilted his head and raised an eyebrow.

"I just wanted to warn you," Zach said. "That my new ally has surrounded your camp completely with no less than fifteen thousand men. Also, my ogre guard has taken the Colorado River, which intersects with a perfect little entrance to Phoenix. So if you expected the magicians to back you up, you're thinking wrong; I have a million at my command there."

John gaped at him.

"Of course, knowing that you are a Quaill, you will survive this attack and somehow weasel you're way around my army at the Colorado," Zach smirked. "I know this and am prepared for it. I am only doing this to delay you. It will take you days to kill that many men. Meanwhile, I would get the orb and you will lose everything."

"Not until we have a stand," John said, mind racing. John knew he might kill his friends if he couldn't scare him. "Our army is moving fast. Your slow phantoms have been defeated. About 10,000 of your ogres were killed. There is no way your million will beat us."

Zach turned and looked around him.

"Your brothers aren't here," Zach spotted. "Where are they?"

John bit his tongue.

"Jerry went somewhere on a dragon," John muttered.

"The entire Locombony air fleet will be after him then," Zach laughed, "the fool. But what about the one holding onto our maze?"

"He was captured by the Kraskull," John said fiercely. Finally, John had said something that made his face pale.

"So … they came … did they?" Zach said.

"Yes," John said. "Did you send them?"

Zach nodded.

"But I sent them on an impossible mission because I was afraid of them. But it seems they'll be back …"

"And you know who else is coming too?" John said triumphantly. "The King Scarlet Phoenix."

Zach clenched his fists.

"It will be too late for him," Zach spat, "the very creature stopping me from using the Rings on the entire world. He will not succeed."

"That was me," John snarled. "Or do you want me to refresh your memory?"

Before Zach could stop him, John grabbed Zach's wrist and pulled back the sleeve to his hand. Three of his fingers were gone to the second knuckle.

"But you ran from that one, too," John laughed. "Always running. Even now, you do not want to fight. You want to hide behind your millions of ogres. You're pathetic."

Zach twitched his fingers and John flew backwards from the magical strike.

"Huh, that little effort shot you back," Zach whispered. "I am in a different class than you, Quaill. You have no idea about my power. Nor do you know how to work the orb. I do. I, who—"

Zach stopped himself.

"Your Phoenix will not stand a chance," Zach started again, looking down at his fingers. "Biting off rings is one thing. It saved you last time. You would have died if my spirit wasn't forced into your body again. The Phoenix, somehow, forced it in. But a little magic trick will not save you this time. And by the time your precious Phoenix comes, I will have the orb and will use it against you!"

"The orb will not kill me," John guaranteed. Then he lied, "That's a prophecy."

Zach stopped speaking. Then he grinned.

"Then before the end, you will wish it had," Zach laughed.

"It won't matter," John said, slightly shuttering for some reason. Apparently Zach's comment wasn't just an insult, it was a promise. "The King Phoenix will win."

"Not if my orb destroys him," Zach said. "This orb has powers beyond your every thought. It can destroy even the strongest pure. And my dream will be complete: I will rule the world as an evil!"

"Not without one last rebellion, you won't," John said standing. "I will fight even if I am stabbed 200 times. This war has yet to finish! Now, if you want nothing else, you have my leave to go!"

"I'll leave when I feel like it," Zach said. "But since I hit many of your soft spots in your tough body, I'll leave. Good luck tomorrow; you'll need it."

Zach left. John breathed very hard and looked at his hand. He had drawn his sword without realizing it. He shook his head and dropped his weapon. He looked at the fast asleep Lino and the ever-peaceful dreaming Joan. John decided not to wake them; he would tell them in the morning. He put his hand on the ground and summoned a shield.

"Is this the twelfth time I summoned one?" he told himself. "I should really keep these things."

He then began work on Lino's protection. He made a pile of small chains appear. Using his magic, he connected each one ...

In the morning, Joan and Lino woke to find John smoothing out a metal shoulder pad. Joan and Lino stood and walked over to him.

"Have you been up all night?" Joan asked.

"Yep," John replied, "preparing for the attack."

"Attack?" Lino asked. Sadly, John told them what Zach had said.

"I made some chain-mail for you," John said, holding Lino up the chain armor that looked awkward for a human. "And I also had some other metal armor I summoned."

They were all filled with fear.

"Fifteen thousand?" Joan asked.

"More I think," John said. "The forest ends a few hundred feet from here and empties at the bottom of a hill. They have the utmost advantage on us."

"Yeah, ya' think?" Lino muttered with disgust, attempting to put on the mail. "But we'll fight anyway, right?"

"Think, if we kill all those people," Joan said, "how that would hurt Zach."

"Don't count on it," John whispered. "Be prepared to be captured. Take out as many as you can before it is obvious we have to give in. We can escape. Keep fighting."

"Alright," Lino nodded. "We know what to do at this point."

"Right," John said, putting in his hand. "For Paul."

"For Locombony," Joan said, putting her hand on top of his.

"For the world and my future," Lino said, putting on his paw. They looked at each other. "Um … what is our partnership called again?"

"Us," John replied, shrugging. They all yelled, "FOR US!"

They lined up and marched into thinner trees. John put his shield on his back like a backpack. He took his sword in one hand and his brother's ax in the other. Lino finished putting on his armor and he looked very humorous. It looked like a dog trying to wear football pads.

"There he is!" Lino yelled. John looked up at the top of the hill. There was a man on a brownish red horse. He wore purple armor. He had a dark purple cape blowing in the wind. However, John was staring more at the horse than the person.

"That horse," John muttered. He looked right at the horse. "It's mine … I raised that horse …. how …. how did he get it?"

"Your horse?" Joan asked. "How do you know?"

"I am positive," John said. "At our house, we raised four horses: Jerry has his, Black Melody, Daniel bought one, Celtic Warrior, Paul lost his, Storm, and mine was stolen. I am positive that's old Dreaded Musty."

John gripped his sword tighter.

"How dare him …" Lino began.

"Let me get my sword into his chest," John said.

"Wait a moment …" Joan strained her eyes at the rider. "Is that … William?"

She nodded. John's mouth dropped. Sure enough, a few obvious barbarian-like soldiers joined his side. Zach's new ally … was William.

John turned and walked across the field. William took out his sword and suddenly thousands of men on horseback appeared behind him. John and the other two continued to march towards their opponent. William commanded them to charge and the legions of cavalry rode at them. John brought his ax to shoulder height and waited. He aimed carefully and twisted the ax's handle. The lightning hit William off his horse. John ran up to the horse and leapt upon it. The extent of the cavalry had not yet come over the hill. John gaped at this. He rode on the horse, hands free, and rode to the men on horseback. Lino was with him at his side.

"Lino," John realized. "They'll eventually capture us. I am needed for Zach and Joan's life will be spared, but you will be killed if you're caught. You must head to the coast."

"No," Lino said, "I will die for you, your country and the world."

"If you leave for the coast," John said quickly, for the men were now in an archer's range, "you will be able to free us."

"How will you know Joan's life will be spared?" Lino said in a hurry.

John couldn't tell Lino. He knew that Joan's life would be spared not by the courtesy of the barbarians, but by the desire of entertainment from the men. He, however, would fight to free her and that he would risk his life to save her. John knew that when the men got tired, they would kill her.

"I just know," John yelled. "Now go to the shore!"

Lino threw him a look, but turned and ran all the same. John looked at the army who was practically on top of him. He swiped the nearest one on his left with his ax and one on his right with his sword. William only seemed dazed from the electric shock that John hit him with.

John looked out of the corner his eye and saw Joan fighting for the first time. She gave Daniel a run for his money – her swiftness rivaled his and she used her magic when the men came to close. She didn't even have to deflect hits from swords because of her quickness.

Dreaded Musty seemed to like his old master to be on his back again for he seemed to help fight. He, like his sister, Black Melody, trampled over fallen horsemen. John knew that now they didn't have two warriors and a horse facing thousands. They had three warriors. John laughed, but then quieted as he saw what William's left wing was doing; instead of coming at John, it circled to be behind him. Glancing at his right, he saw the right wing do the same. The cavalry ahead of him pulled back and joined the circle so that Joan, Dreaded Musty, and John were surrounded. Joan looked at John for instructions for what to do. John looked back at her.

"I thought we would kill more than 50," John simpered.

"You mean," Joan stared in awe, "you knew we would lose?"

"Kind of obvious, isn't it?" William said, beaming in an evil way. "Fifteen thousand against two, that's pretty clear that I would win."

"How dare you talk to me, you traitor!" Joan spat. "You evil …"

"That's enough!" William shouted back, "you will learn to obey us, woman … and you …"

He looked at John.

"… You will be sold into slavery and will never fight in an army again," he sneered. "And that horse belongs to me now. You two, seize them."

Two muscular men ran up to John and pulled him off the horse and bounded him. They then went to Joan and bound her hands. John and Joan's eyes met and John told her through telepathy, *I will get us out of this.* Joan nodded. Dreaded Musty cried out and went wild. William ran to try and control her. John looked at his sword and ax that lay on the ground. He was aghast that he might never take up arms again…

There was a loud horn from the coast. The army quickly turned in its direction. John and Joan looked too. First they saw nothing but the trees. Then the army looked in horror and saw about one hundred thousand brown midgets come at them. John recognized them as Thogs. William gasped.

"You five take them away. We will kill these dwarves quickly," He said. "There's no army that can beat ours!"

Paul hung by his chains at night but didn't sleep. He knew he had to sharpen his knife. All day, during the whippings and other torturing, he was able to sharpen it with his spoon. Not immediate, not effective, but it was sufficient. At the end of the day, it was sharp enough to spread butter on bread. He had to work all night without rest; the Soulhaunts were now able to get him to bleed freely. The torturing was harsh and he was becoming more and more human-like and less genie-ish.

The scraping became louder and more effective during the next day. He woke up with another bad bowl of gruel but ate it fast like before. During the morning whippings, he sharpened the knife on a piece of metal on the post. At the part of the day in which boiling was done, held the knife with his feet and the knife went into the boiling water to soften. Luckily, there was no gladiator challenge. However, the Kraskull did deflesh again and he was fortunate enough not to get caught with it. Plus, he was able to sharpen the knife on a hidden knife on the table (but this one he had to put back for the Kraskull checked their tables afterwards).

At the end of the day, the knife looked nothing less than an iron flat stake. The progress was incredible. Paul examined it in his chains.

"Excellent," Paul said. He examined the chains. They looked old and torn. "I wonder … is it sharp enough?"

He started to cut it. The chains made a whining noise and bits of rust came off of it. He smiled (more of a grimace really) and continued. This is luck, he kept telling himself.

The sun hadn't come up yet …

This is luck.

The chain was just giving off rust …

This is pure fortune.

The Soulhaunts will come and get him soon …

Fortune, Luck, Miracle … call it what you want.

There was a clang and the chain broke on one side. Paul stretched his hand out of the handcuff and pulled it out of the other (the magic connection was not complete since one side was broken). He fell into boiling water, but he was so used to it and so relieved that he didn't care. He got out, with the knife as his only protection, and left the cell to find his brother and the Scarlet Phoenix.

12.) The Orb and The Phoenix

The year was 984. Merlin, the most powerful warlock, had left Arthur, for he no longer needed advice. Merlin was asleep in his bed at night when a powerful vision came upon him. He saw many magicians trying to fight together against a large force of terrible creatures. He woke with a start. The fact that he had seen so many magicians highly surprised him because, at this point, the magician race was almost extinct. However, Merlin knew there was a time when the magician race was large and it could happen again. He contacted his former friends and was able to create the first *Ring* council. On the council: Merlin as the head, Prospero as second in command, Circe as the prophesier, Kewlocke as the strength of magic, Tollund as the warrior, Salazar as the wisdom, Kra as the power, Hecate the goddess and Ambrose the king. They each created a Ring filled with their magic and knowledge.

They gathered together to discuss the matter of Merlin's revelation. Most of them decided that they should do something about this coming war. Prospero came up with the idea of attempting the impossible: finding or creating a pure. There had only been four pures in their history. Merlin and most of the others liked the idea, but thought it might be impossible. They began to work on it, creating a creature from their magic. Merlin gave it his strength, Prospero gave it his magic, Hecate gave it her immortality and Ambrose gave it his virtues so that it would be pure. However, Salazar, Kra, Kewlocke, Tollund and Circe did not give it their powers. They thought it would be better to try and create a weapon to stop the evil army. Merlin only wanted to create the pure to aid the good army.

"But Merlin," Tollund had asked, "what if the pure is not enough? What if it gets killed?"

"A pure does not die," Merlin had replied.

"But if we are successful in this weapon, it would be more powerful than any pure!" Salazar had exclaimed. "Imagine thus – the weapon destroying all evil in the battle and the good would not lose a man."

"Your greed is blinding your wisdom!" Ambrose had yelled. "That weapon in the hands of the enemy would mean only destruction. We can only continue with our plan!"

On that day, the *Ring* council split. Tollund, Kra, Kewlocke, Circe, and Salazar left the council. They tried with all of their might to make a weapon great enough not just to end the war, but to end all evil.

*   *   *

Meanwhile, Merlin and the rest hadn't been able to create the pure. It was beyond their abilities. However, they did make a failed pure. In a ritual, they offered it to the four pures who had chosen to die. Then something amazing happened that none of them could comprehend. The creature came to life in its entire splendor. They had not created a pure, but reborn the unknown pure. Merlin knew little about this being. The pure had been the first creature alive on earth but laid down its life in order to generate the human cell to create life. The pure, however, did not die, but existed in all living cells. Now, however, rising from the ashes, the *Ring* council brought back The Scarlet Phoenix.

Now Circe, Kra, Kewlocke, Tollund and Salazar had much luck. They came across a few eager warlocks who that were willing to help them. Circe, the prophesier, knew that the warlocks would be their downfall, but she kept quiet.

Salazar commanded the eager warlocks to start forcing all of their magic together into an orb (the object which they had chosen to hold the power). The orb became magical, but it wasn't enough. Kewlocke became impatient and began to plan for something stronger. He talked to Merlin and tricked him into pouring all his emotions and magic into the orb. The orb shot back. The few warlocks who had poured all their magic into it were forced into the most evil creatures to walk on the land: Kraskull. Circe named them this because they impressed Kra with their power. Kra learned, however, that the Kraskull wanted nothing more than to hold the power of the orb—that had been completed—to destroy life itself. So he tried to take the orb to be destroyed. However, the Kraskull found him and tortured him until he died. But before he died, he threw the orb to Tollund. Salazar left for another country and was never found by the *Ring* again. Tollund turned on his old friend Kewlocke when he found out that Kewlocke want to ally himself with these creatures. Kewlocke and the Kraskull attacked Tollund. He fought them and escaped, wounded. Kewlocke was never found again. Tollund, fearing his life because of the Kraskull, hid with Circe.

Circe and Tollund fell in love and bore two children. When the oldest reached 19, the Kraskull found them. They brutally murdered all except the 19-year-old who escaped with the orb. At the last second of her life, Circe pronounced: *"One my descendents will find the orb. He will find it and destroy it. That's a prophecy!"*

The magician who escaped, Caleb, was afraid that the orb might go to the Kraskull if he didn't destroy it. However, learning what happened in the past, he knew that only a pure could destroy it. He ran to the ancient Merlin who helped find a good home for the orb: They sent it to the Thogs, who were the near perfect civilization. They never went to war and they knew how to morally live. Caleb gave them the orb. For many years, the plan worked and the orb remained useless, beyond the reach of even the Kraskull.

The Scarlet Phoenix waned and went into hiding. Some had said it went into a magical weapon. Others said it was in space, looking down on the planets. Others said it was merely a legend, and no more should come from it. To this day, the *Ring* council had not made a definitive answer as to whether the Scarlet Phoenix had really existed or not. Either way, the Scarlet Phoenix did not make contact, only supposedly promising that it would come when the time was right.

However, because of the evil the orb brought to Venemay, the Thogs separated into the Thogs and Thogeens and fought against one another. The Thogeens took control of the orb, but didn't know how to use it. Now, the head Thogeen controls the orb but the Kraskull, the Thogs, or the Thogeens do not know how to use it … let alone destroy it …

13.) The Gladiators

John struggled against his bindings.
"You can not escape, so why bother?" the guard said.
"Besides, where would you go if you even did?"
"America," John said. The guard laughed.
"Do you know how far that is?"
John shook his head.
"Well, we're in Peru and America is definitely a long way away," the guard replied. "Well, it's almost time."
They had set up camp somewhere in the forest. John and Joan had separated. The army, however, did not come back. Only one guard had taken Joan, but four remained with John. John hoped, based on her skills, that she would escape within a day. He didn't know what they would do with him.
"Get up!" The guard commanded. "You will now be put to the test."
John raised an eyebrow, but that was all the reaction he gave. He got up, and was led to a building. At a closer look, John saw it was a bar.
"Why do you want me to go with you?" John asked, figuring they just wanted to get drunk. The guard smirked at him.
"Why, you're the whole reason we're going!" he replied. "Don't you realize what this is?"
"A bar?" John said.
"Very perceptive," the guard said. "A Peru bar. And do you know what happens at a few, selective Peru bars?"
"People get drunk?" John guessed. The guard hit him over the head.
"You haven't lived until you have seen a gladiator fight in the Peruvian bars," the guard said dreamily. "Oh, wait, you will, only you will be the very person to experience it!"
John's heart sank.
"A ... gladiator challenge?" He said. "At ... but ... where ..."
"Don't worry, you'll get a weapon," he said as if this answered all of John's questions. John said no more. He and the rest of the guards entered into the bar.

At first, John thought he walked into a concert. There were people screaming at the top of their lungs, there were people spilling drinks on each other, but mostly insanity. But the thing that caught John's attention the most was what the people were screaming about. There was an iron cage in the middle of the bar where two people with knives were fighting. John gasped as one put his knife into the other. The fighter fell dead and the crowd cheered more. John's eyes widened. The guard took him to the bartender.

"We have another one for you, Bob," the guard said to him. "He's strong, trust me."

He added this because the bartender looked at him questionably.

"He killed fifty during battle when they were outnumbered fifteen thousand to two," the guard said.

"Well, we do need another challenger ..." the bartender said. "How about $50?"

"I am worth more then that!" John spat. The guard struck him over the head again.

"Silence! But he's right," the guard frowned. "I am not taking a penny under two hundred."

"For that weakling?!" the bartender sniffed. "Let's see how he does against tonight's undefeated champ. Put him in the ring and then I'll buy him."

John started to breathe hard. The guard unhooked him and went to the door of the cage. The guard forced his knife into John's hand and then pushed him into the cage. John looked at his opponent. He was about seven feet tall, short but massive arms, and his shorts were fading. He had black hair and had missing teeth.

John prepared for the attack. Undefeated or not, John knew how to defeat him. The man had shorter arms then John's long arms. This could be used to John's advantage.

"Kill him!" he heard distinctly from the crowd. "Kill him!"

The man lunged at him. John shot out his hand with his knife and stopped him. John pulled his hand away and then stabbed the man in the stomach. The crowd fell silent. John watched, as if it were in slow motion, the man fall to the ground, bleeding all over. John glanced around quickly to try and find and exit to the cage. There was none. He looked out to the half-drunk people and saw that they were astounded at how calm he looked.

"Now what?" he asked. The crowd cheered.

"He was better than that other guy!" One yelled.

"This is more exciting," another said. "It was boring when only one was winning them!"

"Well, this is a surprise!" the guard said, laughing. "So what do you say, two hundred fifty?"

"Deal!" the bartender said at once in a half surprised, half awed look. He tossed the money at the guards, and stood up on a chair. "Ladies and Gentleman, our undefeated man, Goliath, had been killed! Now we have a new defender! Anyone want to wager their life?"

"I will!" one man said. John took a good look at him. He also had puny arms.

"I will spare you're life if you give me one hundred pieces of gold," he said, after taking off his shirt and getting into the cage.

"I will spare you're life if you get out now," John shot back. The man lunged at him just as Goliath did. John jumped out of the way and cut the man's throat. He rummaged through the man's pockets. He pulled out of his pocket many gold coins.

"Is this enough to buy my freedom?" He asked the bartender. The bartender laughed and shook his head. John pocketed it. "Well, then, I am not leaving. It was a mistake to give me a weapon again."

"Get him, guards!" the bartender said. The nearest one ran and flung open the gate. John threw his dagger at him. It pierced his neck. The guard fell to the ground in agony.

Paul left the cell in a hurry. The Kraskull would be at him very soon. He did not want to think what would happen if we was caught. He ran to the edge of the ship when suddenly a hand reached out and pulled him around. One of the Soulhaunts had caught him.

"*Trying to escape, are we?*" the Soulhaunt rasped.

"Pretty much," Paul said coolly.

"*Very impressive,*" the Kraskull said. "*But now you must die.*"

"What?!" Paul yelled, "what about that ole' 'Zach wanted you alive' thing?"

"*Zach is now beyond his control,*" The Kraskull said, "*Besides, I hardly think that Zach will be choked up about losing one potential ogre. He has many. But don't worry; we will give you a fighting chance. You'll have a rematch in the gladiator ring.*"

"And how do you know I will die from it?" Paul spat.

"*Against us,*" the Soulhaunt finished. Paul's eyes widened.

"With what weapon?" Paul asked.

"*Without one,*" the Soulhaunt said in a finality tone. "*It will be tomorrow. Consider it your glorified execution.*"

Paul was led back to the cell, but the Soulhaunts made sure there was a guard down there at all times. Paul knew he had no way to escape now.

John was eventually outnumbered and captured. They removed his weapon and one of the bartender's guards threw him into a cage.

"Let's get a few rules down, slave," the guard said, "You stay here, you fight all day; you make it, you live. No rebellion, no fighting outside the ring, nothing. Understand?"

"Why do I have to kill people?" John said fiercely. "I hate killing people outside of war. This is murder!"

"You don't have to kill them," The guard chuckled, heading toward the door. "But you have to survive, so do anything in your power to avoid the opponent if you don't like to kill."

The door slammed shut. John looked around the room. The room was small and maroon. There were other cages in the

room, but they were all empty. John had nothing but the pants
he wore. Nothing on his back, no weapon on his belt and no
shoes on his feet. He suddenly felt alone. John looked at the
stale food in his cage, but even though his body was hungry, he
couldn't eat. He killed so many today, and outside of war.
Besides the two challengers, he killed five guards and a
bartender. Still, he didn't kill his "master."

"Maybe I might escape later tomorrow," John said, "and I
still need to help Joan escape. I hope that this will help me
somehow."

Suddenly, his "master" ran into the room nearly crying with
joy.

"We got the Ring!" he said. John at first thought he was
talking about a magical ring of the Ring council. "The Coliseum
in Mexico! They heard of your amazing defeat of Goliath and
they want you to perform in the Coliseum!"

"I guess that's good," John said. Then he thought of
something. "Will you make much money?"

The bartender's face fell.

"I will get fame if you win," the bartender said. "But
because the Coliseum belongs to someone else, I do not get the
money."

"I will give you a deal," John said carefully. "The guards
that captured me last night have another prisoner. She is
amazing and will make you money. Here's the deal: You buy
her from the guards to add to your...'collection,' and I will get
you a portion of the royalties of every person that comes to the
Coliseum."

"You can do that?" the bartender asked curiously.

"Yes, but I will need your help," John said. "And I will
need the prisoner with me to do it. I learned a strong method in
my home town, before I was a slave."

John was making this up as he went along, hoping that the bartender's greed tied with his stupidity would override simple logic.

"You have yourself a deal," the bartender said. "But why do you need the prisoner?"

"We are partners and can think alike," John lied, "it would help us in tough places. So can you do it now?"

"I need to, don't I?" The bartender said. "We are leaving immediately to Mexico, so I better do it now."

He left. John breathed a sigh of belief. But just then, a guard came into the room.

"I hear you are leaving to Mexico," the guard said. "But since your master has one more errand to run, you will fight one more time in the ring."

Paul was taken down from the chains. He was surprised that this would be his death: Being forced to fight the most evil creatures on the earth. *Well*, Paul thought, *it's better that being tortured to death.*

"*You will face our leader*," the Soulhaunt said. "*If you're punny mind can remember, he was the one who betrayed you.*"

"All right," Paul said. He had only one plan: to fight the Soulhaunt with his sharp blade that they didn't catch him with, then try to escape the ring and jump into the water. Paul thought of it as a pathetic and hopeless plan, but it was the best he could think of.

The Kraskull all gathered around Paul. They led him to a part of the ship that was open enough to fight in. One got in front of Paul. The others held out their hands and created a sphere around them so that neither would escape.

John was forced into the cage once again. *Well*, John thought, *this will be the last time I will be in here.* They threw him a knife and the challenger approached him. The challenger had long hair that went into his face. He was looking down, so

John couldn't see his face that well. He was, however, about six feet tall and maybe thirty years old.

"You may begin," the guard said to John. John nodded. He looked at his opponent again and he had looked up. It was William.

"What are you doing here?" John asked in surprise.

"You're little plan worked," William called laughing. "The dwarves came out and destroyed my army. You have won."

It was scary. William was shaking. John saw scars on his face and worn lines under his eyes. His body was bent over a little and he had lost a toe.

"You're mad!" John realized in horror.

"I am not crazy," William growled, spit drooling down from his mouth. "But I must kill you now."

John took a step back. William pulled from his belt a long sword. He took a step near John, but John leapt into the air over him. William turned and stopped John's attempt to kill him. William took two vicious swipes with his sword, both of which John deflected, and then spat at John's feet. John lunged this time, but William's footwork was still good. He stopped John's attempt.

"How did you survive the attack?" John said.

"Good question," William sneered, hesitating for a moment. "Everyone else was killed. My army was my life. You killed my life. You will pay!"

John was forced to the very side of the chicken wired wall. William took swipe after swipe in an attack and John could only barely defend himself. John summed up his magic and shot it at William's chest. It didn't do anything.

"You should be dead!" John exclaimed. William grinned once again and then turned his body into an abnormal shape. John realized a horrible truth, "you're a genie?!"

"One of the last," William shot an attack at John, which he ducked. "You can not kill me. I am invincible."

John's eyes widened. He knew what William said was true. He couldn't kill a genie. John deflected two more and then a particularly strong smack with William's sword sent John's knife flying through the chicken wire and out into the bar. John gazed in horror as William laughed and raised his sword.

John then, having adrenaline pumped into him, had a revelation that would seem obvious to a bystander. Since John had no sleep for seventy-two hours, he couldn't think as clearly. However, the revelation gave him strength and he put his hand behind his neck. *How could I be this stupid to not think of this*, John wondered as he summoned up his favorite sword…

Paul faced his Kraskull with fear, but pulled behind his neck a long knife that he poured the rest of his rejuvenated genie power into …

In Europe, Jerry pulled out his favorite orange sword to swipe the necks of a few goblins …

On the high seas, Daniel pulled out his magical sword to fight a blockade of at least 200 ogre ships …

And far away, in the smallest country and continent in the world, a sword, in the middle of a field cast into a trunk by Daniel Quaill, started to glow for the first time in the world – magic in the sword so powerful that the Kraskull themselves couldn't face it …

The Scarlet Phoenix had risen again.

14.) The Rebirth's Power

John countered William's attack and went in for a swipe at his side. William's eyes widened and didn't have time to defend himself with his sword. He was able, however, to bend away from the attack with his genie powers.

"How can I kill you?!" John practically yelled.

"I was about to ask you the same thing," William growled. "You Quaills aren't too bad. Your brother taking out that dragon, and now you nearly beating me."

"You little ..." John snarled. He could feel the hatred between them rise to an unthinkable level. John never felt so much hatred in his life. He used all of his emotion in his attacks, but William was too powerful. William leapt high into the air to avoid one low attack from John and then brought his sword down on John's shoulder. John grimaced and slid to the ground. He used up all his energy. He was tired and spent.

"Now, brother," William laughed. John's eyes widened in fear. "It's time for you to die."

"You're not..." John whispered through gritted teeth.

"On the contrary," William said, "you fought well, but you must die."

John closed his eyes and breathed. The cage door came crashing down and something knocked him to the ground. John opened his eyes and saw that Lino had saved him again. Lino leapt off William, and he and John ran through the hole in the cage. They ran to the door of the building.

"What took you so long?" John panted as they threw open the door. Before Lino could answer, two large guards ran up to them. John pulled up his sword and gripped it tight. He fought one, and Lino fought the other. He knocked the sword out of the hands of the guard and then, with the remainder of his strength, killed the man. Lino also bit the throat of the man and killed him. John looked at Lino. "I can't go on anymore, pal."

John collapsed onto Lino.

"Come on, big man," Lino said, trying to push John up without any success. John staggered to his feet.

"I'll get you sooner or later, Quaill!" John heard William's voice ring through the bar. "You wait!"

"Come on, John," Lino pleaded. "We have to get out of here."

"I can't," John gasped.

Lino thought crazily.

"Joan is still captured," Lino finally said. John's eyelids jumped up. "We have to save her, come on."

Lino ran ahead, but John turned around.

"No need, Lino," John said in an exhausted tone. "Look."

Lino turned and saw the bartender carrying a chain that was connected to Joan. John approached them. The bartender looked furious.

"Who let you go?" The bartender nearly shouted. John pointed to Lino and then he pulled out his sword, which he had put inside his belt. "Sheath that sword, servant! We're heading to the Ring now!"

John almost laughed at this statement. He looked Lino in the eye and then at Joan. He then turned to the bartender and said, "I don't think so."

He took a swipe at the chain that held Joan and it broke through.

"Feeling generous today," John said as Joan joined them, "I will spare you're life."

"Get back here!" the bartender said as John, Joan, and Lino walked away. "I need that money!"

John suddenly stopped and turned. He reached into his pocket and pulled out a little bit of the coins he had stolen from the man last night. He tossed it at his feet.

"There," John said. John turned and whistled very loud in his old call. He waited a minute and then saw Dreaded Musty come running towards him. "She must have run away from William."

He leapt onto the horse. He looked at Joan.

"Oh yes, I forgot," He reached out with his hand and muttered an incantation and the chain around her wrist disappeared. "Hop on."

Joan was just staring at him.

"What's wrong?" Lino asked.

John leapt off the horse.

"Are you ok?" John whispered to her, glancing into her eyes. He could see she was shaking a bit. John swallowed, "She's in shock, Lino."

John lifted her onto the horse's saddle. He got on behind her.

"I hope you don't mind, but you'll have to stay on the ground," John said to Lino. "And we're going fast. The faster we go, the quicker we'll get there."

"Obviously," Lino said. "Where are we?"

"Not in Phoenix," John said. "And that's all I care about. Musty, you'll have to lead the way … I'm dead tired. Ride on!"

The horse neighed and then sprinted north.

The Kraskull were obviously angry at Paul's trick with his knife.

"*It doesn't matter*," the lead Kraskull said. "*Let him fight. He will lose.*"

"*…,*" one of the Kraskull gasped, "*Master … it's …*"

Though Locombony was far away, a light appeared coming from the ground that both Paul and the Kraskull saw. Something was coming from this beam of light on the island. It got closer and they saw it was an invisible wave. The wave looked like a wrinkle in the air. Paul shaded his eyes from the wave and then heard a horrible sound as if a loud bumblebee had been magnified forty times its normal sound. The wave hit Paul, but he only felt a light breeze. However, when it hit the Kraskull, they all screamed. The hoods fell back but then a blinding light appeared in front of Paul and it prevented him from seeing anything. The Kraskull fell to the ground, one by one. The blinding light stopped and Paul could see the Kraskull on the floor. Paul hesitated no further and jumped out of the boat. Paul, swimming as fast as he could away from the ship, suddenly grinned. Only one thing could knock an evil down and that's a pure. And a pure on earth at this time could only mean one thing: the Phoenix had risen. Paul, draining his genie power once again, made a small raft with his magic. He got aboard it and then slept for quite some time.

He woke up in the morning to find himself near land. He sat up and then swam to the nearby shore. He got to the shore without any problem. Having a proper bit of sleep, he could now think clearly in his old genius self.

Paul didn't see anyone or anything. It looked like he was in a desert area. Studying the land quickly, Paul concluded he was in Columbia. He looked at the sun and then went north.

"This is bad," Paul said to himself. "I am walking by myself in the middle of the desert with nothing but a knife and the clothes on my back. Who knows how I'll survive. But Jerry made a prophesy that he will return on the eighth day of the orb's destruction, so that means we'll have to destroy it. Well, hear goes nothing."

He walked on not having food or water in the middle of Columbia.

"John, slow down a bit, you're horse is going to die!" Lino panted. "And so am I!"

"Musty can hold out a little longer," John said, after he had rested on his horse, "and you can chill out. We have only been sprinting for a couple of hours."

"Only," Lino gasped. "I have never run this fast or far in my life!"

Joan was slowly recovering. She had vomited a couple times during the ride, but that was the only sign she showed of life.

"Wow," she said suddenly. "What a ride."

"Don't talk, Joan," John said. "You are in shock. Just take it easy and rest. We'll be in Arizona in no time."

He lied about this. He knew if they sprinted constantly for 12 hours straight, it would still take them days to get there.

"I can't hold out much longer, John," Lino said.

"Then I'll leave you behind because I am not stopping until sundown," John said fiercely. John knew Lino would never stop if John continued onward.

In three hours, John officially called the sun set, so they stopped and found a place to sleep.

"What a day," John sighed. "I am glad everyone is ok so far. Joan, are you feeling better?"

"I think. What happened?" Joan asked.

"We were wondering that ourselves," Lino asked, "what put you in a state of shock?"

"I can't remember," Joan said, eyes somewhat blank.

"That's ok," John said, "what *can* you remember?"

"I remember being arrested, and then everything goes black until I wake up on a horse with you around me."

"Ok," John replied simply. He knew he had to be very patient with her. "So you remember me and the mission?"

"Of course," Joan nodded.

"Let's sleep," Lino yawned. "I am exhausted. Maybe tomorrow we can go further."

They all agreed and fell fast asleep.

John told his body to wake up at sunrise and it did. John leapt up and woke up everybody.

"Already?" Lino said dazed.

"Twelve hours rides, we ride from sunrise to set," John answered. He woke Dreaded Musty. "But I will give you 15 minutes to get Joan to give you food."

Joan summoned some water bottles and some food for all of them. John took a small gulp of his then gave the rest to his horse.

"You ran great yesterday, Musty," John whispered, patting his horse. "Can you do it again?"

The horse sputtered. John guessed that meant "yes."

"Everyone ready?" Joan asked as she walked up to the horse.

"You seem to be back to your old self, that's good," John said. "Climb up."

Joan pulled herself up onto the horse. John jumped around her and stretched around her to grab the reigns. She twitched again, just like the eve of the Third Stand. Lino turned his head to hide his grin. John didn't move.

"What's wrong?" Joan said.

"I just remembered," John said. "Do you know what today is?"

They both shook their heads.

"It's Christmas," John said. "Oh well. I highly doubt anyone has anything to give each other."

"Not unless somebody would like to stop early tonight," Lino hinted hopefully. All John answered with was a grin and urge of his horse to sprint.

Paul slept badly during the night. The Kraskull had gotten through his idea of thinking of something else and now he had horrible dreams about them.

He got up about two hours after the sun had risen. Paul felt thirsty, but couldn't help himself. Paul got up and trudged on. He couldn't do anything more than to force himself to walk. His genie power was far from rejuvenated. The only thing that pushed him on was the hope built from the prophecy. Paul collapsed a couple times, but no matter what, he pushed onward.

John was about six hours in when another rider came up to him. The rider was dressed in brown robe had a crucifix hanging around his neck. Out of politeness, John let him pass first, but instead, the monk came up to him.

"He has been born!" the man practically yelled.

"Good," Joan said, figuring it was something about his religion.

"He was stopped the Kraskull, I have been told in prayer!" he said. "The end will come soon. Repent!"

"Who stopped the Kraskull? Who has risen again?" John asked quickly.

"The Scarlet Phoenix!" the monk replied. "God sent down an angel to protect us. I have been told in prayer!"

"He has risen?!" John whooped. "Great! We will win this war!"

John looked at the monk and hesitated. John only knew one bible verse, and he didn't even know if it was appropriate for the situation.

"Er … John 3:16?"

"And let he be also with you," the monk nodded. "I am glad to see the day when Christians and Sorcerers unite!"

The monk rode off.

"He was certainly a weird one," Lino said.

"But he has been born again!" Joan said. "This is remarkable!"

"Yes," John said. "But now we have to do our part. Let's get out there and stop Zach!"

John charged ahead. With the Phoenix born again, this gave him knew morale.

"Kind of ironic, huh?" Joan said to him. "Today is Christmas and the Phoenix has been born."

"That is weird," John smiled, looking up to the skies.

At night, Paul collapsed again. He opened out his hand.

"Without water, I'll die," he said, pointing out the obvious to himself. "I need to make water."

Paul concentrated his power onto his hand and in his hand appeared some water inside a glass.

"I wish I were a magician," Paul gasped. "I could create unlimited water."

He drank from the cup and then fell asleep.

John stopped his horse at sunset again. He saw a little ahead of him a log.

"That's strange," John said. "There aren't many trees out here. What is that thing sticking out of it?"

John walked over it. Behind him was Joan. Lino and the horse were already fast asleep. John stopped in front of it and saw a sword sticking out of the log. It was his uncle's sword. The one his uncle had put in the middle of the field in Locombony.

"But that's impossible," John whispered.

"What?" Joan asked him. John explained it to her. "That's strange. Why don't you remove it?"

"I am afraid something might happen," John cautioned.

"Well, I want to find out," Joan replied simply. She reached for the sword.

"Wait," John called, stopping her. "I … I'll do it."

He put his hand on the handle. He removed it.

First, there was nothing to it. Then the sword began to glow white. A rim of white appeared around the sword. It got bigger and bigger. John dropped it and pulled Joan back. Joan's eyes were wide. The rim stopped glowing for a moment.

Then the sword erupted with light and made a noise as if a person had slammed their arm on a piano and hit all the keys. It woke up Lino, and John quickly put his arms around Joan to protect her. From the wall of light, something slowly started to appear. It was a person that was transparent. It stopped right outside the wall and John recognized him.

"Matt …" John said referring to his old friend from the magician school. Three more people came out, "Jimmy … Tyler … and …"

A woman walked out.

"Sarah …" It was John's old girl friend that Zach had killed. One more person emerged. It was John's mother. Words couldn't find him. He waited for a ghost of his father to emerge, but he didn't. "Then … my father … he's …."

The ghosts smiled at him. They then spread their arms out and slowly began to disappear. Not one spoke a word except for a small, gentle, three words from Sarah, "Good choice, John."

The ghosts disappeared, but from the wall came another creature. A larger creature. The creature came out of the wall of light and the wall disappeared. The creature was a bird. The bird was larger than any dragon or any building John had ever seen. Its wing span was over a thousand yards long. It landed close to John.

"The King Phoenix," John and Joan said together. They both fell to the ground in a bow. The Phoenix spread its wings and flapped. A huge gust of wind sent them on their backs and the Phoenix lifted off. It flew higher and higher until it turned around and flew northward. John, Lino and Joan saw it go.

"Wow," Lino said. They all looked at the sword of which it came. John walked over to it and picked it up. It was still glowing white, but much lighter than it was before.

"I think this is the power of a pure," John said, swinging it and then putting it in his belt. "I can beat anything with it."

"Be careful whose hands that falls into," Joan cautioned. John looked at them both.

"So are you guys wide awake?" he asked.

"No, we're dead tired," said Lino quickly.

"I thought so," John said. "That's good, we can get in a couple more hours of running."

John ran up and leapt onto the horse. The horse woke up from the daze, neighed and went up onto two legs. It landed and Joan jumped on behind John and wrapped her arms around him.

"Let's see if we can catch up with that Phoenix," John yelled and he sped off with Lino running close behind.

*   *   *

Paul awoke to the sudden flapping of wings above. It was still dark out. He looked up at the sky and thought he was dreaming: he saw a huge bird descend to him. Paul closed his eyes and then opened them again. The bird had landed next to him. Paul stood up and walked slowly to it. The bird suddenly lunged at him and grabbed him with its talons. The feet were so large, Paul estimated they could crush a large ship. The bird took off and turned south.

"No," Paul said. "I don't want to go that way!"

The large bird flew anyway. It flew about a mile and then dropped, landing. Paul looked up and saw a horseman come riding towards him. There was also something pink running along side him. As they got closer, he recognized the individuals.

"Paul!" John called, running towards him and the Phoenix. "Are you ok?"

"I fine, except this bird can kill an army's worth," Paul panted, struggling.

"'This bird'?! Paul, do you know who that is?" John asked with amazement.

The Phoenix let go of him. Paul took a good look at it and then smiled.

"The Scarlet Phoenix," Paul whispered, kneeling to it. "I am in your debt. You saved me from the Kraskull and brought me to my brother. Thank you."

The Phoenix nodded and then disappeared in a beam of light. The sword at John's side began to glow amazingly for a second before stopping.

"Paul, I am so glad to see you!" John sighed. "I thought you were dead!"

"If it weren't for The King Phoenix, I would be," Paul said. "But I was also worried about you—I thought you would drown."

"If it weren't for the mages, I would have," John replied. "Oh yes, by the way, Paul, this is Joan. She is a mage and is directing us to Arizona."

Joan got off the horse.

"Hi," Joan greeted, nodding to him. "I heard all about you from your brother."

"I would guess so," Paul grinned. He looked at his brother and winked. "Well, now that we're all wide awake, what shall we do now?"

"Well, we can't sprint," John said, and Lino gave him a thankful look, "but we can trot and tell about our stories since we've been apart. But first, what do you have on you? Any supplies that we can use?"

"I have the gold and some medicine," Paul shrugged.

"Great," John said, jumping onto his horse again. "Joan can get on with me and Paul can get on Lino. Let's go."

For the rest of the night, into the morning, after they had a couple hours of sleep, they talked about what happened to each other. After their rest, they continued onward in a dull sprint, making great progress throughout the day.

The next night, the fourth night of the journey, Paul and Lino were asleep. John pretended to sleep, but was actually wide-awake. He finally could no longer stand it and got up to see his horse. He saw it on the ground. He went over to it and stroked its head. He didn't hear Joan walk up behind him. John pulled out his sword and picked up a stone. He started to sharpen it.

"You know," Joan whispered, surprising him. "I've discovered a habit of yours. What are you anxious about now?"

"You can't sleep either, eh?" John sighed. "Well, nothing really. I just am so worried that Zach is so far ahead of us, he'll kill us with the orb before we are able to get to Phoenix."

"Nah, we'll catch him," Joan reassured. "He isn't as insane as you are with trying to get there."

"You'd be surprised," John muttered.

Joan sat next to him.

"Do you want to go for a ride?" she asked.

"Nah," John said, "Musty here is beat. She can't handle another day of this. But I could go for a walk," he added when he realized it would be impolite to turn her down.

She smiled and got up. John sheathed his sword and got up with her. They walked for nearly half a mile. They found a place near a shore. They looked out to it.

"Isn't it beautiful?" John asked. "It truly is amazing. I love the waters. It's probably because I wasn't really near it when I grew up. It was almost always cold."

"I love the sea, too," Joan said. "I grew up near the river so I know a lot about it. It seems like I was with the sea my whole life. It really has been my life. It especially means a lot to me now."

"It really has," John agreed. "It saved my life a couple times, believe it or not. I would have no reason to live without it."

They looked at each other and then looked away.

"We've made such good time," John said, changing the subject. "Look, we're nearly to the end of South America already. Soon we'll be back home in our own continent."

"I hope so," Joan said. "Then we'll go back to being normal people instead of people who are hated."

"We won't be out of the woods yet," John cautioned. "We still have Zyno to worry about. He's the worst."

"Well, we don't have to worry if you're here," Joan said, smiling at him. She looked directly into his eyes.

"We have to head back soon," John whispered, averting his eyes, "or else they'll start getting worried."

Joan nodded. They turned away from the sea.

"You don't …" Joan began, but then paused as she struggled to find the right words. John glanced at her. She seemed very cautious.

"What?" he asked.

"Well, I know what you said about … well, Zach killing your girlfriend," Joan babbled.

John stopped in his tracks.

"It was a while ago … seeing her made the hurting come back," John replied simply. "But she is content."

"What about you?" Joan asked him directly.

John bit his lip.

"I think I've found someone else," John decided.

"You think so?" Joan asked genuinely.

"I … I am not sure if it would be smart to start working on a stronger bond at this point in time," John explained. "But…I can't deny that there is a bond between us. A strong bond that should be developed. But not now."

Joan nodded. She looked slightly disappointed, but they both went back to where they were staying.

Joan and John woke everyone up in the morning.

"You let us sleep in," Lino announced.

"Yes, Musty needs a day of rest so that we can keep sprinting tomorrow."

"Good," Lino said. "And I am glad we're almost out of South America."

John took out his map of the world.

"If we travel all day tomorrow," John said, "for twelve hours, I mean, we'll be in Nicaragua, which is pretty near Mexico. Then after we make it through the day after that, we'll be in about the edge of Mexico. Then it's a four-day journey through Mexico and into Phoenix, that is, if we sprint through it. So we're about a week away and it's not going to be fun. We're not stopping until sunset or eating until sunrise. Of course, Musty and Lino can eat and drink on the way because they are carrying us."

"What?!" Lino nearly yelled. "Who am I carrying?"

"Paul," John answered, "Musty can only take so much."

"You are treating the horse better than you're treating me," Lino muttered.

"I wish we could go now," Paul said, "We're really behind if we do it that way. I bet Zach's already in Mexico."

"Yep," John said. "Well, we aren't going to sit here; we can at least walk all day."

John grabbed Dreaded Musty's reigns and woke her up. Musty stood up as if ready to sprint.

"Not today, Musty," John said soothingly. "We need you to rest; you ran for a long time these past few days."

Dreaded Musty snorted.

"You can't take that much," Joan said, walking up to her. "You'll be beat."

Again, Dreaded Musty snorted.

"Alright, if you insist," John said, trying to control his relief. He was not excited about walking the whole day; he wanted to move out as quickly as possible.

"No way," Lino shuttered as John and Joan got on the horse. "Guys, please. I am beat. Don't make me go through this again."

"You don't have to keep up," John reminded him. "But Paul is relying on you."

Paul got on Lino's back and he sighed.

"Remember, Lino," Paul said, "pain is temporary. When we get there, you can rest."

"Oh joy, I'll be sure and tell you that when you get your arm chopped off during battle," Lino growled.

They all rode off in a quick sprint.

*   *   *

After a couple of miles, they came to something happening in the distance. John continued to urge his horse on. They slowed down when they realized what it was: it was a huge battle scene. There were tens of thousands of ogres and about a hundred mammoths facing dinosaurs, dragons, winged Pegasus, and men that John would guess to be psychics.

"Good," John said, "I have been itching for a battle after that ambush at Locombony's island. You guys up for it?"

"No," Paul and Lino said together.

"You guys stay back then," John called, taking out his sword. "I'll show you how to beat these mammoths, Paul. Oh, yes, Joan I forgot, you don't have a weapon. Have mine and I'll take this one."

John pulled out the Phoenix sword.

"Prepare for the Fourth Stand!" John yelled as Joan jumped off the horse. "Let's kick some tail, shall we?"

15.) The Fourth Stand

John rode into battle with Joan charging right behind him. The battle was not going well: the ogres were annihilating the psychics.

John rode to the mammoths and Joan ran to aid the psychics. Paul and Lino still remained behind.

John rode under a mammoth, holding his sword high in the air. A massive foot threatened to stomp on him, but instead, John swung out of the way and bashed his sword into the leg of the beast. A glowing mark appeared where John swung his sword. He didn't feel any resistance to his swing, as if he had swung it through air.

The glow mark separated and the leg detached from the body. The mammoth started to fall onto its stomach. John rode out from underneath it. Many ogres ran towards him. John turned his horse to the fast approaching ogres. John let Dreaded Musty run over them. He leapt off his horse and ran to the front lines of the psychics. The dragons were beating the mammoths, but the dinosaurs had enough problems with the ogres. There were only 500 psychics left.

John saw Joan aiding them. John turned and saw other psychics falling into a complete retreat. John called to them, "Pull forward! There isn't much left! Hold out!"

The psychics turned. There were outnumbered, 40-to-1, but they saw John's bravery and launched forward. The dinosaurs all charged, and the dragons flew through the air to hit the mammoths head on. Mammoth versus dragon, they were both caught in a stalemate. John reached an ogre and swung. Once again, his sword hit no resistance and the ogre's head flew off.

John realized that he had the power of the Phoenix in this one sword.

I wonder how I summon the full power of it, John thought. He gripped it tight and took swing after swing at ogres without tiring. An ogre ran up to John. John swung the Phoenix sword to parry the ogre's, but instead of making a *clang* noise, John's sword went through the ogre's sword and cut its head off. John looked in surprise at his sword.

"I am invincible!" he yelled. John took dozens of swipes and killed all he took swings at. When he looked at an ogre, it seemed, it was already dead. The psychics were amazed when they saw him go.

John broke through two legions easily. The psychics rallied around him, yelling, and covering his back. John sliced and diced, striking down the enemies. He would occasionally throw a blast of magic at a group of ogres.

If John had not distinguished himself in any other battles, this was where he showed his true colors. He was full of energy, taking down ogre by ogre, until he broke through the lines of attacks. The psychics were ecstatic.

The ogres saw that he was unbeatable and started to retreat. John commanded the psychics to form up again and then to charge all out.

"NO QUARTER!" John yelled as the army started to pass him. He leapt on Dreaded Musty and urged her on. He caught up to the army and led them into the charge. Line after line, the ogres fell.

A few hundred were able to escape and John commanded that they stop. He breathed and turned to his troops.

"Did any of the mammoths survive?" John asked one of the dragons. It shook its heads. He then looked at the psychics. "Who is your leader?"

"He was killed in battle," one responded.

"Well," John sighed. "I can't lead you in battle. I am on a different mission. But I think you can appoint your leader correctly."

"But you could help us," a psychic said. Some of them murmured amongst themselves. Before John could answer, a screech came from above. He turned into the night sky and saw red and black dragons coming in at them, most with riders on their necks. There was about forty in all.

"Oh crap," John swore as they started to circle them. "Psychics, prepare to make your shields. Dragons, open wings and prepare to fly. Dinos, get in an attack position!"

The dragons dove. The psychics put up their magic shields, but it barely worked. Joan ran to John's side.

"Perfect timing," John said to her. Paul and Lino realized they had to help and ran in to do so. "This isn't going to work."

Suddenly, all of the dragons dove down at them. The petrified psychics leapt out of the way, but the dragons grabbed some. The dragons on the psychic's side rose up to face them, but they were also outnumbered, 2-1. John knew they could handle them. One of the last dragons was rising up when John rode over to it and leapt upon it. He climbed up to its neck and said, "You'll need to get me as close as I can to the other dragons."

The dragon roared to signal it understood. Another dragon blasted fire at the one John was on, but it dodged it easily. John stood up on the dragon's head and swung his sword at an approaching enemy. It cut through the neck of the dragon and it fell to the ground. He looked around and then directed the dragon to one attacking the psychics.

The battle raged on for hours. The psychics put barriers around themselves constantly, but they were growing weak. John was doing everything he could, but he could only kill about ten dragons. He finally leapt off the dragon and landed on the ground gracefully. He ran over to his horse and mounted it.

"Full on retreat," he muttered. Joan shouted it and the psychics pulled back to the seas. The dragons closely followed them. They reached the shore and the dragons didn't leave.

"Well, I didn't expect the dragons to just fly away," Paul rolled his eyes. He looked at John. "Can I use that ax of yours?"

John handed him his ax and wondered.

"These scales on the dragons are too hard to penetrate with a simple arrow. Even my magic couldn't hit them down. The dragons must face them. I just don't see how they can win now."

They all looked up and saw dragons on their side falling fast. There was less than ten left on the psychics side but twenty left on the enemy's side. With the attacks from the dragons, there were only three hundred-fifty psychics left. John sighed, and then looked in horror at the sound he heard in the distance. It was an ogre horn. The ogre army was coming back for round two.

"Great," John said. "Psychics, prepare to charge."

The dinosaurs were too preoccupied to help.

"We shall show these ogre battalions that they now must fear the psychics!" John yelled. He turned and saw the fear of the psychics. "What do you have to fear? Death is nothing. But victory is everything. Your challengers wait. If you beat them here, it is clear sailing straight to Phoenix where you can wait for the genies. There you will attack with the largest army and battle in the world. Defeat them here and prove your power! Show them who you are!"

The army cheered. John turned and put his sword in the air. He gave the signal to go all out. As they got closer, however, John realized that this wasn't the army they faced earlier; this was a fresh, new army of thirty-thousand. John stopped the charge. The new army stretched so far that the only place to run was straight back to the ocean. The ogres responded and charged at them. John put his sword out and prepare for an all-out, for-your-life defense. But it wouldn't come. From the right side, another battle cry arouse, this one John recognized.

Paul looked over and saw the largest army he had ever seen. He smiled as his own created Thogs charged at the stunned ogres. The Thogs crashed through the ogre line and were through the first round in a moment's time. Paul clenched his fist and whispered, "yes." He saw John charge right at the ogres. Paul gripped his ax and charged right beside him. Joan and Lino followed suit, as did the entire psychic army. They barely got to the lines when, once again the ogres started to retreat.

"Not this time," Paul said. "John, command our armies to pursue them. This will change from a stand to the greatest attack on a fort ever."

John shook his head smiling. The Thog army lined up along side the psychics. The leader stood in the front and John rode up to him.

"Maurice, nice little army you have for yourself," He said. Maurice bowed.

"At your services 'ah, General Quaill 'ah," He said.

"We have to follow them to their fort and defeat them," John said. He turned his horse and kicked it. The horse ran forward and so did the Thogs and the psychics. John knew that ogres would now fall to the new army. A large red dragon landing on the ground and roaring stopped them, however. The dragon blew fire and scorched a good number of psychics. There were no other dragons that survived. Paul's grin faded, but John's only widened. The dragon had no eyes.

"Marowlog …" He said, "… you survived the attack from my brother … oh well, you'll have to face me. Maurice, continue the attack, I'll handle this one."

Maurice looked at him doubtfully, but ordered his army around it. They noticed their leader going to the dragon alone and they all yelled out a whoop or encouraging call as they passed. They were led away to the ogres. Dreaded Musty walked slowly toward it. Marowlog breathed in and shot fire at John. John easily provided a shield around him and his horse, blocking the flames.

"I don't think that's going to work," John grinned. Marowlog roared in frustration and then attempted to kick him. John shot his sword into Marowlog's foot and then pulled it out.

"That's not going to work either," John said. "Looks like you're out ideas for killing me."

The dragon growled and shot fire at him again. John produced another shield, and then charged at the dragon. The blind dragon could sense his presence and dodged the mighty sword. While John chased it on the ground, the dragon continued to try to pelt the two with fire. It was a stalemate.

Marowlog suddenly dove down at John. John pulled up on the reigns of his horse, coming to a complete halt. Marowlog hit the ground, and John wasted no time. He rode by and took a slice off of the dragon's wing. Marowlog, screaming, went back up into the air.

"Man, I love this sword," John shouted. "Let's test its true power!"

He threw it directly at the dragon's heart. The sword penetrated the scales and went straight through the dragon. John saw it fly out the other end. The dragon slowly collapsed to the ground. John ran quickly and pulled the sword back with his power.

"That was simple," John said lightly. "Now to catch up with the army."

Paul saw in the distance a large barracks that could have held thousands of ogres. The fortress was surrounded with large, brick walls that would be hard to knock down. The Thogs, however, charged at the wall, and the wall came crashing down under the amazing strength of the army. The ogres were prepared. They had had their bows and crossbows pointed directly at the attack. They shot and killed a decent number of Thogs. John charged right behind them.

"Move on!" Joan yelled and pushed at the crossbowmen.

They broke through the first line and more ogres came charging outside from inside the barracks. The right wing of the Thogs clogged the gate and the left wing clogged the one on the left. The body of the Thog army continued fighting through the army. The ogres didn't stand a chance.

The Thogs pushed through the gates and advanced to the second line. The ogres were not as prepared this time, and John led his armies around the ring until every ogre was killed. They then went onto the last and largest gate.

"This is it!" John yelled. "This is the last battle!"

John went through the gates to find the remaining ogres lined up in a box formation to receive the attack. John waited until all the Thogs were ready and then he pulled out his bow. The Thogs pulled out similar bows, took aim and fired.

Thog's shots were always dead-on. The first three lines on the ogres' side suddenly fell because they were hit. The Thogs pulled another arrow out and shot again. By that time, the ogres decided to charge. The Thogs fired one more time and the ogres knew they were finished. The remainder of them (about 2,000 in all) tried to make it over the fence, but Thogs on the other side were waiting for them. The ogres were trapped. Thogs on both side fired arrows until the last ogre was killed. The Thogs and psychics cheered for the victory at the Fourth Stand.

*   *   *

"So how many do you think you have?" John asked Maurice later that night when the army pitched some tents to sleep. Joan, Paul, and Lino were also listening.

"We started with 40,000s 'ah," Maurice replied, "but many of our 'ah women gave birth 'ah and using the super-growth machines 'ah that master made us, we created another 40,000s 'ah. You see, Thogs 'ah give many births at once, like fish producing many eggs 'ah. So we had strengthen it greatly thens 'ah. Also, two years ago, we had sent 100,000 near the river to help guard it from the Australians. Most returned and so we had near 200,000 in our hands 'ah."

"Wow," Lino and Joan whispered.

"But that's just the beginnings 'ah," Maurice said. "Underneath the lab 'ah, we found Thog slaves that were starving. I think they were down there since when Zyno was still free. Us 'ah Thogs 'ah don't need water or food for a long time, but they were dying. We freed them, fed them and had them join our army. That brought us high to 500,000s 'ah. We concluded that Zach had stored the slaves for these battles but had abandoned them when Zyno was captureds 'ah.

"Then, surprisingly, wes 'ah had the women Thogs demand for their rights to fight. We had to accept and that brought us up to about one million Thogs fightings 'ah."

"What about the Thogeens?" John asked. "You just left them?"

"Wes 'ah shall returns 'ah," Maurice shrugged. "But whats 'ah happened to Victor 'ah? Ise 'ah thought he went with yous 'ah."

John and Paul looked at each other sadly.

"He was killed," Paul said. "He was killed by the Kraskull."

Maurice's ears dropped.

"You are the only one left we know," Lino said, "so don't die out here."

"Ise 'ah promise Ise 'ah won't," Maurice pledged.

"So one million Thogs," John grinned. "Zach doesn't stand a chance now."

They all nodded.

"I am regretfully sorry, Maurice, but we must go," John said, standing. "I am glad you are still alive. You know what to do with the psychics, but protect them especially. Good luck, my friend."

Maurice shook his hand.

"We still have a good six days to go," Joan said. "Let's get going."

They ran up to Dreaded Musty and John leapt upon her.

A loud cracking noise shook the earth. It could be heard from every direction. Dread filled their minds for no apparent reason.

"Where is that coming from?" Paul asked, rocking back and forth, trying to keep his balance. But they all knew what it was. In their heart, they knew they were too late. Zach was using the orb.

16.) The Orb's Destruction

"What do we do?" Joan asked, terrified.

"I don't know," John yelled. "None of us are safe. He will kill one group of magical beings. Who will it be first?"

"Forget it!" Lino yelled, filled with adrenaline. "We need to get there now before he destroys the whole earth!"

John urged Musty on the shaking ground. She obviously felt something also, for she sprinted faster than she had ever before.

"Faster!" He said as the shaking picked up. From the distance, a large cloud of black dust was spewing towards them, just as it had done when the Phoenix had risen.

"Oh great Phoenix," John said to his sword, "protect us."

Joan clenched hard to John as the wall of dust came closer. John knew he had little chance of survival this time; Zach was keen to kill the magicians first. Yet something told him that he hadn't targeted the magicians…

Then it hit him. Not magicians, but …

With horror, he turned his horse around.

"This is not happening again," John shouted. He urged his horse the other way, but the wall of dust was going too fast.

"JOAN!" John yelled, suddenly turning his body around and clutching his arms around her.

The wall of black dust overtook them, knocking John off his horse. Everyone else was tossed to the ground as well. The dust cloud didn't stop. It kept trampling over them until it had enough. The air thinned a bit as they saw the cloud of black dust make their way beyond them.

Paul got to his feet. He walked over and saw everyone else on the ground.

"Are you ok?" he first asked Lino.

"Yeah, I think," Lino said, pushing himself up.

"I am fine too," John responded and Musty leapt to her feet again.

Everyone then turned to Joan on the ground. John walked to her and rolled her over on her back.

She was dead.

"No …" John said breathing fast, "No … not again …"

Everyone else walked over to him.

"NO!" John yelled, standing up. "You will pay, Zach. You will pay, you do not deserve life! YOU-WILL-FEEL-MY-WRATH!"

Everyone stepped back. John started to laugh. It was a low-pitched laugh that frightened them.

"John," Paul said quickly, "don't morph again, please!"

John turned around and laughed again.

"I don't need to," John said. A flash of red appeared in his eye. "Sorry, guys, but this is something that I will handle by myself!"

He picked up Joan's body, poured all his magic into his hand. He had never transported before, but he knew he had to try now. He didn't care what happened.

"I will get my vengeance this time!" John yelled and then disappeared. They heard the last words to escape his mouth, "YOU WILL NOT ESCAPE ME!"

They stared in awe.

"My God," Lino panted. "What are we going to do now?"

But it had just occurred to Paul what Jerry's prophecy meant.

"Do you remember what John said about Jerry's prophecy?" Paul said. "About that he would return on the eighth day of the orb's destruction?"

"Yes," Lino responded.

"We had all thought that meant we would win by destroying the orb," Paul said, "but it could mean on the eighth day after the orb *destroys*."

Lino's eyes widened.

"You mean that we might not be able to destroy the orb?" Lino panted.

"Improbably," Paul gasped. "The prophecy doesn't guarantee anything. We must help John in the best way possible. We must hurry to Phoenix."

John's power had a limit, even with all his magic. He transferred himself near the borderline to the U.S. There were guards a little northward that stopped any immigrants from coming over. John carried Joan's body to the gate, sword in hand.

"Excuse me, sir," one guard said as he approached, "do you have your passport?"

John dropped Joan at their feet. He raised his sword.

"I don't think so," the guard said, raising a pistol and aiming at John's chest. "Drop that sword now."

John grimaced at him. He lowered his sword.

"Magicians are immune to bullets," John laughed. He threw out his hand and sent a shot of magic at the guard. The guard went flying through the air and over the gate. Another couple of guards ran up and shot their guns at him. Involuntarily, a magical barrier came around John and the bullets dissolved at impact. The guards lowered their weapons in horror. John raised his sword and in two swipes disarmed the men and killed them.

"Must have forgotten the passport," John said to the corpses. He picked up Joan and walked over the border into Arizona.

*   *

*

"Mr. President," a secretary said, 3,000 miles away, "we have a massacre of people in four different areas including Washington and Philadelphia. The source of destruction is coming from a large tower in Phoenix."

"What kind of massacre?" the president asked.

"We don't know," the secretary responded. "All we know is that some sort of wave of black radiation came from Phoenix and one out of every 300,000 dropped dead."

"Any nuclear reactivity? We are at war with North Korea, you know," the president replied, "they could have nuked us."

"From Phoenix?" the secretary responded. "But that's just the beginning. A large mass of an army was caught on satellite coming from the south right towards Arizona."

The president pounded on his desk.

"I knew it!" the president yelled. "Mexico is aiding North Korea! They must have held their troops there. This might turn out to be World War Three! How many do you think the satellite picked up?"

The secretary took out his handkerchief and whipped his head of sweat.

"Well?" the president said, rising.

"Mr. President," the secretary said. "Come see for yourself. We have the pictures on a monitor right outside the room."

They both left the room and the president reached the monitor at the secretary's desk. Around the desk were some military officials. They all saluted him.

"Where are they?" the president asked. One official pointed to the screen on the atlas. There was huge black mass of something coming right to the U.S. "My God, how many are there? Perhaps hundreds of thousands!"

"Sir, 10 million soldiers wouldn't appear on the map," one official said. "At least, not like that."

"Did we get a count?" the president asked.

"An estimate that would be darn close to the real number," the secretary responded.

There was a pause.

"So?" the president asked.

The secretary whipped his head again.

"Mr. President," the secretary answered in a whisper, "I know this is hard to fathom, but the evidence is indisputable—"

"How ... many ... are ... there?" the President asked slowly and firmly.

"They are projecting ... five billion troops."

There was absolute silence.

"Five—" the president sputtered, "but that's not possible. That would mean every person in the world except for those in China and America was fighting there!"

"Sir," the official said. "Mr. President, those aren't people."

He clicked a few buttons on the monitor and the satellite zoomed in to about four meters away.

"What the hell are those things?!" the president gasped.

"We don't know," the secretary shook his head.

An official from the back moved forward and looked at the video of armies marching towards the U.S. He then looked at the President.

"Mr. President," he said, "I know what they are. They are ogres."

There was a new, quieter silence.

"Og-ogres?" the president sputtered. "General Johnson, this isn't a fairy tale. This-"

"Mr. President, look," Johnson interrupted, motioning to the screen. "Does that look anything that isn't in a fairy tale? Ogres exist, sir. I know they do."

"How?" the secretary asked him.

"I am a magician," Johnson responded. "All magicians were asked to fight a war some thousands of miles away and I refused. They were trying to stop these ogres but it looks like they failed. Mr. President, believe me. If you believe what you're seeing, believe me."

Johnson lifted his hand and a pen at the corner of the desk lifted and came to his hand. They were all shocked.

"The massacre was to stop all resistance to this attack. Now this army is coming to aid this weapon that is held in Phoenix. Mr. President, our armies cannot stop this attack. By the time we fire every nuclear weapon we posses, we would be firing onto American land. Mr. President, this army comes for one thing: the leader hopes to take over the world. If you are to act, Mr. President, you must do it fast."

The screen became fuzzy suddenly. The monitor went blank. Then it changed completely and showed a man in a cloak with red eyes. He stood in front of a large army.

"Mr. President," the man on the screen said. "I am so glad that you finally saw what is coming to you. I hope you don't mind me using the weapon on your soil and destroying Americans by friendly fire. I assure you, we mean no American any harm."

"My foot," Johnson yelled at him. "Then what is the army for?!"

"For your protection," Zach said. "Armies are coming to the United U.S. and I plan to stop them. Don't mind me, I'll do my duty to protect your country."

"Enough of these lies!" the President said. "I got a good look at your army and they have only one thing in mind: invasion. You get your army out of America or we will fight back."

Zach's false grin faded.

"Mr. President," Zach said. "If you deny my army access to this country, you are an enemy and I will destroy every American I see. This weapon that is in my control can do that for me."

Zach raised an orb in his hand.

"This is it, Mr. President," Zach said. "It's your choice. Will you allow my army into your country?"

The president looked at his officials who were all afraid. The president took a single breath, looked at Johnson, and then turned back to the screen.

"If your army comes within 80 kilometers of the U.S.," the president said, "we will unload ever nuclear weapon, missile, and bomb we have onto your army. Then we'll pull our troops to Phoenix and destroy you."

Zach smiled again.

"Very bold," Zach said, "But very foolish. Mr. President, my army is to approach the 80-kilometer mark in about 10 minutes. And now the Americans are an enemy to The Martinet. In only 13 hours, the power of the orb will be rejuvenated and I will destroy all Americans with a simple term."

The screen went black again. The officials all looked up to the president with absolute horror on their faces.

"What are we to do, Johnson?" the president asked. "You are the only one who would know of this 'orb's power'. What shall we do?"

"The orb," Johnson replied, "must be the weapon that destroyed my wife, a mage. In 13 hours, the orb will regain its power and will be able to do another attack, this time directed to Americans, magic or non-magic."

The president nodded.

"There's no other choice then," the president said. "General Smith, order those in North Dakota to deploy everything we got. General Barth, scramble every Marine, Air Force, and Navy pilot we have to those coordinates and bomb them into obliteration. General Richards, contact the governors, and have them order every police officer and National Guardsman we have toward that state. I will issue an Executive Order to mobilize an emergency draft of men and women over the age of 15. Any below that age limit that are willing to join, let them. Impress the Amish and others if necessary. Also, have the children below the age of fifteen go into cellars with provided food and water. Pull all troops out of Korea. We have 13 hours. Get it done now."

All the officials left except for Johnson and his secretary.

"Mr. President," Johnson called as the president turned to leave. "You aren't about to try and stop and army of five billion with only a couple hundred million, right?"

"What other choice do we have, Johnson?" the president asked.

"There are other countries out there, you know," Johnson said. "We could give them the pictures we have of the ogres and they could draft as well."

"For one thing," the president said, "we have too many differences for them to believe us. For another thing, by the time we *could* convince them, it would be far too late and the army would be on top of us. I am, however, about to notify our allies, France, Germany, Japan, Britain, Spain and some other small nations to see if they can send troops over here as soon as possible. Also, I was planning to get Mexico and Canada to take up arms with us."

He turned to leave.

"Mr. President?" Johnson asked. "There is something that magicians are forced not to tell. It's the place that they originated from."

The president turned to him.

"It's a continent called Locombony. It has high technology that can cover itself from satellites. It … it has been at war with Australia, who hasn't let on to its existence. If we could get Locombony to fight, we might win."

The president turned to him.

"Even if we can get this unknown country to fight with us," the president said, "that man will turn its orb on them if he hasn't already. As it is, I am putting millions at risk. It is a lost cause, but it's righteous to fight back. It's impossible to win, but we must fight. We will show these zombies that we will not go out without a defending ourselves."

"May God help us all," the Secretary added.

17.) The Earth's Response

John started to run as fast as he could. His anger had
dissipated, but it had evolved into a new resolved. He still
forced himself on just to kill Zach, to stop the killing and end the
terror. He would transport as often as he could, but it typically
took up all his magic. He would then have to submit to running
a few miles before he would have the magical strength to
transport himself again. By this pace, he would reach Phoenix in
a couple of hours.

Paul had gotten on Dreaded Musty who wanted to ride to
Phoenix with everything she had. She knew her master needed
her. And within Lino's tired and exhausted body was his
resilient heart. This powerful organ shot energy through Lino's
muscles. Lino became enflamed with the passion of protecting
his friend.

With adrenaline, scientists (Zyno studied this at one time)
concluded that, with it, people could perform superhuman
actions. A mixture of adrenaline and magic, Paul, Dreaded
Musty, and Paul were well beyond their capabilities. Dreaded
Musty and Lino sprinted with their whole body towards the
Mexican border.

"Great news, Mr. President," General Smith came in one
hour after their meeting. "The bombs are ready to be fired
whenever you give the command."

"Thrilling," the president spat in discomfort. "Better news
is that, for some reason, there was a massive gathering
happening in Ireland not too long ago. France, Britain, and
Germany had *I-35* jets on standby. Something happened and the
'gatherings' disappeared, but the country's troops were still at
the airports, preparing to launch. They'll send over their troops
in less than five hours."

I-35 was the fastest type of plane in the world. It was a
carrier jet for troops in an emergency. It traveled five times the
speed of sound.

"Just like that? Sending troops?" Smith asked.

"I forwarded the photos we captured, plus the transcript of the message of this 'Zach' character, and needless to say, they acted quickly."

"That's still a rarity," Smith sighed. "To see countries moving that fast."

"Maybe this was a wakeup call," the president shrugged.

"So they are sending troops?" The general asked.

"Those three are sending practically all of their armed soldiers, with Japan and Iraq to back us up in a couple days," the president announced. "How's the militia coming in Arizona?"

"We have 3,000 ready near Phoenix," General Smith replied.

"Does that include some S.W.A.T units?" the president asked. "I want practically every armed local cop, state trooper, and veteran out there."

"I will take care of that," the general said, beckoning over his secretary. He related the message to the secretary.

"That should hold them until the Allies come," the president nodded, "And they shall hold until the Japanese and Iraqis arrive. Then we'll have our military and militia arrive to force back those demons. Finally, we'll have Mexico, Canada and all the rest of the armies in the world come to drive them back to the sea."

The general didn't say anything for a second.

"You are joking, right Mr. President?" he asked. "'Drive them back to the sea'? Mr. President, they will outnumber us by a horrible amount. We *could* hit them with our prepared nukes. All we need is your permission to fire."

"We don't know what these ogres are capable of doing," the president replied. "No, nuking them over Mexico would not send a good message to them. We nuke as a last resort. Besides, we've only used them twice in warfare and then we were desperate. I would like to keep it that way. We have a good chance at this. We acted quickly and we are doing great. I am trying to work out things between Russia and China to see if they could aid us. Let's see what our pilots and army can do against these things first. Then I'll plan what to do next."

"General!" barked a voice over the general's phone. "This is commander Lerkins, leader of the Arizona militia. We are right outside Phoenix with 3,000 armed men. There are ogres patrolling the streets, killing civilians at random. Estimations are about 1,000 ogres total. Can we have your permission to attack?"

General Smith looked at the president who nodded.

"That's what I hired you for," General Smith barked back. "And good luck with these demons. Blast those things back to their maker."

"Yes, sir!" the commander said and turned off his communication device. "Men, permission to move in has been acquired. Let's go!"

The militia nodded and started to move into the city quietly. Most of the army was just stopped on the road and given a machine gun, pistol and ammunition. Some were still in their suits, some were teenagers, some were women, and a few were officers of the law. Barely any used a gun before.

"Quiet when moving, unload bullets when those ogres are spotted," the commander cautioned. "And don't underestimate them. We don't know what they can do."

He stopped them and commanded they hide under something for cover.

"Get your bayonets on," the commander whispered as 60 ogres came marching around down the street. "FIRE!"

The militia stood up and fired.

The commander didn't know it, but there was someone mixed into the crowd who was filming a live feed to the White House. It was the first time anyone had fired a gun at an ogre.

They caught most by surprise, but 20 had enough time to raise shields. The bullets hit the shields and magical barriers came in front of the shields. The ogres pulled back behind a corner. The commander reached for his communication device again.

"General, the ogres have shields protecting them from bullet fire. Should we proceed?"

"Follow and destroy all enemies until you reach the given coordinates," was the answer. "Then blow up the tower."

"Yes, sir!" the commander said. "Follow their path!"

He led the army down the road and turned right. Hundreds of arrows shot right at him. About 20 hit him in the chest and he keeled over, dead. The militia looked in horror as the thousand ogres came running at them, shields raised. The second in command stepped up and fired his pistol. The bullet flew off the shield of an ogre.

"Hold fire!" he yelled, "Prepare to bayonet them!"

The militia moved closer to one another, having a horrible fear in their eyes. Nevertheless, they pointed their bayonets forward.

"Charge!" the commander yelled. They charged forward at them. The ogres shot more arrows at them killing many. The militia got within 10 feet of the ogres.

Suddenly, the ogres brought their swords up to their chests. They charged back. The militia stabbed the first line of ogres, but the second fought them back.

"Fire!" the commander ordered. The men fired their ammunition at the ogres who had lowered their shields to attack. The bullets killed ogres, but shields were raised in response. More bullets were deflected. The commander ordered his men into a retreat. They had killed a decent number, but most of the heavy losses fell on the militia's side. The commander took out the communication device.

"Not good, sir," the commander said, "Lerkins fell, the ogres broke through, these men are frightened and I don't know what to do."

There was static.

"We saw that the bullets aren't working," the general responded. "Bayonet them. Back up should be coming soon."

"Nice try ... sir," the commander said, "that's an old tactic. There's no back up coming, is there?"

There was no answer.

"Oh, well," the commander sighed, "I guess we can take them out. But I don't know where the bombs are so I can't blow up the tower. I'll let you do that, I can check for shields of any sort around the tower."

"Affirmative," the general said, "that is your number one priority."

"Yes, sir," the commander said. He knew what he had to do. He turned to his men. "Alright, prepare weapons and follow me. We'll go around the corner and unload every bullet we have, except one round. Then we bayonet and, when close enough, fire bullets beyond their shield. Understand?"

He didn't understand himself. But his army nodded and they moved around the corner. The ogres we ready. The ogres charge at them.

The militia let their weapons loose, blasting every direction with their automatic weapons. The bullets flew off the ogres' shields, but there was mass confusion and horrible disfiguration for the ogres. This was what the commander was hoping for. His men ran at the enemy and bayoneted the ones that had fallen onto the ground. The commander's plan was working. They drove the ogres back and the commander looked at the coordinate plane on his belt. They were about a quarter of a mile away, straight forward.

"Full power ahead!" the commander said. "The tower is coming up. All you have to do is to protect me from attacks and then we're out of here. You all did great today, soldiers!"

They moved ahead, his militia circled around him. They came within seeing distance of the coordinates when they were heavily ambushed from all around. The commander couldn't see the tower, even though he was near the exact coordinates.

"Hold out, men!" the commander yelled. "Push forward! I need to see the tower!"

The army ran with the commander, bayoneting stray ogres that came out at them. They formed a human shield around the commander, almost as if he were a king.

Just then, the ogres launched a horrendous attack on the north side. It looked like nearly 2,000 ogres, twice the amount of militiamen, had formed up. There was, somehow, a miscalculation in the number of ogre soldiers.

Honorably, the militia charged ahead. The first line of men fell, but the commander squeezed through the gaps of the battle, still guarded by a few well-trained members of the law.

He *needed* to get to the coordinates. The world depended on it. More ogres came charging at them.

The commander stopped. He stood right in front of the coordinates. He looked up to see …

He reached into his pocket and grabbed his communication device as ogres came running at them with no mercy.

"General?" the commander stuttered. "For that … Mr. President? I am … at the coordinates."

"And?!" the president's voice yelled back, "what does the tower look like?!"

"Sir," the commander's last words were before he was struck dead by the overwhelming ogre army, "there is no tower … no building. Just a blank patch of … emptiness … except for … six men … with black hoods … and glowing white eyes …"

And he and the rest of the militia were killed.

18.) The Countries' Victory

The president sent the images of the battle to different countries worldwide. The world responded quickly. North Korea made an emergency treaty with the U.S. to end the conflict that they were in at the moment. Russia promised to move full armies by six o'clock that night. China sent over their best pilots armed with fully armed explosives. Everything was working exactly to the president's plan. Except …

"Did we get anymore information on the tower?" the president said.

"No, sir, we weren't able to do anything with the evidence provided. We know that there is a tower there, sir, and we gave both commanders the right coordinates," General Barth responded. "We are sending pilots over immediately to confirm the existence of the tower. We have set up a rough base of operations near the Arizona-Mexico border."

"That is good," the president said, "but this tower is worrying me. It is not visible to any of us. It is too strange."

General Johnson walked into the room, "Mr. President, how are we doing on hours until the orb is unleashed?"

The president looked at a clock on his desk.

"Six hours left," the president said. "The countries will be here soon. I am just worried that these ogres might have something up their sleeve …"

General Barth chuckled slightly, "You underestimate my fleet. Every aircraft in the world, combined with the best pilots, are heading to the army now. They will arrive to bomb in less than an hour."

"Nevertheless, I want the nukes to be a push of a button away so that we have some back up. Something tells me that the ogres will resist this attack," the president responded.

"You are still shaken from the militia's failure," General Barth replied. "Let me reassure you that the planes we own are not piloted by militia, but well-trained men."

"I still am worried about what could happen," the president said.

"Don't, sir," Johnson said, reassuringly, "let us just see what pilots can do."

A man ran into the president's room.

"General, the aircrafts are reaching the main army," he said to Barth.

"What about the tower?" the president interrupted.

"Confirmation on that as well," the man nodded, "that is a negative on any tower ever existing there."

The president swore.

"I still want photos of the area around there!" the president called.

"Forget it for now, Mr. President," General Johnson said. "Let's have a look at the camera."

The general asked that a camera fly in one of the planes and record the fight scenes.

They left the room. General Barth reached the phone first.

"Lieutenant," he said, "what are your positions?"

There was a lot of static.

"30 Eagles … left wing … 40 Angels right wing … 20 Falcons above … 45 … below …"

"There you have it," General Barth said smiling, "135 pilots flying with full weaponry at them with reinforcements on the right side and left. Plus, we reserved some pilots in case of an emergency."

The president said nothing.

"Objects … in … permission to … fire?"

They looked at the screen and saw ogres everywhere, as far as the eye could see.

"Its worse when it's closer," the general muttered, and then replied, "permission granted. Fire at will."

The pilots recognized their permission by dropping many bombs on the massive army. Then, as the president expected, the ogres pulled off an evasive maneuver – lifting many poles and setting off a button, a large, magical barrier came over the targeted ogres. The bombs hit the shield but had no affect except dissolving into the shield.

The president slammed his fist on the desk and swore.

"I knew they'd have something like this," he yelled. "Those ogres have come so prepared and we were caught unready."

"What should we do?" General Barth said, almost somberly, "the pilots can't do anything, but the ogres aren't advanced enough to destroy our ships. This could be a distraction. I mean, the ogres can't reach them in the air."

General Johnson took a deep breath and pointed on the screen.

"Guess again," he said sweating.

There, in the air in a fierce formation of horrible red and black scales, were dragons.

"My God ..."

"BLOW THOSE THINGS OUT OF THE SKY!" General Barth screamed, "USE AIR-TO-AIR MISSILES! USE MACHINE GUNS! USE ANYTHING, JUST KNOCK THEM OUT OF THE SKY!"

"There are so many," the president said doubtfully.

"I don't care!" Barth snarled. "Let's show these devils that American pilots aren't going to be frightened of these nightmares!"

"... Roger that ..." a voice came from the speakerphone.

Air missiles shot from the planes from all around. They hit the dragon's heads and some of the dragons fell on top of the ogres. But the scales were too tough to be penetrated by mere missiles.

"Fire again!" General Barth said, but there was already a roar of "Fox Two" and more missiles shot at the dragons. "Don't let them approach you!"

Before the missiles hit, the pilots shot another missile, just in case. The first round of missiles weren't locked on because they were only metal-seeking missiles. Most of the dragons were able to avoid the missile shots, but some hit them straight on. The ones that were hit in the face were killed immediately. The ones hit in the stomach fell, but didn't die.

There were still a lot of dragons left. But now, the dragons were very close to attack with their hands.

"Save the last missile for an emergency!" General Barth said. "Use closer missiles! Use the machine guns!"

He looked at Johnson.

"Now they will test their flying skills," he said. They all turned to the screen again.

The pilots shot their short-range missiles and machine guns at the dragons. The dragons responded by forming in a "V" shape and took in a deep breath.

Barth didn't need Johnson to tell him what these "fairy tales" could do next.

"Move out of the way!" he yelled into the phone. The pilots broke formation and went to a separate dragon. The dragons blew out huge fireballs at the pilots, who expertly tried to avoid them. Most were able to, but direct shots burned the wings and sent them crashing at the ground.

The generals looked sadly as slowly, one-by-one, the dragons destroyed the planes. By slashing, blowing fire or smashing them with their tails, the dragons threw the situation out of hand.

The president swallowed.

"Fire everything you got now!" both generals snarled. "Don't leave until those things lie dead on top of the army."

The president turned and wiped a tear away from his eyes.

"There are only a few pilots left," the secretary said.

"Form up," Barth ordered.

The pilots on screen turned and flew into a "V" formation to meet the last of the dragons.

"Aim for the eyes," Johnson said, "Trust me."

General Barth repeated the orders.

"Roger ... that," a pilot said.

The pilots shot their ammunition at the dragons' eyes. The dragons fell by the dozens in agony. The pilots kept at it.

"It's working, Mr. President!" the secretary almost cheered. "We're winning!"

The pilots blasted the rest out of the sky. The generals and the secretary applauded.

"It's not over yet," the president said angrily. "We need to take out those towers. Order the drop of air-to-ground missiles ON the towers producing the shields. Let see what we can do here."

Barth wiped away a tear of joy as he fulfilled the order. He then turned to the president.

"We don't have many air-to-ground missiles left on those planes. Once we destroy the towers, then what?"

"We bring in those reinforcements you were talking about," the president said. "Now move!"

The pilots dropped their bombs on the towers, but all of them hit the shields and had no affect.

"The towers are less than a meter thick," Johnson observed. "It would be nearly impossible to take them down. How many bombs do they have left?"

"We … out … bombs, sir …" came the voice from the speaker.

"Then pull back to the nearest Air Force or Navy airport and reload," the president said. "The reinforcements should attack now."

The generals looked at each other.

"Mr. President," General Barth said slowly, "we sent them in an all-out attack. Our reserve pilots were in the air, preparing to go after our first wave. I figured that the bombs from the frontal assault would penetrate their shields. Then the attack coming from the right would come to take out their middle."

"With the broken formations caused by the dragons," Johnson reasoned, "the plans became a bit skewed."

"Do we have any more pilots?" the president asked.

"Yes," General Barth answered, "but listen—this battle was over quicker than we had imagined. The next wave can't attack for another couple of hours at least."

The president took an impatient breath.

"You mean we have to wait this out?" he snarled.

"Sir!" a messenger said. "They have now passed over the border line. The ogres are now in America."

The president shuttered.

"For once in my life … probably in all of history of presidents, as well," the president muttered. "We have been invaded by an unknown force with no solution to the attack. I do not know what to do or say."

Everyone else was silent as well.

"One last thing, Mr. President," the messenger said, "we have photos in from the coordinates. There is nothing there, but we fulfilled your wishes."

He handed the president about ten photos from an aerial view of the coordinates. He looked through the photos by himself. Then he scowled.

"Nothing but a blank alleyway," he said, tossing them on the desk. General Johnson looked curiously at the photos. He looked at each one and then looked up at the president with a surprise on his face.

"Mr. President?" he said, "You don't see it?"

The president turned.

"Look here," the general pointed to somewhere on the picture, "what do you see?"

"A blank alleyway," the president repeated.

"You don't see the black tower?"

They all turned to him.

"Do you see something we don't?" General Barth asked.

Johnson swallowed and smiled.

"Of course," he said, "It is the tower that is hidden from normal human eyes. I, a magician, can see it. You can not."

They all looked hopefully at him.

"So what does this mean?" the president said.

"It means," Johnson said grinning, "that we may still have a chance in this fight ..."

John finally reached Phoenix. It was very hot, but for some reason, it was storming rain. After traveling miles and miles through dry desert, this was a small consolation to John.

He heard nothing. He figured such a big city would be very loud like the ones back at Locombony. But here, there was silence. Occasionally, he saw a person run from building to building as if he or she was afraid of being seen.

"Something's not right here," He said. John looked around to see if he could see a large tower or building, but he didn't have to look far: The tallest building of all was a large, black tower in the middle of all the tall towers in the city. John turned and headed that way.

He turned a block and stopped abruptly. He saw a large mass of ogres surrounding the tower. There was only a few hundred, but in a packed area of buildings and towers, it seemed to be a lot more.

John quickly stepped backwards behind a building. By doing so, he had run into somebody. He quickly turned around and saw a man crying and his hand halfway towards the door to the building. He looked at John with complete despair.

"They got a friend of yours, too, huh?" the man said, eyeing Joan's corpse. John didn't know why he had carried her so far; did he hope that she might wake up on the way?

John saw the man give him a look of support. "They killed my wife and children as well. I was going to get a drink at the only thing open besides church – the bar. Do you want to join me? I mean, laws aren't important anymore."

John was about to refuse when he saw, behind the glass of the building, other men sipping drinks.

"Only for a little bit," he said. "I need to end this horrible experience."

The man nodded and entered the bar with John. John set Joan's body at the foot of the bar. They walked to the counter where the bartender saw them both full of tears and brought them both a drink.

"Thanks for coming with me," the man said. "Everyone I know, my family, my friends, even some people I disliked … they were all killed. It seems like everything I worked for during my life was destroyed today."

Others looked at them and nodded silently. The song playing in the background, John had never heard, but noticed it was quite patriotic. The man nodded at the song.

"The only thing I have now is my country. My home was destroyed. I fought in the militia, but escaped before I died. I have nothing."

John nodded.

"I felt that way at one time," John said. "My brothers left me, my parents were dead, and my friends have died. Then, the only thing I could fight for was so the earth could survive. Then I met my friend and I fought for her. But now she's dead, and I am alone."

The man next to the one he was talking to started to sing lightly:

The road beyond lies high,
The amount around is nigh,
The ones who loved are gone,
The ones who hate live on,
We have nothing left here,
We are alone in the world,
The last lies on us,
Defend others lies, we must.

John and the man looked at him with sorrow. John felt himself crying. It was as if Joan died all over again. He felt himself fill with despair instead of hatred. He didn't know if that was good or bad.

"Did you love her?" the man asked John. John stared at the bubbles in his mug.

"I barely even knew her," John sniffed. "I've only known her for a few weeks."

There was a pause.

"Yes … " John brushed his eyes. "I think I did love her."

"You see what has happened?" the man called to no one in particular. "We are alone now. It's only us left here. There are the prayers at the churches, but we are here at the bar crying. We are desperate. It is as if we're looking for a solution."

John breathed again. He then stood.

"Sir," he said to the man. "I…"

He didn't know how to close his goodbye.

"Thank you," The man said, "You're brief visit has helped us all."

John wished he was able to say something. He then noticed a gun strapped to his back.

"You say that you fought in the militia?" John said curiously.

"We all did," said the man sitting next to him and everyone nodded.

"Can you help me then?" John said. "I need a distraction as I go into the tower."

"We'll help with anything," the man shrugged, "everything we have is lost."

"Listen," John said, "I will attack the ogres myself and after they lower their shields, you shoot at them."

The men looked at him in surprise.

"You are going to fight them?" One asked.

"They killed my friend, I need to end this," John answered. "Please, I beg you, can you help?"

Everyone stood and pulled their machine guns to their chests in a salute. Even the bartender pulled out a shotgun to fight.

"Thank you," John said, exasperated. "You will get your vengeance. Thank you all."

"We don't need vengeance," the bartender said, speaking for the first time. "Merely hope."

They nodded, now pumped for battle. They slowly exited the bar together, loading their weapons with what meager ammunition they had. John stopped them at the corner.

"I'll run at them first and strike them," John announced fiercely. "I'll yell for you to come and back me up."

John ran around the corner and took a swipe at the first ogre in sight. He avoided an arrow shot at him by somersaulting and taking another swipe at another ogre. The ogres responded quickly, surrounding him.

"NOW!" John yelled. The 20 or so men came charging around the corner. The ogres, thinking a large force was attacking them, formed into a line behind John. John saw the black tower in front of him. At a distance, it didn't seem so frightening. But here, it was the scariest building John had ever seen. It didn't help that there was pouring rain hitting his skin and lightning above him. He took a step towards the building, but remembered the army behind him. He couldn't decide what to do – run into the tower or help the men battling.

John knew he had to help. He turned and, with his Phoenix sword flashing, slashed ogre-by-ogre. The men's bullets hit the ogres' shields and not having any effect. The ogres then charged the men with spears pointing right at them. John leapt over the charging ogres and landed between the ogres and the men. He took swipe after swipe until the ogres realized that the sword couldn't be stopped. The ogres squealed like little pigs and started to run away from John.

"Don't let them escape!" he yelled. The men sprinted after the ogres, shooting them with the rest of their bullets and stabbing them with their bayonets. The five ogres that survived were able to run off. John looked at the men.

"Thank you all again," John said smiling.

"First off," his friend said, "thank you for stopping the ogres from charging and over running us. And second, you could have taken out those ogres by yourself."

"Who are you anyway?" John asked.

"I am James Lerkins II," John's friend said. "Third in command to the militia. Who are you?"

"John Quaill II," John said. "Third in command to the Locombony's Magician Rebellion battalion."

John made up this title, to support his modesty of being a good warrior.

"Tell your leader or president or whatever," John commanded, "that bullets will barely work on these opponents. You need to train with more spears, swords, and medieval weapons to beat these guys."

"Will do," Lerkins Junior said, "and thank you for giving us hope."

"We will win," John said. "I promise you that."

John walked up to the tower's doors. John grabbed the rusty handle and took a deep breath. He threw them open and entered.

He was welcomed by a large growl. In front of him was a large creature (about seven feet) that held a large sword. It was bent over, having a hunched back. The creature had orange skin with red splotches on it and teeth as sharp as a sword. John recognized it immediately.

"The first Thogeen," John challenged. "The Evil that can't be killed."

19.) Inside the Tower

John held his Phoenix sword in front of him, preparing for any daring attack. The creature grinned in a malicious way and removed from a sheath on his back another large sword. It now wielded two enormous swords.

The Thogeen lunged at John. John stepped away from the spot and swung low, near its legs. The creature, instead of trying to parry it with its weapon, leapt over it and, using the momentum, sliced high through the air. John ducted and pulled back.

John realized the creature had been informed that the Phoenix sword couldn't be parried. This would mean the only way to avoid John's attacks were to step away from them.

John lunged forward and the Thogeen leapt over him and swiveled to strike John's lower back. With magical instincts, John flipped backwards and landed facing the creature, sword flaring. John swept back and the Thogeen slowly pursued.

"You are quite the opponent," John breathed. The Thogeen only snarled in reply. "I can see why Jerry had trouble fighting you way back then."

John slid to the left with the Thogeen copying his movement. John waited for it to attack first, because if he did, John figured it would remain in a stalemate.

"So, rumor has it that you were the previous owner of the orb," John questioned. "What made you work for Zach?"

The Thogeen didn't reply. John had never heard a Thogeen speak, and he wasn't expecting an answer this time, either.

After a moment, when the Thogeen didn't attack, John saw no other alternative. He leapt high in the air, bringing the sword close to the monster's head. The creature rolled to the right and John went flying to the ground. John somersaulted quickly and bounced to his feet in time to see the Thogeen strike with one sword high and the other low. John hopped up and led his sword into the Thogeen's. The Thogeen's sword was cut in half from John's sword. However, a second later, the Thogeen pulled from its sheath another sword. John held his sword low, inviting the Thogeen to attack. The Thogeen took his message and lunged in high. John did a back flip and bounced off the wall with his legs over the creature and swung at it waist-high.

John even surprised himself at this move, but the creature reacted quickly, ducking to the floor. It turned and approached John who started to retreat. John stopped suddenly and then spun fast, sword in front of him. The creature was too slow and it resulted in another useless sword. The Thogeen took a swipe at John's leg, which John easily parried, cutting the sword.

It looked for a second that John had won, but the creature, yet again, yanked out two more swords.

"Obviously you came prepared," John nodded, breathing hard.

John leapt forward and swung high at the creature's neck. Instead of trying to back away or even block the attack, the creature slashed John's leg instead. John fell in pain and rolled to his left, hitting a spiral staircase. He climbed up a few steps and saw the Thogeen coming towards him slowly. John let it come close as if giving up. The creature snarled triumphantly and raised his swords above his head.

Immediately, John stabbed him right in the chest. The creature howled in agony. It fell to the ground dead. John breathed a sigh of relief and sheathed his sword.

"I lost that one," John said, holding his leg. The Thogeen had pierced his leg about half way from cutting it completely off. John rummaged through his pockets to see if he had but one healing pill. He had none. John wasn't as good of a healer as his uncle, but he tried with all his might to heal the wound. The flesh started to come back in place and the skin came together again. John stopped exhausted. "I can't do this. I am not trained that way. I am trained only in fighting and apparitions."

John slowly got to his feet. He could barely walk on it, let alone fight.

"Let's hope there are no more enemies here," John grimaced. He hobbled up the flight of stairs and looked at the second story. He did a double take.

"Finally," his opponent said, standing, "we have met again, Quaill."

William snapped his fingers and a trapdoor slid from behind John to have him avoid any escape.

"How'd you get here before me?!" John nearly shouted.

"Simple," William replied, "Zach."

John clenched his fists.

"First the Thogeen and now you," John snarled.

"Yes," William said, removing his sword. "You see, Zach wanted to delay you in every way possible to the last second. So he placed the only creatures that you could lose to on each flight. You had help to defeat the Thogeen and me. But now, you're alone."

John jerked his sword from its scabbard.

"I don't need help to kill you," John responded, waving his sword. "En gard, William!"

William approached him sword twirling. John spun his sword on his palm, awaiting his attack. William roared and swung his sword at John's left. John lightly moved his sword and split William's sword in two. With another wave of his sword, John cut off William's hand holding his sword. William fell to his knees.

"Sorry, Billy," John sneered. "But with the Phoenix sword, you can't beat me. I'll make sure you'll never sword fight again."

John raised his sword and cut off both of William's arms. He wailed in agony.

"Never try to stop a Quaill again," John nodded.

Choosing not to kill his bleeding opponent, he started to hobble the stairs again.

"Believe it … or … not … QUAILL!" William called. "We … will … meet again!"

John slowly walked the stairs, supporting his leg. He started to lengthily move upward.

Finally, he reached the third story. He looked up and saw his opponent. He gasped. It was a Kraskull.

Or was it? No, John realized, a Kraskull's eyes glow through the hood of its cloak. This was just a darkly robed person. Looking closer, John also saw that it was a hologram. He approached it.

"That's right, Quaill," it said. "Take me on alone. You can't beat me."

The words rang through John's mind. They were familiar …

The hologram removed behind his cloak two swords identical to John's Phoenix sword.

"It's a hologram of Uncle Dan!" John said, removing his sword carefully. "But how do I destroy a hologram?"

Then he remembered how easily Flaminetore fell to the Kraskull's evil swords. John stepped forward to engage the attack. The hologram charged at John and, in large sweeps of its swords, had John on the ground. John was barely able to deflect the attacks from the Phoenix swords. John slowly drove the hologram off of him and he stood up again.

"You are a good opponent," John said, "But you are merely a hologram. You cannot kill me."

John, forgetting all his pain, leapt high into the air and landed behind the hologram. Right after his foot hit the ground, John pushed off forward towards the wall to rebound, for the hologram already turned to take dangerous swipes at him. John rebounded off the wall spinning, deflecting the attacks shot at him. John landed and attacked right and left at his opponent. The hologram leapt and fought more than John, but John was able to deflect the attacks from the two swords.

Finally, John leapt into the air and landed crookedly. The hologram shot at John, both swords twirling. John ducked the swords and pierced the hologram on the left hand. The holographic arm flew off with the sword with it, but no blood issued. John seized the dropped sword in the air and fought against the one-handed hologram. John attacked the right side and, when the hologram turned to deflect the sword aimed at his weak side, John's other sword hit the man's last hand. The sword dropped and John went in for the simple, last move. He beheaded the hologram and all the holographic things disappeared. John collapsed, the pain reinstated.

"That was the worst," John said, "But I guess they'll all get worse by each flight of stairs I take."

He sheathed his sword. For the third time, John went up the stairs. He looked out and saw a robot that looked like a human, merely silver. It seemed to be shut off.

"Maybe if I am quiet, I can sneak by it," John whispered. He slowly headed for the stairs when the robots eyes lit in a piercing glow. The eyes stared right at John.

"*Item found*," It said in a robotic voice, "*Termination must be complete. Preparing for eradication.*"

The robot's arms flew to the swords at its holsters.

"I don't think so," John sputtered, removing his sword. The robot flew into battle with the help of boosters on its back. John deflected each shot thrown at him, but he had to admit, they were hard to avoid.

The robot landed and spun its sword in a circular motion and headed right towards him.

"I saw this in a movie once," John said, "How did he beat it? Oh yes…"

John lunged forward and cut one of the swords in half.

The robot paused for what seemed like a millisecond before it attacked again, this time trying to avoid John's sword. John slashed at the hand without a weapon, but it pulled it back and brought out another sword from a holster on the robots waist. John got frustrated and spun his body forcing the robot back, but not far. The robot leapt over John and shot an attack at his back. John's magician instincts told him to fall to the ground and he obeyed, missing the sword by inches. John spun on his back and, with the momentum, struck the robot's arm and it flew off.

The robot paused for another millisecond and another robotic arm appeared in its place with it holding a sword.

"It's learning while fighting!" John realized. John went forward and tried to attack, "It's gained every piece of information on how to fight against a person and then uses it in battle. When it comes up with certain things that have never been used before, it learns and never makes the mistake again. That means I have to pull some moves I don't even know exist."

John did a back flip and bounced from the ground right back at the robot putting his sword in front of him. The robot spun away and launched his attack. John stepped back and shot an attack at its hand and cut it off with a swinging attack directed with his knee to confuse the robot. The robot paused and then, in a robotic voice spoke.

"Object not annihilated," it said, *"Absolute measures reached. Complete destruction passed."*

The robot, instead of growing another arm, grew many on its right side. On its left, a lot more grew on its left. They all were armed with weapons.

"Oh crap …"

John stepped back. The arms suddenly all swarmed at him. John stepped aside as each one passed. He struck one sword with his and it cut in half. The robot didn't even pause before striking again and again. John desperately struck down each one and stepped back. He held his sword at the ready. The robot's eyes glowed and suddenly lasers shot at John from them. John held his sword up and deflected them right back at them. They hit the robot and shot it to the corner. The robot got to its feet and charged at John full speed.

Then the answer came to John: a new type of strike that *he* had used before, but barely any other warrior knew about. And it was one of John's greatest weapons: his magic. John opened his palm and concentrated hard on a force of magic. His eyes grew red and his cape started to blow back as if a large gust of wind. He released the magic at the robot. The blast hit the robot and slammed it against the wall again, this time much harder. The blast rocked the tower for a moment.

John wasn't sure if he defeated the robot or not, but he ran to the stairs as if he did. He charged up the steps through the pain. This flight of stairs was the highest yet. John tried to count how many circles he did, but he lost count at two hundred.

Finally he reached the top. John took a step out and looked around for his, hopefully, last opponent. John saw him, leaning against the wall. It was another cloaked man, but this time it was not a hologram. It leaned forward as he saw who it was.

"Well, John, I am surprised in many ways," he said.

John took a quick step back. It was the first time somebody called him by his first name in some time.

"I am surprised by the way you were able to defeat all of number one's challenges up to me," he said, "I am also surprised that you have mastered the power of the Scarlet Phoenix. And lastly, I am surprised at how much you have grown up since I last saw you. Let me introduce myself: I am Number Eleven, last survivor of Number one's army of sorcerers."

John nodded at his opponent. He still had his sword in his hand.

"You are probably wondering how I know you," Number Eleven said.

"Not really," John said, "just wondering how someone like you would be so high up in the challenges."

"Sarcasm," Eleven said, "yes, that passed through your family, didn't it? Well, you'll have to see the answer to that in a second."

The man swished his cloak back and removed a long black sword. John recognized it immediately as one of the Soulhaunt's swords.

"You're a..." John began.

"I am not a Kraskull, no," Eleven finished. "But I need an evil sword to fight against a pure sword."

"A pure sword will still cut an evil sword," John grinned.

"We'll see," Eleven, John could sense, smiled.

John made the first move. He came in low at his legs. Eleven struck the Phoenix sword with his Kraskull sword. John's sword bounced off. John stepped back in surprise. He quickly recovered and slammed at Eleven's side. Eleven countered and swung at John's left side. John parried and spun around and struck high. Once again, Eleven parried it. John sensed something.

"You aren't trying!" He said angrily.

"Why should I?" Eleven said laughing, "You can't beat me. I can beat you without trying."

"Then I'll make you fight hard to beat me," John snarled.

"Bring it," His opponent said, drawing back.

John let out a battle cry and leapt high in the air and landed behind Eleven. John did a backwards somersault between Eleven's legs. John straightened and attacked. With instinct obviously magical, Eleven dropped to the floor and spun forward. He twisted around and faced John again. John charged in again. Eleven sent a strike of magic left and right, both of which John was able to avoid and parry. John blocked a blow aimed right at his head and they froze in that stance for a moment.

"You are indeed trained," Eleven breathed, "But I am not yet going full out on you."

"You know that you are," John grinned. "And you are trained just as good as me."

"That's an insult," Eleven snarled.

"It's an over-exaggeration," John snapped back.

They pulled their swords back and returned to smashing swords at each other, neither pulling the upper hand and both getting more and more frustrated. John blocked strike after strike coming from Eleven, each getting progressively harder. John realized that staying on defense was no way to win.

He blocked one solid attack on the left and reversed the attack to his opponent's neck. Eleven switched to defense and evaded each shot at him. John faked him by making him think he was about to strike high and he actually struck low at the leg. Eleven reacted quickly after the Phoenix sword hit his skin. He did a back flip back to avoid getting cut more.

"Nice shot," Eleven said frustrated, "You'll get my best now!"

Eleven roared and spun quickly at John. John repelled his attack. John marveled at how Eleven could sense which strike would be blocked and which wouldn't before it even occurred. It seemed as if the blades had barely touched before Eleven slashed at a different area. John found it very difficult to keep up with him.

John felt himself sweating harder than he had ever done before. He relied on his skill and magical instincts to lead him through each defense. However, he was growing very weak. John blocked one aimed at his feet and, once again, they stayed where they were (which meant that they were going to insult each other again).

"I am going all out and you are still blocking each one," Eleven snorted.

"I have to admit," John gasped, "You are indeed the greatest swordsmen I have ever seen. I mean, faced. I still haven't seen you."

The man laughed and removed his hood to show a man with blue eyes, gold hair that went down his neck and a beard that was kept well. He looked very similar to Uncle Dan, but John had no more living relatives... even though the look of this man seemed vaguely familiar from his childhood.

"Well, we'll still have to finish this," Eleven said, "And I admit now, before you're captured, that you are the best opponent I have ever fought since my brother and I clashed."

John didn't have enough time to calculate what he had said before he was thrown into another fight. Eleven sliced his sword into John's so fast that the swords were blurs to each other's eyes. John tried to concentrate on the battle, but it was so difficult to go on when his leg was full of pain and he had been battling constantly for hours. I *must rely on the Phoenix to guide me*, John thought, *only then will I beat this evil; I cannot simply kill him by myself.*

Drained from energy, John brought magic from deep inside of himself. He felt his body about to give out.

"Will you surrender?" Eleven sputtered, retreating.

John was half-tempted to say yes.

"You'll have to kill me for that," John breathed.

Eleven shook his head.

"Actually, I won't," He said, "Number one gave me specific orders to give you to him alive."

"Then I'll face him myself!"

John lunged forward with all his strength. He could feel his legs turn to jelly, as he struck as hard as he could at Eleven's side.

"You can't beat me now," Eleven said, easily parrying the blow, "You have been fighting constantly and I have not. And now I have worn you down so that you have no more strength when I go all out again."

"I wore you out enough for you to be unable to go 'all out' again," John responded, retreating back to the wall. He leaned against it for a brief second to recover some strength.

"Look at you," Eleven snarled, holding up his blade, "You can't even stand up."

John held up his sword as well.

"Nevertheless," John sputtered.

John tried to strike with his sword, but Eleven slashed at the John's hand holding his sword. John fell to the ground, holding his hand, defeated at last. John looked at his opponent in agony.

"Who could be so good," John said nearly crying, "to be able to defeat me in such away that could kill the devil himself?!"

Eleven raised his sword to John's neck.

"One of your only living relatives," he answered.

"My brothers and uncle are the only family I have now," John whimpered, "My grandparents are dead, I have no cousins, my Aunt is dead, my parents-"

He stopped suddenly. The horrible truth dawned on him.

"My mother died …"

"And your father?" Eleven said, ironically smiling.

John looked into his enemy's eyes and then drooped his head.

"Joined with my arch-enemy and defeated me."

20.) The Jail Room

John just couldn't believe it. His own father that, until just recently, he presumed to be dead, joined with Zach. The truth stung at John's heart like a heated blade.

He had always imagined his father to have died valiantly. John learned some time ago that his father was a mighty magician, one of the most powerful. Indeed, his magical powers rivaled those of both Zach and the *Ring* council. John thought his dad was killed trying to save someone or died in a secret magical war.

He would have never imagined this.

John was lifted up by the neck of his cloak. His father carried him like this up the next set of stairs. There, waiting for them was a Kraskull.

"*At last, the mighty Quaill has lost,*" it said in a ghostly voice, "*The Phoenix could only take you so far. It is now time to finish what has begun. Hand him over to me, Eleven.*"

John's father looked at the Kraskull in half surprise and half terror.

"Zach gave me specific orders to take the child directly to him. He did not say to kill him."

"*Nevertheless,*" the Soulhaunt whispered, "*Hand him over to me and I will take him to Zach.*"

"Liar," John snarled, "You will kill me. And you will also kill Zach."

The Kraskull looked at him in the eyes for a brief moment. John felt a tidal wave despair and fear all around him. It was the magical effect of the Kraskull. But as soon as it looked away, the despair and fear left him. The Soulhaunt was now looking at his father.

"*I will ask this one more time without a fight: HAND HIM OVER!*"

"NO!" John's father yelled, drawing his sword. "Zach said to take him to him directly and that's what I'll do!"

The Kraskull drew his sword with a *zing* that hurt John's ears.

"*Do you dare defy the Kraskull?*" It whispered.

"I only obey one master, if that's what you mean," John's father said with defiance John recognized.

"*Then you will die,*" It said simply. And with a clang that echoed around the room, both swords met in the air.

They held the swords in that position for a long time. Then, to John's amazement, they both, at the same time, lowered their weapons.

"Together," His father said. John looked with amazement to the Kraskull. Surely the Kraskull would only obey its own wishes and not one of another? But the Kraskull sheathed its sword and gave a shadow of a nod. John's father grabbed him by the arm and dragged him up the flight of stairs. The Soulhaunt followed behind them.

After many other flights of stairs (all of them had empty rooms), they reached the end of one where there was a trapdoor above them. His father called out, "it has been done, Number One!"

There was a pause and then cruel laughter came to them from behind the trap door. The trapdoor opened and John, his father, and the Kraskull entered into the room. John found himself in a dark room. The only light appeared from a spherical object on a small circular platform. The object emitted blue light that looked like a lighting storm inside of itself. The blue light danced dimly on the walls, but other than that, John couldn't see anything.

"Well, well, well," came a voice from across the room and John leapt. Coming into the light of the object, Zach's evil face come into John's line of sight. "Well, well, well. I would have never thought anything less from you, Quaill. You rose above the rest, but were defeated by one of the greatest magicians of our time: your father.

"I expected nothing more from a Quaill. However, you did lose eventually. You were valiant, but it isn't enough to be just valiant when there're lives at stake, you know what I mean?"

Zach laughed.

"No matter how fast you ran and reappeared in different areas, you were still too late. The orb has won."

John realized at last what the object on the table was.

"In exactly one hour from now, I shall order the new and rejuvenated orb to destroy every American on this earth. After that, millions of people will die.

"And why do I do it slowly, you ask? (You should really control your mind, Quaill, I can read it like a book.) But I will answer; I like to see people suffer. It would be no fun, see, to say: 'Oh, destroy everyone except me and those who will always serve me as ruler.' I must destroy them nation-by-nation and see the outcry from other people.

"Also, it is a lot of fun to watch futile attempts to stop me. The US air force? That was a joke. The Phoenix militia? I was surprised that lasted over forty seconds. The treaties for a united attack against me? That is quite laughable. There are too many strong ties to the past for that to work."

"You won't get away with this, Zach." John snarled. "That orb will be destroyed. It was prophesized so."

Zach laughed.

"Ah yes, the prophesy. But did it ever say *when* the orb was destroyed, boy? You see, in order to fulfill the prophecy, I plan to destroy the orb when I have full control of the world."

"No."

Everyone looked at Number Eleven.

"You are not of the same line as Caleb, son of Tollund. Only those of the same line as Tollund can destroy it. It is prophesized that way."

Zach stared at him for a moment.

"And who is of the line of Tollund?"

"All I know is that the line always bore one son in each generation. They never had twins and never had more than one. You had many brothers in your family, Number One; you couldn't be of that line."

"Nevertheless, Quaill," Zach said as though no interruption had happened, "Even if this descendant of Tollund destroyed my orb, you are still surrounded by five billion troops that could form a line and destroy everything in its way. It would be slower, but it will be done."

John gaped at him.

"Five Billion?"

"You heard me," Zach said simply. "All will obey my command immediately."

John was speechless. A few million troops were hard to beat, but possible. But five billion and a weapon that destroys all opposition?

"But now, story time is over," Zach said. "And it is now time for you to go to the jail room. You, take him there."

He finally addressed the Kraskull.

"*No, Zach,*" it said. "*Your servant can take him there. You and I need to discuss what will happen when you rule the earth.*"

Number Eleven grabbed John and quickly led him down the trapdoor and hastily shut it behind him.

"You don't want to be there when those two get in a fight," his father said, "it gets intense."

"Who is from the line of Tollund?" John asked, forgetting completely that his father was a traitor. "I could tell you knew something that Zach didn't."

His father flinched. John recognized it as the flinch that his uncle gave three years ago when he refused to give his true name to them.

"It's us isn't it?" John whispered. They both stopped. John looked him in the eye. "We're the descendants of Tollund, aren't we?"

Slowly, his father nodded.

"You knew this?" John said, realizing what he was nodding at. "You knew you had the power to save the world and you didn't?"

"I do not care about the planet," Eleven replied, "It is a broken and crippled world. The majority of it is selfish."

"So is that a reason to kill it?" John snarled, "Because it is weak?"

"You wouldn't understand."

"But I do now," John said. "You betrayed our family. Didn't you care about our family at the least?"

"I didn't like it at all," Daniel said, "I loved your mother, as I loved my children. But the ties to the past too strong, as Number One said. The line to the past forced me to hate myself. I broke the code. It was supposed to be that only one to carry on the name. I had let three."

"But you and Uncle Dan!" John almost shouted. "You didn't seem to hate him—"

"We were twins," Eleven interrupted, "I was younger than him by about a minute, but I was still the second child. I still broke it. I made it worse by having a family. Now, I can set things right."

"By letting millions die," John said angrily, "Letting millions die to try and satisfy a stupid code. No code is worth that. No code is worth losing a family over."

They both stood in silence.

"Mother is dead," John said, "Jerry is probably somewhere in Europe, maybe even dead. Uncle Dan is probably dead trying to get here. And Paul…he is in Mexico, near the billions of ogres. He could die also. And now, after this hour, Zach will kill me too. The Quaill Chain will be destroyed anyway. You can earn back the honor of our ancestors if you help fulfill the prophecy."

"It is too late for that now," Eleven said in a final tone, "I have already lost."

"Well, I hope you're content now," John spat. "Because of your master's orb, the one I had loved is dead."

They stood in silence with one another. Then Eleven grabbed his arm again and led him down the stairs to a room. He led him to a wall where John found himself facing a hammock. John's father thrust him onto it.

"There you will stay until Zach releases you or kills you," Eleven said. The ropes on the hammock glowed red slightly for a moment and then John was forced to lie on his back. "Of course if you do escape, you cannot enter the orb room anyway, it is sealed with magic that Zach personally has to open."

His father left. John tried to move, but he was stuck on the hammock. The hammock seemed to be made of a sticky material. John glanced around for something to escape with. Then he saw on the ground something glittering: a sword! John tried to grabbed it with his magic power, but couldn't. He tried again, but still no luck. The sword stayed untouched on the floor.

"I already tried it. It didn't work," a voice rang out in the chamber. John looked around and found another hammock identical to his own with a prisoner in it. The prisoner was somewhat tall, had dark skin, and had short, brown hair. He was slightly younger than John, but seemed very, very thin.

"It's bound with the magical spell that that man laid on it," the stranger said. "It's impossible to break. You can't use magic while on these."

"Who are you?" John asked.

"I was a friend of your brother at genie school," he answered weakly.

"You're a genie?" John said impressed.

"Hybrid, they call me, 'cause I am not completely a genie. I am half genie, half magician," he responded weakly.

"Wow," John said. "But what are you doing here?"

"Trying to stop Zach from using the orb," Hybrid answered, "But I was stopped by that thing on the first floor."

"Well, you needed a proper sword," John said, glancing at the one on the ground, "but how did you know about the orb?"

"My dad told me," Hybrid responded, "he is a general for the President of the United States. He is a magician."

"I see," John said. "Well, Hybrid, thanks for the tip, but nonetheless, I need to get out of here."

John swung the hammock back and forth.

"The spell indicated that you stay there," Hybrid said, "And there you will stay."

John grinned.

"To the quick, less informative mind, yes," John responded, trying to reach for the sword. "But if you listened carefully, I can escape."

"How?"

"As an afterthought, he mentioned that if I *could* escape, my plan would *probably* be squashed," John emphasized the two words carefully. "I'm famous for loopholes."

"That doesn't seem to be the only thing you're famous for," Hybrid said, smiling.

John turned the hammock upside down. He pushed his hand out to try and grab it. He was mere inches from it.

"Come on!" John gnarled his teeth. "Come on!"

John saw the blade move slightly. John looked at his hand in surprise. It was blood red. He was overriding the spell. The blade moved another couple centimeters. John reached with all his strength.

The hammock shot upwards in John's haste to grab the sword. John's hand closed around the smooth handle of the sword as his body came up.

"Yes!" John half-shouted. He looked at the sword in his left hand. "Now, it's time to face Zach and those Soulhaunts."

John sliced against the ropes. His left arm came free to move around. He sliced the ropes binding his right arm. Then both his feet, and finally his neck. John fell to the ground. John got up and crossed the room to Hybrid.

"I will only free you on one condition," John said to him. "You will go home immediately. Or better yet, you will join my uncle and fight in the battle against the ogres."

"I swear it," Hybrid sighed. "I only wish I could help you."

"Sorry, you can't," John said. "I need my Phoenix sword one floor down, so I guess I can see you off."

John sliced the bindings to Hybrid. They both jogged down the stairs.

"How long have you been here?" John asked.

"Three days," Hybrid said, "and I am starving."

"I can't help you, man," John muttered, sympathetically, "I am a weak magician."

"Oh, I highly doubt that," Hybrid smiled, "you are one of the most powerful."

John smiled back. He spotted his sword immediately on the ground. He grabbed it and attached it to his belt. John turned to Hybrid and handed him his sword.

"You'll need this," John said, "But now it's time to end this battle with the orb."

"I hope to see you again," Hybrid proclaimed, extending his hand. John took his hand firmly. "Good luck, buddy."

John gave him a short nod and ran up the two flights of stairs. He reached the trapdoor and he gripped the handle of his sword tightly.

"In the name of the Scarlet Phoenix and the planet Earth," John shouted, "I demand that you open this door!"

The door flew open immediately by Zach, but he wasn't looking at John.

"We had a promise!" Zach yelled at the Kraskull across the room. "We wouldn't use it to destroy everything!"

"We are getting tired of you, Zach," The Kraskull said in a low voice. *"Times have changed. You are too slow. Your weak army is bound to fail if you don't use this orb with them."*

"I wouldn't dare, the enemy would get it!" Zach said, shaking.

"You are a coward," the Kraskull snorted, *"Which is why we'll take this orb from you."*

Zach took a step back.

"You're...going..." Zach stuttered. "You...can't..."

"Watch me," The Soulhaunt took a step forward and put its hand on the orb.

"I won't let you!" Zach shouted frightened, "The world would be completely dead! I will have no servants!"

"Then you need to reflect on the true meaning of evil," The Soulhaunt instructed. *"You are weak, Zach."*

"Hand that over," John said, taking a step into the light so the Kraskull could see him.

"I am tired of you, too, Quaill," the Kraskull said, letting go of the orb, grabbing the hilt of its sword. *"I believe it's finally time for you to die."*

"AFTER YOU!" John said, whipping out his sword.

The orb's glow was added by the near-blinding light of the Phoenix sword. The Kraskull's white eyes narrowed slightly.

"That's right," John announced, approaching the table. "Your dreaded enemy, the Scarlet Phoenix, is with me. If you dare approach to stop me—"

But the Kraskull already leapt at John, hissing like an angry cat—the desire for the orb outweighed the Kraskull's fear of the Phoenix. John gripped his hilt hard and countered the attack. In a slash of black and gold sparks, the duel started. Each blow hurt his wrist, but John continued to stop each attack.

"Zach!" John yelled over his shoulder, "Grab the orb and run!"

John never thought he would say those words, but he would much rather have Zach take the orb at the moment, rather than the Kraskull.

It took a second for Zach to comprehend what John said, but then he lunged for the orb. However, the instant he moved closer to it, the other five Kraskull appeared in front of him, swords out. Zach stopped in his tracks. Zach drew his sword and John's father followed suit. John watched as the Kraskull shot ferocious attacks at his father.

He paused too long. The Kraskull he was facing cut his shoulder slightly. John leapt back, but he dropped his sword.

At that moment, another Kraskull disarmed John's father.

Without thinking, John shot out his right hand and pushed his sword at father. His father caught it and it took the Kraskull by surprise. Eleven sliced the Soulhaunt in half.

The hood fell back on the Kraskull and John saw its face for the first time. He screamed and shut his eyes in horror. There was no face. There was only bone; black, rotten, old bone. The eyes that John had seen through the hood were not from eyeballs but from the absence of them. There were flecks of thin hair on its head.

But it was not these features that made John scream. It was its mouth.

It was grinning. John couldn't think of anything less like a grin, however. It was so horrible to see something that dead, sneering. The terrible thing didn't stop grinning even after it hit the ground, forever finished.

There was a world-ending pause. Everything was perfectly still.

John looked into his father's eyes. John was astonished to see what he saw: a final, everlasting comprehension. His father, at last, learned the true depth of the evil.

And then suddenly, with a short nod, John's father leapt over the four Kraskull in his way and landed on the table. He picked up the orb and closed his eyes and said:

"And so, with final strength, John Quaill, one of the last descendants of Tollund, the greatest warrior ever to walk on this earth, with the power of Scarlet Phoenix, the first and final pure, destroys the evil orb and all power and strength attached to it!"

John watched in awe as the sword glowed a miraculous bright white, stretching over the entire room, lighting it up like a star. The Kraskull recoiled in obvious pain.

In what seemed to be slow motion, John Quaill the First shoved the Phoenix sword into the orb.

21.) The War Begins

John looked in absolute wonder as the blade entered into the orb. The orb set off a bluish lightning that snaked quickly up the sword. It crawled up John's father's arm and covered his body. Eleven issued a deadly scream, but didn't release the orb or the sword. The lightning increased until it looked as if Eleven's entire body was hidden beneath the blue lightning.

John was watching so intently to what was happening to his father that he didn't watch what was going on around him. The rest of the Kraskull's hoods fell back to show there faces. They looked as if they were suffering the pains of the orb as well.

The orb changed color from blue to red. It started to vibrate so violently that the room itself started to shake. John felt the vibrations from where he stood.

Eleven's screeches increased. The red orb turned suddenly to bright white, but not as bright as the Phoenix sword. The orb remained intact, but a large split could be seen from where the sword had sliced. The lightning subsided a little, but each bolt seemed to have a greater effect on Eleven. John could see every ounce of pain his father was experiencing, but he didn't see how he could help him.

Eleven's eyes shot open and he looked at his son. He became more determined and shoved the sword in further. The lightning bolts ensuing from the orb ripened to a stronger state and Eleven started to shake violently. He had trouble even standing on the small table he was on. However, he sliced it more and the split became more pronounced. Eleven quickly shot the sword out of the orb and brought it down with all his remaining strength onto the split.

The fission was completed and the orb split in two.

The aftereffect John would remember all his life. He was certain what was going to happen next. He quickly conjured up a small, circular barrier around himself as a blast of blue lightning erupted in every direction of the room. The walls of the room burst apart and everyone, including John, was sent flying out of the tower. John tumbled in the air and struggled to keep his barrier alive. John saw the ground come closer and closer.

The impact almost killed him. The barrier was able to prevent death, but not injury. John hit the ground with his feet and they collapsed beneath him.

John raised his head a few inches and looked around him. He looked up at the tower. The tower was swaying from the blast—John thought it looked like someone shaking their head. At last, with one mighty groan, the tower slowly started to fall, level by level. The first was crushed, followed by the second, third and fourth until the whole thing was destroyed. As the last black brick fell, John slumped over in exhaustion.

He awoke sometime later, not knowing how much time had passed. He opened his eyes, which seemed to bleed from pain. He lifted himself up and looked around at the rubble.

John's head fell back. He couldn't remember exactly what had just happened. Then it all came back. He jumped to his feet, but then collapsed again. He compromised by crawling with his hands towards the tower. He could barely make someone out by the rubble. It was his father, but he was on the ground unconscious. John quickly crawled up to him. He turned his dad onto his back. His eyes were shut.

John looked around for the Phoenix sword. He found it lying a few feet away. John grabbed it and looked at it. He saw a small ghost form of his father right above it, shining pearly white. It was smiling.

"Thank you, John," it said in an echo of a voice. "You saved my soul from becoming a phantom, a tortured eternity."

John just stared in amazement and grief. To see his dad like this only meant one thing…

"Oh, I am not dead," It said, reading his mind, "but my life is over. I am complete."

"No," John pleaded, "if you're not dead, please…"

"I can't live," His father sighed, "it would be complete pain for the rest of my life. I will now be in union with the Phoenix. However…"

John looked up.

"Life is a horrible thing to waste," The ghost said, "I can use my remaining living parts to return your friend from the dead."

A ghost form of Joan appeared. John's dad touched Joan and she floated to her body next to the bar where John had left her. John looked back at his father. It would be time now.

"It was a pity I couldn't raise you as my child," The ghost of his father said. "John…remember this: no matter what happens, no matter what anyone says or does, you will always be the world's most powerful magician."

His father looked him in the eye.

"Your magic will always be with you. As will we." John's mother and friends appeared out of the sword. "Remember that."

They all vanished and the sword lost its glow. John closed his eyes in pain. But he opened them a moment later. He was beyond the crying stage now. He had taken care of that before he entered into the tower. He stood up and walked over to the body of Joan. She sat up quickly.

"John-wait…where…what—" she stuttered.

"It's over, Joan," John said, kneeling down beside her. He was smiling kindly. "The orb is destroyed. Zach and the Kraskull are killed. It's all over."

"John…what happened to me?" Joan asked.

John took a deep breath.

"You were killed by the orb's power. I came here and tried to stop Zach from using it again. The tower and the orb collapsed and Zach and the Kraskull were destroyed because of their attachments to the orb. The Phoenix sword revived you in reward."

John vowed to himself to never tell anyone about his father. It was best to keep that up to the imaginations of his brothers.

"I'm—alive?" She breathed. John leaned in and kissed her quickly on the lips.

"Yes," He said quietly.

Just then they heard fast hooves approaching. John adjusted himself and helped Joan up. John saw his horse accompanied by Lino sprinting at break neck speed right at John. John's brother pulled on the reigns and made Dreaded Musty stop. Paul leapt off and ran up to John.

"We're here," he breathed. As he said that, both his horse and Lino fell onto the ground. "We had to come. We'll be ok."

Paul fell into his brother's arms. John looked at Joan.

"Do you still have that potion in your pocket?" He asked.

She reached into her pocket and gave John the potion she found. It was green, but John hardly looked at it as he poured it into Paul's mouth and then to Dreaded Musty's and Lino's. He came back to Paul who was sitting on the ground.

"What happened?" John asked.

"I was about to ask you the same thing," Paul asked, looking at the rubble of remains of the building.

"Well, the orb was destroyed and the Kraskull went with it," John answered, breathing hard at what he was repeating.

"Well, Zach can't be dead," Paul spat unceremonious to the information just given to him. "When I was inspecting those dead ogres when we were fighting with the Thogs, I noticed a chip inside of there bodies that is an artificial attachment. Zach has one similar. If he dies, so do all the ogres."

"Then the ogres are dead then!" John said excited.

"No, they're not," Paul said, "I saw them less then a mile away. Millions of them."

John cursed and put his hands in his face.

"No, Paul," John said, "Billions. Zach told me about this. He was expecting the orb to be destroyed. He raised an army of 5 billion ogres, starting when he was a child. So this is not over yet."

"On the contrary," Joan said as Lino got up and walked carefully to John. "The war for the orb is over. The war for the world has now begun."

Dreaded Musty trotted to John. They all looked up at the sunrise.

"The second day of the orb's destruction," Lino said quietly.

Paul then noticed his father's corpse on the ground.

"Who was that?" He asked John.

John looked down at the body and then at his brother.

"A valiant warrior."

22.) The Two Generals

"How will we prepare for this attack?" Paul asked his brother.

"We will have to move to the Gila River," John said, pointing at his smudged map. "There we will meet our troops of magicians and genies and everyone else."

It was three hours later and Lino, Joan, and Dreaded Musty were taking a well deserved sleep.

"What if they don't come in time?" Paul asked.

"I was thinking about that," John said, smiling. "Paul, look at the map. The ogres are close to us now. If we beat them to the river, we can blast the bridges. We can ask the Americans to blast the bridges around the other rivers. If you look at the map…"

"There are rivers surrounding us everywhere!" Paul exclaimed. They would all be—"

"Trapped, I know!" John said, getting excited. "And I highly doubt if they can swim well. That would give us enough time to get our troops organized with the rest of the world to fight them."

"A perfect plan!" Lino said, sitting up. "Let's move now!"

John and Paul looked at Lino in surprise.

"Maybe I was up to late last night," John said, "But did I hear you correctly? You *want* to go?"

"How far is it?" Lino asked.

"Just a few miles from here," John said.

"I have supplies ready," Joan said, sitting up as well. "Right here."

She gave them a stack of clothes, food, bottles of water, and knives. John and Paul looked at the clothes. They were all the same, only different sizes. They were shiny silver material that was quite light. On the chest was a red phoenix head.

"Uniforms," Joan explained, pulling hers over her clothes. She did the same with her pants. She pulled on her boots.

"I am catching on," Paul said, repeating her action and then strapping his belt on.

John connected his sheath to his belt. John felt behind his back and found a hood.

"You remembered everything," He said, pulling it onto his head. He shoved the knives into his boots. "I think we're ready. I guess we can let Musty catch up, she's probably tired."

But at the mention of her name, Dreaded Musty leapt up and neighed.

"That horse is strong," Paul said, "some might say that it's a super horse."

"I know it's so," John said, stroking her mane. He leapt onto her saddle. "Do it again, Musty."

Dreaded Musty performed the classic two footed stand and then knelt back down. Joan leapt on behind John. Paul leapt on Lino. They both charged ahead.

It only took a few minutes. They reached the river in no time. John and Joan leapt off and headed to the bridge. Paul followed.

"One problem with your plan, John," Paul said to him, "How are we going to contact the US commanders?"

"I was thinking about that, too," John frowned. "I was hoping that we would see that general again, but it doesn't look like it. I guess this is the only bridge for miles."

He pointed at the sign near the bridge.

"I guess we could just defend this bridge until they come," Joan said. "The powers of our mages are truly remarkable."

John and Paul looked at each other.

"Joan," John said, "The orb destroyed all the mages. That's how you died."

Joan looked at him.

"I am the last mage?" She asked.

"Yes," John said sadly.

She clenched her fists.

"The genies have died out to near extinction," Paul sighed, "The psychics will not help us much. We must then rely on magicians then."

"There are too few," Lino commented. "We do have the mythics, though."

"Also too few," Paul said. "We don't have enough soldiers."

"We have the humans," John shrugged. "At this point, they are the only ones in which we can rely. John walked onto the bridge. The others followed.

He crossed it and then saw houses.

"We could form a militia from the humans," Lino suggested.

"I need to use a computer to contact Uncle Dan," Paul said. "I would be able to do it, I just need a computer."

"I bet someone has a computer in those houses," John said. "Ok, we'll split up. Lino will stay with me. Paul goes alone. Musty will go with Joan."

They all separated. Paul went up to a door and knocked. A person answered.

"May I borrow your computer?" Paul asked. "It's an emergency."

The bald man scratched his head.

"I never had a computer," He said. "'Can't help you kid."

"Maybe you can," Paul suggested, "Do you know where I can use one?"

"My neighbor probably has one," The man said. He was about to close the door when Paul said, "Listen sir, a war is about to brew and we need to start a militia."

The man stared in amazement.

"Listen, kid, I don't know what movie you were watching, but there is no war here unless you count 'Korea."

Paul breathed impatiently, "Sir, do you have a television set?"

"Yes," He said.

"Turn on the news," Paul commanded.

"Listen, kid—"

"JUST DO IT!" Paul snarled.

The man turned on the TV behind him. The news showed huge slaughter of people in large city.

"Well, citizens," the newscaster said breathlessly, "there is a large evacuation in Phoenix on the way now. All citizens are called to get guns, knives, any weapon you can get your hands on and prepare to get called for duty. The president will give a speech later on this morning, but people in Phoenix must get out."

The man turned off the TV.

"This is no children's crusade kid, this is an invasion," The man said. "It is dangerous out there."

Paul finally took out his ax and showed the blade to the man.

"You see that?" He asked the man. "That's blood on there. I have slain hundreds of these things along with my brother. I am a war hero. You must believe me."

The man looked at him hard. Then he nodded.

"I got my old .45 caliber from the Dessert Storm battle a few decades ago," He said. "I can get my neighbors. They'll believe me more than you."

"Get everyone from eight to seventy," Paul said, "I'll check the neighbors for a computer."

John used the same method as Paul. Entire families got their rifles, shotguns, display swords or even sharp knives from the kitchen. John went from house to house saying that the war was coming. Those who had seen the news left their homes and followed John.

Paul got into the neighbor's house. They must have already evacuated. He turned on the computer, logged onto the Internet and went to his home site. He typed the code in and the screen went black for a second. Then red letters came across the screen saying:

F2 Uploading

Please Wait. . . .

The screen appeared in color again. Paul was now on his computer. He clicked around for a few moments and then accessed his uncle's computer.

His uncle felt his computer in his bag vibrating. He opened his laptop and found his nephew looking at him.

"Paul, are you ok?" Uncle Dan asked.

"I am fine," Paul said quickly and briefly explained what was happening in Phoenix. "We are building a militia, alright?

We need to defend the bridge long enough for you to use the river. How close are you?"

But Uncle Dan didn't answer.

"Who thought of blockading the ogres using rivers?" He asked.

"John did," Paul said impatiently.

"It's an excellent idea," Dan said. "General-ship worthy. And you are smart as well. I am appointing you and your brother Generals of the Phoenix Militia."

Paul grinned.

"Isn't that name copyrighted?" He asked.

"The Scarlet Phoenix Militia, no," Dan said. "Make the right decisions. I will be there in a few days."

"Right, I'll keep you informed," Paul said. "I'm out."

He was shut down the communications and was about to shut off the computer when he turned back to F2. He scrolled down a list and finally found the name he was looking for: Victor. He was about to double-click it, bringing his holographic friend back from the dead. However, as he was reaching for it, a vivid picture reappeared in his mind…with the Kraskull piercing the sword into him…seeing the look of horror in his face…his last scream of pain…

Paul shut down the computer. Joan ran up to him.

"John has everyone in this town ready for battle," Joan said, "But a lot of them evacuated."

"How many do you estimate are here?" Paul asked.

"Forty or fifty," Joan responded as they started to walk to where John was standing. John ran to them.

"They're scared, all of them," he said.

"Aren't we all?" Lino asked him.

"True enough," John said, "but I think they're expecting me to make a speech. Here's what's going to happen: Paul…you get that bridge battle worthy to our advantage. Joan, summon up some more uniforms. Lino, stay near me."

They all obeyed their orders. John got on his horse and rode over to the militia. He looked out at all of them. The whispering stopped. John swallowed.

"I admit," he began, "I am not as good a speaker as my brother, who isn't here right now. My girlfriend Joan will give all of you uniforms to put on over your clothes. With it, you will become a member of the army. But before you do, remember what this means. This act will be your oath. You will follow my orders and remain loyal to me, even in the face of death. You may turn now and leave, evacuate and save your families. But the world depends on your help. Please, we need every soldier to fight against these demons. Please come forward and pledge yourself."

Nobody moved. Then a small child from the back, no older than ten, stepped forward. He walked slowly towards Joan. He looked at John and then said, "For daddy, I will fight."

He grabbed a uniform and put it on. He stepped behind John. A minister then stepped forward and grabbed a uniform and said, "For God and my country, I will fight."

He put it on and stepped next to the child. Slowly, everyone present put a uniform on and lined up in front of John. John looked at them.

"You are all courageous and I thank you with as much thanks as I can offer."

John took a deep breath and said in a fierce tone that was unlike him.

"I do not know much about your country and customs. I do not know much about this area. I do know how to fight. I do know about these ogres we are about to fight together. Soon people across the world will stand up and draw weapons with us and fight back. Thousands have already died trying to stop them. But we cannot die. We must protect this country. We must fight. True, some are children and some are veterans of World War II."

Some people chuckled at his exaggeration.

"But nevertheless, we will win. We can hold them enough until others come. We will go to battle together. Together we win, together we flee, together we fall, no matter what, we must remain together. Let us now show these ogres that the US is not something they can take. Let us go together!"

John drew his sword. The militia held up their weapons. John turned and commanded his horse to trot to the bridge. Paul and Victor were waiting. They had set up obstacles on the bridge and blocks that they could hide behind. Victor had his bow out and Paul his ax.

"Separate behind an obstacle," John commanded. He got off his horse and turned to it. "I know how much you like battling, but you can't be with us this time. You can't give away our position. You must hide. If I die, then you will find a new master, all right? That's a command."

Reluctantly, the horse turned and trotted away. John sighed. He turned to see who was next to him behind a block. It was the child who first stepped up.

"Thank you for volunteering," John said.

"My dad was fighting in an army," the kid said sadly, "and he died."

"You will get revenge," John promised. "Take it out on the ogres."

The child looked at him.

"I am not here for revenge," he said, "I just don't want anyone else to die."

This statement took John aback. He had always fought for survival. But mainly what people were inspired by in war was their own satisfaction or revenge. What this child proposed was a new way to fight—to save lives.

"Well, I can't promise people won't die," John said, "But by fighting, you do prevent death. It's very complicated, but it's true."

The child nodded.

"John!" Paul whispered behind a block behind him. John looked around his defense and saw ogres slowly coming onto the bridge. It wasn't a large amount, but it was more than seventy. *Not too shabby,* John thought. The militia loaded their weapons quietly. The child gripped his knife. The ogres got closer. John pulled his shield closer to himself. The ogres stopped.

"*I smell a human,*" one said.

"*So do I,*" another said.

"*There's fresh meat here!*" the first one said, starting to run. John held his sword steady. An ogre ran past him. When he saw the second, he leapt at it, yelling. He knocked it to the ground. John shoved his sword into its chest and stood up. Paul sliced the first one with his ax. He ran up to John to stand side by side.

The militia stood up and those with guns (a considerable few) shot their bullets at them. John charged with Lino, Paul and Joan at his heels. An ogre reached for his horn, but Paul leapt up and blasted the ogre apart with his lightning.

Joan removed her two samurai swords and took the right side of the lines. Joan spun in the air like a propeller and cut ten ogres before she hit the ground.

Lino completed a sort of doggy-paddle in the air. He leapt from one head to another, slicing them with his long claws.

Paul did his classic lightning-and-slash attack that killed many. Between the five of them and the militia, the army was cleared out within minutes and none of the ogres we able to signal to other ogres that they were under attack. None escaped.

"That's strange," John breathed to Paul, "why didn't the ogres shields deflect the bullets like magicians' shields?"

"I think those shields are strong, rare and expensive," Paul panted, "I saw some at the lab. I think Zyno was creating them."

"So that's why the ogres attacked the lab so many times," John said, "they wanted to create more."

"It is an advantage," Paul agreed. "That's what the US is specialized in, right? Guns?"

"I guess," Joan said, wiping her swords off of blood. "I just hope these ogres come in small numbers like these did. It would be quite easier."

They all nodded. They headed back to the blocks. The militia was already reloading.

"Anyone wounded?" John asked.

"I have a cut, but it isn't that bad," one man said, holding his arm.

"That's the spirit," Paul said. "Keep it up, guys!"

"I know they're scary," Joan said, "But just ignore looks and just shoot them."

John grinned. Joan came back to him.

"That's the way to talk to them," John said. Then, quite suddenly, more ogres came charging onto the bridge. Joan stepped away. "You're right Joan. The war for the world has begun."

23.) Reinforcements

Paul spun his ax and stretched away from a few dozen arrows that were fired at them. Paul squeezed his handle and zapped a few ogres into the water. Lino leapt over him to cover his right as he fired yet another bit of lightning at his opponent.

"How many do you think are there?" John shouted above the ogre's snarls.

"Four hundred left!" Paul estimated. "Watch your back!"

John turned, but the child John had met stabbed it with his knife.

"Thanks, kid!" John shouted, pushing the child back as ten approached them.

"Right side!" Joan said leaping to John's aid.

"I can take it, defend the others!" John ordered. Joan obeyed after she killed the one on his right. John concentrated. That was two he didn't see. Was he getting slow?

"Look out!" Lino shouted to a civilian as an ogre shot an arrow at them. Lino intercepted the arrow with his teeth.

"They're running out of bullets!" Joan shouted at the two generals.

"How many now, Paul?" John asked again.

"Four hundred or four twenty," He answered dodging a blade. "They're actually gaining numbers! Their net numbers are—"

"Pull to the back!" John commanded.

They all obeyed in a hurry as everyone sprinted to the end of the bridge.

"Further!" John shouted.

The people moved to beyond the houses. Paul held his stomach and Lino panted hard. Joan leaned on her swords. John sheathed his sword and peeked around the corner. The ogres had covered the bridge.

"Everyone, take a breather," John said. He nodded at Joan, "Have some water at then I'll give out some melee weapons."

Joan summoned a few dozen water bottles and handed them out. They started to whisper nervously at each other, some saying goodbye to others. John bent down to the small child.

"Hey, kid, what's your name?" John asked him.

"Jerry," the kid responded quietly.

"Well, Jerry," John said, "I have a brother by that name. He is quite a warrior. You actually remind me of him somewhat."

The child just nodded.

"You're a very good soldier," John said, "I hope you remain with us after this battle."

"I will," the kid said in a high voice.

John stood up and said, "Everyone had a good rest?"

Everyone nodded reluctantly. John stretched out his hand and concentrated on a pile of swords. Swords appeared on the ground.

"Everyone grab one and we'll go quietly forward to attack them," John said, "with any luck we'll beat most of them before they notice we're there."

They snuck forward, close to the ground, weapons at the ready. John saw the nearest ogre and he had his back turned. He went up to it and stabbed it in the back. Paul snuck around and cut off an ogre's head.

"*A HUMAN!*" an ogre shouted as it hastily fumbled with its horn. John showed his face and yelled for everyone to charge forward. As the ogre brought the horn to its lips, John grabbed it with his magic and thrust it in the water. He pulled his shield forward, sword held high.

"YAH!" Joan said from behind. John turned and saw she was standing, with ease, on Lino's back as if riding on a skateboard. She jumped high into the air when they got close to the orbs and did a double flip. She kicked into a split as she knocked two ogres aside. She landed on another ogre. She thrust her swords into the ogre and somersaulted forward, striking another in the stomach. Four strikes in one jump.

"Save the moves for the ballet!" John shouted at her as he kicked an ogre into the water.

"It worked, didn't it?" Lino said, showing a toothy grin that was dipped with blood. John grimaced. He turned towards his militia. Almost none of them were trained with weapons as Paul, John, and the rest were. The ogres were also stronger, so they were able to disarm the militia without really trying.

The ogres were beginning to win. Paul looked away for a moment to concentrate on an ogre who was able to avoid his lightning. When he turned back, almost the entire militia had been killed. Only his brother, Joan, Victor, Lino and three other members were alive.

"Retreat!" Paul called out. John hadn't been concentrating on the militia. Everyone turned and ran off the bridge. An ogre growled in victory. John caught up to his brother.

"Thanks, bro," John said, panting, "I didn't see what was happening."

"No problem," Paul said, "the problem is now we don't have any militia left."

"Don't say that," John said fiercely. "We can win. Remember that battle against the Thogeens three years ago? Our first battle. Two hundred versus forty. We won, didn't we?"

"Yeah, you bring that up every time something goes wrong, and it never doesn't help," Paul said, shaking his head.

"Nonetheless," Lino said, "we still have a problem. The ogres are lining up and are about to attack us."

John looked back and saw the Lino wasn't lying. The two hundred or so ogres were lining up forming a box and were starting to march towards them. John looked at his militia. Jerry was still alive, plus the first man Paul got and another teenager John didn't recognize.

"Draw your swords everyone," John said.

"Are you CRAZY?!" Paul said, eyes widening.

"Line up in a line," John said, ignoring his brother.

"Come on," Lino said, standing up. "Listen, I know you're brave ..."

"We'll charge at them to stop them from escaping the trap they got themselves in," John said. "If they escape, the world is in jeopardy."

"I'm backing you 100 percent," Joan said standing next to him. Everyone lined up in a single line.

"Let's go," John said, his mouth dry. He turned and ran at the opponent. The line behind him followed in a charge. The ogres stopped in amazement. John reached the ogres and sliced his way through many. The wings of the box charged forward and met to surround John and the others.

"Form a circle!" John said, getting shoulder-to-shoulder with his brother and Joan. The ogres pointed their spears inward so that the militia had inches to move about. The row behind them drew arrows and pulled on the string.

There was absolute silence.

A shot arrow could be heard.

John felt the whisper of it zoom past his left ear. The arrow struck an ogre right next to John. The arrow was gold. Just then, from on top the roofs of the houses came a flash of red and many gold arrows shot out. They struck ogres right between the eyes. John marveled at the accuracy of these shots. They seemed to be better shots then any Thog hoped to accomplish, which Thogs were renowned for their archery.

The ogres tried to see where the shots were coming from, but looked confused and scared. Thinking the attack came from the militia, some ogres charged at John and the others. Paul got in front of his brother and shot lightning to protect his brother. Ten ogres fell from the lightning. More gold glints came flying past the militia by millimeters. The ogres, not sure where the shots were coming from, and having no luck with the militia, retreated. They left the bridge screaming. John and Paul turned to the rooftops. Many men, dressed in red cloaks jumped down from them. They all reached the bridge when they stopped, save three.

"It seems like the Red Purloiners might fulfill their duties after all," One of the three said.

"Quite a greeting," Paul said, raising an eyebrow, "who are you?"

"We are the Red Purloiners," Another repeated, "We were formed two and half hundred years ago by the British army. We were supposed to come when called by Britain to support the British in the fighting of the 'Revolutionary War'. We were sent behind the colonies to attack the rear and take the thirteen by surprise. However, the British never called us. For two hundred years, we have been waiting, generation by generation, for the British to call for help when fighting in America. We are the ancestors of the greatest warriors in the world."

"Why are you staying hidden?" John said, while Paul was still trying to comprehend this. "Why not reveal this to the British?"

"The British sent us here in exile," the Purloiner said. "We were magicians, or what the old ones called warlocks. We were banished and would only be used in battle. That was our punishment instead of being burned. Each generation is trained to fight by the generation before them."

"Why were you using arrows instead of bullets?" Lino asked.

"We ran out of bullets during training, so we used arrows instead," another Purloiner said. "And now that the world is gaining allegiance to fight this terror in America, the British are calling all troops to fight, and that means us too."

"Well, thank you for helping then," John said. "We seem to have a lot of luck with this war."

"Well," a Purloiner said, "we have helped others before, helping those who are being attacked by thieves and things like that. We are referred to many times as the Angel Army."

"How many people do you have?" John asked.

"Five hundred," another Purloiner said. "All trained with the bow and sword. We are now here to serve."

The Purloiners knelt down on one knee.

"Thank you," Paul breathed, overwhelmed. "Line up on the bridge. The ogres will be back."

The Purloiners positioned themselves behind blocks and boulders pointing their bows outward.

"As for the militia," John said, "stay back. Let's see how good these Purloiners are."

John had a lot of confidence in the Purloiners, but the ogre number came coming back to haunt him: Five *billion*. That is still a large amount, John thought.

A horn could be heard closer than ever to the bridge. John clenched his sword and it started to vibrate as if it were dying to be used in the battle. The Red Purloiners armed their weapons and pointed them at the edge of the bridge.

Ogres came charging out of the bushes in an uncomprehending number. The Purloiners shot their gold arrows and killed the first set instantaneously. The ogres tried their best to put their shields up in time, but most arrows were too fast to see. John watched in awe the Purloiners slaughter the ogres with their arrows, either firing one, two or even three at a time. The ogres fired back, growling in frustration. The Purloiners' great eyes saw them coming and avoided them. John saw some magic fly from the arrows and strike other ogres.

In short, ogres were not doing so well. The ogres that could even get to the front lines were able to swipe their sword once before it was killed. No Purloiners were killed yet. Unable to make more progress, they retreated. John walked up to one of the leaders.

"Great job, I—"

But John was interrupted by a rush of wings above. They looked up and saw red and black dragons descending upon them.

"I thought we killed them all!" Joan said in surprise.

"Obviously not," John said, readying his shield. "Aim for the eyes!"

The Purloiners raised their weapons and fired arrows at the dragons. Some hit the eyes, but the attack didn't stop the dragons. The dragons took a breath and blew fire at the bridge. The Purloiners ducked for cover, but many were unlucky. They turned their weapons and fired at the dragons' scales, but the arrows simply bounced off them.

"Keep at the eyes!" John shouted, throwing his sword at a dragon. "We can stop them that way!"

"It's not working!" one soldier called, shooting wildly at the dragons, "They're flying blindly!"

John cursed in despair. He grabbed his sword and threw it at another swooping dragon. It hit it square in the head and the dragon fell into the water.

That made three dragons.

Quite suddenly, just when everyone else was giving up, there was another zoom from above. All, including the dragons, looked up to see what it was. Two hundred or so jets came screaming across the sky, heading straight for the dragons. All of them fired missiles into the air that screeched through the air.

"More reinforcements!" Lino shouted in triumph. Dragon after dragon fell victim to the incoming missiles. The force knocked them into the water. John leapt onto the knocked down one and sliced its head off. John looked up and saw a dragon about to blow fire at him. Just as it was about to blow fire, a missile came out of nowhere and struck it in the head, knocking it to the ground, dead.

The dragons turned in the air and shot towards the planes.

"There's nothing more we can do now," Paul said, looking at the aerial battle. "Our arrows can't shoot them down, so we must rely on the jets."

Paul just finished his sentence when the rumbling of the bridge meant a new arrival of animals. Mammoth after mammoth came onto the bridge.

"GET OFF THE BRIDGE!" John shouted, hurrying off the dragon corpse. "It will weigh too much!"

John was right. No sooner had they gotten off the bridge than the mammoth's weight crippled the bridge. It was no longer usable. Paul turned to his brother.

"We have to head for the next bridge over," Paul said. "I know you'll hate to hear this, but we should split up."

"We can cover more ground that way," Joan agreed. "What do you say?"

John was hesitant.

"I really don't like the sound of it," John said. "We are stronger together than separated."

"I don't like it either," Lino said. "We shouldn't separate the Purloiners anyway."

"Listen, Paul," John said, "our numbers won't hold. Get to a computer or phone far away and contact the right people. We need to join our armies together if we are going to win."

"Who should come with me?" Paul asked.

"Lino should give you enough protection," John said, grinning. "Joan and the Purloiners will stay to defend the other bridges. Good luck, Paul."

Paul turned to leave, but turned back at the sound of his name.

"You can have this," John said, removing his non-Phoenix sword. "It's the one I got when I had to fight the Thogeens. Use it well."

John grasped his brother's hand firmly. Paul, Lino, and Victor left. John sighed.

"Captain, we should leave," the little Jerry said.

"You're right, kid," John said. He whistled and his horse came trotting towards him. "Follow me, everyone."

John kicked his horse and it went off in a run. The Purloiners struggled to keep up.

The next bridge was several miles away. As they all approached it, they saw a mixed sight of good news and bad news. The bad news was the ogres were all over the bridge, covered with about 400 armed soldiers.

The good news was what was coming up the river bearing the magician flag.

24.) The Third and Fourth Day

A man sat in the shadows of a cell, looking down. The gate opened and he looked up.

"You are free, master," the came a voice from near the gate. The man stood and walked out of the shadows.

"You have done well, Will," the prisoner said. "You shall be rewarded. I have the machine ready. I take it you had no trouble locating the jet?"

"None," William said, limping into the cell. "I just had a little trouble with that Quaill …"

The prisoner laughed.

"Yes, he does tend to do that," he said. "But your arms will be replaced in time. You will make a very nice replacement for Zach."

William paused.

"What are you talking about?" he asked.

The prisoner came into the light. He was wearing a dark purple jumpsuit.

"Pending who succeeds in this war, Zach is no longer a member of our trio," Zyno whispered. "… which will soon be four."

Another man came out of the darkness.

"And what of Dan?" he said. "He will not merely walk over to our side."

"You know that our imprisonment was just so I could work on this chemical. It is complete. Dan will join us if he takes only one sip of this potion."

Zyno Wayne held up a glass beaker.

"*Shrinky* is finished also, then?" William said.

"As well as Roboblast," Zyno said. "But this newest machine is the greatest of all of them."

Zyno held up a syringe that had a blue liquid in it.

"Finally, the magic traits of a magician can be held," he said, "to be injected with magic—"

He looked at both of his apprentices.

"—Or sucked."

Magicians were leaping out of boats onto shore quickly. They were shooting fire and magic balls at the ogres who returned fire with arrows. There were seven magician ships in the water with hundreds on every ship.

John could look back and still see the aerial battle going on a few miles away.

All our armies are winning.

Purloiners shot arrows into the air wildly to strike down the ogres left and right. More ogres continued to swarm onto the bridge. The Purloiners lined up onto the bridge and shot arrow after arrow at the ogres.

"Leave the fighting for the Purloiners!" John shouted at the magicians. "Go seek shelter away from here! Hey, Joan, lead them somewhere safe! Away from here!"

Joan nodded and shouted orders to the magicians. The magicians obeyed without hesitation.

John sliced through many ogres without tiring. Purloiners stopped firing arrows and pulled out their swords. They were long, maybe four and a half feet, John estimated. The Purloiners must have been out of arrows.

"Aim for the necks!" John shouted over the charging cry. He turned to face the other side of the bridge to find more ogres. "I guess I better get used to infinite number of ogres; there's still billions left to go."

Paul picked up a phone at an abandoned house. He had checked out the White House's number on his computer. He just hoped he wouldn't get a secretary.

"This is the President's secretary speaking, if you would like to state a message for the President, leave it now," this was the answer Paul got.

"Ogres, Phoenix, Dragons, Orb, five billion," Paul said. There was a pause on the other end. "May I please speak with the president? I have important things to ask him."

There was some scuttling of some feet.

"There is probably some chain of command I have to go through first," Paul muttered to himself. But after a few minutes passed, Paul was convinced his message of urgency was well received and that he was about to speak to the most powerful man in America.

"Hello?" said a deep voice from the other end.

"Mr. President, I am the General of the Scarlet Phoenix Militia," Paul said, "I have information for you. But you must follow some orders."

"We'll see," said the stern tone of the President, "What information do you have for me?"

Paul took a deep breath.

"Our armies, coming from the south, are facing the ogres as we speak. We have the ogres stopped at the Gila River. To stop them completely, we plan to cut off their way around by blowing the bridges. If we do this, they are trapped. It will stop the rushing and give more time to organize. We need help from you. We need you to send planes to blow up the bridges. Is that all understood?"

"What do you want with my armies?" the President asked.

"Place them a little north of the Gila River," Paul said. "So you got all that?"

"Affirmative," the President said. "Armies will be at your disposal in a day's time. Thank you for your advice."

"Thank you for your soldiers," Paul replied. "You seem to trust me very easily."

"You sound like you know what you're talking about," the President sighed. "I, on the other hand, am a loss for words."

They each hung up. *That was easier than I thought*, Paul pondered, *it must just be the war scaring everybody and I sounded like I knew what I was doing.*

"What now?" Lino asked Paul, breaking into his thoughts.

"Well, I can check on each of the armies," Paul said. He turned on the computer again and accessed Flaminetore. He called the genies first.

"What's your positioning?" Paul asked the leading genie. The genies appeared to be on a ship.

"At your command in one day, General Quaill," he responded and signed off. Paul clicked the psychics next. They told Paul that they would also be there in a day.

"And lastly, the magicians," he said, calling them. His uncle answered.

"Two and a half days," Uncle Dan said. "Please don't call again, unless it's an emergency. I am busy."

"Nice to hear from you again, too," Paul muttered sarcastically, scowling. He hung up.

"Let's move to the next bridge," Lino suggested. "We need hold off these ogres at least until the Thogs come."

"You're right," Paul agreed, removing his ax. He left the house to find a horse standing in front of him. Paul approached it carefully.

"St-Storm?" Paul called incredulously. The horse neighed. It was pure white with a beautifully combed mane. "How'd you get here?"

"Who's this?" Lino asked.

"The horse that I was promised when I was born," Paul whispered. "I can recognize it anywhere … it's a perfect white."

The horse just stood there. Paul mounted it, no saddle.

"It must have been traded to this family," Lino said. "It's the only logical explanation."

Paul conjured up (with his genie magic) some reigns for the horse and attached it to it.

"Let's go," Paul said in a half whisper. The horse charged forward and leapt over the fence. Lino walked through the open gate.

"Nice," Lino said. "Let's just get there, ok?"

Paul grinned and kicked his legs hard.

John keeled over and vomited. He had never fought so hard for so long. The blood of many ogres was spread on every Purloiner's sword.

John stood up again and wiped his mouth. He charged ahead, swinging wildly. Ogres fell faster. Finally, the ogres stopped coming.

"Good," John said, and he collapsed. The Purloiners slowly went up to him and poured water on his face. John opened his eyes. "Blast the bridge and leave for the next one," he responded.

The Purloiners carried him off the bridge and settled themselves away from it. With their magic, they blew up the bridge.

"How many dead?" John asked weakly.

"Thirty-seven, sir," the Purloiner said. "Lost count on how many ogres, but I can check with the rest to determine the total."

"Thank you," John said, slowly rising to his feet. He leaned on his horse and mounted it. "I must see to the magicians. Continue onward."

John rode off as the Purloiners gathered again. He rode to what seemed like miles, barely keeping his head up. He saw Joan coming to him, but it seemed to confuse him what she said.

"We found a safe spot for all the magicians," she said, "about 900 in all. Your uncle is not amongst them; he must be on a longer route."

"Thanks," John said, taking some water that she offered him, "Nine hundred well help a little, but I am thankful nevertheless. Is there a captain?"

"No," Joan said, sighing, "None of them have leaders."

John looked up at the sky. The sun was high.

"What time do you think it is?" He asked.

"Noon," she said. "Does it matter?"

John didn't respond. It mattered to him a great deal. When was the second day going to end? It will take forever for his brother to get here.

"Come on," Joan broke into his thoughts, "let's meet these magicians. Besides, we all need rest."

John obliged and went with her. They went on for another few minutes before getting to an old, large building.

"It was the only structure big enough to hold everybody," Joan explained.

*   *

*

Paul found out about the building through much "telephone," but finally found out where everyone was staying. Lino and Paul came to the building, and Paul quickly dismounted. John greeted them, looking absolutely exhausted. There were dark rings under his blood shot eyes, his body was limp, and he had a deep cut on his arm he hadn't noticed.

"I found Storm in somebody's back yard," Paul explained. John didn't look surprised. They both walked in.

Paul took a deep breath.

"Air conditioning," Lino sighed contently.

"Yes," John responded. "We received contact from the Purloiners confirming two more bridges blown. What is the word on the armies?"

"The Thogs will get here quite soon; they were right behind us," Paul reasoned. "And the magicians and genies are two days behind. The humans from all around the world will also send their armies into deployment tomorrow—I am not sure their exact amount, but I know it's in the millions."

"Great," John said, forcing a smile. "Now get some sl—"

"You should talk—you're a wreck!" Lino said. "You need to sleep or you're really going to get hurt!"

"I can handle it for another few hours," Paul said. "Take a nap. That's an order."

John grimaced and walked up the stairs. Lino said he would like to speak to some of the men and Victor needed to recharge. Paul went up to Joan.

"Are you ok?" Paul asked her.

"I am great, thanks," she said to him kindly.

"Are you sure?" Paul said nervously. "I mean, not just physically, but …"

"You mean the 'last mage' thing?" Joan said sadly. "There will be a time to mourn later. You and I both know that tens of millions of lives will be lost in these final battles for earth. If we mourn for each one, we will lose. We cannot concentrate on death alone."

"You are strong in that way," Paul whispered. "But that wasn't exactly what I meant. I meant about you and my brother."

She looked at him hard as though he interrupted her.

"He was hurt very badly when you died," Paul continued. "You guys must talk to each other. The thought that both of you might come out alive is … well …"

"I understand," Joan said, nodding. "I hope sincerely that we both do. For I am confident that John knows—"

"Are you positive?" Paul questioned her, "because he almost lost it again."

Joan turned to him.

"Again?" she asked him.

"Yes, but I will leave explaining it to him," Paul answered. " Please talk to him. He cares about you. I know you care for him."

"Listen, Paul," Joan said a little more sternly. "I know you are trying to help, but please, this is between the two of us. We'll just hope we both come out of it alright."

Paul knew that the conversation was closed. He nodded to her and walked away. He didn't know what to do now. He had two days of doing nothing but waiting. He walked amongst the troops (all of whom now had donned their uniforms) and talked to them. As it turned out, most of them had been spread around the globe, and then rendezvoused to Locombony because of the message of the *Ring* council. It wasn't until the fortieth person or so that Paul saw an old friend.

"Hybrid!" Paul said.

"Hey, man," the tall, dark man replied. They shook hands. "Your brother sent me here. Did you have a smooth journey up to this great country?"

"By smooth, you mean tortured, kidnapped, nearly killed from heat exhaustion, and various other types of graceful attributes, then yes, a splendid journey!" Paul spat in a serious tone.

"Don't forget starving to death," Hybrid replied. He began to explain to Paul what had happened to him.

As they were conversing about the tower, John approached, looking much better.

"Good to see you again," John said to Hybrid. He beckoned Paul aside. "Paul, I woke up to a phone call. The Purloiners wiped out every bridge in their sight. They are transporting back here as soon as they get in range."

"How did they go across the state so fast?" Paul whispered urgently.

"Magic," John responded simply. "They have to get into their transportation range, though. They can't go far on that alone. That's why the magicians traveled by boat."

"That was my next question," Paul said. John pointed to his head. "Ah, yes, mind-reader."

"But anyway, contact the government to see—"

"—If they can blow the bridges, already done," Paul interrupted. "So that's all the bridges. The ogres trapped themselves in."

"Now," John said, sitting, "the plans."

They worked for hours, using a new map of the South. They used little plastic toys to represent armies.

"… No, no, no, if the genies attack with the psychics, who would back up the ones who attack northward?" John said. Lino walked up.

"Nice," he said, examining the toys, "who is Superman?"

"It's just a representation," John said impatiently.

"So, does that mean we don't have to dress up in tutus?" Lino said, pointing to a ballerina.

"No," Paul said. "If you don't want to participate, you can leave."

"Ok, fine," Lino joked, walking away. He added in an undertone just loud enough to hear, "Don't invite me to your tea party."

Paul rose halfway. John leaned on his fist so that he didn't let out a laugh.

"Anyway, so if we move Super—I mean, the Thogs …."

"Ah, Paul, I think I knew what Lino was getting at," John said.

"He was making fun of us?" Paul asked.

"Paul, he was saying we are working too hard," John sighed, "and he's right. I think we need to relax a bit."

"Yeah, right," Paul said. "Ok, sure, what do you want to do?"

John lay on his back.

"How about dreaming?" John suggested and he quickly fell asleep. Paul sighed, sat down next to him, and fell asleep on the hard, cold floor as well.

Paul and John woke up at the same time at the sound of rumbling feet. They lifted their heads a fraction to see the magicians lining shoulder to shoulder. To the left in the corner was the Red Purloiners leaning on the wall out of sight.

Joan was walking up and down the isles, as if inspecting them. She noticed they were awake and walked over to them.

"Good evening, generals," Joan said to them. "The Thog general is arriving in a few minutes."

"Maurice!" John said, leaping to his feet. Paul got up, as well, and looked at Joan.

"How'd you know?" he asked her.

"Our spies," explained Joan, "told us not too long ago. The rest of the mythical creatures are with the psychics."

"How many?" Paul said, stretching.

"Psychics, about 5,000," Joan answered, "The mythical creatures hold at least that many and the Thogs …"

"One million," Paul answered for her.

"So …" John started to say.

"So our 'headquarters'," Joan looked around in disgust, "is not big enough for that many people. I am going to try and conjure up a basement large enough to hold 50 million men. That will be enough for the mythical creatures, psychics, and maybe Thogs. After that, I can make a connection to a new one that holds equal amount so to hold the magicians, genies and the militias created around here will stay there."

"You'll need a lot of magic for that," Paul pointed out.

"No kidding," Joan said, grinning, "That's why I assembled the magicians to help me. You can, too."

"I will," John said. He glanced at Paul's watch. It said 11:45. "How long will this take? I have never conjured that much power before."

Paul gave him a skeptical look but Joan said, "I don't know, I haven't either."

John went over to the middle of the huge room and opened his hand at the ground. He focused intently on the word "Basement" and a trapdoor appeared right below his feet. He opened it and he found a small, dark basement. Magicians slowly started to jump down to help. When Joan and a good number came down, the magicians started to concentrate their powers on the basement. The basement suddenly transformed into a large dungeon that could hold thousands.

"Then we'll just have to create more rooms," Joan said, as the magicians started panting. "At least a hundred more, I am guessing."

After they had finished, Paul's watch said 3:10 a.m. They walked outside the building to see all the Thogs spread out everywhere outside with some confused looking psychics amongst them. The Thog captain stood at the front, looking fierce. Paul and John went up and greeted him.

"Maurice, my friend," John began, but Maurice interrupted him.

"The armies are at your command, general," Maurice said, bowing. "All one million 'ready. We met up with almost an equal amount of ogres at the border but we fought through without many injuries. Don't worry, we are all prepared."

"Maurice!" Paul said sternly. "You're a friend and a general, you don't have to talk as if we are in charge."

"It's the war," John explained to Paul, grinning, "'Gets his face on."

Paul nodded.

"Head inside, we're almost ready," John said to Maurice.

"For what?" Maurice asked as the army slowly started to head into the building.

"Tomorrow we plan to attack the left flank of the formation containing a billion ogres, distracting them from the southern wing," Paul answered at once. "The rest of the magicians will attack then, wiping out a good portion. Then the rest of the world will attack straight on in a frontal assault at their strongest point. With luck, we'll back them up."

"Right," Maurice said. "We'll be ready."

"Hey Maurice," John said as Maurice started to head in. "When did you learn to speak perfect English? It's very good."

"The psychics taught me on the way," the Thog said, pointing at the psychics. "The mythical creatures, before I forget, have been reinforced a bit. Half way through Mexico, I saw some attacking The Coliseum. They agreed to join us. They'll stay out and guard us if that is alright with you."

"No problem," Paul said. "We need to get some sleep now."

Paul looked up at his watch. It read 4:48 a.m.. He rolled over. He knew he needed his sleep for the battle ahead. But up against the windowsill, on the ledge looking out, was his brother. Without looking at Paul, he noticed he was awake.

"If you're hungry, the Thogs have prepared some food for us to eat when we get up," John said, pointing behind himself. Paul looked at the bag and then back up at John.

"This seems oddly familiar," Paul said, staring at John.

"Thog world, three years ago, before our first war?" John reminded Paul.

"And you suspected Zyno," Paul said, recalling what happened.

"And I was right," John said sighing.

"Well, what's going on now?"

"Its just something that d-someone told me recently," John whispered, catching himself before he said "dad". "That I will always have my magic, always. But it seems … I don't know, that something's out of place about that statement; about this war actually."

"What is it?" Paul asked.

"Well," John said, without a change of expression, "Zach told the Kraskull and me that he wished to destroy all those who would fight against him and save those who wouldn't. He wanted to make himself the supreme power to himself, forcing all others to follow."

"What's surprising about that?" Paul said.

"Well, think about it," John said, "Where does Zyno fit into all this?"

Paul chewed on it for a moment.

"The Kraskull said Zach would release him, that this whole war was just a diversion," Paul said finally.

"Yes, but something's not right about it," John said impatiently. "Don't you see it? Zach has put a lot in this war. You told me about the chip in his skull. If he dies, the whole plan goes under. This is just too much for a diversion. This is treason against his master.

"He probably planned the attack on the world and gave the blue print to Zyno. Zyno approved it and helped catch the genies to turn them into the ogres. Zach had claimed that his plan was a mere diversion, but he was lying. After a bit, Zach had his army, and the deceptive motive of attempting to get Zyno out of jail. What he really wanted was absolute power."

"But John," Paul countered, "there's something's wrong with *your* plan. Zach had his army; why did he wait for Zyno to step aside? What was it that made him stay?"

"There must have been some—," John started, but then stopped. "Of course! The technology for the war!"

"Which technology?" Paul asked.

"Well, first off," John said, counting on his fingers, "the shields that make bullets bounce off, the holograms for the tower, the contacts for the armies …"

"Very good theory, but I have answers for all that," Paul said triumphantly. "The magic is cast on the shields as an enchantment, the holograms were easy to find in the lab, and you only need a cell phone for the contacts."

This finally stumped John.

"It's just a feeling, that's all," John said, "that we're missing something crucial and it has to do with magic and this war. There are things surrounding this war we have no control over and that I fear might come to pass."

John lifted up his nearly shoulder-length hair and revealed a long scar on his face.

"I was right about the maze, wasn't I?" John said, and then he revealed his ears as well. "Well, I know magic is involved here, but one much stronger, a more powerful force."

"There's nothing more powerful than magic," Paul said firmly. John grinned.

"Knowledge and skill can get you only so far," John said. "Let's get some sleep. We'll need it."

They woke at noon. There was a large, dark black storm raging on outside.

"It will give us more cover," John responded to the psychics when they asked why he was looking jubilant. "Surprise is a helpful ally I have learned."

"The bridges are complete," Joan announced to the three generals and the tiger. "Let us go…where are we going?"

Paul looked at the map.

"It is an offshoot valley from a large splitting land called the 'Grand Canyon'," He answered, "don't ask. These Americans come up with the weirdest names. Don't get me started on the money."

John coughed to cover his chuckle, but Joan ignored him.

"Either way, the main Canyon is located at the northern tip of Arizona…we have quite a journey in front of us. The enemy, so our spies say, is not prepared in the least. They have hundreds in the valley, around it, on the ledges, pretty much everywhere but they're in their own camps, not as one force. They are sleeping, eating or arguing."

"I didn't think they could argue," Lino said, "let alone talk. It mostly sounds like a forced effort of grunts."

"Next," Joan said loudly as John and Paul had to turn away, "we should attack the ones at the highest point so we control the valley."

"Right," John said with a straight face. "The army should be at our disposal if we take the top. They only have about a thousand times our amount."

"Can we just go?" Maurice suggested as Paul, John and Lino burst out in laughter.

"Good plan," Joan said crossly. "Lead the way, Captain."

She stared hard at John with a look that he read as a *can-we-be-serious-for-a-second-please* look. John straightened up and called over his militia. The Purloiners followed, and then the magicians, followed by the Thogs.

"Too bad we don't have gliders," John said. "It might have been helpful to attack from the air."

"We have dragons," Paul reminded him.

"Yes, I suppose," John sighed, looking disappointed.

They came to many bridges that looked like they were set up the night before. They all walked across cautiously. John looked back and saw that the Thogs still hadn't fully immerged from the building yet.

"I guess there was more than I thought," John told Paul as more and more came out.

It was a long way to the valley. When they finally got to a torn sign signaling the canyon was a mile away, the armies spread out to form a line.

"I just hope there are enough arrows for everyone," John told Joan.

"I made sure of it," she responded with an encouraging smile. She pulled him aside as the armies passed them.

"What?" John asked quizzically as he saw that she waited to be out of earshot.

"I just wanted to say goodbye if this is our final battle together," Joan said and kissed him. John looked impatiently at her.

"You didn't have to pull me aside for that," He said.

"I know, but …"

"And also, there was a prophecy promising I would see my brother on the eighth day of the orb's destruction and the Phoenix gave you life again. I would doubt that it would give you life for one battle."

Joan pondered the ideas.

"Don't you think I would have considered all this?" John asked her.

She didn't answer.

"Come on, we need to be there for the horn charge," John said, "You're leading the assault, didn't you know?"

John handed her a large horn. They ran up ahead of the army. The army had halted in the large crevice made by the boulders around them. Peering out, they saw, not only countless ogres, but also Thogeens, dragons, goblins, and other terrible creatures. The soldiers were spread out through out the valley, on every level of the canyon, and many were patrolling the area above.

John removed his sword and readied his shield once again, preparing for the attack. The plan was to fight as long as possible and then retreat. It wasn't a very strong plan, nor did he hope for it to work, but this was merely to cripple one of Zach's major flanks. It would be this area that the rest of the world would focus on; therefore, it made sense that John's soldiers soften the attack for them.

The storm was still going on up above. Joan stood upon a rock and, just as lightning lit up the sky, she blew on the horn which echoed across the land. John stood up and raised his shield and sword above his head. The army responded with a shout of battle. Hundreds of thousands of arrows shot into the air right at the opponents, which the enemy gladly returned, with millions of black arrows. Thogs fell left and right in agony as they were struck down. Dragons charged down at the enemy, blowing fire and breathing smoke. The Thogeens suited up with their armor and removed their five-foot swords.

"Fire at them!" John shouted at the Purloiners who had assumed the first rank. "Take them down now!"

Regardless of how swift the Purloiners were, they could not reload fast enough for the charging Thogeens. They swung back their cloaks and removed their swords. All started twirling fast, stopping the approaching Thogeens.

At this moment, all one billion of Zach's north flank started moving for battle. John had never seen so many in one place. Ogres swarmed up the Grande Canyon (which nobody had the time to view properly), and all around the evil creatures started to wake up and fight. Thogeens, who were much stronger than the Thogs, shot their arrows straight at the attackers.

John lined those without arrows into the front to attack the other armies. As he did, the ogres lined up as well. The psychics and magicians shot magic at the ogres as they darted forward.

"Let's move, guys!" John shouted at Lino, Paul, and Joan. They had stayed behind until John shouted for them. Apparently they were lost in shock at the number of the enemy.

John struck the first line with his sword twirling so fast the gold shine was a blur. He slashed 10, 50, 100 and then he lost count. As before, the army could not stop the Phoenix sword. Many shot arrow after arrow at him, but the combination of skill, magic and the Phoenix power helped him slice each arrow into twigs.

Paul twisted hard on the handle of his ax and thought of his loyalty going so far as to fight a billion ogres. Lightning shot out of his ax like the legs of spiders. The lightning avoided the psychics and magicians, but snaked through to hit the ogres and Thogeens. With one blast he killed at least 50.

Lino had been training all the time he had off. He leapt high and backhanded two ogres. The strike was so strong it forced them out into the canyon. As he landed, he donkey-kicked two more onto the ground. Lino twisted and sliced them with his claws. He roared loud and jumped at a Thogeen's throat. The Thogeen couldn't stop him in time.

Joan spun her duel swords so fast it looked like she grew propellers on her arms. She ran back and forth, killing as many as she could see. Some goblins tried to slide through the swords, but were fatally unsuccessful. Joan killed 100 in a matter of minutes.

Thogs shot arrows high into the air, knocking off ogres, goblins or anything they hit. The magicians shot magic forward and over their shoulders behind them to hit anything nearby.

Friendly fire casualties were huge. Magicians couldn't see where there shots were going and Joan was so fast that if anyone got in her way, they would have been killed. Paul's ax was of such high technology that it could differentiate between good and bad. The lightning also worked as a barrier against the arrows shot at them.

The fighting continued into the night. The armies started falling by the thousands on both sides. The Thogeens were falling off the cliff, trying to avoid the lightning. Everyone was tired, weak, and injured in some way. The sun had just set. John could barely lift his sword up. He cut another ogre's head off. He finally couldn't take it. He took the horn from around his chest and gave it a good, loud blow with the rest of his breath. John hurried down the hill as the ogres gave a victorious roar that rang out everywhere. Most of the dragons had been defeated.

John hurried his troops to get away from the ogres. The last thing he wanted was for the ogres to find their headquarters. They crossed the bridge in a hurry. The line seemed to go a bit faster than last time, John found to his sadness.

They clamored into the building. Paul threw open the trap door and all the Thogs and psychics tumbled in. The magicians stayed on the higher levels as a guard.

"I call all generals and top officers to the second floor for a meeting!" John shouted over the rumbling of feet. Maurice, Paul, a Purloiner, and a psychic and magician representative followed John up the stairs. "Lino and Joan, you may come as witnesses."

"Witnesses, that's all we are?" Lino muttered, but barely anyone heard him. They were all half asleep and could almost not get up the stairs. Nobody cared about this meeting, nor about the war—they did not care about anything except that they needed sleep. John conjured up a table and chairs with difficulty.

"Have a seat," John said after half of them had sat down. "I am not going to deny it, we are all tired."

"Amen!" Lino said.

"However," John said, and they gave him long faces, "we must take a count of our casualties. This is most important."

"Can't they all get some rest first?" the Purloiner said, "They are tired and deserve rest. We asked the impossible of them."

"True enough," John said. "Five hours and then roll call. We must be ready to fight again."

"We lost most of the dragons and dinosaurs in that last battle. It really cut us back," Maurice said. "And a great portion of my Thogs we killed today. In fact, if it weren't for Paul's ax here, we would have all been killed. It was very fortunate."

"Our morale is low, sir," the magician said. "Our men are wondering when we will be backed by these ghouls you promised us. And what happened to the other magicians under Daniel, huh? When are we to be backed then? And the genies, the other psychics, and all the other armies that were to be reunited with us? We are not happy with this setup, sir."

John stood up.

"Sit down," Paul said calmly, and then he turned to the magician. "Daniel is our uncle. He has never failed us yet. The ghouls? They are fighting the other ghosts on Zach's side. Their presence will be known soon, for the better or the worse. The genies, psychics, other mythical creatures and the humans will all be here tomorrow. Why do you doubt us? Do you think we don't know what we're doing?"

"Well, you are children ..."

It was Maurice who rose first. He pulled a dagger out of his sheath and leapt across the table at the magician, all sleepiness lost. He pushed the magician onto the ground and put the knife at his throat.

"THEY ARE OUR LEADERS UNTIL DANIEL COMES!" Maurice shouted at him. "DON'T YOU DARE CALL THEM CHILDREN! THEY FOUGHT IN MORE BATTLES THEN YOU COULD HOPE TO DO IN YOUR LIFETIME! YOU DESERVE—"

"That's enough!" John said loudly. Without realizing it, he had removed his own sword. "If anyone fights against their friend from now on, they shall be judged with this sword! Nobody challenges the general's decisions and nobody fights with each other again, UNDERSTOOD?"

Maurice glared at the magician, who at this point looked horrified. Maurice got off of him.

"Six hours," Paul said, "and then we'll meet here again. No use denying the enviable, as the general said."

  *   *   *

John forced his body up after the six hours were up. He counted all of his militia and saw that only one was left from the original 40. Nobody had to guess who.

"I am really tired," the little Jerry said.

"We all are, but we must count how many have been killed," John said. He checked in with the other generals within an hour.

"Three legions of 2,000 each," Maurice said.

"One hundred dead here," the psychic said.

"Another hundred for the magicians and 70 dragons and dinosaurs," the magician responded.

"Twenty, sir," the Purloiner said.

"Twenty?" John said in disbelief.

"And because of our magical abilities, we remember everyone we killed," the Purloiner said, "about 200 each, with our arrows recycled."

"And you have 400 men?" John said, writing this down.

"Yes, sir," the Purloiner said, walking away.

John looked out at the army. They looked bruised up and hurt from their last battle, but they seemed ready for the next battle ahead. John formed them up into perfect rows and marched outside the building. John and Paul grabbed their horses. They mounted and marched off, confident this time.

Little did they know that there was another large army sneaking behind them, unnoticed.

25.) The Massacre at Prescott

John led them on for at least six hours. The army behind him was tired, and he could sense it. The hot rays of the noon sun beat down on them and he couldn't yet see the canyon. John was lucky to have so many talented magicians amongst them – a few thousand of them were able to conjure up water sacks for each of the soldiers.

Even better, a few of the magicians conjured up a black cloud over the army for shade. It certainly helped.

Even with all of this, however, the conditions were less than ideal. The dirt was blistering in temperature, the air was quite dry (John's lips had cracked multiple times), and the open landscape and soaring earth-made structures seemed to mock their inability to enjoy the beauty around them.

It had been decided by Paul and John that their strategy would be to make sure that the core of Zach's army stay weak. They, therefore, chose to strike at the same point that they had the day before. They figured that Zach was spreading his troops, and by now, the flank they had weakened yesterday had moved more north—hopefully where the world's armies would be waiting for them. It wasn't very reassuring to hear that they would be going up against a fresh set of one hundred million soldiers, so the generals kept it quiet.

At this point, they reached the canyon's battle field once again.

"Form straight lines," John commanded to Paul and Joan. They barely hastened to enforce it.

Finally, the canyon came into view. The ogres were set up in infinite stretching lines. Most had hundreds of arrows.

"Draw swords," John said. He had prepared a new tactic that he hoped to try. His plan was to run through the arrows to strike at close range.

"CHARGE!" Paul commanded. Hundreds of thousands of Thogs charged first. The ogres grinned and fired their arrows. Thogs, with their great eyesight, jumped away from each one. As they got closer, the ogres became more and more scared. The Thogs struck the first line of ogres while jumping through the air. They looked like they were ballerinas, just leaping everywhere, slicing with their tiny daggers.

"Purloiners, next!" Joan said. Their red cloaks left behind because of the distraction, the Purloiners swiftly drew their swords and sprinted ahead. They had attached another sword's handle to the original handle by magic so that it was now double bladed. They matched the Thog's power with their swiftness.

"Magicians, mythics, and psychics, now!" John said, raising his gold Phoenix sword. The dragons rose up and faced the enemy dragons once again. Both magicians and the psychics ran at the ogres.

The first line fell in less than two hours. They lost almost nearly a thousand warriors, plus the dragons, which the more experienced enemy dragons were killing.

John felt his body near the exhaustion stage as he sliced his two hundredth ogre. Lino was on the ground, bleeding from the side. Paul was beside him, bleeding from the nose and lip. John took out his horn and blew loud in retreat once again. John picked up Paul and Joan lifted Lino. They all ran back. By the time they got out of arrow range, the dragons had been stopped.

John was then surprised to see William's former army waiting for him at the rendezvous point. However, he was even more surprised to find what flag they were flying under: the magician's flag.

"We will explain later," the leader said. "But I have heard word that you are needed at the city of Prescott. The Americans are there."

"How can we trust you?" John said. "You fly under the magician flag, yet you were under Zach a few days ago."

"We were under William, not Zach," the general said, "We follow what higher orders say. General Jerry said to fight with him, and we follow orders."

"Good enough," Paul said, "Turn to head to Prescott!"

The armies moved northward.

"We will hold off Zach's army here," the commander reassured. "We will make sure they do not advance, but I am not promising a victory."

"Hold on, Paul," John warned, grabbing his brother's shoulder. "Is this smart? We promised Daniel that we'd be ready to back him up when he comes, which is soon."

"He is a general, he can take care of himself," Paul replied. "We need to back up the Americans; they seem to be more in need then he does."

"The Americans are strong too," John said, "Remember, they helped me stop the ogres long enough to help me get into the tower."

"I have a feeling," Paul said, pointing to his head.

"You're mocking me, aren't you?" John said, scowling, but he continued with him.

Prescott was a long way away. It was late into the night by the time they got there. There was a large lake at the bottom of a steep hill.

John saw it first.

"It's a gun," Paul whispered. It was lying on the ground. "Funny, you'd think there'd be ..."

He just saw the corpse on the ground. It had a bloody mark on its body, right above its chest.

"He's dead," Paul said. He found another corpse right next to it.

"I'll see what's on the lower part of the hill," John said. Paul realized what happened before John shouted: *we are too late.* "Paul! Look!"

Paul, with a heavy heart, followed slowly by Lino and Joan, looked over the hill. There were hundreds of thousands of dead bodies of people scattered around the hill. There were no survivors and the striped American flag lay without honor on the ground.

"It was a massacre," John said in shock. "Look, there are about 20 dead ogres. The armies must have crossed the river."

"The Northern flank of Zach is at Prescott," Paul pondered, looking at his map. "They must have crossed the Verde River last night. It could have taken the Americans completely by surprise."

"Not to mention the technology used on both sides," John panted. "Remember, this is practically Zyno's technology against the American technology, it's like comparing the eighteenth century with Rome."

Joan merely sighed.

"If the Northern flank pushed across the river," Lino said slowly, "would it be safe to assume that eastern Arizona has been crushed as well?"

"I think so," Paul calculated. "The ogres are pushing forward now. If they are not stopped, the body will start its final pushing as well. At least we know where it's heading—West, towards us … Zach knows we are his last major threat."

"We don't have enough warriors without the Americans," John sighed.

"This isn't all the Americans," Joan said quietly. "There must have been more."

"That's right," John said brightly. "Zach mentioned something about the world binding against him. This can't be the world's army."

"This must be a section of it," Paul said. "Nevertheless, our trap failed, they escaped."

"So, now what are we going to do?" Lino said pawing the dirt. "Now we are back in the same situation – our armies are split too far apart."

"Let's head back; this was a waste," Paul said. "I'll send a message for the Americans to support us to the West; it's obvious now that we must play defensive to win."

"Defense will never work," John said, kneeling down. "We must keep attacking him or else he will think he won."

They all walked back where their confused-looking army was sitting everywhere.

"These thousands seem like so much," Paul said, gazing over them all. "I just can't imagine a billion."

"We killed at least that many," Joan said, "With all of our arrows gone, we fired at least three billion arrows."

"That's amazing," John whistled, nodding. "That means we have four billion to go."

"Let's go."

They turned to leave when John stopped.

"Do you feel that?" John asked Joan and Paul.

"What?"

"The earth was just vibrating," John replied. He turned quickly, but saw nothing. Then, from all directions, the pounding came harder. John and Paul could tell that they had been completely surrounded by something they couldn't see yet. Then they both said the same thing out loud.

"Mammoths."

"Draw your weapons, hurry!" Joan shouted at them. The warriors already had their weapons out. "For a circle, large pikes outward!"

"Good thing she keeps a cool head in battle," Lino said, rolling his eyes at John.

They formed an enormous circle and held out long spears for the Mammoths to hit. The mammoths charged at them as soon as they came into view. It was more than Paul had ever seen before in one place. Hundreds, maybe even a thousand of them.

"Steady!" John said, but half of the word got caught in his throat from fear. He mounted his horse and Paul his. "Paul, do you remember our bet?"

"Not now," Paul called, a bit dazed, "I can't remember anything."

The mammoths were within a thousand yards.

"I already killed two," John reminded, gripping the Phoenix sword. "I need thirteen more to win. I am charging out at them. Will you follow me?"

Paul just shakily nodded his head. Lino did also.

"Let's go then," John said. "FOR PRESCOTT!"

He kicked Dreaded Musty's side. He lifted up his sword high into the air. Musty charged ahead, underneath a mammoth. With one mighty swing of his sword, the creature's leg came off and it fell. John hurried out of the way. He saw the first of the mammoths hit the circle of warriors. The pike went straight into the front of the mammoth. Cries from all around signaled that the armies were not about to surrender so easily.

Paul climbed slowly onto Storm and ran behind John. Lino left also, but couldn't do much. John pushed out his hand and (his hand and eyes turning red) pushed two mammoths to the ground.

"I got these!" Lino said, leaping at the fallen animals. He cut each of their throats.

"Watch your left side, Paul!" John called out to Paul, who was trying to push a mammoth away with his lightning. Paul turned quickly and barely moved his horse away before the tusk went into Paul. The blow knocked Paul off his horse. John gasped, but was forced to continue onward.

As four mammoths approached John at the same time, he stopped his horse. He readied his sword.

At least 200 arrows flew by John's horse and struck the mammoth all over. The mammoth staggered and fell to the ground. John looked back and saw that Joan had sent the attack, ordering the Purloiners.

Paul slowly got up and ate one of his healing pills. The wound healed and he climbed up onto his horse again. Paul circled around and threw his ax at a mammoth that was approaching the broken circle of armies. The ax went into the neck and shocked it, killing it. Paul could now see the fear in the armies' eyes now. With all the combined efforts, they had only killed about 50. They couldn't stop them all.

The mammoths stopped and reformed into four long lines. They were waiting for the opportunity to attack.

"The massacre at Prescott," Paul said sadly.

"Yes," John said, squeezing his handle. "But we will not go silently into the night. I am taking out as many as I can."

John ran ahead of all the armies to the 800 or so mammoths.

"King Phoenix," John called quietly as the mammoths stirred slightly. "I need you're help. Our armies can't beat Zach if you don't help us. We will be killed.

"So I ask of you this: will you fly? Will you help?"

A large blast erupted from John's sword. The white light flew through the darkness. John held it up high, but instead of the Scarlet Phoenix coming out, hundreds of other small, red phoenixes came out. They broke into song and then shot fireballs at the mammoths. It caught on the mammoth's hair and scorched them.

"That'll work," John said to his sword. "Can we keep them?"

The light died down. The phoenixes remained. John figured that meant, "yes".

John looked forward. The enraged mammoths took off again, intent on flattening the armies. The phoenixes continued with their aerial attacks, striking with their talons and magical fire.

John came within one hundred yards of the mammoths. He pulled his boots out of the stirrups of his horse, planting them on the seat of the saddle. Slowly, maintaining control of his reigns, he stood up on his horse.

"Musty," John commanded. "You know where to go when I'm off … stay safe!"

The mammoths came within striking distance. John leapt off his horse and brought his sword down upon a mammoth. It slid right through the skin. John grabbed onto the dying mammoth, ran across its back, and leapt onto the next mammoth. He, in turn, struck down upon this mammoth's skull. The result, however, John was not prepared for; the mammoth immediately tumbled, throwing John off of it.

As John was falling, he could see the trampling mammoths pass him. He knew he was about to die …

A shadow was thrown over John, and suddenly John could barely see what was happening around him. A person had thrown themselves over John, covering him from the mammoths. It took him a moment to realize it was Joan. She was near his body, casting a shield around them both. The mammoths tripped over the barrier.

John relaxed.

"Thank you," he whispered.

"No problem at all," Joan replied, glancing down at him.

Slowly, the rumbling stopped. Joan lowered her shield and gazed out. The phoenixes had stopped the mammoths before they reached the soldiers.

"What do we do know?" Paul asked Joan and John.

"We must go back to William's former army," Joan answered. "I didn't get enough information from them about why they're helping us."

"And we need to also back up our uncle, he should be here by now," John added. "We need to stay united, that will be our key to victory. It is almost midnight of the Fourth Day. Jerry will return in four days. We can hold them for that long."

"Hopefully," Lino said. "Can we at least rest here? We have been traveling day and night almost."

"I agree," Joan said. "Let's set up camp."

Paul checked his watch on his second shift. It read 4 a.m.. After two, almost everyone was asleep. They had to check role call, which took a long time. They were barely scraping a million warriors (not counting the phoenixes).

No sound was made anywhere. It was a large desert in all directions. Paul could barely keep his eyes open. The only way he was able to stay awake was to read his journal that he wrote in right after the maze. He was on the section of the last world (which was the most intense part, keeping him awake). He remembered every second of it in detail. He couldn't wait to get back there.

"We might not go back there, Paul," came John's voice from behind Paul, startling him. Paul realized that John read his mind again.

"Why not?" Paul said, "with the prophecy and all ..."

"As we have sadly learned," John responded, sitting up, "the prophecy can be misread many different ways. The prophecy didn't promise we'd make it out of here alive. Jerry could come back, but one of us might be killed."

"We can't die ..." Paul said. "We just can't ..."

"The truth is Paul," John sighed, "we can. I have a feeling that one of us, someone close, won't make it out of here alive."

"Who, John?" Paul asked him.

"Paul, I promised I would end up killing Zach," John said. "I don't know what that involves or what that means for the family. But I have promised I would. I vowed I would, some way or another. But Paul, if I can't, you must kill him. I might not be strong enough. I would be too busy saving the person I think will die."

"Who will die, John?" Paul repeated.

John looked him in the eyes and smiled sadly.

"Me."

26.) The Rise of the Castle

They left at daybreak. John walked rather rode, but his pace was just as fast. He had a grin on his face as if he was enjoying something big. Paul was surprised that John was even smiling, considering what they talked about last night. Paul ran up and matched his pace.

"Hey, um…John," Paul muttered to him. "Why are you so happy?"

John turned to him.

"I was given another vision last night," he replied.

"What did it say?"

"Well," John said, slowly, "We get all of our armies today, The Fifth Day. Uncle Dan is here, the countries have sent all of their armies, and we are all united now. It's almost over, this war."

"Does your vision say when?" Paul asked.

"Three days," John said, "Either Jerry is going to come and we're going to lose, or he's coming and we are going to win."

"Hopefully the latter," Paul said, nodding.

"No kidding," Lino cut in, coming up to them.

"We have a battle coming up, guys," John said. "This next battle where we're all united will be like nothing you have ever experienced. I have a feeling my first vision will come true."

Paul stopped. He tried to think back to John's first vision, but couldn't remember it. He looked back at Joan who was riding Musty. In the sunrise, Musty's hair looked reddish. Paul patted John's horse slightly and examined the army behind him. He was ready for back up right now.

John and his army moved forward for about six hours. When they came to the land where they had been only the day before, they saw that land had completely transformed.

"Oh my gosh…" Joan whispered, eyes as big as dinner plates. "What…happened?"

John just bowed his head. He had prepared himself for it.

The land, the little bits that had trees or a bit of grass had been burned so that the land looked even deader than before.

There was still fire in some of the trees. The houses were on fire, everywhere, fire.

"Is...this, this thing what you...imagined?" Lino gasped with difficulty.

"Yes," John said, turning to his brother. "I had imagined...the whole world like this...if we lose."

They all looked around saw nothing. Nothing living survived.

"Uncle Dan's here," John interrupted their thoughts, "I can feel him."

John moved forward and felt the ground. He picked up some sand and felt it in his hand. He stood up.

"He has an army...much larger than the Thogs," John said, turning around. "They are near...There!"

John pointed far away on a large hill where they saw his uncle on a strange colored horse. The wind was blowing in his face, kicking the hair out of his face. He looked as fierce as ever. John wiped away a tear at the look of his uncle; it reminded him of his father.

The Phoenix sword glowed amazingly for a second. But as quick as it did, it left.

Daniel's horse pranced down the hill with an army of millions slowly following.

"Order the salute," Joan said. Paul got off his horse, and mounted Lino. John mounted his horse and Joan mounted Storm. They all rode up to Daniel. He stopped short. Daniel looked around at the army behind them and then back at them. He got off his horse and walked up to them. They all dismounted and went to him as well. He looked at Paul and surprisingly hugged him.

"I...I...can't believe..." Daniel sputtered, "I set you... up...with... with Zach...What was I thinking? You..."

"Uncle Dan," Paul said. "It's ok."

"I am responsible for...you guys," Dan said. "It's my fault..."

"Uncle Dan," Paul stopped him, sounding quite serious. "I am going to say this once to you. We're not children anymore. We grew up...we grew up three years ago. No one has to look over us. We are men. We are strong. We are adults. We will win. We *will* win."

Daniel looked at John. He made a movement towards John, but John glared at him.

"Number Eleven," John said. "I met him."

Daniel stopped. He put one of his hands in his face.

"I'm so sorry," Daniel whispered really low. "I should have told you."

"Told us what?" Paul demanded.

"Paul, listen …"

"I told you, Uncle Dan," Paul said interrupting. "We are men. That includes me."

Dan quickly looked at John. John nodded.

"Paul," Daniel said, "Your father … he …"

"He's alive?!" Paul said, taking a step back.

"No, Paul," John whispered.

"Paul," Dan explained, "he was killed. Your father joined with Zach."

Paul closed his eyes.

"No …"

Joan and Lino looked away. Paul opened his eyes.

"It's over, then," Paul said.

"What?" John said.

"We're attacking them now," Paul said, removing his ax.

"Paul, we must wait for the countries," Dan said.

Paul turned and ran.

"No, this must end NOW!" he shouted. John turned and raised his hand, but it was another magic that hit him first. Paul fell to the ground. Joan walked over to him.

"Paul, listen to me, now," Joan said, rolling him over. "Carefully. Your father made a mistake. But I have no doubt in my mind that he wouldn't have wanted you to run off by yourself into war."

"I know what's best for me!" Paul yelled as he got up again.

"Shut up," Joan commanded. "Listen …"

She calmed herself.

"I know you are an adult, and I hope you find that I treat you as an equal," Joan lectured. "You have to be one of the most intelligent people I have ever met. But wisdom does not stem from intelligence. And it certainly does not stem from emotion, either. You need to understand the situation. When this war is over, I am sure John will explain everything to you. But for now, keep a cool head. Accept the facts. There will be time for discussion later. But now, time is a limited resource."

John wasn't sure if he liked Joan's response. But it certainly did calm down Paul, making him refocus.

Suddenly, there was a large roar from up ahead. Paul stopped in his tracks.

"Let's investigate," Lino whispered, but John stopped him. "No …" John said. "I will."

John moved by Paul. He crossed the long, narrow bridge. There were no more roars, but obviously a lot of commotion. He passed the large defenses the enemies were building and looked out across the land.

It was just like in his dream. There were large dragons stretched all over the sky, black clouds were all around, ogres, Thogeens, and goblins were everywhere—but the most fearsome of all things was in front.

A large, black castle had been risen up from the ground. The flag on top was the Kraskull's sign, obviously an honorable, last commemoration. But on top the colossus was a large throne in which Zach himself was reigning.

It was madness. Fire everywhere made it ten times worse. The evil around him made John shiver. He quickly left for the bridge.

As he turned to leave, a voice entered into his head.

"*You can't hide from me, Quaill,*" Zach's voice said. "*Soon you will all know the meaning of power!*"

John ran away to where Daniel and the others were standing.

"The power of Zach has stretched around the land," John announced. "I don't know what to do."

Someone else came into view. There were many behind him.

"We are the Brothers," The leader said. "We are the world's warriors."

The others looked behind him. Indeed, it was the world, in all its wonder.

At least one hundred million men were behind him, all with loaded guns and many swords. There were some tanks, helicopters, and other types of machinery. John did not recognize some of the amazing weapons, such as large tube-like man-cannons, vertical take-off and landing planes, vehicles that looked to be a cross between an off-road car and a tank, and various other mechanisms.

The Band of Brothers, stretching out as far as the eye could see, all looked confident. John and Paul turned to their uncle.

"Um…we're not exactly sure what to do with all these men…" John answered.

"So good luck," Paul added.

Daniel gazed upon all the armies.

"I don't even know what to do," Daniel said, letting out a breath. "We're all here. I never thought we'd do it. Genies, psychics, magicians, humans…we're all here."

"Don't forget Thogs and Purloiners," Lino added.

"And a mage," Joan said.

"I heard about the mages," Daniel consoled sadly, "I'm so sorry."

"Don't be," Joan said. "We'll come back again."

"I hope," John nodded.

"Well, we must prepare," Daniel said. He turned to the humans. "March your men behind mine. You will clear them out once we're done."

"Roger," The general said.

The armies moved away, which took many hours. The magicians formed into small boxes. The genies took the first line. There was only about a couple hundred. Next came the psychics and then the Thogs. Then the magicians (including the Purloiners). Lastly came the humans. However, after assuming the positions, they did not move. Daniel said they would attack immediately the next day.

John and Paul woke early the next day. John examined his shield and made sure it was ready for a lot of smashes. He checked Dreaded Musty. Daniel's horse was right next to his and he got to see what color it really was. It was green.

"It's not naturally like that," Paul explained. "The plague hit us hard one year and it was affected. It is lucky to be alive."

John nodded. It looked strong enough nevertheless. He saddled both his and the plagued horse. John knew he was leading them into battle with the phoenixes. He was beyond thankful that the Scarlet Phoenix gave them to him.

He checked on everything to make sure nothing was out of order. Everything seemed to all right (besides the obvious fact that they were outnumbered fifty to one). The soldiers were of fairly good health, the weapons worked properly, and the battle stations had been uniformly organized by a system of proper hierarchy.

"I have everything set for battle," Paul said. He clicked a button on the laptop his uncle had brought him. A holographic battle board appeared suddenly.

"Here are our armies here," Paul explained pointing to one section. "Our enemy lines up unprepared. Here's our plan: You lead the phoenixes and the Purloiners in and then we follow with genies and psychics. After that, they will spread to the flanks, and we attack with magicians and the rest of the mythics. We only have the pegasuses and unicorns left. Let's hope that our luck against the dragons changes."

"The plans," John reminded.

"Anyway, after we got them jumbled up," Paul continued, "We retreat and then the Brothers come in and start blasting them with everything they've got."

"And do you think we'll win?" John asked.

"Oh, of course not," Paul said, laughing. "We're going to get crushed. But I just want to weaken the army down for Jerry."

"So you're putting your faith in the prophecy again?" John said.

"I am not giving up on Jerry. Jerry knows we'll lose by the numbers," Paul replied simply.

"Two and a half days, huh?" John said sighing, "We're going to lose so many."

"Yep," Daniel said, surprising them. "But we're fighting anyway."

Paul got the feeling that he had been listening the whole time.

"Are you sure this is the best way?" John said, as he mounted his horse. The phoenixes were behind him.

"I hope," Paul said. He gave John's horse a swift smack in the hindquarters and Musty ran off. The phoenixes followed.

"Here goes nothing," John said, as he crossed the bridge. He came through the unfinished defense. He took out his sword and horn. He blew hard on the horn and the Phoenix sword lit up, showing brightly in the ogre's faces. John looked as scary as ever. *Either way*, John though, *two and a half more days...*

The phoenixes went up high and faced dragons, but some remained behind to attack the ogres. John struck the first ogre that got in his way. His horse trampled the ogres as he killed many with each swipe. The ogres finally started to line up.

The next sweep of soldiers came swiftly. Paul was leading on Storm. All the genies were looking equally as strong as the ogres. The genies each had their weapons out and were starting to spin them fast. The armies ran at their opponents gladly. John sighed, but quickly had to refocus. *You're in battle now*, John reminded himself. He shot magic at approaching ogres.

Suddenly, everything became quiet. All the phoenixes, instead of making tons of musical growls, had silenced. John saw the reason a second later. All the phoenixes, in a matter of minutes, had been struck down. There were the bodies everywhere. The dragons had won again.

But that was just the beginning. All the genies had died in the few moments that John had turned his head. Even his brother was wounded. Through the silence, John could hear Zach's menacing laugh. Then John wondered something.

Where were the Purloiners?

He was answered instantly. To his right, something that silenced Zach's laugh happened. All of William's former men and the Red "Angel Army" appeared. They all rode in on heavily armored cavalry. The horses had spikes on their armor that pierced through the ogres. They took heavy damage, but the ogres fell by the hundreds to thousands. The magicians came with a boom. They shot magic everywhere. Paul unleashed his ax and Daniel and Joan came riding in. John finally got to see them compete.

It was a close match, even though the ogres outnumbered them heavily. Paul thought it might be a good time to retreat soon, but Daniel gave no sign of it. Paul suddenly had an idea. He went to his brother.

"John!" He yelled. "Let's climb the pegasuses and face the dragons in the air!"

John nodded and dismounted his horse and quickly mounted a winged horse. It shot upward. There was a rush of wings behind him and he found Paul had joined him. But he wasn't alone.

"Sheen!" John shouted. The large green dragon joined the two of them and they attacked the dragons (about a hundred). To top it off, more screeches in the sky signaled the coming of the Brother's pilots. John raised his sword and, as an approaching dragon opened its mouth, John took off its head. He swung around on his horse and pulled away from a fireball. He threw his sword into a dragon's neck as missiles shot from the sky. The missiles struck down many. The dragons answered harshly. They turned and hit them all with fire. A lot of pilots were unlucky.

Paul shot his lightning at dragons. A lot was ineffective, but it distracted the dragons—which was what Paul was going for. He aimed for the eyes, as always. With the combined efforts, they had only killed about fifty. John pulled them down. The land army had wiped the land clean of a lot of ogres and creatures, but at great cost. To make matters worse, John gazed out and saw square, black box formations in the distance coming forward, signifying Zach's reinforcements. Legions upon legions were beginning to pour in and push the magicians back. In a manner of a few minute's time, the armies found themselves to be in a stalemate: not a positive stance for Daniel.

It was time to retreat. Daniel signaled it. As they left the battlefield, the ogres thought they had won. When they had gotten out of the way, the humans ran forward with each banner held high.

"It's an amazing sight," John breathed.

"And we'll beat them, too," Daniel reassured. "I know we will."

"We better," Paul added. "The world's time is almost complete. Jerry will be home with us soon."

They all sighed. This was all wishful thinking. For the large castle still loomed down at them, signaling its unwillingness to move. Zach had won this round.

27.) The Loss of the Dead

John and Daniel asked the magicians how they were doing. Most were in shock, but they all responded that they were alright. The only ones that didn't make any answer were the Purloiners, who were recovering. They were meditating, and while doing this, John could see the magic regaining inside them.

It was still early afternoon on the Sixth day. The humans still hadn't returned from fighting. They were worried about that.

"Are you sure this is a good idea?" John asked Paul. "To just leave the humans on their own?"

"I am questioning that myself," Paul said. "Do you know what we really need?"

They both shook their heads.

"The ghouls," Paul said simply. "I bet they beat the phantoms."

"I wouldn't count on it," John said, but he raised his arm anyway. He shot a green fire up to pop three times. A flash of light appeared and about twenty ghouls appeared.

"What happened to the rest?!" Daniel asked in surprise.

"We were defeated," The head ghoul answered. "Even with everyone on heavy cavalry, we couldn't take them all down. There are still hundreds of them."

Paul stared at them in amazement. Daniel looked away in frustration. John, however, was in deep thought.

"Paul, how many dragons do we have left?" He asked, but Daniel answered.

"We have two including Sheen, but they are scouts, not warriors," Daniel answered.

"Call over the other dragon," John said. The dragon came to them after Daniel called for it. "Now, Paul...do you see where I am going with this?"

Paul didn't.

"Imagine this to be a horse," John reminded.

Paul understood. He stretched up and attached wires to the dragon's head that went to his computer. He pressed a button and the dragon suddenly looked stupid and full of despair. John removed his Phoenix sword and sliced the dragon's head off. Daniel swung around in rage.

"That was our last dragon, we needed him!" Daniel said. John turned him towards the corpse. Rising from the corpse was a large dragon ghost.

"Scan, F2," Paul said. "Create...number? Five."

Another huge blast came forth from Paul's laptop that was equal to when he created a thousand horses. It shut down his computer.

"Will this help?" John asked Sire sarcastically. Sire was in awe. "Do you think you can take them down?"

Sire nodded, biting his lip.

"We're counting on you," John said. "I couldn't use the orb. I am sorry, but we need you to beat them by yourselves. If you don't, we're done. We lose."

Sire nodded. One of the stray phoenixes that had survived came over to John. John mounted it (it was large enough) and said to them, "I will lead you in."

The phoenix rose up, with all the rest of the ghosts behind him. The phoenix spread its wings and soared over the battle between the humans and ogres below.

Above it all, there were the phantoms, set with their weapons pointed towards the ghouls. The ghouls charged ahead of John and struck the phantoms hard.

John pulled up on the phoenix he was riding.

"I wished you guys had survived," John murmured to the phoenix. The phoenix suddenly dove. John grabbed onto its feathers. It came within twenty feet of the ogres when it suddenly blew a huge amount of fire at the ogres. The fire didn't have any effect on the ogres. But rising from the fire were many other phoenixes, almost the same amount they lost.

"I love phoenixes," John said, smiling. "Always rising from the flames …"

He stood up on his, and put his shield forward. He sliced and cut ogres as the phoenix approached it. The phoenixes behind him started blowing real fire at each of the ogres. As John turned back for a second, he could see the humans' gratitude.

John looked up. The phantoms were almost out of warriors, but then again, so were the ghouls. But without a doubt, the phantoms couldn't destroy the dragons. The dead were almost defeated.

John concentrated on killing ogres. He and the phoenixes were making remarkable progress. They had killed at least 2,000 already. John leapt off his phoenix and started swinging his sword wildly. He cleared out a circle of 50 in seconds. From the north, suddenly came more of William's men.

"Boy, you guys come in handy," John said as he did a back flip to avoid an arrow shot at him. Four phoenixes with riders came to John.

"No fair, you can't start without us," Lino said. Joan, Paul, and Daniel were with him.

"Wouldn't dream of it," John said, grinning. "Let's get moving."

Daniel removed his sword and kicked an ogre to the ground.

"Let's go then," he said. Joan went forward and spun her swords in her signature move. Lino leapt around, cutting his opponents faces, Paul blasted his ax and shot many oblivious ogres to their deaths. John simply zipped the ogres' swords in two with his unstoppable sword. He glanced up at the ghouls again. With triumph, he saw that the ghouls had almost won. There were only a few dozen phantoms left. John called a phoenix over and he rode up to them. By the time he got up there, the phantoms were finished and the ghouls had won.

"Go down and help us out!" John said. The ghouls were so happy that they obeyed orders without hesitation.

John couldn't describe the ogre's fear. They charged down and all the ogres couldn't stop them. Row by row, they were killed instantly.

Finally, Zach interceded. He stood on his throne, hooded so no one could see his face. He formed a magical sphere larger than a house. He summed up his strength and shot it at the ghouls.

John saw it in time, but the ghouls didn't.

"Scatter!" John said, pulling his phoenix up to charge out of the way at top speed. The magic ball hit the ghosts, blasting them away, in hundreds of pieces.

"How'd he do that?" John asked himself, looking in awe at Zach.

Zach just sneered at him and sat down again. Then John remembered something Zach had said in the forest: *"I am in a different class than you, Quaill. You have no idea about my power."*

John pulled his hair in frustration. Was Zach really this powerful? How could he compete with someone of this status?

John realized something, though: the ghosts were no longer necessary; the phantoms had been killed. There was no more death to fight. *It would have been nice, though*, John thought, *to have some people that couldn't be stopped.*

John flew back to the four people on the ground.

"How are the humans doing?" John asked Daniel who was fighting a ferocious Thogeen.

"They are doing fine," Daniel said, "if you say being outnumbered, scared out of their minds and four hundred times weaker is fine."

John got the message. He leapt on his phoenix and flew over to the humans.

"RETREAT!" John yelled out at them. He summoned up a magician flag to show them the signal. They all ran back. Joan, Daniel and Paul followed him.

When they had all crossed the bridge (still about 40 million left), John saw a terrible sight. The ogres were following them. All of the ogres, Thogeens, or goblins were swarming inwardly for the bridge. John glanced up at Zach. His hand was raised, pointing at them.

"It seems Zach had enough," John showed Daniel. "They're following us. His invasion has started."

"PULL BACK!" Daniel shouted. "Everyone move! We must move or we'll be defeated!"

He woke up the psychics, magicians and all the others.

"WE MUST MOVE!" Daniel and Paul were shouting.

"I'LL HEAD THEM OFF!" John said. He mounted Musty and Joan mounted a phoenix to help him. John charged the horse forward to the bridge. He was trying to be as swift as possible, but there were so many ogres. Slicing many ogres to the ground, Joan reached the other side and John started on the other end. No matter the process, the swiftness of the warriors or anything else, there were just too many organized troops storming across the bridge.

"We can't hold them!" John shouted, returning to Daniel. The ogres were feet away. "What are we going to do?"

The phoenixes dove and intercepted the ogres. It gave the warriors enough time to get up and moving.

"We have to pull back," John said to Daniel. "The phoenixes will slow them enough for us to get a good head start. Then we can march against them together."

Daniel nodded. He mounted his horse and Paul his. The three charged ahead of the armies and led them forward. John looked at the sun and saw it had set. It was the end of the Sixth day.

As he was began to slow down, once they had a reasonable distance between the Zach and themselves, John realized how tired he was. He saw why: he was carrying the war on his back with only a few people taking it as bad as he.

"How long should we travel?" Joan asked nobody in particular.

"Maybe eight hours," Daniel said. "Then we all need rest and then … well, I don't know what happens next."

Paul looked like he was about to fall asleep on his horse. He was nodding and his mouth was slightly open. John rode up to Daniel.

"I don't know how much more we can all handle, Uncle Dan," John said. "Paul's tired. I'm tired. Lino and Joan are tired. Our army is tired."

Daniel nodded, "I know. I am, too."

John looked back to his horse, which was also exhausted.

"John, you never told me how my brother died."

John looked quickly at his uncle. He looked down again.

"Do I have to tell?" he asked.

"Sooner or later," Daniel said, "I will find out anyway. I would prefer it your way."

"As opposed to …" John asked.

"Zach's way," Daniel said. John nodded.

"We were facing the Kraskull," John retold. "They had betrayed Zach's orders. I joined Zach to fight them."

Daniel smiled at him.

"John, you truly are wise," he said. "Someone else might think that Zach and Kraskull we at the same level. You saw forward to the consequences of each event. Seeing that Zach was still 'Bad' and the Kraskull were 'Evil' proved that you could truly see people for what they are. You can separate people into groups, while a lot of people can't."

"You said 'was still bad'," John noticed. "... was?"

Daniel refused to answer.

"Continue with the story," he avoided.

"I was fighting a Kraskull when my father was disarmed," John resumed. "I tossed him my Phoenix sword. He killed a Kraskull and saw its true horror. It finally woke him up and he leapt up onto the table and completed the prophecy of the orb. He cut the orb open and the building collapsed upon him. Zach and I survived, but my dad died and the Kraskull ... disappeared?"

"Were removed from existence," Daniel corrected him.

"Either way, it removed all evil," John said.

Daniel shook his head.

"I am sorry, John," he said. "But it couldn't have destroyed all evil. There is still evil out there. You have heard 'no two wrongs make right'."

He chuckled.

"Evil will always exist, somewhere, until the end of the universe. Ever since its existence, evil has always been out tormenting the innocent to become just like them. Some are strong and resist. But no matter how strong, nobody can defeat it. But we fight it so that *all* may have a choice."

John didn't really understand what this last statement meant. He continued onward, nonetheless.

*   *   *

When they finally stopped, it was not soon enough. Nobody even bother setting up a defensive perimeter; they just fell down and slept for hours. Paul and Daniel woke early though.

"How many enemies do we have left do you think?" Paul asked.

"Your strong people killed at least a billion," Daniel said, sleepily. "Then the second attack, I would guess you had killed

400-500 million. The humans and ghosts and stuff, I would guess killed another billion."

"So we're half way there," Paul said. He looked back and sighed. They had lost much more than half of their armies. "We have a huge deficit to overcome here."

"Two and a half billion armies," Daniel said in amazement. He took in a breath and said, "I can't see how we can do this. No amount of strategy can do that."

"It is statistically impossible," Paul said. "They have 2.5 we have .035. That's like for every one we lose, they must lose 70."

Sheen came charging full speed at them. He began speaking in dragon. It was translated on Paul's computer. Paul leapt up.

"The ogres didn't rest! They are coming … almost two miles away!" Paul read.

Daniel and Paul woke everyone in a hurry. They took off again in a much faster pace.

After another few hours of traveling the armies stopped. The armies went straight to sleep again. Paul, Lino and Joan went to sleep right away, but John kept his uncle up.

"Uncle Dan," he said, "If we keep this up, we will end up at the California coast, with nothing but the ocean to move to. When we went upwards towards northern Arizona, we noticed that Zach's armies had gone through Prescott. That means there is a possibility that the Northern flank could have swung around. We are in a bad position. We can't keep fleeing."

"Paul read the statistics to us," Daniel said. "We don't have enough men. We just don't."

"And moving will have us gain more?" John said. "Face it, Uncle Dan, we have everyone. We have everything that can possibly be coming. There is no more back up coming."

"Jerry is still coming," Daniel suggested.

"Yes, and we're all looking forward to that day," John replied impatiently. "But that isn't enough. We will reach the edge and then what? Jerry will return and we'll all be trapped. And who said Jerry isn't coming alone? This might be a hopeless wait."

This silenced Daniel.

"I have a plan for you," John said. "Charge out to the enemy. They will be waiting. Zach will be there. We can be fighting when Jerry comes."

"It will be a 70-1 deficit," Daniel reminded him. "I can't see us winning."

"There's your problem," John said. "A day ago, you told me about evil. Well, this might not be evil, but as close as you can get to it. If Zach wins, he will *force* everyone to worship him. 'Force' is the key word here. You told me that evil can't be defeated. But we fight to give everyone the choice. Running from evil will never work. But fighting ..."

Daniel nodded with pride.

"You're right, John," he said. "We'll charge out at them tomorrow."

"Maybe it won't be that long," John said as Sheen came flying at them again.

28.) The Last Stand

John helped rally the troops. The final strike was obviously right here and now. The run was finally coming to an end, one way or another. They couldn't believe it. John checked with Sheen and the enemy was only a few minutes away. But they were ready. The three horsemen were on their horses.

John took out his Phoenix sword and started to sharpen it with his dagger.

"You know," Paul said as the Phoenix sword started to cut the dagger into small shreds, "that's kind of pointless."

John smiled slyly at him.

"I know, but I don't have any more swords," John said.

"Is it just me, or is that sword brighter than before," Paul asked cautiously.

"It's not just you," John replied, peering at it, "it looks different to me too."

"What do you think it means?" Paul asked, feeding his horse some food.

"I think it means the Scarlet Phoenix is going to fly soon," John answered quietly.

"But it already did," Paul said. "It carried me to you, didn't it?"

John considered this.

"But Jerry's prophecy said 'before the King Phoenix flies'," John said, pondering hard. "So what does this mean?"

"You can ask him," Paul said. "He'll be here by sundown tomorrow, right?"

"We're in for a long day," John sighed as the ogres came into view for the hidden armies.

Joan stood behind them lining the lines for battle.

"You know, Paul," John answered, smiling a little. "This could be our final battle. But I wouldn't be lying to say this might have been our best journey of all."

Paul looked in the eye.

"John," Paul began slowly, "I guarantee that our greatest journey is yet to come. It might be soon."

"You know what," John said, "Death is just another journey, perhaps the greatest. I'll see you there."

Paul nodded sadly. Daniel turned his horse around and tried to speak to the men many times. But no words came out. He finally turned his horse around and moved in front of John and Paul. Sheen rose up and moved away from battle as planned. If there were to be any survivors, they would take Sheen to live as long as they could.

Suddenly, an enemy dragon (one of the last survivors), came into view and blew fire all around the armies. It came close to torching everything, had it not been for Daniel. He raised his arms just in time and made a barrier that John thought he could never do. The barrier stopped the attack, but Daniel could barely maintain it. Finally, Daniel was able to push the fire outwards away from the warriors. It hit anything else in sight, making the path clear for the ogres to see. There was nothing but empty land as far as the eye could see.

"We'll fight first," the Head Purloiner said. "We'll protect the lives once again, and for the last time."

John lifted his sword. He led the way into battle. *Just one more day*, John had to keep thinking as the ogres came steadily closer to him. They were more endless than he could imagine. Over the desert area, it looked even more deadly.

Paul aimed his ax for the first line of attack. When he was close enough, he shot lightning at the ogres. Ogres fell in high numbers with just Paul's ax.

John's passion mounted. It just wasn't fair that Zach had this many warriors. It was nearly impossible. This was it, though. The end of Zach's reign.

John slashed his sword back and forth on either side of his horse, breaking through many lines. He turned to the Purloiners.

There were two dozen left. The next line was the cavalry belonging to William's former army. As soon as the last Purloiner fell, they charged out, full sprint, to the enemy. Their spears struck many down. In fact, they almost caught up to John. John noticed this and pushed harder through the ogres.

It went well into the night. The cavalry had long fallen. The magicians were on their last legs. The psychics were killed. Almost all the phoenixes were killed again, and the mythics were long gone. All they had in great number was the Thogs and the humans.

But the ogres were defeated. All of them were dead. It was over on John's last slice of an ogre's head. He turned to his rigid and tired army. He got off his horse and it went immediately to sleep. He walked over to his family who miraculously survived.

"We won," John breathed, "it's over."

Daniel turned to him and shook his head. John's heart fell.

"It's … not over?" He asked.

"This isn't all of the troops," Paul said. "Not even close. I did the statistics and a mass of soldiers that has five billion soldiers has the volume of the entire state of Arizona itself."

"The army would be that big?" John asked in awe.

"We barely killed two billion, if that much," Daniel said sadly. "We're done. Even with every other person in the world showed up, we would still not have enough. They have four billion. We have a couple million at best."

"1 to 2000," John said, nodding in defeat. "We lost."

The truth came to them. Daniel chuckled.

"What was I thinking that we would have a chance against Zach?" He sighed, putting his hand onto his forehead. Their uncle, who was in his late thirties, looked 20 years older. "We were all bound to lose anyway. But now he knows he didn't go unchallenged. We made him work for his victory."

"Let's go into exile, then," Paul decided. "Let's keep running from him, all our lives. The orb is destroyed; he has no way of tracking us. We can live in loyalty to the truth and could build another rebellion someday."

This sounded logical and safest to everyone. In silent agreement, they knew that it was the only way to survive. Finally, John spoke.

"It's the eighth day, or close to it …" He said. "By noon, Zach will have no challenge up against him. There's nothing to stop him from taking over the planet. He has the potential to do it, now that we are out of the way.

"The thing is, guys, you say that we could run. Zach is good at getting what he wants. He could line all of his soldiers, shoulder to shoulder and march across the globe and destroy everything that is not loyal to him. True, if only one survived to pass it on, there is still a prayer that we could win. But it isn't going to happen. We have to stop him before 'The Last March' so to speak."

"And what happens once we fail?" Daniel said. "What happens when there are no more loyal people to this cause?"

"Oh, there will always be people with a conscience," Lino broke in, "always. No matter how evil or corrupt the world will ever become, there will always be good people. Our failing won't change that. That's the thing. There will always be people to fight with us, in this world or the next."

"Well put," John said.

"And what is your plan?" Joan said. "The classic, 'wait for the prophecy'?"

"Jerry will come, and not alone, either," John said loyally. "All of you have stated this at one point or another."

"Oh, we already went through that," Daniel said, "Even if he brought every living person on this earth to help, though, we'll still lose."

"He will come, with many," John promised.

"So what do you propose in the meantime," Daniel said. "Charge at Zach head on? With his four *billion* troops?"

John stared him in the eye.

"That's precisely what I want to do," John said. "A half day's march, and a five-hour battle, and before the sun sets – Jerry comes. Paul stated that Zach contains a chip in his skull that is also in every ogre. If Zach dies, all the ogres die. That way, no one can come after him if he should fail. But he left us an easy way to defeat his armies: kill him, and we kill his armies.

"You call killing Zach easy?!" Paul gasped. "You should know better than the rest that we have better luck killing all the ogres with our couple million!"

"Then, let's try both, and with Jerry, we should be able to succeed in at least one of them," Lino said simply.

"Well, we might just put it to the vote," Daniel said. "All in favor of exile, raise your hand."

Daniel raised his. Paul and Joan did, too.

"Majority rules," Daniel said, apologetically.

John sucked in some breath and with a loud, carrying voice said, "All in favor of making one last stand against Zach and rely on the greatest warrior to return to us, raise your hand."

John and Lino raised theirs, but all of the troops behind them –all of them –raised their hand in favor … for the Final Stand.

29.) The Eighth Night

In the lines formed, all the armies went forward to attack the enemy one more time. John sent Sheen out to see if he could find Jerry. This was it. The Eighth Day.

"We have come a long way," Daniel said. "And in one way or another, this is it."

"Our last stand is over," Paul added, "This is our attack, the attack to save the world."

"Let us ride in," Joan said. "Going out fighting instead of hiding."

"We'll show Zach that he was not unchallenged," John said. He mounted Musty. "Here we go, Musty, Celtic warrior, Storm … are you ready?"

"Everyone is," Daniel replied. "I know everyone is strong and willing, but it's pointless."

"I don't care," Lino said. "We should always try."

They moved out.

"It will be a six-hour journey from what I see," Paul said. "That means Jerry comes six hours after we fight. Can we hold that long?"

"Hopefully they will," John said. "While I go in alone to kill Zach … well, if Paul is willing, he can come too."

"How do you plan to do that?" Daniel asked him. "We have been trying to do that for years."

"We distract them," John explained, "And Paul and I will go into the castle and kill him while you guys fight outside. He'd never expect this plan."

"Why does Paul have to go with you?" Lino asked. "We might need him out here."

Paul remembered why.

"Paul knows," John said shortly. "Is that alright with you guys?"

"We were kind of hoping that you would stay down here," Lino whispered, sadly. "The people like it when they have courageous leaders to lead them."

"That won't be a problem," John patted Lino's head. "They have that."

"We can hold the field for a few hours," Daniel said. "Come on, Paul, let's make the plans."

John glanced at Joan. The others moved aside.

"Well, after this, I don't know what's going to happen," John said. "If we die, we die together. If we live ... well, what do you think?"

"I think we should go back to Locombony," Joan said.

"Locombony," John whispered the word. "I have been so caught up with Zach, the orb, Kraskull and the USA that I almost forgot about Locombony. Well, when we get back, it will be ruled by Australia, right?"

"Nothing much we can do about that anytime soon," Joan replied sadly. "But we will return ... one way or another."

"I hope," John said. "Even if we do win, the journey home might be long."

John looked at Joan for a long time.

"Joan, I am probably not going to return," John said to her. "Zach is the most powerful magician as Uncle Dan said. I will weaken him enough, though. Push through the ogres as much as you can."

"I lost my family and friends," Joan whispered, holding back tears. "I don't want to lose you too."

"You won't lose me," John promised, "I will always be with you."

John kicked his horse harder and it sped ahead of the rest. Paul looked and saw him go ahead. He caught up with him.

"So what's the plan with Zach?" Paul asked.

"I don't know, wing it I guess," John shrugged. "There is no plan Zach isn't ready for."

Paul was right in two instances. One was that it did take six hours to get there. The second ...

"Oh my gosh," Joan gasped, looking out over the hill. Zach's army, who a day before barely had a gate up, had set up an entire fortress, the size of the state. None of them could see the end of it. Ogres roamed the land everywhere. John looked behind them at the bottom of the hill where their army of one or two million stood in a vast array. John turned to Paul. He nodded. They both turned to face the enemy. They rode down alone to the gates, which, to their luck, was open. They looked in and saw ogres everywhere. John glanced one more time at Paul.

"For the Phoenix," John said, removing his gleaming sword. "And all it believes in!"

He ran into the enemy lines. Paul pulled out a pair of identical axes and charged in as well. He caught up to John, who stopped in the middle of a bunch of confused ogres. John, with one hand lifting a sword in the air, pulled a horn to his lips with the other. He blew into it giving the charge to the others behind the hill. The ogres scrambled around in fear. They never imagined that the army would attempt to attack them with the army being so highly outnumbered and not to mention exhausted. Paul and John spotted the castle immediately. They ran through the mess of ogres to get to the castle. They almost ignored the ogres in the rush to get to the castle. Zach was barely visible on his throne. They reached the doors of the castle and came upon two ogres and two goblins with weird looking weapons. John did a flip off his horse and kicked an ogre to the ground. He stabbed it and approached the other ogre. Paul aimed his two axes at each goblin. He threw them both. One was killed with its lightning, but the other one dodged it. Paul slid off his horse and stretched his arm and grabbed his ax. With another stretch of his arm, he punched the goblin to the ground.

He sliced his ax against the goblin's throat. He looked up to John and saw he killed his guard. John nodded and they went into the castle. It was very old with rotting walls.

"What do we do now?" John asked his brother in haste.

"We have to go up, for one," Paul said.

"There aren't any stairs, though," John said, walking around the hallway.

"Keep looking," Paul answered.

They went down the hall. It was dark, only lit by occasional torches. John moved cautiously through the room.

"There's some stairs!" Paul pointed, taking a step forward. John's magic instincts tingled mildly, but it was enough.

"Paul, down!" John said, tackling his brother. At least twenty arrows missed their heads by inches. In the shadows of the darkness stood many goblins. John and Paul got up and twirled their weapons in an intimidating way. The goblins ran at them, bows raised. John took the first step and wiped the first line of goblins out with one strike. Paul leapt over John and removed the last row. Together, John and Paul killed the rest.

"Up the stairs then?" Paul whispered. John walked to the wall that was hidden in shadows.

"Wait," he answered. "There is a ladder here. Which one holds the true path?"

"Well, it comes to the split again, doesn't it?" Paul said sadly. "I go one way, you the other."

"Splitting up is the worst way to beat Zach," John said. "But I guess it was destined this way. I will weaken Zach as much as I can. You finish him."

"You're not going to die, John," Paul stated firmly. "You are stronger than Zach."

"Promise me when I fall, you will kill Zach."

"You're not going to die!" Paul said, almost laughing at the idea. "It's not going to happen!"

"Will you?" John said seriously.

"If I can," Paul said, sighing, "and if you don't kill him first."

"You have to," John encouraged. "The fate of the world depends on it."

"No pressure then," Paul called as he charged up the stairs. He could feel his brother smiling below him. Paul tried to calm himself as he reached the top of the stairs. He didn't find anything except a small room holding a ladder.

"I guess I am going up then," he said.

John climbed the ladder and found himself face to face with 20 Thogeens. Without hesitation or misstep, John attacked each one and sliced them to the ground. He moved slowly towards the door at the end of the room. John quickly opened it and readied his shield. No attack came to him. He lowered his shield and walked into the room. There were no creatures, but a door to his right.

"Almost a maze," John realized. Then he chuckled to himself, "Well, it's a good thing I am good at this."

He opened the door and came within a couple centimeters of an arrow. He jumped up and attacked an ogre. He cut its bow, and then it head. There was only one. John took the next door (to his right again). No creatures, but there was a long hallway. John came to the end of it and opened the next door that happened to be black.

Paul kept climbing up ladders, but didn't have to fight many creatures. The worst that he had to fight was a Thogeen guard, but nothing else. Even Thogeens were nothing to Paul anymore. Paul was determined to prove John's vision false. It had to be … there was no way that his powerful brother could die.

Paul reached the next level and found a ladder standing in the middle of the room with a trap door above it. He took a breath and climbed the ladder. He knew this would lead to the roof, to Zach himself. He opened the trapdoor and pushed himself through it. He faced the back of the throne. He readied his ax. He ran gripped it tight and jumped so that he was facing it. He gasped at what he saw.

Or rather, what he didn't see.

*   *   *

John looked into the room. It was pitch black. He took a step in and the door behind him closed on its own. There was absolutely no light now. John removed his sword. It was not glowing.

"Please, Phoenix," John whispered. "I need you more than ever. Dad ... please intercede for me."

The sword lit up for John. It was shining only a little, but it was enough for John to see what was in front of him. He saw nothing in the room. It was empty – no door, no ladder, no stairs.

A light sound, the touching of soft boots to the ground, was heard behind him.

John turned as fast he could, moving his sword in a wild way. Zach stood in his way. The contrasting-colored swords of the Kraskull and Phoenix met in mid air. The clang of metal to metal echoed around the room.

"First time you heard that in a while, I imagine," Zach growled in the darkness. "With that filthy sword of yours cutting through my troops."

"Sorry to disappoint you," John said.

"Disappoint?" Zach said, pulling his sword back. "You fulfilled everything I could have hoped you could do, Quaill. You have passed every test I put you up to, even killing the Kraskull. And now that they're gone, I have nothing but clear sailing to the end! You're father's performance gave me my lifelong dream –...absolute power! You see...when the Kraskull fell, I gained their power. With the orb destroyed, their spirits were removed from existence. But their strength lingered... I gained it, and the crushing rocks did not kill me. And now that all other power has been removed, your pathetic rebellion crushed, I can conquer everything!"

"I can't see how you can do that," John spat, "When you keep lowering your defense!"

John, with lightning speed, shot an attack at Zach that he only just dodged by throwing himself to the ground. Zach looked up to him.

"You think you're so clever, Quaill?" Zach asked sarcastically. "Then let me give you a rude awakening to your dreams."

Zach summed up a great ball of magic and shot it a John. John put up his shield just in time, but it knocked him to the ground. The rest of the ball went at the opposite wall, blowing a titanic hole in the castle. John got up a little shaken.

"You missed," John gloated, smiling mockingly.

"I wasn't aiming for you, Quaill," Zach yelled, "Look outside!"

John glanced out, and then looked back in a stare. His large army, the one that once held millions, had not even five hundred men.

"Now you see?" Zach spat, "you cannot win. Your stupid plan failed."

John's heart and morale just sank to his boots.

"Your girlfriend probably died down there," Zach said. "Last of mages, wasn't she? I wonder how her family died?"

John's breathing increased.

"Your brother?" Zach added. "Won't you think he will make a great ogre? I have the materials to do it. The Kraskull attempted to do it on their ship, but your brother was too strong. Not for me, though."

John started to shake with furry.

"And your father…he died after the fall, didn't he? He wasn't really dead yet…you might have saved him but you didn't…he was too weak, wasn't he?"

John yelled out in pure anger. He swung his sword in passion and Zach deflected it. John whipped his sword around and swung fast, but Zach was faster than John has seen anyone be. John struck back and forth, but Zach deflected every strike.

"You can't beat me, Quaill," Zach said. "Nobody can beat me! I was trained by Merlin himself!"

John pushed the Phoenix sword hard on the Kraskull sword, but Zach pushed him to the ground.

"Merlin was more than a thousand years ago!" John said. "He couldn't be still alive!"

"Who do you think started the great Thousand-Year War? Who do you think had the idea of the orb? Who had pushed the image of war into Merlin's dream?" Zach screamed all this.

"Who do you think is the mighty, the most powerful sorcerer in the universe, in all of its history, the great Kewlocke?!"

John took a step back. He had studied about the wizards of the past… even about Kewlocke…about Zach.

"You destroyed my creation! You … you betrayed your line of Circe! You cannot beat me now! *I am evil!*"

He said the last three words with the deepest voice John had ever heard. Zach ripped off his hood. John hadn't seen his face after the battle of the tower scene. It had changed. His eyes were of a deep red and the outer tips were now pointed. His former skin was now a layer of black scales. His head of dark, snake-like hair was gone, revealing a bald head. His pointed nose was shriveled up. His lips were almost gone, but he had pointed teeth all around. He raised his hand which John hadn't seen in the darkness, but now saw. His nails grew so that they looked like claws. The moon on his hand glowed a magnificent gold now. The three fingers that had been bitten off were now back, fully intact.

"You can not defeat me now, Quaill," Kewlocke said. *"I have accomplished my goal of being evil. I care nothing of the living. Only my ogres will survive my wrath! Time for you to die, Quaill!"*

John was so horrified about the change in Kewlocke he had dropped his sword. John fell to the ground in fear. He grabbed for his sword, but Kewlocke kicked it away. John summoned it with his magic. He slowly stood up.

"Pure beats Evil any day!" John said, lunging at Kewlocke who dodged and sliced. It struck John's arm, but only left a small mark. Yet no matter the size, it burned so hard John thought he would die from the pain.

Paul got to the door holding Zach and John. He reached for the handle but couldn't open it. He pulled back and tried blasting the door with his ax, but nothing happened. He could feel his brother was in trouble but couldn't help him.

John got up slowly. He looked outside the hole again. The sun had almost set. The armies were almost gone. John could feel Kewlocke raise his sword. He turned quickly and deflected the sword. John fought him hard, but Kewlocke was too fast and powerful.

"You can't beat me either, Kewlocke," John said. "Do you remember how I defeated you last time? Well get ready."

I vowed never to do this again, John thought, *but I have to do it now.* He started to morph.

"No, Quaill," Kewlocke said, *"I am the last evil. You're morph isn't going to stop me!"*

Kewlocke stopped his morphing with his magic and knocked the sword out of John's hands. John lay defenseless on the ground. Kewlocke put his foot on John's chest. Kewlocke raised his sword and John breathed out. He knew what was next. But he was ready.

"I am ready to die for the Phoenix," John said. The sword glowed a magnificent color of white. Kewlocke looked in terror. A figure rose from the sword …

Paul kicked the door one last time and broke through. He saw the crystal color of his father come forward from John's sword.

*   *   *

John pushed Kewlocke off of him and he got up. His father picked up the Phoenix sword and approached Zach.

"I still have life in me to fight you, Kewlocke," the ghost of their father said. "The Phoenix will be raised against you soon!"

John reached for a knife in his boot and pulled it out. Paul raised his ax, but their father shook his head.

"Someone else is here to see you guys," he said to them. He nodded towards the hole in the castle. They looked out to the big hill they had recently charged down.

John later describes the scene as, "the greatest warrior in the world on the black horse came upon the hill with the strength of a thousand men. With the orange sword blasting its flame, the man ran down the hill at top speed with hundreds behind him."

Paul looked out as he saw his third brother come down the hill. Paul felt the water from his eyes flow down his cheeks. He looked at John who looked in awe back at him. He nodded slowly and they both jumped from the hole to the ground to meet their brother.

30.) The Flight and the Miracle

They landed softly on their feet and ran to their horses. When they mounted, they rode through the large mass of ogres to get to their uncle who was still alive. He saw them and mounted his horse. He commanded that all retreat. They charged backwards, the hundred or so that was left. The three horsemen met with the fourth horseman on the top of the hill.

"Where's your army?" John asked him.

"Nice to see you too," Jerry said. "Right here."

He pointed to his side, nothing there.

"Where?" John asked.

"They're invisible … the last of the ghosts," Jerry said. "They're called Specters."

Suddenly tons of ghosts appeared to them. They all had some weird ghost-like weapons. They ran down at the approaching ogres who started to run away at the sight of the ghosts. The ghosts hit the ogres and started to march through each line. There was nothing that could stop them.

"How'd you get them?" Paul asked.

"I'll explain later," Jerry promised, looking nearly as exhausted as everyone else.

"As the four horsemen, I suggest we move in, shall we?" John nodded.

They all rode in on horseback to the castle, by which time all most a quarter of the ogres were killed. They all saw the battle between their father and Kewlocke.

The ghostly image of their father was radiating a strange red light, as if the King Phoenix were inside him.

"You will finally fall, Kewlocke," he said. "You are evil, no more!"

Kewlocke smiled as their father kicked his sword out of his hands.

"You may kill me," Kewlocke said, "but the ogres will never be killed."

Kewlocke pulled from his sleeve a small dagger. He brought the dagger to his forehead and cut out a piece of his flesh. Inside lay a small chip that Paul had predicted. Kewlocke pulled out his wand.

"Never will you see the end of the ogre race!" He shouted and made the chip disappear. "You'll never find the chip and raise the Phoenix!"

The Quaills' father grabbed Zach by the collar.

"*He is risen*," he whispered and stabbed him in the chest with the sword. Kewlocke screamed as he fell lifeless to the ground.

The next scene was hard to describe. From the ghostly image of the Quails' father flowed a red cloud. The same image pulled itself out of the sword in Kewlocke. The specters, in turn, flowed upwards into the massive red cloud. All the soldiers standing for good and pureness felt a strange sensation as if they, too, were being pulled towards this massive cloud. They became bound to it, perfectly unified.

This formless shape slid together into the massive bird. The bird was no longer red, but a perfect color they could not find on the color spectrum. It was just light, power and wonder. Its features were of the most perfect nature. Its cerulean eyes shined and the feathers whisked in the wind.

Now they all knew the meaning of the King Phoenix's rise.

It soared above the castle and through the ghosts. With the chip gone, the ogres ran for their lives.

Jerry rode out, nearly alone, with the magnificent bird. He brought his sword up to full height and began a glorious chant. No one could make out his exact words, but one thing was clear: This was no battle cry. It was a bellow of awe. He and the Phoenix fought the enemy with great haste and efficiency. Jerry took down ogres as if they were standing still. The Phoenix used both its wingspan and its fiery breath to wipe out sections of thousands of ogres.

Panicking, the ogres ran in all directions, fearing for their lives. Daniel barked out orders to trap major divisions of the ogre chaos. Thousands of the ogres went at the approaching army, but the Scarlet Phoenix clashed against them. Similar to how the sword was, the great bird produced devastating damage to those who went at it, but did not itself receive any injury whatsoever.

Opening its wings to full length, the Phoenix let out a piercing screech. For the armies of men and magicians, the sound was welcome to their ears. They felt more peace flow throughout their veins and their hearts filled with contentment. However, it was harsh to the ogre's ears. They buckled down, howling at the noise. It was loud, louder than any horn or bellowing army.

The battle continued on and on, but it seemed to be a very one-sided battle. The Phoenix set out a magical mantle of protection to each soldier as they continued. Ogres fell in quick numbers. By now, the ogres were trying to escape from their impending doom.

As their numbers fell down past 10 million, past a million, past 500,000, eventually, they began to escape. The ogres ran in all different directions. The Quaills could not contain such a large quantity of them.

Soon, the soldiers realized the ogres were no longer a threat to their race. The Quaills called them off and allowed the remaining ogres to flee into the setting sun.

An enormous cry ensued from all the soldiers, magician, man, and Thog alike. They had succeeded.

"We did it!" Lino called, dancing around.

"Well done," Paul said, patting his friend, Hybrid, on the shoulder.

Jerry raised his sword high into the air. Many of the cheering soldiers lifted him up onto their shoulders. Tears flowed down his face as he glanced around at his welcome party and then let out a loud call to the heavens.

Daniel, however, stood by himself, gazing at the magnificent Phoenix, who seemed to be in a state of joy. It lowered its head to Daniel's height. Daniel took to his knees.

"You help us beyond any of us could do," Daniel blubbered. "For that … we thank you."

The Phoenix nodded. It turned and lowered its wing, beckoning them to get on. The Quaills and Joan got on and as Jerry did, he said,

"And so, as it was, Jerry Vincent Quaill mounted the Scarlet Phoenix, the ogres race diminished, and the Phoenix flew as the last day of earth sets and a new planet will rise from the ashes, united as one."

They all grabbed hold tightly and the Phoenix rose up and flew above the clouds. Many of the people below began to chant: "Scarlet Phoenix! Scarlet Phoenix!"

When the bird came down from the clouds, they were above water. They came close to the crashing sea.

"So tell me, Paul," John said, smiling as Sheen came soaring next to them. "How is it that Sheen's saliva is a healing power?"

"Captain," a man said to the general, "the city is almost taken. The Thousand-Year war is almost over. Australia will rule the island."

"I know," the general said, "About how many more troops are left?"

"They have about 50, sir," the other man answered hurriedly. "We have about two sentries."

"Excellent!" He said. Quite suddenly a large shadow came upon them. They looked up in time to see six figures fall to the ground.

"Locombony will live," One of the six said. With a glowing sword, he approached and killed the two men. They ran in and together each killed 20, securing the victory for Locombony. As the last was slain, John Quaill looked up to his uncle.

"The war is over. The journey is over. But the ogres survived and we must hunt down each one. You know this was a miracle. We are actually back on this island."

"We all are not taking this for granted," Joan said. "Don't you start worrying about that."

John walked away from the group. He looked out over the sea that he had looked at mere weeks before. He was joined by his older brother, who threw his arm around him.

"Stunning," Jerry whispered.

"Jerry," John asked, "What was the deal with the specters? How did you get them to join with you?"

Jerry sighed, a sad smile appearing on his face.

"Those specters…they were not strangers. I had traveled to Europe to find a specter who could properly explain the situation to me—you know, how they become who they are. They told me of a certain chant that could be performed to call a specific ghost or ghosts. It reminded me of the orb. Well, it was an upsetting prospect, but I knew what I had to do."

"Which was what?" John asked. "And what do you mean the specters 'weren't strangers'?"

"The specters … I had called them based on one attribute," Jerry breathed. "I called only those who had died in the war on our side."

There was silence between the two of them.

"More had died, though," John shook his head, confused. "There were only a few thousand in that bunch."

"I know," Jerry whispered, voice cracking slightly. "Those were the ones who had died without being given a chance. They were not ready to die. These people were not soldiers. They were innocent … that the ogres had murdered."

John gasped.

"How many?" John asked.

Jerry stared at the ground, "Over half a million."

John caught a sob in his throat and choked. He couldn't believe it. He had done so much…and yet 500,000 people died without even involving themselves with the war.

"That's why you waited so long," John realized. "You waited until the last minute…to get every last soul."

"I am sorry, John," Jerry apologized, completely weeping at this point. "It sounds terrible, but it had to be done."

John hugged his older brother. It was a hard philosophy, but things began to fall into place.

"How will we remember this?" Jerry wiped away his tear. "What shall we name this tragedy, and yet blessing?"

"The War of the Scarlet Phoenix," John stated instantly.

Jerry nodded, saying, "That's appropriate."

John shook his head, breaking the eye contact.

"Not in the way you're thinking, Jerry," John explained. "What made the Phoenix? Our love. Our passion. Our faith. Our magic. Every positive blessing that we've been given, we offered back to the one who died in order to start the evolution process of a one-celled organism – you know and I know that the one was the Scarlet Phoenix. The Phoenix was an angel. We gave him its power. Through each of our daily sacrifices, we bring the Phoenix out. Each thought of vengeance turned to justice, we allow the Phoenix to conquer. With each selfish act replaced by humility, we win battles. We don't need the Phoenix in the bird-like form. He came to us to prove that he was with us. He went away from us when we were called on our mission. And he came again when it was time to end it all. It is a beautiful process … and the King stayed with us the entire time. Many died in these past weeks, because of the Phoenix. Not for the bird, maybe, but for the Phoenix inside of them."

John paused.

"The 'Scarlet Phoenix' refers to the color of the place we went," John concluded. "Blood was spilt in the land of Arizona. In the city of Phoenix. Scarlet lands from the sacrifice of the soldiers and the innocent. Scarlet, in the land of Phoenix … The Scarlet Phoenix."

"Something doesn't add up, though," Paul said to Daniel. John and Jerry eventually came back to the discussion. "Didn't you say something in the building about Zyno, John?"

It all came to them.

"Zyno," Lino whispered. They all ran for the city jail. They burst open the doors.

"We need to check cell number 145236 … it's an emergency!" Daniel said to the guard.

"I can't let you in with those weapons," The guard said.

"This is taking too long," Jerry said. He pushed the man to the wall with his psychic powers.

"Grab the keys," Lino instructed. Paul leapt over and grabbed them. They all ran towards the door. Paul opened it and ran towards the cell Zyno was put in three and a half years ago.

The cell was empty.

Daniel banged his head against the jail door.

"We should have known!" Daniel yelled. "One of us should have stayed back. He could be anywhere!"

John approached the cell bars. With his sword, he cut a hole. He entered the cell. He looked on the floor. On the floor was a note addressed to Daniel. He picked it up.

"It says this," he read as he showed the piece of paper to them all,

"   *Dear Daniel*

If you are reading this note, then it means that you have
passed *Further than Zach's clutches, the traitor. He has*
      Delayed you for me, so that I can get to the US leaders
      If you want to try to catch me, be my guest. Your nephews
are
      Going to pay the price for your attack. The
      Loyalist army will come and kill
      U and your family, whatever is left of it.
      Remember, fear anything that has purple.
      Evil will reign in the end as you know
      Nightmare of yours forever,
          Zyno Wayne

          "

Epilogue

The evil did spread throughout the lands. The loyalist army that Zyno had promised was actually the leftover parts of Zach's army. The Phoenix sword was restored to the trunk of the tree, forever to remain. The Quaills talked to their father one last time before he and the Phoenix went away for good. John and Joan – though young – felt they loved each other. They bought a house from the help of their brothers, and it became John's work to help fight the Loyalists. Paul went back to the lab and started to write to the countries about their new medicines, for the Locombony Island was no longer a secret. Jerry was promoted to head of all the armies in Locombony and as his first act, he offered peace treaties with Australia. Daniel went forward to the U.S. to try and find Zyno's whereabouts. Nobody seemed to know anything.

Meanwhile, the rest of the world tried to recover from the hardest loss in world history. A total of 1.3 billion people died, wounded or were missing from the war – almost one sixth of the world's population. However, it was decided that it was the war to end all wars, for peace was finally accomplished. Lino figured that it was not a coincidence that when pure evil tried to take over, the entire world united under one common ground. For even though, as John, Jerry, and Paul learned, there were good and bad people, they were all on the same page–neither pure nor evil.

Who knows what the future will bring? That is the view of the Quaills at this moment. They believe the most powerful of the trio has been killed, saving the world, but little do they know the future will bring them to saving things beyond the world ...beyond all worlds.

For the Scarlet Phoenix was only the second of their Perpetual Journeys.

About the Author

John McClellan created his first two books before leaving grade school. Since then, he has published two works, and completed a third, *The Four Kings*. John hopes to teach middle school math, but continue writing on the side.

The Four Kings is set to come out in the Fall of 2010. The fourth book—which is unnamed thus far—will come out in the Summer of 2011.

To get a copy of this or other books by John McClellan, contact him at: legendarywarhero@yahoo.com